# Agnes Somerset

# Agnes Somerset

## ❧ *A Victorian Tale* ❧

## Ann Maureen Doyle

For permissions, please contact the author at
*AnnMaureenDoyle@gmail.com*

Published by Ann Maureen Doyle

Cataloguing data: FICTION, Literary, Romance—Historical—Victorian, post-Civil War, New York State—Dutchess County, Victorian era
Author: DOYLE, Ann Maureen

*Book design and cover photo by A. M. Doyle*
*Author photo by M. E. Doyle*

Events in this story, as well as all characters, are fictional.

*This book is dedicated to the memory of*

*Anna Burns*
*Died February 19, 1878*
*and buried beside the blue waters of*
*Saint Augustine, Florida*

*"She was a kind*
*and affectionate wife and mother*
*and a friend to all."*

*May as much be said of us.*

# *Acknowledgments*

The author wishes to warmly thank the people who encouraged her as she researched and wrote this story: her husband Michael, whose enthusiasm never flagged; the writers group at Homer's Coffeehouse, who kept her producing chapters to read aloud at each meeting; friends Becky and Rod, who stayed up much too late night after night reading the first draft and jotting notes in the margins; and literary agent Susan G. and her staff, whose insightful critiques resulted in many improvements.

# Contents

# *Prologue*

*Brookside Estate, Dutchess County, New York*
*Early 1880s*

Agnes stood motionless at the foot of the stairs. She had just come down from putting the baby to bed for a nap, and his dribble cloth lay across her shoulder. She looked at Phillip and knew why he had come.

He stood in the dim foyer, turning his hat in his hands. "I have good news," he began abruptly.

The words he was about to speak she could not hear. She knew she should sit down but feared that if her feet moved they would carry her away at a run. Better to stand steeled for the next blow. She was vaguely aware of Fettles working behind her, quietly lighting the lamps against the darkness of the autumn afternoon. She looked at Phillip's dark eyes and beautiful brow, the careless hair, the magnificent angle of his shoulders, and for the first time wanted to put her fists into him.

He had come to begin prying the baby from her. Agnes felt herself standing there, between the two of them, as though blocking the man from mounting the stairs to where the mysterious little bastard slept in sweet ignorance of the swirling violence his existence had ignited in the grown-up world below him.

How strange, Agnes thought, that the passage of less than half a year could pull a woman through bliss she had never imagined and dash her into dark chasms with hardly a foothold. She turned her gaze toward the tall eastern window, trying to steady her mind. The lawn stretched out damp and brown, and the sky was threatening rain again. Only a few months ago, how green the view had been, when a glad sun coaxed every blade of grass into growing, every bud into opening, and warmed the gray stones of the terrace. For a moment only, the whole scene lay before her clothed in the glory of summer, but tiny, like a cameo, as though seen from a great distance. Indeed, the bright vision grew smaller with every swing of the pendulum in the implacable old clock behind her.

No, they were here now, thousands of miles from last summer, with no way back—even the truth about the baby upstairs would probably make no difference, could they ever even know it . . . .

# *Part I. As the Wild Bird Flies*

# Chapter 1

It was one of those days in early June that, despite their rarity, stand in our memory as the quintessential summer day. Agnes directed the staff to throw open all the doors, which set the draperies to gently flapping, the edges of tablecloths fluttering, and newspapers and writing supplies taking flight until paperweights were rounded up to secure them. The sky was a luxurious blue interrupted by high, white clouds sailing briskly to the east. It was tremendous luck that brought such fine weather on this, the first day guests would be arriving for Brookside's hundredth anniversary.

By mid-morning the house was nearly ready. Flowers had been cut and arranged, guest beds made up with scented linens, the dinner menu finalized, and the croquet course freshly mowed. Agnes swooped from room to room, her dark blue work skirt swirling about her legs, as she checked every detail, issued instructions, and lent a hand where needed.

In the foyer she paused across from the grand front doors that she had ordered propped open to let in the air. She slowly surveyed the space as the breeze stirred her hair and brought in the smell of climbing roses blooming just outside. Something was not right, but what? Then she saw it. "Marie," she called to the young woman spreading a heavy red cloth over the mahogany dining table, "Where is the umbrella stand?"

Marie approached, her thin dark hands smoothing her white apron. Agnes could not help noticing how handsome Marie looked, with her black hair pulled tightly back from her smooth brown face with its magnificent cheekbones and lavish mouth. "Ma'm, Mrs. Williams thought it needed polishing and took it to the kitchen. And, the weather being so fair, we probably won't be needing it for a while."

Agnes turned a cautionary gaze on her maid. "So we are now able to forecast a week's weather, are we?" Marie was silent. "Well, you may both be completely right, and I hope you are, but do me the favor of asking Mrs. Williams to finish polishing the stand and replace it by lunch time, please." Marie nodded and hurried to the kitchen.

Agnes loved opening the grand house to guests each summer, but the details nearly drove her to shrewishness in the days leading up to their arrival. And this year the expectations were all the greater since they were celebrating the century mark of her family home. On top of the usual preparations, this year called for a celebration dinner, a reading of "The History of Brookside" (researched and written by herself), a hunt, and extra invitees.

Urgent footsteps approached from the main hallway, echoing against the gray and white marble tiles. "Madam, a moment, please."

It was Fettles, looking more alarmed than usual, his coat flying open, his wiry gray hair blown back from his narrow face. The butler paused to catch his breath as he stood before her on his impossibly thin, black-stockinged legs, his hands shaking just the slightest bit with the tremor that had set in during the past year.

"Fettles, you're just the person I was looking for. Have we safeguarded our more valuable pieces? You remember that the Duke is coming . . ."

"Oh, yes, madam," Fettles said firmly. "Reassembling one seventeenth-century Polish pitcher was quite enough for me." (The Duke of Gloucester, who lived just up the road, had on a previous visit knocked the pitcher to the floor while making a sweeping gesture to describe his enthusiasm for American politics.)

"And what were you going to say?" asked Agnes.

"Madam, the strong air through the house is, I'm afraid, posing difficulties for the floral arrangements. Mrs. Williams requests that we might close the doors and windows."

"Does this mean that Mrs. Williams is not able to engineer a bouquet that can withstand a summer breeze?" Agnes affected an incredulous look.

"Well, Madam, it's just that she has designed a particularly complex arrangement for today's decoration, making it more delicate than her usual."

4

"Fettles, I applaud her zeal, but I cannot let concern for our bouquets shut up the house on this glorious day. Please tell Mrs. Williams that we will be very happy indeed with her habitual brilliance—a few collections of durable flowers will suffice."

Fettles rubbed his fingers together and waited as though more precise instruction might be coming. Hearing none, he blinked and turned to retrace his steps with a murmured "Yes, Madam."

Agnes heard phrases float back to her as he retreated—"won't be easy . . . why *I'm* always elected . . . hurricane . . ."—and smiled. Fettles had a heart of purest gold, but the butler was even more prone to upset than his mistress during their bigger events. He had served the Somerset family since coming at age seventeen to work as a groom in her father's stables. He proved totally unsuited to working with animals, but his earnestness could not be overlooked, and, much to the horses' relief, Agnes's father offered him a position in the house. Fettles executed every task he was given quickly and with merciless attention to detail. Her father felt his conscientious bent owed much to a strict Catholic upbringing.

Agnes consulted the solemn clock that stood counting off the seconds in a corner of the foyer. Ten forty-six. In just over three hours the guests should start arriving, beginning with the Bairnaughts and followed shortly by Aunt Vera, accompanied by Vera's friend and traveling companion, Mr. Schmidt. In two days, by Wednesday, the house would be nearly full.

Agnes started for the stairs to check on the guest rooms but stopped on the first step. She turned her head and listened. It was getting louder, the certain sound of carriage wheels on gravel. Impossible—no one was due before two. Fettles, returned from his mission and ever alert, had also heard it. He edged cautiously sideways to look out the open door.

"Oh," he winced. "Mrs. Thorne's carriage."

"What?" snapped Agnes. "At this hour? The woman has no consideration whatever!" She looked down at her simple work clothes, started to smooth her hair, and stopped. "Well, if she wants to pay visits in the middle of the morning, I am not going to worry about it. She gets me as I am."

"She does it on purpose, you know, Ma'm," put in Maria from the dining room doorway.

Agnes let out a low, exasperated sound. "It was too much to hope that she would not appear this week."

"Shall I tell her that you are indisposed?" asked Fettles.

Agnes put her fingers to her temples. "No, I had best get this over with. She'll be outraged, of course, that she is not part of our festivities, even though she has not invited me to a single thing. Oh, why can't this woman just disappear?"

Fettles looked at her sympathetically. "She is indeed the Thorne in our side."

Agnes smiled despite herself. "Of course, if she sees me like this, she will take in every disheveled detail and recount them to her circle of magpies. Show the woman in. I will appear by and by," she said and hurried upstairs.

Moments later, after a deft refinement of her coiffure and the addition of a smart poplin jacket, Agnes came down to find Mrs. Sherman Thorne sitting stiffly in the first parlor. Both of her delicate hands rested on a well-ruffled parasol as she stared at a sweeping painting of sturdy Italians harvesting olives. As usual, Claudia's dress was designed to stun the viewer into speechless admiration. Today she was a pillar of ivory in varying tones. European lace embraced her throat, shoulders, and arms. Below her impossibly narrow waist, cascades of ruffled satin fell to the floor. A simple, wide-brimmed hat protected her pale face from the day's sun and concealed her masses of silken hair. (Claudia's hair was famous and was often described as the color of wheat just before harvest.)

The siren turned her head mechanically at Agnes's approach and rose. Agnes extended her hand, grateful for Claudia's gloves that prevented contact with the skin of this poisonous woman. She looked neutrally into the cold face, into the gray eyes set wide beneath the perfect brows. Claudia tilted her fine chin forward and broke open her a dazzling smile.

"Agnes, do forgive me for calling so early. I was just on my way into town and thought to stop for only a moment. It looks as though you are making preparations for something rather grand. I had no idea."

"Not at all. It's a small fête with mostly family and friends of my parents," Agnes explained, allowing no space for a mere enemy such as Claudia. "We are marking Brookside's hundredth anniversary."

"That *is* a special occasion," Claudia enthused. The two women seated themselves across from each other. "I will not keep you. I simply came by because Sherman's mother finally left for Europe"— she drawled the word *finally* to ensure an understanding of how burdensome her mother-in-law could be—"and at last I have time to attend to calls I have long neglected."

"How lovely that you and Mrs. Thorne keep up such close relations," smiled Agnes, "even with Sherman gone."

"Well, he was all she had. So now it's me, I suppose." Claudia smiled wanly and pulled gently on a dangling curl. Claudia had declared herself a widow a year earlier, after her husband had been missing for eight months. Sherman had left with his trunks, telling her that the French had recruited him to assist in building the canal in Panama. She was used to—and even relished—his far-flung travels, as his career kept him away the greater part of every year, engineering bridges, tunnels, and seaports. Devotion to his work was one explanation, but many felt that he accepted long assignments to remote places as a refuge from his wife. For her part, Claudia took advantage of Sherman's absences to indulge in amusements he would neither enjoy nor approve of. On the rare occasions when he was at home, Claudia threw parties to put him on display and demonstrate that he was more than a myth. He spent those evenings sipping hard liquor and saying as little as possible.

But this trip was different. After several weeks she had received neither letter nor money. When her own letters were returned unopened by the canal administrator, Claudia demanded answers. After several more weeks, the French Director General of the operation sent her a telegram from Panama City stating in no uncertain terms that they had no knowledge of her husband, had never hired him, and had no reason to, being fully confident of their own engineers' ability to build the daunting waterway. Claudia declared the director either a liar or an incompetent who did not even know the engineers they had engaged. Still, she chose not to request a formal investigation and concluded that Sherman, in his selfless effort to bring progress to that barbaric part of the world, must have met his end either by fever or headhunters. She resigned herself to her new status of singleness, wearing black for only a month with the explanation that she found that ritual "far too depressing."

Most people felt that Sherman was not dead and secretly cheered for him in his new life. Overall, his disappearance served Claudia well. She had found that, after working to secure Sherman as a husband, his mathematical mind only bored her more each day. She had not realized that the qualities required of a good engineer do not include creativity or anything like reckless abandon. He did not care what pictures she hung on the walls or what local scandals were bubbling, and he proved incapable of surprising her with anything but the depth of his dullness.

Agnes speculated that Sherman had married Claudia for her beauty and possibly her dowry, which was her parent's estate upon their death. Claudia's mother had died of tuberculosis shortly after the wedding, and her father welcomed the couple to live at Beaujour with him. He had shamelessly spoiled his only child since her birth and constantly referred to her as "the prettiest thing breathing." He sent her in her teen years to the same academy Agnes attended, where Claudia enjoyed a campaign of subtle persecution upon the intelligent, quiet girl. Afterwards, Agnes's theft of the desirable M., (a man she could not even manage to keep, Claudia had often pointed out at the time) only increased Claudia's antagonism. Claudia took her marriage to Sherman as a personal victory over Agnes and gloated over her neighbor's continued spinsterhood.

"Well," smiled Agnes, "you are very kind to drop by."

"Of course, I can't stay. A widow's affairs just have no end, it seems. Lawyers, bankers, architects, there is always someone demanding a meeting. But, as a single woman, I am sure you know how that is."

"I do indeed."

Claudia smiled. "Oh!" she exclaimed. "There is one thing I have been meaning to ask you. I've heard that you are thinking of . . ." Claudia leaned closer and dropped her voice as though sharing a secret, "selling Brookside?"

Agnes felt the words run over her like ice water. "Selling Brookside?" she repeated slowly. "What—what would possess me—"

"Oh, I have no idea, it's just something I heard," Claudia laughed lightly, drawing back.

"From whom?"

"I really don't remember now. But I thought I would ask. It is a lovely old place, but I would understand if you were growing a bit tired of keeping up with it all." Claudia waved her folded parasol around vaguely. "It is, of course, old-fashioned and would need a lot to bring it up to date, but it still is a very fine property. You know, I have about finished the improvements at Beaujour. You must come by and see it! I spared no expense," she confided, winking at Agnes as she adjusted her gloves and rose.

"Well, I am off. Do come by, won't you?" she repeated as she headed for the open door, then stopped. Turning, she tossed out "I hear that the Duke's son is back from India. Have you met him?"

"Not yet, but the Duke has promised to bring him to the festivities."

"You *are* the lucky girl!" exclaimed Claudia. "I'm told he is quite the fascinating young fellow and rather dashing. He should make a colorful addition to your grand event. I am gone!" she concluded, waving a lacey hand in the air, and glided out the door to her waiting carriage.

As it clattered away in a swirl of dust, Marie approached and touched her mistress's arm.

"Beware of this woman, ma'm. I feel danger from her."

Agnes looked into her maid's dark, serious eyes. "You need not warn me, my dear. I have long understood that Mrs. Thorne is capable of nearly anything."

A sudden shriek pulled their attention sharply away from their departing neighbor. A house maid, just crossing the foyer, stood against a wall with a hand to her mouth.

"What is it?" Agnes asked.

"A snake, ma'm!"

"Where?"

"It went down the hall."

Fettles dashed to the front doors and pulled them closed. "It is a morning for unwanted visitors," he declared. "I will do my best to find it, and enlist the footmen."

"Oh, you must, Fettles!" cried Agnes. "We can't have a serpent in the house! Oh, my Lord, it will be greeting our guests as they climb into bed or slithering between them at dinner."

"Yes, madam." Fettles called, already flying down the hall after the legless intruder, his heels clicking crazily down the passageway to the kitchen.

Agnes shook her arms and let out an exasperated noise. She should not have forgotten, but it had been so long since a creature had sneaked into the house that she had let herself relax too much in leaving the doors open. The raccoon had been hard enough to trap, but a snake . . . . You cannot relax, she stormed against herself, and you should have known better.

But there was no time to dwell on her mistake. She heard again the sound of carriage wheels rolling toward the house. "Oh, who can it be this time?" she cried. "The first guest has not set foot in the house and already I need a bromide!"

From the corner of her eye, Agnes thought she saw a black, satiny form slither under the parlor doors and disappear. The footmen, she realized, had been bested.

# Chapter 2

In the dingy dressing room hung with exaggerated costumes, Rupa finished painting her eyes before a tall mirror cracked from top to bottom. Beyond the door a gay piano piece led six dancers across the wooden floor in perfect, pounding unison. Rupa drew a steady black line just below her lower lashes. She wrapped herself in the last layers of her sheer orange costume and stretched her legs, her arms, her neck one more time. She looked around the chaotic room, stale with the smell of sweat and grease, and thought how far away India was, how far away her father's house. No one must find her here; surely no one would look in a place like this. She hugged herself, counting up what she had lost and what she had gained by the hard decisions made in her sixteen years.

Here, on a narrow street in Marseilles, just a stone's throw from the docks, sat the tavern that had become her home. Like everything in this port city, it catered to crews tumbling off ships, rough men eager for food, drink, and the smell of perfume. On this particular evening, Monsieur Vaudin, proprietor of La Coquette, had just finished hanging the new sign he had ordered, featuring the establishment's name skillfully painted onto a wooden replica of a woman's calf. And tonight he would be introducing Rupa to his clientele. It had been a long time since his troupe had included an Indian, not since the last one ran off with a captain from Istanbul. But this girl was better in every respect: younger, prettier, a gifted dancer, and more docile. When she came to him two months ago she was almost skeletal, but even her jutting bones could not disguise her beauty. He had fed her and fattened her to an attractive size, although she would always be small. He had watched her practice with the other girls and could not help noticing a natural grace and fluidity to her movements. He dubbed her La Petite Violette. Tonight she would debut with a solo performance of a veiled dance for which he had gone to some expense with a silk merchant two streets over.

By eight o'clock the tavern had filled up, as usual, with a handful of locals as well as captains and crew from ports dotting the edges of the Mediterranean. Many were regulars, but others had been drawn in by flyers that promised a new talent performing a never-before-seen dance that would set even the sternest seaman's heart thumping. Come see for yourself La Petite Violette.

Rupa heard the piano player hammer out the final notes, heard the audience whistle and stamp their feet. In a great rush six girls tumbled into the dressing room, jostling each other in their bulky skirts. They fell exhausted onto benches and wiped the perspiration from their faces and arms. Unfastening the hooks of their bodices, they glanced expectantly at Rupa. They could hear Monsieur Vaudin intoning her introduction. Rupa tiptoed through the open door to the dark curtain beside the stage and waited for her cue. Monsieur Vaudin's voice stopped and the plaintive notes of an Asian flute took its place. Rupa looked back at the oldest girl, who stood in the doorway watching.

"*Vas-y, vas-y,*" the girl encouraged her, making a shooing motion with both hands. "Go on. You'll do fine."

Rupa held her breath and stepped into the harsh light of the stage, carefully keeping her eyes away from the men spread out before her. She felt their eyes on her and smelled the sting of tobacco, catching her breath as the smoke entered her lungs. She felt exposed, like a fleeing fawn forced into an open field. But no one could know her here. She somehow remembered what the girls had told her—forget the audience and listen to the music. Closing her eyes, she drove her attention back to the mournful flute and arched her back. She took the first step, the second, and let the music pull her along. Little Violette danced, her sheer veils floating around her with each liquid swivel and leap. Before she realized it, the dance was over, and she looked out on the men as they roared their approval. She felt frightened, almost in peril, until she caught sight of Monsieur Vaudin in the back, applauding slowly and nodding his approval.

The second show went more easily than the first, and Rupa found herself smiling as she bowed gracefully at the finish with the last notes of the flute trailing off. Her head pounding from the smoke and excitement, she made her way up the tight staircase to the little room she shared with two other girls. A small window faced the sea that glittered darkly beyond the tiled rooftops. She went to it and stood with her elbows on the sill looking out to the water and wondering which way she would sail to find a certain man who had saved her from one fate without dreaming she would run to this.

And she thought about the tiny baby left in a basket by the convent's kitchen. The nuns had been so good to her, and she flushed when she thought of how she had run out on them. But she could not stay at the convent where Phillip had brought her—although thousands of miles from India, it was still too easy to find. Her father might pick up the scent any day and fall upon her. She pictured his eyes, round with rage, and his terrible strength. The last time she saw him angry, their servant had barely survived the beating, and she remembered the sound of the blows as her father brought down the baton on his back and head.

Rupa pressed her hands to her eyes to push back the tears. Was all this pain worth the mad flight? Had she made a terrible mistake? In answer, an image of herself as the disgraced daughter—or worse still, as Manindra's bride—flashed into her mind, and she knew that she was willing to run her whole life long.

# Chapter 3

Maria looked out a foyer window between the pane's deep etchings.

"Guests, Madam. I see trunks on top. What shall we do?"

"Oh, my." Agnes instinctively tucked loose strands of hair up and under. "The Bairnaughts must have found a quicker connection. I do wish people would not improvise in the middle of traveling, it throws things off so."

"Ma'm, I believe it's your Aunt and her companion. I think I recognize her baggage."

"Oh, well that's easier at least. You absolutely never know with Aunt Vera, anyway. She could arrive two days early or a week late.

The carriage, which was now directly in front of the entrance, turned off to the right. "Oh, they must be headed for the porte-cochère," observed Marie.

"That's very much Aunt Vera—keep them guessing, even about which door you'll come in."

Fettles reappeared, slightly out of breath, to report that the footmen had the snake cornered in the pantry and should have no trouble bagging him.

"Very good, Fettles," sighed Agnes in relief. "I thought it had eluded you. Well, it seems my Aunt and Mr. Schmidt have arrived well ahead of schedule. Would you please welcome them and offer them some tea, of course, while I dress. Do you know whether Mrs. Williams remembered to put Mr. Schmidt at the other end of the hall from Aunt Vera?"

"Oh, yes, they are in the distant corners. Your aunt has the ivory room, as you requested, and Mr. Schmidt looks out toward the stables."

"Excellent. Oh, and Fettles--" Already proceeding to intercept the early arrivals, Fettles stopped himself.

"Close some of these windows, please."

"Of course."

Agnes took a step. "And one more thing," Fettles caught himself in the passage doorway and turned again. "Ask Dahlia to get a light lunch together for us to eat in about an hour. But no chicken—Aunt Vera refuses to eat it since she saw one killed behind the kitchen last year. And send Marie up if you see her—I don't know where she has disappeared to."

Fettles waited. "That's all. Thank you, Fettles." The butler bolted away in his usual manner, like one sprung from a trap, to check on the efforts of the footmen.

As Agnes hurried up the stairs, she heard the distant exclamations of her aunt. If Agnes's life had been one prescribed by duty and tradition, her aunt's was the opposite. No experience was too risky, no taste too foreign, for Vera to try it on. Twenty years earlier, she had cut her hair and dressed in homespun to sign up with the Union Army at Albany. Being of rather boyish proportions, she was accepted and uniformed without question under the name Julian Howard. Vera's hobby of marksmanship stood her in good stead at three battles, from which she emerged with no more than scratches. But the endless marches and lack of sanitation became more than she could stand. When the captain asked for volunteers to staff a field hospital in Virginia, she raised her hand. The captain had noticed a certain daintiness about the recruit and doubted he would last on the trail much longer, so with a warm handshake and best wishes, he gave up the odd marksman to service as a nurse. Before arriving at the hospital, Vera peeled off and buried her filthy Union uniform, bathed in a creek, and donned a dress she had stolen for the occasion from a soldier's wife at their last encampment. (She did, however, leave two dollars clipped to the clothesline where the dress had hung.)

She arrived at the hospital late that day, after rubbing the letter "n" off her paperwork, presenting herself as Julia Howard, nurse volunteer, ready for duty. The hospital was a once glorious plantation home wrested from its owners and pressed into service for the North's dying and wounded. Vera would say that she met the only man she ever loved there, where he lay in a corner of the dining room, bandaged about the head and missing a left arm and foot. She tended him for six weeks, falling in love with his stories and his soft eyes, those eyes that followed her as she stepped gently over the soldiers, handing out water and changing dressings. What she did not know was that the hand he lost had worn a gold band that was now tucked into his jacket pocket, a memento he never revealed. When a letter from his wife finally reached the hospital, it fell to Vera to read it to him, owing to his sight being damaged from the explosion that took his limbs. That torture had a lasting impression on her—reading a wife's declarations of love and news of their children to a man who had in every way possible encouraged her affections. She never again trusted herself in the matter of men and pursued a life of independent adventure.

By contrast, Agnes felt her own life was narrow and hardly deserving of comment. She had few stories to tell. And time was passing faster and faster, still with no husband to share the work or joy of life.

Lately, Agnes had taken to looking more closely into the mirror on her dresser. Sometimes she picked it up and moved nearer to the window to check the lines forming at the corners of her eyes, the definition coming into her brows, the hardening of her mouth. She had always told herself that she would not be a woman to fuss over age and run from wrinkles. Gray hair had a beauty of its own, and she would be perfectly happy when it came time for her deep brown waves to lose their color.

"A woman must walk into winter gracefully," her mother had often said, "or she'll look the fool, wearing her summer hat to an ice-skating party." And mother had managed that feat of grace like no one else. Mrs. Somerset's long hair had turned gray early, and Agnes remembered no other color on her. Her mother wore it piled on her head with jeweled combs setting off its own dull shine, combs Agnes's father brought home from his distant travels.

But it was different for Mother, Agnes brooded in her moments of self-pity. She had Father. They married young when she was beautiful and he was dashing; she was not, at thirty-two, trying to win a man. Mother knew who she was and what she had to do, every day. Life did not scare her—life, rather, was at her service.

Agnes had not inherited her mother's beauty or her tall, delicate body. She mirrored instead her grandmother's short, sweet frame with soft, rounded shoulders and full hips. She even had Grandma's gentle brown eyes, her dainty mouth, and beautiful hands. No, Elizabeth was the one who took after Mother in nearly every way. Agnes adored her older sister and still felt a dull shock to her chest whenever she remembered how swiftly the infection had carried her off, leaving her one daughter on the verge of marriage, their darling Stella.

As she stood before the wardrobe unbuttoning her work clothes, Agnes imagined the lunch she was about to share with Aunt Vera and Mr. Schmidt. They would sit on the terrace and listen to Vera's latest tales, laughing and exclaiming, and this was wonderful and as it should be. We can't all be adventurers, she reminded herself; some must stay home and keep things running. Day after day and year after year. But Agnes knew in her heart that this life suited her well and only occasionally did she wish for more. That is, besides having a man to call her own, and that particular emptiness pulled harder at her heart each year.

Agnes took from its hook the rose-colored chambray dress with pale blue bows running down the sleeves, one of her favorites. Marie, who was a genius with a needle, had converted several of Agnes's best dresses, including this one, to the new slimmer look by removing the bustles. Agnes was thus spared the expense and aggravation of ordering an entire new wardrobe while enjoying immensely the liberty to now sit properly against the backs of chairs.

A soft knock came at the door, and Marie entered. "Oh, your pink, ma'm, it's still missing a bow on one sleeve."

Agnes dropped the dress over one arm and put her hands over her face. She drew a slow, deliberate breath. Marie waited.

"Maybe this was a mistake," Agnes confessed from behind her hands. She peered at her maid over her fingertips. "Don't you think so, Marie? Once again I am probably trying to do too much. Who decreed that we needed all this ado over our hundredth anniversary? Well, I did, of course! I set myself and everyone else chasing through several circles of hell to make something grand happen, but why, really? And then we're all exhausted by the time it begins."

"Ma'm you are hardest on yourself," Marie asserted. "All of us are doing fine. It's exciting to have a party now and then, and if there's a little extra work, no one minds."

"*You* don't mind. I don't think you speak for Mrs. Williams or even Fettles. They both look like they are getting up a mutiny."

Marie laughed. "How you talk, Miss Agnes! That's not anywhere near true."

Agnes held out the pink dress. "I doubt anyone will notice the missing bow—it is surely the least of our flaws. I'm in the mood for it, Marie, so I'm wearing it! Have you seen my little silver cross? It was missing yesterday."

"Yes, ma'm, I just put it back in your drawer last night. I polished all your silver things."

"Marie, you are a gift." Marie helped Agnes into her dress and fastened the delicate silver chain behind her neck. Agnes sat down in front of the mirror and straightened her sleeves. "I think this dress is getting too young for me. I might send it to Stella. I wish she would have come, it's been so long since I've seen her."

"We are a long way from Chicago, ma'm, and her being in a family way makes it hard, you know."

"Oh, but she's only a few months along and feeling perfectly healthy. She said so in her last letter. I suspect her husband is being overprotective and worrying her with all sorts of disasters that could befall her if she travels. You know that once the baby is born it will be a long time before she'll want to take a trip out here. Traveling with children is so difficult."

"Yes, ma'm," Marie braided Agnes's dark hair and wound it artfully into loops that hung across the back of her neck.

Marie knew about traveling with children. Some twenty years earlier, at the age of eight, she had traveled with her mother and baby brother, along with the remnants of the family that had owned them, to New York City. Half starved, they had turned their backs on their Mississippi home, the burned crops, the graves of their men, and headed north to find work—any work. Marie had loved Mistress Dickinson and learned reading and arithmetic at her knee. Her owners' daughters were almost sisters to Marie except for the chores that never fell to them. She did not know until later how fortunate she had been compared to most of her black brethren. Together, in that crisis, the ragtag group operated more like an extended family than slaves and masters, and lived together in the huge, pounding city for several weeks until different fates pulled them in separate directions.

"You do have beautiful hair, Miss Agnes. It sure does remind me of your mother's, may she rest in peace."

"Yes, and it's turning her color at a frightening rate."

"No, ma'm! I don't see but a strand or two of silver, and it's always the same—never more."

Agnes turned her head from side to side in the mirror. "I choose to believe you, Marie. All right, let's go down and hear what new revolution my aunt has lent her hand to."

# Chapter 4

Agnes found Vera stretched on the terrace, her small feet clad only in white stockings and propped on a chair. Two cast-off yellow boots lay on their sides as their owner leaned back with a smile on her lips, surveying the splashing fountain, the riot of crimson roses around its basin, and the crisp, green fields beyond. Mr. Schmidt stood examining the foliage of a caladium in a nearby urn. The pink-and-white Newport teapot sat on the table flanked by half-finished cups of tea with a rose petal floating in each.

"So, am I keeping up the old place to your liking?" smiled Agnes as she stepped up behind her aunt and kissed her warmly on the cheek.

With a small shriek, Vera leapt to her feet, clasping her niece in an embrace whose strength belied Vera's small size.

"My dear! How impossibly beautiful everything is! And you don't know how desperately I needed this refreshment, away from that infernal city. I swear it's twenty degrees cooler here. And just look at your roses! They were babies the last time I was here, and that was only a year ago. What have you been feeding them? But how are you, my dear? You look irresistible, as ever. What a wonderful dress, and it suits you perfectly—Paris?"

"New York."

"Good girl! I very much support buying from our own. And our designers have gotten so good at copying what's being done on the Continent, why buy foreign merchandise?"

"Your aunt has become quite the patriot these days," Mr. Schmidt put in, walking forward with his hands behind his back—a posture that had grown more difficult in recent years with his increasing circumference.

"What do you mean, 'these days'?" frowned Vera. "You forget whom you're talking about."

Agnes put out her hand. "Frederick, how lovely to see you again." Agnes had looked forward to seeing Frederick Schmidt almost as much as seeing her aunt. His quiet firmness and simple wisdom acted like an anchor, steadying any situation and balancing Vera's flights of feeling. Even when he sat and said nothing, his generous frame and settled gaze made people feel they could relax into his good hands.

"And you, Agnes. I will reinforce your aunt's admiration with my own: your gardens look sumptuous. I congratulate you and your gardener."

"The praise goes entirely to Ned," smiled Agnes, sitting and pouring herself a cup of tea. The two visitors resumed their seats. "He is a genius with a spade. I give him some sketchy ideas about what I like and what I don't like, and he makes our landscape bloom like a magician. Also, this spring has given us a perfect balance of sun and rain. But it is mostly Ned. Do you see that patch of purple bells there? They are supposed to flower only every other year, but Ned has somehow managed to make them bloom every summer for the past three years. And speaking of Ned, he is probably at work inside the house now, trying to bag the snake that slipped in this morning."

"Oh, my!" exclaimed Vera. "Do you know what kind?"

"The quiet, hard-to-catch kind. And it's black."

"How large?" asked Frederick.

"Bigger than a garter snake. I was so foolish to leave the doors open. And not only that, but Claudia decided to drop in this morning, of all times."

"Ah, speaking of serpents . . ." said Vera.

"Do you know, she said the most remarkable thing. She asked if Brookside were for sale!"

"What?" cried Vera.

"Yes, she said she had 'heard' that I might be selling. Then she called the house old-fashioned and invited me to drop by Beaujour to see all the wondrous changes she has made there. As though I would ever be caught on her property!"

Fettles appeared between the open French doors. "Madam, lunch will be ready in fifteen minutes. Would you like to take it in the dining room?"

Vera interceded. "Oh, I can't possibly leave this terrace! Can we eat right here, Agnes?"

"Fettles, my aunt has spoken. We shall enjoy lunch where we are. Any news on finding . . . ?"

"Not yet, madam," Fettles confessed as he noiselessly gathered up the extra tea things. "But Ned and Isaiah have it cornered in the kitchen." After brushing the crumbs from the table, he retreated into the darkness of the house.

"I wouldn't worry about Mrs. Thorne," Vera resumed. "She is probably bored and just wants to stir something up—anything to occupy her tiny mind. But Fettles is looking well. Is the tremor any worse?"

"No, thank heavens, and I can't bear to think that one day it might be. He is simply indispensable. And you, Vera, you grow more glamorous every time I see you. You must share your secret with me—I am going to need it very soon. For now, tell me how was your trip. You must have left the city early or made exceptionally good time?"

"Your aunt has been so excited at the prospect of seeing you that she decided yesterday that we should leave on an earlier train," Mr. Schmidt explained, casting a restrained look upon his traveling companion. "It took a little doing on my part to finish things up in time, but I was happy to oblige. You know how she is. Once she decides something can be done she must do it."

"I hoped you wouldn't mind too much," said Vera, leaning forward, "but look how well it's turned out—here we are, about to dine together on this glorious afternoon!"

"I couldn't be happier," Agnes reassured.

"Well, everything went as well as you can ever expect," Vera recounted, "except that we nearly forgot your gift on the train. I was so excited that I left it on the seat beside me, being distracted by two nettlesome women who kept asking directions of us and then ignoring the answers. We'd gotten to the carriage stand when I remembered. Luckily, Frederick was able to run back and get it just before the train moved on. My heart would have simply broken if we'd lost it; you'll know why when you see it. When I laid eyes on it, I said to myself, that's for Agnes, she must have it."

Vera's enthusiasm on any subject outstripped that of all women Agnes had ever known. Both small and large delights thrilled her equally. While easily angered and even more easily hurt, she bounced back quickly and forgave easily. She was the younger sister of Agnes's mother and some 15 years older than Agnes. Vera's hair had kept its color, a light brown that bordered on orange around her face. Her eyes displayed an intriguing mix of green and brown, and from their corners a set of fine lines radiated, marking a generosity of smiles across the years.

"I can't wait to see it," said Agnes. "Now bring me up to date. How are things going in your 'infernal city'?"

"Oh, please don't say it as though *I* had any responsibility for it," protested Vera. "Of course, electrifying the city is the latest *cause célèbre*, which will be fine if it can be made to work reliably. Everyone will be happy except the gas companies, who are already complaining that they will starve to death as casualties of progress. Of course, now we're tearing up all the streets to put in conduits to carry the current to every mouse hole in the city—no telling how much that's costing Mr. Edison! That's probably why he's charging a dollar for every one of his silly light bulbs. I don't think I'm ready to pay that."

"You may not have a choice before long," warned Mr. Schmidt.

"They'll have to drop the price—people just won't buy them. Let's see. My neighbor has joined the cause of temperance and wants me to go to meetings with her. I certainly agree that alcohol is a wicked thing when it destroys a household, but I so enjoy a glass of champagne now and then that I don't feel I can endorse the cause wholeheartedly. Fannie has a personal interest in the subject, with a husband who has to be carried home three nights out of seven. If it weren't for her money, which she has very wisely protected from him, she and the children would be sewing aprons for pennies a day."

"Poor woman!" sighed Agnes. "I've come to feel quite the way she does about alcohol. So many lives ruined . . . I won't keep it in the house these days. It's just a temptation for the servants."

"So you're having a gala without spirits of any kind?" asked Vera.

"Oh, heavens, no," cried Agnes. "Can you imagine Grandma Brown without her sherry? Or worse—Wilbur and Eleanor without their after-dinner brandy? I've ordered in enough for the week and then some, but when it runs out, that's that."

"Very wise," Mr. Schmidt complimented her. "My physician tells me it's poison, plain and simple. I gave up spirits myself several years ago. I found my memory and my energy both improved accordingly."

"Oh, Agnes, are Wilbur and Eleanor coming?" moaned Vera. "They are such a caustic couple. I feel positively pitted after the shortest conversation with them."

"I wish I could say they weren't. Grandma certainly cannot travel on her own, so their presence is required. She is such a dear. I can't understand how she tolerates them. But we will just have to do our best, I suppose."

By now the sun was high, and Mr. Schmidt had begun mopping his glistening forehead and bald crown. Fettles announced lunch, and the party moved to a table at the other end of the terrace, still shaded by a house wall. Aunt Vera rejoiced at everything she was served, all the while recounting recent travels and bracing experiences. After finishing with cheese and fruit, the three friends adjourned, the guests to their rooms for a much-needed rest and Agnes to ensure that everything was ready for the next arrivals. As she crossed the foyer, a telegraph messenger stood in the front doorway. Marie came toward her with an envelope.

"For you, ma'm."

Agnes took the thin envelope and opened it slowly. No bad news now, she prayed silently, not this week. The snake is quite enough. All I ask is seven days without a crisis.

# Chapter 5

As she read, Agnes's face brightened. "Oh, how wonderful!" She crossed quickly to the messenger. "Please send a return message: Delightful news. Come immediately. Signed Agnes." The young man jotted the words quickly, took his payment, and was gone.

"Stella is coming!" Agnes announced to Marie. "I had a feeling that she would find a way. Oh, we must make sure she has a fine room. Marie, do you know where Mrs. Williams is?"

"Upstairs, I believe."

Agnes looked at the clock—1:45. She flew up the stairs, clutching her skirts, and found Mrs. Williams in the peach room, setting down a fresh bouquet. The head housekeeper was a stocky, unflappable woman, whose steady eyes and gracious smile sometimes belied a thin streak of perversity. When she was in a mood, Mrs. Williams was known to withhold important bits of information unless you knew exactly the right question to ask. As far as Agnes could tell, this was the housekeeper's only major fault, but more than once it had driven her to nearly throttle the woman. She hoped that Mrs. Williams was not in such a mood today.

"Ah, Mrs. Williams, I found you. That's a beautiful arrangement." Mrs. Williams smiled, poking stems into their proper positions in a deep blue vase. She took pride in her skill at flower arranging and considered it a valuable bonus to her employer. "I just received news that Stella will be coming after all, arriving in two days." Agnes paused cautiously for a reaction, but the housekeeper only smiled benignly. This often signaled, to the initiated, rough water ahead. "What rooms do we still have empty?"

The housekeeper held her smile but stiffened almost imperceptibly. "I know of only two, Madam. The small room over the kitchen and the walnut room."

Agnes asked which one she would recommend, to which the housekeeper replied impassively that she was sure the mistress would know best, being better acquainted with her niece. Agnes made another sally. Which room was in better condition to receive a guest without a great deal of extra preparation by the already busy staff, to which the reply was that "they will both take work, Ma'm."

Agnes felt her temperature start to rise. There was no time for this parrying, with guests due any minute. Like a rescuing angel, Fettles appeared in the doorway. He opened his mouth, but Agnes plunged ahead. "Fettles, what do you think? Stella has decided to come after all, and we must put her in the best room possible without causing undue effort. Mrs. Williams—who is being very careful to make no recommendation— says our choices are the room above the kitchen and the walnut room, neither of which has been used in some time, I believe. What is your opinion?"

Fettles looked at the housekeeper, whose look had gone from one of quiet power to undeserved injury, and back at Agnes. Extending his thin fingers one by one, he reviewed the other guests and their assigned rooms: Mrs. and Mrs. Bairnaught, the McMeeds, the Rockwells and their daughter, Aunt Vera and Mr. Schmidt, Grandma Brown, and the Wilbur Browns. With the names now penciled into his mental floor plan, Fettles explained that, in his opinion, the room over the kitchen could get too hot for a young lady to stay in comfortably, and he understood besides that it had been prepared in case cousin Wilbur decided to bring along his valet again. The walnut room was more commodious but somewhat gloomy, and a hinge on the window had never been fixed, making that window unsafe to open. "And the Bairnaughts have just arrived, " he added.

Agnes twisted the fabric of her skirt in her fingers (a habit she had kept from childhood) while thinking. Suddenly she looked up at Mrs. Williams. "Where did you put the Wilbur Browns?"

"In the mosaic room." This was Agnes's favorite guest room, a small, sunny chamber named for its fireplace done in hand-painted Italian tiles of blue and yellow.

"I assume that's because they have complained about every other room they've been given in the past?"

"Yes, ma'm. It's a bit small, but the décor is beyond reproach."

"*We* might think so. Wilbur and Eleanor will find something to object to. I propose, since we can't make those two happy, let's not waste the room. They don't arrive until the day after tomorrow. Fettles, can you get that hinge repaired by then?"

Fettles eyes twinkled. "Are you quite sure you want me to?"

"I'm afraid so. Mrs. Williams, if you could, please prepare the walnut room for the Browns. It will suit them as well as any, and we shall put Stella in the mosaic room."

And so the afternoon proceeded with last-minute adjustments that kept the staff bustling throughout the great house. For the next two days carriages pulled up to the pillared entry and discharged their passengers and trunks were handed down and trundled upstairs to the various bedrooms and many hugs were exchanged and exclamations heard as people who had not laid eyes on one another for many months or even years got a look at how time had changed—by a little or a lot—everyone and everything.

As for the Wilbur Browns, Agnes was very glad she had not squandered the mosaic room on them. The couple arrived in the late afternoon on Wednesday, a gray day without rain but thick with humidity. The guests had just gathered for tea in the main parlor, where the men had loosened their collars and the ladies fanned themselves in the oppressive air, but chatted nonetheless excitedly, as those newly drawn together always do.

Above the bubbling flow of their conversations, the sharp sounds of a commotion began to rise from the foyer. Added to several raised voices came the barking of dogs. Agnes excused herself and left her guests with their teacups in mid-air. Entering the foyer, she stopped. Fettles was trying to lead two silk-jacketed greyhounds back out the front door without success. The nervous dogs, lean black-and-white brindles, darted this way and that, tangling their leashes and nearly toppling the delicate butler. At the same time, he was trying to convince the Browns that it was not customary to allow dogs, no matter how well dressed, into the house, and that they would be much better off in the kennel. Eleanor and Wilbur were loudly defending the sterling character of their animals and declaring they were no more suited to be kept in a damp kennel than Fettles was. Wilbur was trying to take the leashes from Fettles, who was not letting go.

"Wilbur! Eleanor!" Agnes cried. "You're here. And you've brought some unexpected companions, I see."

Wilbur drew himself up and forced a smile. He nodded curtly to Aunt Vera and the small crowd standing quietly in the parlor doorway. Putting off for another minute the confrontation that was about to unfold, Agnes asked Wilbur the whereabouts of Grandma Brown.

"Surely you did not leave her behind in Philadelphia?" she asked brightly.

"Marie showed her to her room, ma'm," Fettles spoke up. "She asked to be excused until dinner. And," he added, with a "didn't I tell you" look, "Isaiah is showing Mr. and Mrs. Brown's man to his quarters."

"Well," said Agnes, "why don't we all step outside where we can talk? I'm afraid it's a bit noisy for the guests if we stay here in the foyer." Agnes led the way out, past the struggling Fettles, who grudgingly ceded the reins to Wilbur, and the small group gathered on the front drive. Agnes groaned silently at the prospect of an entire week ahead. This was just the beginning, and already the circus had begun.

# Chapter 6

"So whom do we have here?" Agnes asked as cheerfully as she could, eyeing the pacing dogs. She could not help admiring their jackets, which covered their backs and bellies and buckled smartly to one side. One wore a sumptuous shade of green silk and the other an exquisite red with a gold fern pattern through it. Their bodies were startlingly lean, and they displayed such intense alertness that it was hard to imagine they ever slept.

Eleanor spoke first, adjusting the dark, gauzy scarf around her shoulders. She was a tall, spare woman with abrupt cheekbones and a wide, thin mouth. She wore her dark hair pulled tightly back and pinned in an elaborate knot behind her head. Eleanor seldom smiled unless she was describing one of the couple's latest *coups* such as a wildly successful dinner party that the governor had attended or the addition of a new wing to their Renaissance revival mansion they shared with Grandma Brown outside Philadelphia. This not being the moment for such stories, she remained somber and introduced the dogs.

"Surely you received our wire? About bringing Empress and Napoleon." Eleanor's deep-set eyes fastened on Agnes.

"No, I'm afraid not," Agnes replied. She doubted there had been any wire. These two were not above bald-faced lies and were unlikely to go to the trouble of warning her of their planned imposition.

"Oh, yes, we sent word a week ago, wasn't it, Wilbur, that we had just acquired these darlings and could not possibly leave them behind. Greyhounds—purebreds, of course—are such sensitive animals, you see, they certainly would have felt abandoned." She bent down and took each dog's chin in her hand and kissed their noses in turn. Her eyes shone with maternal solicitude.

"The question at hand seems to be," Wilbur pronounced, "one of accommodation." Like his wife, Wilbur was tall, lean, and angular. At one time he could have been thought handsome. But Agnes noticed his lackluster pallor and a new touch of gray—he looked almost gaunt and certainly older than the last time they had met.

Beyond doubt, he was her least favorite relative. Wilbur was the only son of her father's half-brother, Uncle Thaddeus—he was not a

Somerset. Grandma's first husband was the flamboyant James Simon Somerset, who went down with his ship somewhere between Liverpool and the New York harbor. Grandma and James had been married just a few shining years and had produced one child, Benjamin, Agnes's father. A dainty and charming lady, Grandma spent only two years a widow before attracting the attentions of Aloysius Brown, a man of even greater wealth than James. This marriage was a short and unhappy one for the bride, who found a few weeks after moving into her husband's mansion outside Philadelphia that Aloysius could not be content with just one woman—this man who wooed her like his very life depended on it was soon making new conquests and sleeping in other beds.

Within three years his deeds caught up with him. The husband of one of his lovers came to visit Aloysius one day and shot him dead where he sat in his library chair. All parties were satisfied to report the death as an accidental suicide, the grievous result of careless pistol cleaning. Grandma made a special trip down to the Schuylkill River and threw her wedding ring in the day after its purchaser went into the ground, and for the rest of her life wore the band her first husband had put on her finger.

Grandma had borne one son to Aloysius Brown, an engaging boy named Thaddeus, who took after his mother in face and faculties. He grew into a lively and generous man, well loved by everyone who met him. Sadly, he died at the age of 45 in a mountain-climbing accident, shortly after the death of his wife. (Some said his fall was no accident but rather his way of escaping the overwhelming and undiminishing grief of his wife's absence.) He left behind one child, Wilbur, a taciturn youth just emerging with a mediocre record from Harvard College.

Wilbur showed an early affinity for forging connections among society's top rungs. At an exclusive ball for Boston's best, Wilbur noticed Eleanor; her chilly grace and regal bearing drew him to her. She, from a humbler background than Wilbur's, was also on the climb, and so their ambitions meshed. They married and took their place alongside Grandma at Montefiore, the Philadelphia mansion built by the extravagant Aloysius. The Italianate monstrosity was the pride of the Brown family, and since Aloysius had secretly amended his will to leave it to his son Thaddeus and his issue—Wilbur—

Grandma could not refuse the new couple entry. They allowed
Grandma to remain, of course, but Agnes supposed that the dear old
woman stayed far away from these two in the great reaches of that
residence and was thus able to preserve her good cheer, for which the
grand old lady was legendary. She would probably see more of them
over the course of this week than she did in a month back home.

Wilbur looked significantly at Agnes and raised his brows
slightly.

"We've made up the walnut room for you both, and I do hope
you'll like it," Agnes offered.

The Browns exchanged a dark glance. "The dogs, Agnes," said
Wilbur. "Your man here—" indicating Fettles with a slight toss of the
head, "tells us that you have some rule against dogs in the house.
Which I would understand if we were bringing in mud-caked hounds
fresh from the hunt, but as you can see, Empress and Napoleon are
cleaner than most people's children."

"I've not doubt of that," agreed Agnes. "They are splendid. But
they are also dogs, dear Wilbur, and Fettles was quite right about my
stricture against animals in the house. But we do have the kennel and
the stable, which my people keep exceptionally clean and well-aired."

Wilbur looked down at his prized dogs, then back at Agnes. "I'd
sooner sleep in the stable myself than put these two out there!"

"I can prepare as many stalls as necessary," muttered Fettles.

Eleanor turned. "What's that?"

Agnes spoke up. "Wilbur, I wish I could budge on this, but it's
simply impossible. You know I'm allergic to anything with fur, and I
assure you that Empress and Napoleon will have no complaints about
their accommodations."

Eleanor took up the cause, explaining that the sensitive dogs slept
in their owners' rooms (as anyone would imagine, her tone
conveyed). "What will they think if they find themselves at night
alone in some rough, drafty stall? And there is their health to
consider—these are delicate animals."

Agnes offered to assign one of the stable hands to spend the night
with the dogs if they thought that was necessary. She assured them
that in June the nights did not get so chilly, and the dogs would find a
bountiful supply of hay to snuggle into if they wished. Wilbur
continued to foam at these suggestions, and the debate could have

continued for hours if just then a young man had not ridden up to the house, unnoticed until his horse was nearly beside the group. The man slid nimbly from the saddle and stood holding the reins, looking at them all amicably. The ride had left his sandy hair windblown and himself and his horse breathing hard.

"Good afternoon," he announced at length, smiling with the ease of one who was among friends he had known for years. The smile was irregular— a full moustache almost hid the scarred left corner of his mouth—but nonetheless charming..

"Good afternoon," said Agnes, looking at the newcomer expectantly. When he remained cheerfully silent, she ventured, "Lord Phillip?"

"Oh, indeed!" he replied as though just reminded that he was among strangers. "I am the Duke's son. So very thoughtful of you— are you Miss Somerset?—so very thoughtful of you to have invited me."

"It is a great pleasure to have you with us," answered Agnes, extending her hand. "I would like you to meet my cousin Wilbur Brown and his wife Eleanor . . . and their companions Empress and Napoleon. This is Lord Phillip Aspen, the Duke's son newly returned from India."

"India?" asked Eleanor, tilting forward. "How exotic."

"Import export?" asked Wilbur.

"Not exactly," answered Phillip. "Missionary to the heathen."

"Indeed!" remarked Wilbur. Wilbur did not believe in God any more than the greyhounds did, but he seldom betrayed this in public. "Fascinating work, I imagine."

"Oh, yes. It keeps one humble. I just didn't seem to be much good at it. Greyhounds?" Phillip asked, looking down. "Fine animals, these. Do you race them?"

"Not yet," answered Wilbur. "We only just acquired them two weeks ago. We haven't quite decided whether we want to put them on the track or not."

"Well, they will no doubt do you proud no matter what you decide."

"Right now we are trying to decide where to put them." Wilbur smiled tightly.

Agnes began to twist her skirt and glanced at Lord Phillip. For a moment no one spoke.

"Then you are probably on your way to the kennel," declared Phillip. "I say, would you mind if I accompanied you? I'm considering a dog myself, possibly the Italian variety, and I'd like to get your opinion if I could."

Wilbur was clearly torn between continuing to insist on better lodging for the dogs and the opportunity to be treated as an expert by a titled Englishman. His vanity won out, and he and Lord Phillip, accompanied by the confused dogs, walked slowly toward the kennel as sluggish drops of rain began to fall. Isaiah the footman, just arrived from stowing the Browns' luggage, hurried forward to show them the way. Agnes watched Phillip's back as the men retreated, noticed his head cocked toward Wilbur at an attentive angle, and thought she noticed a barely discernible limp on his left side. She then turned her attention to Eleanor, who was saying something about dreadful weather, and led her into the house. Agnes presented her to those in the parlor, where Mrs. Bairnaught befriended the new arrival with compliments on her dogs and questions about the latest renovations to the mansion. Mrs. Bairnaught, an old friend of the Somersets, did not care a twig about Eleanor's projects but knew that someone had to adopt the unpopular woman so Agnes could unwind from the scene that had just taken place. Agnes thanked her warmly with a look and sat down to enjoy the last of the tea. She hoped her face did not reflect the worry she felt over keeping peace in her home without sealing two of her guests in the cellar.

# Chapter 7

The storm that had threatened them all day broke loose after dinner. Torrents of water washed the north windows while brilliant gashes of lightening announced thunderclaps that made the china shake. After dessert, Grandma retired to her room with her good friend Mrs. Bairnaught, who would help salve Mrs. Brown's rheumatism and read to her. The damp air tormented Grandma's hips and back, evidenced only by the matriarch's sitting a bit too quietly through dinner. Wilbur, as the self-appointed male host for the evening, led the gentlemen who wanted cigars into the study. The ladies, along with those men who preferred to take their coffee and cognac free from tobacco smoke, followed Agnes into the music room. Vera, succumbing to loud urgings, seated herself at the piano, whose polished rosewood with brass medallions of lute-playing cherubs glowed a warm welcome in the lamplight. Mr. Schmidt took up a position beside the instrument in happy anticipation of hearing his companion play. His face wore a suffused glow as if to say, "You will see that she is marvelous."

Eleanor, spectral in a narrow black gown, drifted from the guests and stood before a dark window, staring anxiously at the night. Her fragile dogs were out in the kennel, probably quaking beneath a mound of straw as the thunder cracked above them. But going to comfort them was out of the question until the storm slackened. Agnes called to her. "Eleanor, won't you join us? Vera has agreed to play a *Gloria*, and we need your soprano to balance Mr. Schmidt's bass." Agnes had no idea whether Eleanor could sing a note. Reluctantly, Eleanor left the window and approached the piano.

"I don't sing, I'm afraid. But I have heard that you sing like an angel, Agnes. I'm sure we would all like to hear you and Mr. Schmidt in a duet." Her rigid face kept the words from sounding like a compliment.

Vigorous approval rang from the group, so Agnes took her place beside Frederick. Vera's fingers began dancing over the keys of the proud old Chickering, and the singers raised their voices in an interwoven melody that softened everyone in the room far beyond the ability of the cognac.

"How about a round?" asked Mrs. McMeed, putting down her coffee as the song ended.

"Oh, indeed," put in the Duke, "Those are delightful! I should call in Phillip—he needs to learn some. But I doubt I'll get him away from a good cigar."

The rest agreed to rounds, and so they sang a set accompanied by the unpredictable percussion of the thunder. When their energy flagged, the Duke toasted the pianist and mused aloud, "How is it possible that this woman has eluded some man's net? Mr. Schmidt, I wouldn't let her get away if I were you."

Frederick reddened and Vera threw back her head and laughed. She rose and took her friend's arm. "My dear Frederick already values me more than he ought, I assure you."

"A good friend makes the best spouse," intoned Mr. Rockwell from his deeply upholstered chair. "Friendship first. It's the thing that lasts until the end. But these days—" he paused to remove a crumb from his moustache—"a husband must keep a tight rein. Modern women look for that insubstantial thing called romance and then busy themselves with all kinds of mischief rather than tending to their duties, that's what I see."

Abram Rockwell had been the business partner of Agnes's father and still ran the major portion of their "financial empire," as he referred to it, speaking of themselves in the same Olympian terms that might describe Carnegie or other captains of industry. He spoke with his coffee cup held just below his chin, the saucer very properly just beneath the cup. His gray hair ran in two swatches on either side of his rather pointed head. Mr. Rockwell's nose and ears gave evidence of the natural law that these features continue to grow into old age, while the head does not, giving them ever-increasing dominance over a man's appearance.

Mrs. Rockwell, a stout woman never guilty of chatter, sat across the room from her husband, her large arms straining the seams of her dark satin sleeves. Her coarse gray hair was pulled back in a simple style, but such was the hairs' vigor, it maintained a sort of tension around her head, making one wonder if it might spring out of its pins at any moment and arrange itself as it pleased. Mrs. Rockwell had once admitted to Agnes that she secretly wrote letters to the New York legislature regularly advocating property and voting rights for women. The Rockwell's daughter and only child, Sarah, submerged in a complicated gown of rich blue silk, sat beside her mother, watching. Suddenly Mrs. Rockwell decided to speak.

"Abram, have you been reading that Frenchman Proudman, or whatever his name is?"

Her husband stared. "What do you mean? To whom are you referring?"

"I think you mean Proudhon," volunteered Vera.

"A mixed-up fellow, that's what," continued Mrs. Rockwell, swelling further with indignity. "And those are just the kind to get the biggest following, aren't they? 'Man is three to a woman's two,' whatever that means! And our brains are smaller. Well, what of it, I say. A cat's is smaller than a bull's, but which would you rather have around the house?"

Mr. Schmidt put a hand on Vera's arm. "You can be sure that Mr. Proudhon never met a woman of your wit or ability, my dear. Otherwise he would have had to reverse all his theories on the nature of women."

Mr. McMeed, as though feeling this was a subject too grave to address while seated, rose and set his cognac on the piano. He grasped a lapel with one hand and cleared his throat. Although he had entered the second half of his own personal century a few years earlier, he maintained the lean form and dark hair of a much younger man—favors he occasionally complained about as standing in the way of the respect his years deserved. He was always clean-shaven, and his hair framed his upper face in short curls. Simon McMeed had entered local politics at an early age as a representative in the state capitol. A nephew to Mr. Somerset by marriage, he had faithfully represented the interests of his uncle in the chambers. A personable, articulate, and often outspoken man, Mr. McMeed quickly rose into a position of power and had recently run for the office of governor only to lose narrowly. Having learned valuable lessons from the experience, he now had his sights set on Washington, and his wife had practically started packing for their relocation into the rarefied atmosphere of Potomac society.

"Proudhon and his chaps seem to be spreading like a fungus, don't they?" McMeed pronounced. "Anarchists and atheists. They are all the fashion."

Mr. Schmidt's face darkened a shade. "As bad as he is, he's better than that scoundrel Marx."

"Must we choose between them?" cried McMeed. "Any man who declares 'Property is theft' can hardly be recommended."

"Yes, he subscribes to most of the Socialist rot," admitted Frederick, "but at least the Frenchman allows the farmer his land and the craftsman his tools. If the Marxists had their way, none of us would be left with a thimble to call his own."

Mrs. McMeed, an otherwise pretty woman whose eyes always looked too wide open, said, "Well, let's hope that nonsense stays in Europe. We don't need it coming over in the hold of a ship like the plague."

"Margaret, I'm afraid your caution comes too late," laughed Agnes. "It's here."

The Duke frowned and waved his cognac. "I have no taste for Proudhon myself or his petty bourgeois sermons. This was all covered before him by Britain's own simpletons, anyway. Haven't you noticed that the French are forever running about claiming to have invented things that have been kicked around for decades?"

"They did invent the guillotine, I believe," put in Mrs. McMeed.

"A perfect example!" exclaimed the Duke. "Monsieur Guillotin simply copied devices that were already chopping off heads in England and around the Continent. But the French made the greatest use of the thing, to be sure. Barbarous race, if you ask me. And worse still—totally unoriginal."

"Except for fashion, of course," Eleanor corrected. Everyone knew (because she made sure to tell them) that she went to Paris every other spring and ordered her gowns while Wilbur tried his luck at the casinos.

"Indeed!" Thunder rolled above the house as though punctuating Vera's exclamation. "The French concoct the silliest costumes imaginable and then export them, trying to make us look ridiculous. As soon as we buy them and struggle into them, the *illuminati* of Paris change their minds and we are all instantly out of style. Isn't that so, ladies?"

"Speaking of which," warned Mrs. Rockwell, "I hear the bustle is returning next season."

"You can't be serious!" gasped Agnes.

"How does one sit down in those things?" asked the Duke. "I've never understood it."

"And I hear they will be bigger than ever," the young Miss Rockwell chirped.

Mrs. Rockwell put her hands to her face. "Heaven help us. Here we are, fighting for the vote, and they're making us look more absurd than ever." At which her husband shot her a dark and suspicious look.

"Who's absurd?" asked Lord Phillip, casually entering the lively group, his hands in his pockets.

"Ah, Phillip," declared the Duke, "you should have been here for the singing."

"We heard it all the way in the study," smiled Phillip.

"So why didn't you come and join us?" asked his father.

"I was rather busy trying to defend the better part of Christian history from Wilbur's flaming arrows. I'm afraid I had to give it up at last; logic and mere fact held no sway."

Phillip's father threw his arms behind his back and began to make apologetic noises to Eleanor about his son's frankness while Agnes laughed quietly.

"Oh, no" Eleanor declared straight-faced, "please don't feel you need to apologize. Many others, I assure you, have failed to breach his walls on that subject."

Phillip turned to Agnes, who was gently clearing her throat in an effort to subdue her laughter. She sat on a burgundy chaise longue, her russet skirt spread across the cushion and her hair gleaming in the gaslight. Creamy lace covered her shoulders, and around her neck shone her mother's topaz necklace, a gift Mr. Somerset had brought back from Spain. Agnes smiled back modestly at Lord Phillip, then lowered her eyes as his gaze remained fixed. He stood this way, seemingly unconscious of staring, even after she struck up a conversation about the future of fashion with Mrs. Rockwell and her daughter. At a fitting point in their dialog, she sought to soothe the awkwardness with, "Maybe Lord Phillip would tell us his view of fashion. He has such interesting—"

But turning to where he stood, she found him gone.

# Chapter 8

The rain had nearly stopped and thunder only mumbled in the distance when the guests finally said good night to one another. As Agnes passed Grandma Brown's room, she was surprised to see a light still shining and hear quiet laughter. The door was ajar, so she knocked once and put her head in. In the corner, seated on either side of a small table, sat Grandma and Mrs. Bairnaught, on whose lap the Bible lay open to the book of Psalms. Grandma was dressed for bed, with a cap pulled over her snowy hair. A lamp of exquisite yellow Venetian glass bathed the room in a delicious glow. The ladies, who had been reminiscing together, smiled expectantly at Agnes.

Mrs. Bairnaught, about twenty years younger than Grandma, was something between a friend and a daughter to the venerable old woman. The two were brought together in the course of Mr. Bairnaught's friendship with Agnes's father, meeting for the first time at a Christmas ball thrown at Brookside. By then Grandma was widowed for the second time, and for the Bairnaughts, hopes of children were growing dim. The two ladies took to each other immediately. They became friends and confidants and traveled far and wide together while the gentlemen pursued fortunes for both their households.

"Come in, Agnes, come in," cried Grandma Brown. "I'm sorry I was such a bore at dinner. Everything was splendid, dear girl, and you are beyond beautiful this evening. I remember that necklace, I think. Do sit down for a moment."

Agnes drew up a chair. "Father gave this necklace to Mother shortly before he died," she explained. "He bought it in Spain for her birthday but couldn't wait to give it to her, so he put it on her pillow the night he came home. Every time I wear it I remember that night and how excited we all were to have him back, especially Mother."

"We were just talking over old times ourselves," said Mrs. Bairnaught. "There's nothing old women enjoy more than recalling moments from all the years gone by."

"Memories are a treasure," admitted Agnes. "They are delightful to recall with a friend and good company when one is alone.

Grandma, how are you feeling?" she asked, taking the matriarch's knobby hand.

"I'm feeling quite wonderful," she said. "The good company is doing wonders for my rheumatism, which is lucky since the doctor's tonics are useless. You have assembled a delightful mix of guests, my dear, and so interesting."

"Tell me," said Mrs. Bairnaught, leaning forward as far as her dumpling figure allowed, "what do you know about the Duke's son? A handsome young man, for sure, and so cheerful, don't you think?" Mrs. Bairnaught liked nothing better than romance, and sought to fan it wherever she thought it might be kindled into a good marriage.

"I know almost nothing," replied Agnes. "He returned from missionary work in India last month. He'd been there several years, I believe, and it sounds like it did not turn out well. He is single and seems to enjoy riding. He is also looking to buy a dog. That's all."

"Did he tell you that—that he wants to buy a dog?" asked Mrs. Bairnaught.

"I heard him tell Wilbur that as we were discussing where to put the greyhounds before dinner. Lord Phillip asked if he could sound out Wilbur's opinion on Italian hounds, and they went off to the kennel together, thank heavens."

"Oh, Agnes, I am so sorry about the dogs," said Grandma. "I told Wilbur that dogs had no place on a visit here, but you know how he is. He simply told me that I was old-fashioned. It bothered me all the way here, but I finally made up my mind not to worry about it because I had such confidence in your ability to handle any situation. And so you have." Grandma's face relaxed, and Agnes admired the soft wrinkles of her cheeks.

"You know," resumed Mrs. Bairnaught, "I'm surprised Lord Phillip said he was shopping for a dog."

"Why is that?" asked Agnes.

"Well, I was talking with the Duke earlier today as a few of us walked the gardens. He told me a very interesting story about his son." Mrs. Bairnaught proceeded to recount how Lord Phillip, at the age of 16, had just dismounted from his horse when the two family Dobermans dashed up to him, snarling. They did not recognize him at all. Whether it was the scent of wild lavender from the hill he had rolled down, or that he rode back in just his breeches, his other clothes stuffed into a saddlebag on that warm day, no one knew. But the dogs charged him, knocking him into an excavation. They proceeded to maul him until the stable master and two other men managed to beat them away, but not before they had inflicted lasting damage to the boy's face and hip.

"The Duke said that Phillip learned you can never trust dogs, even your own. It was years before he would go near one again."

"How terrible!" exclaimed Agnes. "Then I wonder why he said that to Wilbur."

"He probably said it to rescue you," said Grandma. "I bet Wilbur followed him to the kennel like a lap dog himself, didn't he?"

"Yes, he certainly did."

"How long has the Duke lived here?" asked Mrs. Bairnaught.

"Oh, a few years now. You know he has the property just two miles up the road, Fellcrest. He bought it when the old patriarch, Mr. Snowden, died and none of the children wanted it. The place had slipped into near ruin by then, so the Duke got it for next to nothing, I hear. He has absolutely transformed it."

"But hadn't you ever met Phillip until now?" asked Grandma.

"No, he was always abroad with one thing or another."

"What became of the Duke's wife? An American, I believe," put in Mrs. Bairnaught.

Agnes recounted how, when the Duke was a very young man back in England, the daughter of his Latin tutor proved quite irresistible. The Duke fell in love with her and she with him. They kept it a secret for four years, until he was on his own and had his inheritance, but their engagement created a scandal. There were the usual rumors of impropriety and the worst sin of all, marrying below one's station. They got married anyway and shortly afterwards moved to New York City, where she had relatives, after the Duke sold off everything in England.

"That is a great deal to give up," put in Mrs. Bairnaught. "I believe dukes are at the very top of the ladder in English aristocracy. But why is his son called Lord Phillip? Shouldn't he be a marquis?"

"Oh, I understand it was New York society that mistakenly gave him that title," explained Agnes, "and it stuck. The Duke was not interested in preserving the trappings of English peerage on American soil, so he never corrected them. They had two daughters and one son,

Phillip—which makes him the heir. When the wife died, the Duke bought Fellcrest. He said he never liked the city and he certainly lost little time moving to the country. He says it reminds him more of England, except for our winters."

"I can't blame him," said Grandma. "I ran out of patience with cities a long time ago. When I was a girl I thought they were so exciting. I loved nothing better than a trip to Philadelphia or Chicago or New York. Now all I see is pandemonium, the jostling of cabs and the smell of horses, all that noise all the time, everyone with something to sell you, and not a corner to rest in. Do you know, I haven't been to Philadelphia in almost a year, and it's only a few miles down the road. Which points to the fact that I am old. And an old woman must get to bed, my dears."

Agnes and Mrs. Bairnaught rose and helped Grandma into bed. "Shall I leave the lamp on just a bit, Grandma?" asked Agnes, tucking her in.

"Yes, my peach, just a bit. I often wake up in the middle of the night these later years." Grandma turned her head on the large pillow to face her granddaughter. Agnes thought how small her grandmother looked in the great mahogany bed, just a bump in the sheet, really. "Without a light I'm sure I won't know where I am and wake up the whole house by tumbling down a stairway," she chuckled.

"Goodnight, Grandma. I'm so very glad you came." Agnes leaned over and gave her grandmother a kiss. The ladies left, closing the door softly behind them. Agnes turned to Mrs. Bairnaught.

"Does she seem well to you, Mrs. Bairnaught?"

"Yes, for the most part. Of course, her rheumatism gets a little worse every time I see her, but that's to be expected. But Agnes," whispered Mrs. Bairnaught, placing a hand on her arm, "your grandmother seems anxious about something. I asked what might be troubling her, but she only said it's a matter she needs to talk over with you."

Agnes frowned.

"Just be sure to find some time alone with her," advised the older woman, patting Agnes's arm. "I can't keep Mr. Bairnaught waiting any longer. Good night, my dear. You looked absolutely stunning tonight."

Agnes stood alone in the upstairs hall. Behind each door came the muffled sounds of people preparing for bed. She crossed her arms and gripped her elbows, pondering Mrs. Bairnaught's words as she headed for her own room. Passing Lord Phillip's room, she stopped to listen. She heard his voice softly singing, and it sounded as though he must be pacing back and forth. The melody stirred her heart though the words were inscrutable—an ancient, swaying hymn in the language of the Hindus.

# Chapter 9

The morning rose up clear and cool. Flower stems hugged the ground, beaten down by the night's rain, and droplets hung heavy from every leaf. After the warm stuffiness of the previous day, the guests were delighted to find the windows thrown open and all the promise of the day riding in on the morning breeze.

As Agnes descended the grand staircase to breakfast, she glanced through a clear pane of the stained glass window that dominated the landing. There on the sodden lawn stood Wilbur, putting Empress and Napoleon through their paces, alternately patting their heads and shaking his finger. He almost looked relaxed. She was reminded that some people's hearts warm more to animals than to humans. Why was he so awful to people, she wondered. The only kind thing she could remember him doing was when he bought her a basket of pink roses one summer many years ago while he was visiting Brookside. A ferocious summer cold had kept Agnes in bed, making her miss a ball she had bought a new dress and shoes for, and she was inconsolable at her bad luck. The gift had the effect of puzzling more than cheering her as she tried every which way to understand why a spiny character like her cousin would do such a lovely thing. She suspected at last that he had bought the arrangement for some other young woman who had refused his advances, and he then took the ready excuse of Agnes's illness to dispose of the unwanted bouquet. But she never knew for sure.

As she entered the dining room, guests had already begun serving themselves from the platters spread across the sideboard, and Isaiah was refreshing cups of coffee and tea. Fettles stood just outside, conferring with the stables staff on the timing and details of the hunt. The dogs knew that something was afoot and could be heard barking expectantly from the kennel.

Agnes took a sweet roll and cold ham while Isaiah poured her tea at the head of the table. Mr. and Mrs. Bairnaught sat down with crowded plates beside Agnes, and the mister set to slurping his coffee with relish. Agnes carefully cut open the warm roll and buttered it. "I hope you both slept well."

"Not at all," replied Mr. Bairnaught without completely raising his head. "But it's my wife's fault. She didn't read to me. Stayed up too long chatting and visiting. I was asleep when she finally came to see me, but I woke up all through the night."

Agnes looked at Mrs. Bairnaught questioningly and tried to conceal her amusement.

"It's true," smiled Mrs. Bairnaught, patting her husband's shoulder, "I neglected him shamefully. I'll do better tonight."

Mr. Bairnaught was a man of few words but great gusto, one who enjoyed life with both hands, as his wife was fond of saying. He measured just below average height, partly because nature had denied him the benefit of a neck, and remained, even at 65, powerfully built. His features forbid nonsense, and Agnes could not remember hearing him laugh. Nevertheless, a more solid friend the family never had. Both he and his wife were devoted to Agnes's mother and father, and they proved invaluable to her when her parents passed away within months of each other.

Mrs. Bairnaught clung to her husband as a barnacle to its ship, traveling with him wherever he went. She barely came up to his chin and, before her lovely shape widened with the years, she was often mistaken for his daughter as they walked arm in arm through public places. Now with her two chins and rounded shoulders, she was recognized as a wife, and, though she never admitted this, it had smarted for years when people stopped making the mistake.

"You are in the habit of reading to Mr. Bairnaught?" asked Agnes.

"Every night. It helps us both to sleep and we learn so much. I can't tell you how many wonders we have discovered between book covers over the years."

Agnes pictured this couple in their nightclothes, propped up against a bank of pillows. The gates of foreign cities opened before them as they looked with fascination at the strange landscape of an undreamed-of place "And what are you discovering now?"

"Emerson," answered Mr. Bairnaught, looking directly at Agnes as though to emphasize the importance of the name. "Rereading his piece on self-reliance. Brilliant man, but I'm not completely comfortable with his message. Transcendentalist, you know."

45

"Oh, dear, more philosophy," said Mr. McMeed, who was just taking a seat. "I don't know why, but any discussion of it stirs me up so. One can hardly eat a meal while talking about it." His linen was, as usual, exquisite this morning, and his chin shone from a meticulous shave. His wife sat beside him in a yellow dress that could not be ignored.

"I know what you mean," agreed Mrs. Bairnaught, "but his views are very popular. May he rest in peace."

"He died?" asked Mr. McMeed.

"Just a month or two ago, I believe."

"But what was wrong with him?" asked Mrs. McMeed.

"Well, I don't know, age probably took him."

"I mean his thinking."

Mr. Bairnaught briskly stirred more sugar into his coffee. "Caught the philosophical bug from his brother, I understand, who contracted the infection in Germany. Brother came home and convinced Ralph that the miracles of the Bible probably never happened. From there it was a short leap to putting God aside. Rely on your 'inner self' for truth. Dangerous idea, really."

"Well everyone has his own ideas about what's right these days," remarked Mrs. McMeed, looking wide-eyed at everyone in turn. "I feel that's all right, as long as you are sincere about what you believe. It all comes down to sincerity and everyone getting along, don't you think?"

The group was relieved from answering by the appearance of Wilbur, who strode into the dining room with a loud "Good morning," and, without sitting down, raised a cup and saucer toward Isaiah for coffee.

"Good morning, Wilbur," said Agnes, "I saw you outside exercising Empress and Napoleon. You must have worked up an appetite. Do help yourself to the sideboard."

Wilbur glanced at the gleaming platters. "Thank you, Agnes, I don't eat breakfast. Coffee is all that's needed in the morning. Eating before noon slows down the body and the mind."

"Indeed!" cried Mr. McMeed. "Then you should have the advantage in this morning's hunt since we are just finishing stuffing ourselves with this delicious fare." He nodded appreciatively at Agnes.

"Ah, the hunt," smiled Wilbur, walking to the window while balancing his coffee. "Yes, I heard the hounds. But isn't this a little late for a hunt? I should have expected you all to have dashed off hours ago."

"Group decision last night," returned Mr. Bairnaught. "After a late evening it's no use promising to get up at five in the morning." Heads nodded around the table. "We voted to go out at a civilized hour and just see what we could find."

Wilbur grunted and said he would not be joining them on that "archaic adventure." It was a practice, he explained, that had long outlived its utility. Chasing down a fox or hare just to show you can do it, along with a troop of horses and a pack of hungry dogs, no, not the sport for him. He returned his cup to the table and informed Agnes that he and Eleanor wished to make a jaunt into Chesterton to pick up a few things they did not find in their room, and he hoped her man could see his way to getting a carriage up in about an hour. "And if anyone would like to join us, you are welcome," he added, with an uninviting look around the table. Agnes assured him that she would make the arrangements.

Wilbur headed for the door and stopped. "But here's an idea," he exclaimed. "Who would like to wager on the outcome? I'll put money on the fox. Anyone for the hunters? We'll have Fettles hold the wagers for us and see who comes out on top at the end of the exercise. Shall we say twenty dollars?"

Wilbur's eyes had taken on an unwonted shine. "Anyone? Of course, we could open up the croquet tournament to some speculation and put a little flavor into it also, couldn't we?" He looked cheerfully at Agnes. The breakfasting guests stared at him without speaking.

Just then Phillip walked in, smoothing his hair with one hand and buttoning his waistcoat with the other. He stopped just inside the silent room and looked around uncertainly.

"Look who's here," exclaimed Wilbur. "Now I take you to be a betting man, Lord Phillip. I was just suggesting that we enliven today's hunt with a little wager on who might emerge the victor. Or even lay odds on the old croquet tournament. Are you in, old man?" Then, putting a finger to his lips, "Oh, wait, I forgot! You're a man of God, aren't you? I suppose gambling lies outside your field of allowable activities."

Phillip replied coolly, "It's true that I have gambled in my life, but never with money. I'll have to pass, 'old man.'"

Wilbur's eyes narrowed almost imperceptibly. "Indeed! A man who never gambles with money. Well, what stakes do you prefer? Commodities? Loaded pistols?"

Phillip, who had headed to the sideboard to investigate breakfast, turned around, smiling. "Are you proposing a dual?"

"I wouldn't dream of taking such advantage. It's simply that of all the things one might take chances with, a simple wager on the outcome of a fox hunt is about the safest way to enjoy oneself." Wilbur's eyes sparkled malignantly, but his voice carried a tune of pure merriment.

"So, then, no one?" he asked once more, surveying his confused audience. "Well . . . ." He nodded carelessly toward Agnes and left the room.

Mr. McMeed waited as long as he could before breaking the spell. "Well, that's awfully rough."

"Now, Daniel—" his wife warned.

"Well really! Agnes goes to all this trouble to show us a fine time and he comes along like a Turk with a toothache and tries to spoil it. I guess that's what comes from being modern—maybe he's a Transcendentalist—no respect for people's feelings or anything else, and you can say anything you damn well feel like."

"Those are the nihilists," Mr. Bairnaught corrected.

"Whatever he claims to be, he's a cad for sure. I know he is your cousin, Agnes, and I apologize, but it's a shame. And then to think of making wagers on the outcome! What's wrong with him? Well, let's clear the air." Mr. McMeed dropped his napkin on the table and rose. "Who's up for hunting?"

"Here, here," affirmed Mr. Bairnaught, raising a finger into the air.

"I wouldn't miss it," exclaimed Vera, whom no one had noticed in the pantry doorway, eating a lemon ice pilfered from the kitchen.

With perfect timing, Fettles stepped into the dining room to remind those joining the hunt that they would be departing on the hour. There was a sudden pushing back of chairs as some hurried off to change and others to enjoy the freshness of the morning from the terraces or gardens. Amid the tumult, Lord Phillip quietly layered his plate with eggs, cold meat, toast, and raspberries.

Agnes remained in her chair and silently took in his firm shoulders, the squared line of his chin, and the way his hair fell over his collar. She spoke up, "Lord Phillip, are you hunting today?"

He looked at her and smiled broadly, his features showing no trace of the barbed conversation he had just endured with her cousin. His eyes shone with a kind of innocence and gratitude she had not seen in a grown man. It was as if no armor covered him, and he stood before her unprotected.

# Chapter 10

Phillip came toward her and bowed modestly. "Hunting? Well, ma'm, I do love to ride, but I'm afraid it's all a little too chaotic for my nerves—the hounds and all, the chase. It's a fine sport for those with a thicker skin," he laughed easily. "However, I have done a bit of hunting in my own way already this morning."

"Oh?"

"Is anyone by chance missing a snake?"

Agnes's eyes widened and she caught her breath.

"One found its way to my room and we had quite a bit of sport between ourselves when I insisted that he remove himself from the comfortable armchair that I needed for putting on my boots."

Agnes was white, her hand over her mouth. "What happened? He didn't bite you, did he?"

"Oh, no. I finally convinced him that my laundry sack was a cozier place and in he went with just a little assistance."

"He is there now?"

"Oh, yes, quite safe and sound. Looks like one of your black rat snakes if I had to guess—not dangerous, unless you are a rat or a vole or some such thing."

"Lord Phillip, I am so grateful. It got into the house yesterday and I've been worried sick. You were very brave to trap it."

"Quite easy, really. I had a good deal of practice in India. The place swarms with snakes, so one has to get used to taking the upper hand with them."

"Well, then, after such an adventure, I hope you would join me for some breakfast on the terrace," Agnes offered. She had barely taken a bite of her meal before Wilbur's entrance, and her plate was still full. Phillip smiled his consent, and Isaiah carried their breakfast out to the terrace. Swiftly with a white napkin he wiped off the water, twigs, and leaves the storm had deposited on the table and chairs.

Phillip held a chair and Agnes took her place. She felt strangely self-conscious as she spread plum preserves over her toast. What is wrong with me, she wondered. She added a spoon of sugar to her tea, forgetting that she had already put one in. She was keenly aware that the dark coral color she had chosen to wear that morning did not flatter her as much as some others. She had not felt this prickly nervousness for years, and she did not welcome it. After all, she was a mature woman in her fourth decade. She had entertained a number of suitors and knew how to master her emotions, whatever they might be.

However, none of those men had borne any resemblance, in body or in manner, to the one sitting across from her now. There had been the railroad tycoon twenty years her senior with a penchant for singing off-key whenever a piano was played. There was the handsome but exceptionally dull army captain from Virginia who wanted her to move south with him to his family's tobacco plantation. There was the shy and thoughtful heir to a lumber fortune who kissed her once and, in great confusion and embarrassment, fled to St. Louis. Then there was M. She no longer thought of him even by his full name, because it pulled up in her mind his image, complete and seeringly vivid, and she did not want to remember.

"I feel I must apologize not only for the snake in your bedroom but also for my cousin," Agnes began. "That was a terribly rude display, but not exceptional for Wilbur."

"Do you think he dislikes me, or does he just hate God?" Phillip asked.

Agnes looked up, surprised by the directness of the question. "Oh, I don't know anyone he does like," she returned. "But God is certainly near the top of his list of villains. I can't say whether Wilbur hates Him or just finds the whole idea of a deity unbearably silly, along with all us poor souls who believe in Him."

"Well, if you enjoy doing any number of things that God has forbidden, it's essential to shove Him into the category of the ridiculous. Then you can carry on quite freely. It's a popular practice."

Phillip raised his coffee to his nose, smelled it, then took a sip. He proceeded to do the same with his eggs.

"Do you always smell your food before you eat it?" Agnes asked.

"Usually," he replied. "If you don't smell it you only get half the benefit, don't you think? The smell of eggs with ham, of fresh coffee, well buttered toast, that's a great part of the pleasure. If you just tear ahead swallowing everything in front of you, well, it's all over too quickly."

"You make a good point," Agnes conceded. "I will be careful to remember it."

Phillip looked at her earnestly—just a degree more than the way he looked at everyone—and saw that she was not laughing. "Thank you. I've gotten rather used to being ridiculed for ideas like that one."

"Well, don't let that concern you," Agnes reassured him. "You simply have a fresher outlook than most of us. It is a terrible rudeness as well as an ignorance to laugh at an idea simply because you are not used to it or you don't understand it. People given to ridicule rarely learn anything of importance."

"Very true!" agreed Phillip, raising his eyebrows and sniffing his toast. "Which explains why—I don't know if you agree—most people are quite unconscious of many ordinary truths that surround them." Phillip went on to explain how it does not occur to such people to observe things and then base their conduct on those observations. Instead they follow along in the stream of what everyone else is doing and talking about and wind up with very little first-hand knowledge. Then, to reinforce this poverty, they laugh off the practices of any friend engaged in objective investigation and discount his conclusions. "However," he drank off some coffee, "if those same investigations and conclusions appeared in print these same people would be declaring them brave and brilliant and would spend at least a week trying to apply them in their own lives."

Agnes laughed. "You are quite the student of human nature, Lord Phillip."

"People are endlessly fascinating, and you will never run out of depths to plumb no matter how long you study them."

Agnes poured herself more tea and wondered how many observations he was making about her. "I understand you have returned from India very recently," she resumed. He did not reply, but watched a sparrow hop forward to grab a crumb of fallen bread. "How did it strike you?"

"India?" Phillip held his fork and knife still and looked at his plate. "That question could require a very large answer. Most people don't have room for it. What size answer would you like?" he asked, looking at her.

Agnes paused as well. What a question, she thought. Who is this man? Is he rude or something else altogether? He demanded honesty from the very start. He did not allow a person the usual slow ascent; no, one immediately faced a steep climb, searching for footholds and making each step count.

"If need be, I can be free until dinner," she replied.

"Hah!" he laughed. "never have I been so indulged. I would not keep you that long, however. I might run out of things to describe by tea time."

"Somehow I doubt that."

Phillip glanced at her and saw again that she was not laughing. The baying of dogs being freed to lead the hunt made him snap his head around toward the stables, where the smartly dressed hunting party launched their mounts across the wet field. They both watched until the riders disappeared behind a gentle rise, the dogs' cries dying in the distance.

"Hot," he suddenly announced, returning to his plate. "So colorful it hurt." Then Phillip described to Agnes the masses of dark-skinned, shirtless men, the gaggles of women in brilliant saris, the marketplace's bags of orange and yellow spices, the violently green fields, the piercing blue sky. At times he longed for the refuge of a cool New England wood full of browns and muted greens, with soft beds of pine needles underfoot rather than dirt baked to a rocky hardness. But then the rain would come and they would all be standing in water up to their ankles for weeks, and then he longed for sun and dry land and clean clothing.

"I understand that you went as a missionary. What brought you back?" Agnes asked.

Phillip leaned back in his chair, having finished his food, and stretched out one leg. Agnes could not help noticing the outline of muscle beneath the gray pants. "There are two answers," he confided, dabbing off his moustache. "The one my father tells people and the more honest one. With you, I somehow feel like starting with the latter." He looked at her keenly, and his eyes sparkled like a man's do when he is about to take a risk and embraces it.

"You honor me," said Agnes, looking down to cut her last slice of meat. "I myself feel that anything short of honesty is usually a waste of everyone's time."

"I agree—when you are dealing with people of substance, that is. Which, of course, you are, Miss Somerset."

Agnes laughed. "You've hardly had time to find that out, have you?"

"Not at all. My father has told me much about you. He esteems you very much. And I have observed quite a bit during these two days that tells me he is correct in his opinion."

Agnes cleared her throat and sat back. "Well, then, why did you leave India?"

Phillip put down his napkin and rose to his feet. "I will tell you. Shall we meet, say, just after tea, on the bench in the topiary? I'm afraid I have an appointment just now—Ned has offered to show me his butterfly and nest collections."

Sitting up straight, Agnes considered her schedule. "I will be delighted to rendezvous after tea to hear the answer. Nothing could keep me from it."

His Lordship bowed, laid down his napkin, and ran off across the lawn.

Agnes sat for several minutes, feeling her heart pound. Above her, a giant elm bent its wet branches over the terrace, letting occasional drops splash onto the dirty dishes. A fresh breeze blew from the north and stirred the fine hair around her face as she mused. On the west lawn, Fettles was overseeing the establishment of the croquet course, pointing out necessary adjustments and pacing off to check the distance between wickets. Through the open doors behind her, Agnes heard dishes being cleared and the quiet laughter of the kitchen staff as they hurried to make way for lunch preparations.

Agnes reviewed the conversation that had just transpired and concluded that the Duke's son was a singular character whom she was not sure she liked. Was he the most mature man she had ever met, or the most childish? Spearing the last of her breakfast, she rose and went inside.

# Chapter 11

Lunch in the dining room that day was a small affair. The hunting party was still out, eating from hampers on the field of battle. Wilbur and Eleanor had gone to town after persuading the Duke and Lord Phillip to accompany them. (The Duke never hunted due to a violent allergy to poison ivy, which he unfailingly stumbled into whenever he strayed from manicured paths.) Nothing buoyed the Wilbur Browns so much as mixing with English aristocracy, even its displaced members. No tonic could impart to them the same glow, and the two were nearly giddy as they hunted for their necessaries in the small shops of Chesterton. Of course, no suitable merchandise was to be found anywhere in that provincial city, but even this frustration could not dim the couple's spirits, and they bravely remarked to the Duke that they "knew how to make do."

The group took lunch in the dining room of Chesterton's best inn, which came highly recommended by the dry goods merchant and the drugstore owner alike. "This should prove interesting," Wilbur winked at the Duke as they entered the clean but somewhat shabby dining room set with limp tablecloths and sturdy dishes. The Duke returned from this outing thoroughly drained, but Phillip beamed, having tucked away in his mind a myriad of new observations regarding a known type, the toadying critic.

In the meantime, a carriage bearing the last guest arrived at Brookside while Agnes shared a cold lunch with her guests in the dining room. Hearing voices out front, she excused herself and flew to the door. A young woman stepped down gingerly from a carriage and, with much relief, enfolded her aunt in her arms. The pleasure of being on solid ground almost overwhelmed the unsteady traveler. Agnes took her niece's face in her hands. "You are paler than ever, you poor little thing."

The exhausted young lady was the daughter of Agnes's sister Elizabeth. Stella favored the redheaded strain that ran through their line. Her skin was like a doll's, perfect and nearly translucent, but with pale freckles sprinkled across her nose, a nose that seemed just the slightest bit too large for her small face. A generous mouth, large eyes of faded blue fringed with tawny lashes, and thick red-orange hair lent Stella a dramatic look more powerful than beauty.

"I'm fine," Stella assured her aunt. "It's just my condition. I had not realized how difficult all the motion would be."

Agnes felt a wave of guilt and selfishness roll over her for urging this budding mother to make the trip from Chicago. "I am so sorry," she groaned, putting an arm around Stella's waist and leading her up the steps. "I am a selfish and ignorant woman. I will try to make it up to you while you are here. How long will you stay?"

"Two weeks, if you'll have me."

"Oh, not nearly long enough!" cried Agnes, and she led Stella upstairs after ordering that tea and toast be brought up. At the top of the stairs, she led her to a door and softly pushed it open. Stella gasped, forgetting her fatigue. "The mosaic room!" Years slid away and she was eight years old again, kneeling on the hearth, tracing the patterns of the Italian tiles. She remembered the Christmas she proudly gave her little paintings as gifts to her admiring family. "I like to think that my painting career started right here in this room," she smiled, unpinning her hat.

Tea arrived, and Agnes offered to let Stella rest, but her niece insisted that she stay. Agnes opened Stella's trunk and began hanging dresses in the old German wardrobe that seemed alive with its profusion of roses and birds cut deeply into the dark wood. Stella sat before a matching mirror and refastened her hair.

This is how Vera found them as she strode into the room with barely a knock. Stella jumped to her feet and was about to grab her great-aunt in a hug when she stopped short. Vera had brought back from the hunt a generous covering of burrs, and dried mud besmeared her riding pants and jacket. She explained matter-of-factly that one of the hounds wandered into a briar patch and could not figure his way out, so she had volunteered to work her way in and lead him back, losing her footing more than once on the muddy slope.

"Frederick of course wanted to go in my place, but as I was the smallest person in the party it only made sense for me to do it," Vera explained. "It was really the highlight of the whole outing, besides Mr. McMeed dismounting and chasing the fox on foot when he had completely lost confidence in the dogs."

"Did you catch the fox?" Stella asked.

"We had him cornered nicely, but Mrs. McMeed went into such a wail about how darling he was and what about his family somewhere, so no one could shoot."

"Did anyone explain that I brought that fox in expressly for the hunt?" asked Agnes. "That he was raised for this purpose and had no one waiting at home?"

"It would have been useless. Mrs. McMeed was too overwrought. I don't know what she imagined a hunt was all about." After kissing Stella carefully, Vera excused herself to change.

Alone again, Agnes fell to asking Stella question after question about her life in Chicago, her daily routine, her health, and her husband William. She noticed that her niece's voice stuck a bit in places and made her doubt the exclamations about how fine life was. Agnes leaned back in her chair and studied the face before her.

"What's wrong, Stella?"

After a short silence the young woman walked to the window. The afternoon sun turned her hair to flame and made her squint as she looked out across the brilliant lawns and flowerbeds.

"It's so beautiful here, Aunt Agnes. I already know that I won't want to leave."

"And I know that I won't want you to go. But I sense that your wish to stay will have more to it than just your love of Brookside. Stella—you don't need to pretend about anything with me."

Stella stared outside as though looking for the words somewhere just out of view. She worked her hands, sliding one over the other. Agnes waited. A squirrel scolded from a limb just outside the window and distant laughter drifted in from somewhere. Both women became aware of a world busy with itself as they occupied this little room, concentrated upon one life. Stella drew a breath. "I feel sometimes like I am . . . disappearing."

Haltingly she let out the story of the past two years in disjointed pieces interrupted by frequent reflection and apology. William was an excellent husband. Her mother had been right about him, and he worked hard to advance their fortunes. But sometimes it seemed too much, staying ten to twelve hours a day at his business in the stockyards, checking on a rumor of disease or meeting with railroad men about shipments or dining privately with investors. But it was not as though she found herself with nothing to do in his absence—

quite the contrary. She had been catapulted into a world of dinner parties and teas and ladies' clubs and supervision of a household. Although she had watched her mother perform these duties, she found that she was unprepared for the rigors of seemingly endless social obligation. At every turn she had a dozen questions and her mother was not there to answer any.

Stella recalled how she was the girl with her hair always coming undone and her hands dirty, a girl to be found either high in the branches of an apple tree or standing at an improvised easel painting a wildly colored landscape. Now she never ran, never painted. With the baby coming, time would be scarcer still. Some mornings, when she sat down at her little desk to answer a small pile of invitations and inquiries, she imagined packing a bag and disappearing, just for a while, to a place where she could breathe and stretch her legs and sketch the countryside.

"Do you feel that William loves you?" Agnes asked.

"Oh, yes, I know he does. He apologizes all the time for being gone so much and says it won't last forever. But he is ambitious, Agnes. That's something that drew me to him, I think, that energy. For a time it was directed toward me, though, and now . . . "

Stella went to her bag and pulled out an envelope whose worn edges showed that it had been opened and closed many times. From it she drew a paper heart printed with dark roses and trimmed in a thin green ribbon that laced its way around the edge. She handed it to Agnes, who took it carefully and read:

> *Let me Dwell in the light of thine eyes,*
> *Let me find a sweet home in thy heart!*
> *For my soul like a wild bird flies,*
> *To linger wherever thou art—*
> *As night gives place to the day,*
> *And darkness before the sun flies,*
> *So my sorrows will all melt away,*
> *When I live in the light of thine eyes.*

"This was his valentine to me two years ago, four months before our wedding. And this year . . ." Stella turned up her palms, empty.

Agnes studied the card. "Do you take this with you wherever you go?"

"When I travel, yes. I like to look at it whenever I am feeling sorry for myself. I know I am being selfish, Aunt Agnes, but I can't help it—this isn't what I wanted, this isn't what I thought married life would be."

"What did you picture?"

She had pictured happiness—a river of happiness that they would float down, each day more blissful and refreshing than the last. He would cover her with kisses each morning and she would spend the day painting pictures for him to praise when he returned in the evening, pulling her into his arms and whispering how much he had missed her. They would go to dinners and balls and be admired as the couple most in love. Children would come along to be purred over and taken on picnics every weekend. They would pack the happy brood into a buggy and bump along under leafy trees, past exuberant spring meadows, drunk with the richness of loving family life. Stella smiled with embarrassment and sank into a chair across from her aunt.

Agnes cocked her head. "In this tableau there are no runny noses or soggy picnics or clothes that smell like the stockyard?"

"Naturally!"

"Stella, you know that I am not laughing at you." She handed back the precious valentine. "I think you might simply need a rest. Can you stay with us a while?"

Stella stared at the paper heart. She would write to William and see. Maybe she could. She did not admit to her aunt that she had brought along in the bottom of her trunk a small set of paints and brushes and far too many sheets of heavy paper for just a two-week visit.

# Chapter 12

Fatigue filled Agnes as she left Stella's room. She knew she needed a nap, especially since tonight she would be reading aloud her history of Brookside after dinner, and a lackluster performance was out of the question. She had put too much work into it for that. She would go to her room, ring for Fettles to check on the state of things, and lie down until tea. But as though anticipating her thoughts, Fettles approached from the far end of the hall with a tray bearing a single card. He held it out to her without a word.

Agnes picked up the rich ivory card. *Mrs. Sherman Thorne*. She looked at Fettles with mild alarm. "Now? Again?"

"In the parlor, ma'm."

Agnes exhaled hotly. "Tell her I am not at home—no, tell her— oh, why does she insist on dropping by at the absolutely worst times?!"

"I can send her away. I would be very happy to."

Agnes thought. "No, I feel I must keep an eye on her. Let us just get this over with. And no tea, Fettles, whatever you do. We don't need to prolong the agony."

Agnes found Claudia displayed to advantage in a deep brown dress with a finely worked lace collar. Above it, her perfect chin tilted upward as she beamed a benevolent smile.

"I spoke with the Duke on my way in," remarked Claudia without rising. "He looks very well. He was a great friend of your father's, wasn't he?"

"He was," answered Agnes, perching on the edge of a facing chair, "although they knew each other a fairly short time before Father's death. But our families' friendship has continued."

"Still not remarried, I assume?"

"That's true."

"Well," confessed Claudia, "I hope you'll forgive my just popping in once more, especially in the middle of your lovely fete, but—" dropping her voice, "I was wondering about the Duke's son. Did he come?"

"Yes, he did. He was kind enough to come along and stay with a crowd of people he has never met, which is very brave, really."

"I'd like to meet him."

Agnes shifted in her chair. Failing to offer any refreshment to her visitor was only a small affront given the busy circumstances, but to refuse to introduce her to Lord Phillip was not possible. She rang for Fettles and asked him to request a moment of Lord Phillip's time. In moments he was leading the young gentleman into the parlor. Phillip looked slightly bewildered and registered no amazement at the spectacle of the legendary Mrs. Thorne. Agnes introduced them, watching Phillip closely. He took Claudia's hand briefly with a small bow and began a subtle study of her person. Agnes could see him taking in her feathered hat, her face, the costly earrings. She could almost hear his pen scratching notes.

"Agnes has scored a great victory having you to herself this week," Claudia cooed. "Everyone is talking, we are all so anxious to make your acquaintance, Lord Phillip. I trust you will be generous enough to visit the rest of us as soon as time permits? We would so love to hear about India."

"Would you?" asked Phillip, holding his hands behind his back. "When?"

Claudia stammered. "Well, any time you like, I'm sure."

"The Wednesday after next?"

Claudia for once was caught off guard. "Yes. That would be delightful. I shall expect you, then?"

"I shall be there."

Agnes felt her cheeks flush. That would be a week after the end of his time at Brookside. Why was he so anxious to leap into this woman's web? Was he smitten? He didn't look like it. Was this just more research? Either way, she recoiled at the idea of his sitting comfortably across from Claudia, enjoying a light lunch, sniffing his entrée and sharing his observations on the Orient.

"I should go," Claudia was saying, "and leave you to your guests."

Agnes smiled.

"May I show you out?" offered Phillip, extending his arm. Claudia poured a satisfied look over Agnes, took his arm, and swished away. Agnes heard the bubbling laugh.

She did not get her nap, and Phillip did not come to tea. Agnes occupied herself by introducing Stella, who felt much improved after a short rest, to those she had not met and listening to accounts of the hunt. Several people offered slightly different versions of Mr. McMeed's behavior and his wife's interference with the fox's destiny, but it was clear that everyone had enjoyed himself enormously and would tell the story many more times to other audiences.

Agnes dawdled over her tea, drinking three cups rather than her usual one. She sat afterwards with Stella on the terrace for nearly half an hour before excusing herself to find Phillip in the topiary as they had agreed.

Shadows lengthened over the lawns as Agnes walked slowly toward the gardens, breathing in the delicious early evening air. She pulled her skirts close as she passed through the old arches draped in white climbing roses and stopped to put her nose in one. They gave off their sweet scent so freely at this time of day, and it hung in the air above the fine gravel path. The delicate blossoms clung to the stone pillars and twined around the heavy black chains between them. She passed white, pink, and red roses set on thick, twisting stems that had been widening their reach for the better part of a century. Beyond the climbers came her favorites, the English roses, with their densely layered heads and sweet aroma. Vicious thorns covered their stems completely, and she had learned painfully as a child that these could not be picked but needed the shears of the gardener to separate them from the bush. Admire us, they seemed to say, but do not try to take us as your own; do not stand us in crystal vases in stuffy rooms. Gather your hybrid teas just down the path—they were grown for sacrifice with their long stems and garish blooms.

The path led her into the topiary with its old boxwoods and dense yews trimmed into hedges, balls, and obelisks. On the far side of this strict garden, behind a hedge six feet high, was a sheltered corner at the edge of the estate's high ground. Nestled against the ancient greenery, protected from view, was a stone bench enjoyed exclusively by Agnes. Two marble statues flanked the bench: a modestly robed Venus and her blacksmith husband, Vulcan. The spouses gazed at each other, forever longing, forever separated by the stone slab where living lovers might sit whispering between them and look out over the distant hills to the west. Agnes loved this secluded spot and came to it often to collect her thoughts or simply to dream, especially at sunset when the sky lay spread before her, shot through with pink and orange. Sometimes she stayed to watch a perfect ascendancy of blue creep from the horizon to heaven's immeasurable vault and see the first stars prick the darkening sky.

It was on this bench that she sat immobile for hours when M. left, when her chest felt like its center had been carved out and taken away. The coward, the deceiver. Where was he now? Had she been fully replaced, and how many times over? Was he romancing another innocent maiden? Oh, but he could make her laugh. And his eyes, they looked inside her and saw what no one else had been able to find. Scoundrel! I hope he's been lost at sea, made a slave to pirates, blanketed by coursing lava, eaten by wolves—

Hurried steps approached down the gravel path behind the tall hedge. Agnes sat very still, listening, and wondered why she had not told Phillip about this hidden bench behind the hedge. She had to admit that somehow she intended to test him, to see how hard he would look for her. The steps stopped momentarily. Then a voice called over the perfect silence of the late afternoon.

"Agnes? Agnes, are you here?"

Oh, my goodness, she thought, he is calling for me like a child playing hide-and-seek. Fearful that a guest might hear him and join in the search, Agnes rose and hurried around the hedge, nearly colliding with him on the other side. He stood smiling and clearly amused. Carefully he held out a tea cookie.

"Another step and you would have made me drop our cookies. I brought some along for us."

"How very thoughtful," she stammered, taking the proffered cookie. "You must enjoy anise as much as I do."

"No, I don't like it at all. Are these anise?"

"Yes, they are Dahlia's specialty cookies. She is rather well known for them."

"She's done a good job of covering up the anise, then." Phillip brought one close to his nose then popped it into his mouth. "Where shall we sit?"

Agnes paused. Should she guide him back to a bench in the heart of the garden, where they might be observed and overheard by others? Or should she admit him to her private place between the gods, where he might look for her again, making that magical spot no longer a secret, no longer an assurance of solitude?

"The view is best from over here," she said, taking his arm. "But you must promise," she warned, looking him steadily in the eye, "to tell no one. This is my private retreat," she explained as they continued around, "and you should consider yourself flattered in a spectacular way to be admitted."

"Your confidence is safe with me, madam," Phillip assured her as they settled themselves onto the cool bench.

Now you've done it, Agnes told herself. She felt the sharp pang of having given away something before it was earned. She scolded herself, but it was too late.

# Chapter 13

Phillip gazed at the deep green hills and the patchwork fields laid out between thin lines of trees, tiny in the distance. A lone bird winged its way home across the vast sky. Phillip took in the stone lovers on either side of him, looking first at one, then the other, and back again. "Forever separated," he observed. "Your retreat is a place of yearning, then. And great beauty."

"You see why it is so special to me."

Phillip leaned back into his corner of the seat and arranged his arms and legs comfortably.

"So what do you want to know?"

"Everything you are willing to tell." She looked at him expectantly.

Phillip took a long breath and began. Some ten years ago an appeal had been sounded for missionaries to central India. The church wanted single, healthy males who were looking for adventure, loved God, and had a natural boldness that would allow them to talk about Christianity in a wild place among people who already had more gods than they could count. Phillip knew this was his calling. His extraordinary curiosity, which had gotten him into endless trouble since he learned to walk, could now be indulged. He would observe a totally new culture, with no one shutting up his questions or forbidding him from poking about where he did not belong. His father approved the trip as a providential solution for what to do with an intelligent son who did not seem to fit into any occupation he had tried—or even into polite society.

The voyage had been exhilarating. For weeks he traveled, first across a stormy Atlantic, then through the enchanting Mediterranean, and on through the Suez Canal. At the Suez you knew you were entering another world, he reminisced. Passengers were told to change into their tropical dress, and a new energy ran through his travel-weary shipmates. Whether they were bound for India to make their fortune, take up a government job, or serve with the British army, a sense of eagerness gripped them all as they pushed into the Indian Ocean and made for Bombay.

The year was 1874. The Brits had sent the last Mogul emperor packing years earlier and now held direct control over two-thirds of the country. Entrenched princes and maharajas ruled the other third in scattered states, having pledged allegiance to the crown. It was to one such state that Phillip was headed, Hyderabad, to a small mission at its southern border. He already knew that the ruling nizam was among the world's richest men. Reports abounded of the splendor of his court, the egg-sized emeralds that decorated his throne, buckets of pearls and golden plates and a different silk robe for every day of the year.

By contrast, the mission—and the town and countryside around it—existed in the simplest way imaginable. Arriving in late April, the hottest month of the year, Phillip was stunned by the scorching sun. The land was dry and water precious as the population waited for the relief of the monsoon rains.

"I came to reinforce a Welsh missionary who had been at his humble post for five years, the last two years alone since his assistant had died of cholera," Phillip explained. "When I asked him after a few days how he stood the bristling heat, he scowled and said 'Do you want some rain, then? Be careful what you ask the good Lord for, my friend.' I didn't know what to make of that at the time."

"We had a small chapel adjoining our rustic residence. It contained a few benches and a rough cross nailed above an altar that we draped in a piece of white cotton. Every Sunday Gregory, my taciturn superior, said a simple service at nine in the morning, attended by a changing mix of curious children and one very dark old man who told Gregory each week that he was thinking about converting. Gregory told me he was a spy for the local Hindu priest."

"So you made no converts?" Agnes asked.

"Not there in Hyderabad, not while I was there. The Hindus listened to us politely but went away chuckling at a religion that relied on a single god. And one who had come to earth as a mere man with only two arms and two legs like the rest of us. Our tales were not tall enough, our holidays not colorful enough. And the local Mohammedans had no more use for us than the Hindus did."

Agnes asked whether he ever found out what his superior had meant about being careful what he prayed for. Indeed he had. They baked like pots in a kiln until June. Phillip was sitting in the scant shade teaching a few urchins some English from the Gospel of John, when the clouds slid over the mission. The next morning they let loose their load of water. He thought they must all drown. The hardened dirt of the mission yard was transformed into a slippery bog, and waterfalls fell from the roofs of every building. In many places the water lay ankle-deep, in others it rose to their knees. The rain continued until September, by which time he could not imagine the land ever drying out even if it never rained again.

As the land recovered itself, Phillip could not ignore his growing restlessness. He received Gregory's permission to travel around a great part of India, taking copious notes on the people and their customs, sharing the Bible with any who would listen.

"Did you see the Taj Mahal?" Agnes asked eagerly. Once at her aunt's house she had seen pictures of it through a stereoscope.

He had, and made several sketches. He asked if Agnes knew that the emperor Shah Jahan had it built of white marble in memory of his beloved wife, who died after giving birth to their fourteenth child.

"Fourteenth!" Agnes gasped.

"And he himself would have been buried in a temple of black marble just across the river. Unfortunately, his third son interrupted his plans by throwing the father into prison and beheading his older brothers in order to crown himself emperor." India, Phillip said, was a land of extremes. Drought and flood, excess and want, generosity and cruelty, beauty and barbarism.

"Not a place for the faint of heart," observed Agnes.

Phillip was silent a moment, his brow contracted as he surveyed the deepening colors of the sky. "Maybe not a place for those with any heart at all."

Agnes held her breath. Now he might be on the verge of telling her why he had left. The real story, not the varnished one his father gave out.

# Chapter 14

She studied Phillip's profile, so close she could make out each soft eyelash. The dying breeze blew strands of hair against his temple and cheek. Agnes watched them dance there as she fought an inexplicable urge to reach out and tuck them behind his ear.

Low voices approaching from beyond the hedge broke the spell. Phillip looked at Agnes as she put a finger to her lips. The voices came nearer while the two sat as still as the statues watching over them. Wilbur's low tones floated on the cooling air.

". . . not at all the time to talk about a thing like this."

Eleanor answered, her voice tense with urgency. "You promised me that you would tell her on this visit. You know I wanted you to make a clean breast of it weeks ago, but  you said"—her voice going pompous—"'This is not something you put in a letter.' Well, which is it? We're here and you can tell her face to face."

"My love," Wilbur replied, just inches behind the dense hedge, "she's my cousin. I should know how to handle this, don't you think? And wouldn't I be a cad to spoil her anniversary party with such a discussion?"

"If you don't, Grandma will. Do you think for a moment that she is going to leave here without letting Agnes know? If she sees you keeping silent?"

"You need to trust me with this, Eleanor," Wilbur put down firmly. "And for heaven's sake, don't play the righteous wife." The voices thinned as the couple moved off, leaving behind them a domestic sort of anger that hung in the air like smoke.

Phillip looked at Agnes with concern. "What do you make of that?" he whispered.

Agnes clamped her skirt in her hands. "I've no idea. But it sounds like I should have a conversation with Grandma Brown first thing tomorrow." Agnes remembered Mrs. Bairnaught's advice to her the night before. "It appears I have some things to look into," she said distractedly. Collecting herself, she smiled at Phillip. "But now I want to hear the rest of your story."

Phillip sat back. "Where was I?"

"Beheadings, and not a place for those with a heart."

"Well, let's see. You remember what Gregory told me? About being careful what you prayed for? Well, I learned not to wish for rain or against it." Phillip told how the monsoons were a force to reckon with, indeed, but their absence was worse. In 1875 the rains failed across southern India. The population scratched out an existence, waiting for the next season. But the next year they did not come either. By then, the price of the little food that remained was horrifyingly high, out of most people's reach. Britain was slow to respond, with the viceroy in charge declaring that a free market would be the best way to ensure an adequate supply of food. By the time they set up refugee camps they were too few and too late. The mission closed, and Phillip went to lend a hand in a camp 50 miles to the east.

"On the road I came across flocks of children wandering alone. Walking skeletons. I couldn't understand how these little ones kept going. And they did not just walk along themselves—I saw so many carrying children smaller than themselves, wasted down to their bones, too exhausted even to speak. Scores of them arrived weekly at the camp. Often those who clung to one another were not even related but had come from the same village where their parents had died of famine or cholera or had simply abandoned them in search of food."

"We brought some back to life. Others got only as far as our gate. They would deliver their little burdens into our arms, then lie down . . ." Phillip's voice failed and he looked at the ground. Agnes took his hand and pressed it into hers.

"I cannot tell you all that I saw. I must not. No one I suppose will ever read a full account. It's as one missionary told me, that a man's pen sticks at writing down scenes that have made his blood run cold."

Agnes waited, watching a band of noisy blackbirds find their places in the treetops. Finally she asked softly, "How long did this go on?"

In earnest, eighteen months. It seemed an eternity. The rains finally found Madras again in '78, in June. He returned to the little mission, but nothing was left of it. Gregory had been killed on a solitary outing by a murderous band of thugs, hoping no doubt that his bloody death would placate Indra. That mercurial goddess would then release the monsoons and end the famine, or so a talkative passerby had told him.

"So I walked into town and stood in what was left of it. Half of the inhabitants were dead or gone. What to do. I decided to pay a visit to the family I remembered as the wealthiest in the area and see if they would help me rebuild the mission. I had no idea why they would—I just thought I'd give the hand of God an opportunity. I hadn't the least idea what else to do. The father, Dhanesh, being a good man of business, spoke very fine English. He was genial and sat me down. I remember he said with a grin" (here Phillip adopted an authentic south Indian singsong) "'Why do you waste your time here in Madras? You are a young man, strong, intelligent, but you are getting older every day and you are alone. It is not good for you. A lizard who comes to live with the turtles will never teach them to be lizards. And the turtles just wait for him to leave one day. You are understanding me?'" Phillip smiled. "I was understanding."

"So you left?"

"No. You might say I should have." Phillip glanced at Agnes, then away. "He had a daughter."

# Chapter 15

Rupa was fourteen and well into marrying age. Her father suspected every man in the province of wanting to wed her for her beauty and the family's money, and indeed, she had many suitors. Her mother envied the daughter whose radiance grew as her own faded. She had noticed how lately, when they walked together through town, her daughter stole the attention of men who only a handful of years ago looked approvingly at her, the lovely Neela. So Neela soothed her injured vanity by scolding the girl for failings large, small, and imagined. Three brothers, all older, delighted in teasing Rupa and setting up elaborate schemes to frighten her. The father joined in the hilarity, and even though the mother condemned this campaign of shock as going too far, her sons had long ago developed an immunity to her high-pitched harangues.

Being a hospitable Hindu, Rupa's father invited Phillip to stay in his home while deciding what to do next—that is, when to leave the country and by what means. They gave him new clothes (his own were in rags), fed him, and instructed him in the glories of their many gods. Reclining on silk cushions, Dhanesh talked to Phillip long into the night about the proud history of India, about what Marco Polo really found on his voyage through that country, about invaders and emperors and the craftiest warrior of all ages, the Lion of Punjab.

Rupa kept her distance from Phillip but he had caught her watching him from corners or behind curtains. He assumed that he might be the only man who did not stare at her or order her about or sadistically frighten her.

"One day," recalled Phillip, "I took a basket of melons from her and carried it the rest of the way to the kitchen. I could see that this confused her, especially when she saw that I wanted nothing from her. The next day, in my broken Hindi, I told her the story of Mary Magdalene, and how Jesus was probably the first man who had loved her without wanting something in return. I tried to explain how Jesus was like that, a servant, and yet God. Of course, this was very difficult for her to imagine. She asked me to tell the story many times over, and sometimes I would substitute other parables—the Good

Samaritan, the rich young ruler, the good and poor soil. Her mother watched us with suspicion. Her father laughed."

"He did not see you as a threat, I imagine?"

"Not at all. I believe he saw me as a mangy cub he had taken in until I could be released back into my own habitat."

"Did she fall in love with you?" The question startled Agnes even as she said it.

"She would have fallen in love with any man who was kind to her."

"What happened?"

One night Rupa crept to Phillip's bed and begged him to take her back home with him. She would marry him, or be his servant, anything he wanted. He could never forget how her wet eyes shone wildly as she knelt beside him in the moonlit room. She could not stay there, she said. Her father was in final negotiations to marry her to the son of a minor prince, a young man only ten years older than her but already famous for his wickedness.

"What could I do? I could not leave her there. I had met her betrothed earlier at a festival in Hyderabad—I was walking through the market when his man pulled me over and asked me to translate an inscription inside a ring. Manindra, the fiancé, stood there, handsomely dressed, with a great sword hanging at his side. He held the ring out to me without a word, and his eyes were like a dead man's—there was no light in them. They did not seem human, really. I've never seen eyes like them."

"What was the inscription?" Agnes asked. She had always needed every detail colored in when hearing a story.

"It was Latin: *Misere mei, Deus*."

"Have mercy on me, Lord."

"Yes. I could not help imagining that the ring came off the finger of a Catholic priest, and probably not with his consent. I gave him the translation and he slid the heavy ring onto his middle finger. Then he paid the seller and smiled at me in the strangest way. Even in that miserable heat, a chill ran through me."

Phillip described the plan he devised with Rupa. In two days they would steal away during the night to a town ten miles south, where they could catch a train to the coast. They would travel posing as man and wife. In Bombay he would find a friend of his father, who could be counted on to lend him enough money to transport them to France. Once there, he would leave Rupa in the care of nuns in Rheims, a refuge he had heard other missionaries tell about.

They waited through the next two agonizing days, afraid that someone, somehow, might read their minds and snatch Rupa away to the prince's household for safekeeping. Instead, the family continued in its routine, the mother scolding everyone and fussing over wedding preparations while the brothers left a dead lizard in Rupa's shoe, and this was all very reassuring.

Just after midnight, with only a sliver of moon to guide them, Phillip and Rupa slipped out of the house. If they were caught, it meant certain death for Rupa and something worse for Phillip. They hugged the shadows along the road going south, hiding from the late-night carts that rattled along that lonely stretch, reaching the train station just before dawn. Rupa kept her veil spread over her face and walked with the dignity of a married woman, adorned with jewelry befitting a young bride. She had taken the finery from her hope chest kept in her mother's room the evening before, along with enough money for food, the train trip, and any bribes that might ease the journey.

Phillip purchased two tickets to Bombay. They wandered through the marketplace for an hour, concealing themselves amid the crowd in case any one had come looking for them already. At the last possible moment, they returned to the station and jumped on the westbound train, settling themselves away from the windows. A conductor eyed them suspiciously above his massive moustache as he took their tickets, staring intently at Phillip before moving on. As he walked back through the car, he stopped again beside them.

"You are missionary?" he asked, narrowing his eyes.

Phillip's jaw tightened but he replied as evenly as he could, "That's right."

"You have been in Anayesh, in Madras?"

"Some time ago, yes." It might end here, Phillip thought. This man could call the guards and pull them off the train. "God, help us!" he silently implored.

The conductor's sun-darkened face relaxed. The small man grabbed Phillip's hand and squeezed it. "You are good man!"

Phillip slowly let out his breath while trying to retrieve the man's face from memory. The conductor explained that Phillip had taken his child from him when they arrived at the relief camp a year ago, his wife already dead along the way. He reminded Phillip of how he had fed the man's little girl for several days as he himself, too weak and sick to care for her, lay on a mat and watched. His daughter was now healthy, he said, and living with his mother while he looked for a new wife.

"I remember you tell me, in heaven, no caste. For Jesus, we all are same. I like your Jesus," he whispered, dropping his head close to Phillip's ear. Then he was gone.

Agnes saw Phillip's face brighten as he recalled the scene. He turned ruefully to her. "My only convert!"

The rest of the journey went incredibly well. They found the Duke's friend in Bombay, still at his old address. After listening closely to Phillip's story, he took from a little locked drawer in his desk the money needed to reach France and pressed it upon the young man. Seeing this, Rupa reached into her bag and drew out two gold bracelets as partial payment. The good man held up his hands, but she insisted, and he knew better than to refuse. They all shook hands warmly, and their benefactor sent the couple off with his best wishes and greetings for the Duke. The boat sailed, the wind blew fair, and by the time Phillip and Rupa reached the Suez they had stopped looking over their shoulder. In France they found the convent right where the missionaries had described it, spreading quietly beside a humble stone church. After a long embrace, Phillip left Rupa at its gates, in the care of the nuns.

Unwilling to present himself to his father in the state of turmoil and exhaustion that the adventure had left him in, Phillip made his way to the home of his godparents (artistic ex-patriots from New York) just south of Paris, there to recover and re-acclimate himself to the civilized life of sitting at a well-set table, wearing clean clothes that fit, and communicating in his native language.

"This is a wonderful story," Agnes breathed when he had finished. "Why should your father tell any other?"

"Have you heard the axiom that no good deed goes unpunished?" asked Phillip. "At least in this life."

"I have both heard it and experienced it," she assured him.

"There is another version of my story afoot. And for some reason it seems more credible to people than the actual one. Maybe because so many people enjoy thinking the worst. At any rate, Rupa's father complained to the British governor, and word got around that I had a romantic entanglement with a young girl and had dishonored her in the worst possible way, then spirited her out of the country."

"Were you called to account for it somehow?"

"Oh, yes, the Raj tracked me down and asked for a full explanation, which I provided except for any disclosure about where I left Rupa. As it was my word against her father's, nothing could be proven, so they have left me alone. Nevertheless, the ugly version of this tale has somehow found its way into certain pockets of society, so I am for some a man with a soiled past." He glanced sideways at Agnes and pushed at a buried rock with the toe of his boot.

"So," observed Agnes, "your good works have earned you a penalty you did not suspect at the time."

"Correct."

"The consequences truly never occurred to you?"

"I knew her family would be furious, but I counted on distance to protect me from them. That the story would follow me home and besmirch my name here was a surprise. I am, you will see, that most exasperating of human creatures, the slow learner."

Agnes felt her heart throb with affection for this man, but she kept her mind steady.

"And what reason do I have," asked Agnes coyly, "for believing one tale rather than another?"

"None at all," he answered, rising. "You may believe whichever one appeals to you." He held his arm out to her. She looked up into his face but had trouble making out his expression in the dusk.

Suddenly a realization struck her. "Oh, my!" she cried, jumping to her feat. "The dinner! I still need to dress. Look how you have distracted me, Lord Phillip."

"Then let's away, madam—let's run!" Agnes took his arm with one hand and her skirts with the other and ran as lightly as she could ever remember through the gloom of the garden and toward the great house where golden light now shone from every window.

# Chapter 16

Agnes took a moment on the terrace to catch her breath. Phillip had slipped away to enter by another door and thus avoid any raised eyebrows at their entering *ensemble* after such a long absence. Looking through the French doors to the dining room, Agnes saw the heirloom candelabras blazing on the main table and sideboard, and prisms sparkling in small circles on the chandelier above. Hunting scenes and still lifes hung against the red and gold wallpaper, giving the room a rich and permanent look. The table was set with the family's gold-trimmed ivory china and complicated silver, all freshly polished. She swelled with pride at her family, at what her father had achieved, at the fine things her mother carefully collected, and the beautiful experience she could now offer her guests. She felt deeply happy to be a Somerset, honored to carry their traditions forward in her own hands.

She tiptoed in and went straight to the kitchen. There she found Fettles deep in conversation with Dahlia, who was trying her best to ignore him into disappearing. They glanced up as she entered the too-warm but deliciously scented room.

"Ah, there you are!" exclaimed the butler with an arch look. He was clearly waiting for her to explain her tardiness, but when no excuse came, he continued.

"There is a problem, ma'm. Three bottles of Chateau Plessy are missing—poof!" He motioned with his fingers that something had suddenly turned into nothing. "This leaves us without enough to serve during the second course. And I have a good idea what happened to them." Fettles turned to the cook.

"It's all nonsense," Dahlia protested, her sleeves rolled back on her sturdy arms. She stirred four sauces in rapid succession then motioned for an assistant to take over. "He thinks my nephew, the new boy, is to blame, but I know him, and he'd never do any such a thing."

"Madam," said Fettles, turning to Agnes. "He was put in charge of sweeping the wine cellar just last week against my better judgment. All the wines for tonight were there at the time."

Agnes picked up a buttery pastry from a pile beside the stove and smelled it. "I doubt we will solve this mystery tonight. The question is, what will our guests drink?"

"Precisely," returned Fettles.

"Don't we have anything else that will do?"

"We have an inferior claret that is similar but certainly not up to the mark. Aside from that, there is nothing. Even with that, there's nothing."

"Well, we seem to have no choice but to follow the advice of the wine steward at Cana," Agnes observed. "Serve the Plessy on the first couple of rounds, then substitute the other. By then, with any luck, our friends will not be able to distinguish between claret and apple cider."

"And Fettles," Agnes added as she turned to go, "the dining room looks marvelous. It is just as I'd hoped. Thank you!"

Unable to keep his starch under this shower of appreciation, Fettles cleared his throat and excused himself to double check the seating arrangement. Agnes took the back stairs to avoid any entanglements with her guests and flew to her room, where she found Marie laying out the sapphire silk gown they had chosen for this special evening.

Despite her hurry, Agnes stopped to gaze at the shimmering dress spread across the bed. She had ordered it from the City just for tonight, and it had arrived only yesterday. Agnes had put it on immediately so Marie could make adjustments in the little time left, but by a miracle, it fit perfectly. Tonight the tiny black beads that trimmed the wide neckline twinkled in the lamplight. Agnes admired the cut of the dress, with dark vertical piping that would flatter her figure. She loved how the yards of deep blue silk gathered themselves up at intervals into two rows of black rosettes, each with beaded centers. Suddenly she had misgivings.

"Marie, do you think it's too much?"

"What do you  mean, Miss Agnes?"

"Too much for me, for the occasion."

"If you mean too much beauty, how can that be? This is probably the finest dress I've ever touched. And you get to wear it tonight and be the most beautiful woman in the world."

Agnes laughed and let Marie help her out of her day dress. She hastily freshened herself, and, with Marie's help, worked her way into the subtly twinkling gown. They agreed on a simple upsweep for her hair and then earrings only, with no necklace to distract.

The hostess and her guests formed a glittering congregation at dinner, the ladies in their best gowns and the gentlemen displaying their finest linen. Conversation rolled easily back and forth across the table as they consumed generous servings of soup, roast pork, new potatoes, and fish. Their wine glasses were continually refreshed course by course, so that by the time dessert and sherry were served, everyone felt on the very friendliest terms with everyone else. No one noticed the wine substitution, or at least they gave no sign of it. Agnes watched Wilbur and Eleanor closely throughout the meal, but they betrayed none of the anxiety expressed earlier in the garden and gave every sign of enjoying themselves as much as they ever could.

Of course, the natural centerpiece of the evening's chatter was Lord Phillip's recent adventures in Asia, which Mrs. McMeed eagerly inquired about shortly into the first course. Phillip, impossibly handsome in black and white, with his neatly combed hair already beginning to stray along one cheek, finished his mouthful of iced grapefruit and looked knowingly at his father. To Agnes's eye, his look said "Don't worry, I will be careful." Phillip then regaled the company with the same tales he had told to Agnes, minus unsavory descriptions of the famine or any reference to a beautiful, desperate young woman.

"So," put in Wilbur when Phillip seemed to be finished, "I am not clear on why it was you left."

The Duke adroitly stepped in. "Neither am I," he smiled, leaning forward confidentially. "I had hopes he might make a career of good works among those poor Mohammedans and Hindus, but here he is again, the dear boy. But with that climate, I can surely understand. Disease everywhere, drought one month and monsoons the next—it doesn't seem a place for civilized people, after all."

"I would have needed to be made of sterner stuff," Phillip concluded. His eyes met Agnes's with a sensation that was almost physical. How many times had she caught him looking at her that evening? But this time he did not look away and she had to reluctantly break the connection by inviting Grandma Brown to tell them (a propos of other cultures) about her impressions of Paris when she went there on her first honeymoon so many years ago.

After dessert, the guests adjourned to the drawing room, where Agnes arranged herself beside the fireplace as her guests settled back with cups of steaming coffee. With only a few glances at her notes, she delivered her History of Brookside. She led her listeners from its construction by her great grandfather Phinnaeus—who had made a small fortune in coffee after the colonists patriotically switched from tea—through the family's ups and downs across the decades and the tumultuous years of the War Between the States, up to a tender conclusion with Agnes's account of the deaths of her dear parents and older sister in the years just past.

Aside from Grandma Brown, who went quietly to sleep in the first few minutes of the recitation, not a female eye was dry by the end of the tale. Mr. McMeed could be heard sniffing audibly in a far corner, and Mr. Rockwell, feeling so many memories stirred, had to blow his nose several times. Agnes's finish was greeted with loud applause and hearty commendations, and many hugs were exchanged all around.

It was late, and the party soon retired to their own rooms, leaving Agnes to quietly congratulate the staff, still busy in the kitchen, on a job well done. She felt the fatigue that had been building over the last few days. The presentation over, the grandest dinner of the week a success, she allowed herself to slip into a wonderful sleepiness anticipating the comfort of her bed. She headed across the thick, blue oriental in the foyer toward the grand staircase. As she did, the smell of pipe tobacco met her nostrils. She turned her steps toward the library, where a lamp was burning low, and looked in.

There he sat, a book open on his lap, the lamp beside him just bright enough to read by. Phillip pulled at the pipe thoughtfully and took no notice of her.

"Madam." A voice from behind startled her and she spun around. Fettles stood apologetically in the gloom. "Did you wish to start the croquet tomorrow at ten or eleven?"

"Eleven."

"Very good."

The butler disappeared as silently as he had come, and Agnes wondered as she had so many times if he ever slept.

Phillip was looking at her appraisingly. "A wonderful evening, Miss Somerset," he said, rising and taking the pipe from his mouth. "If you will allow me, you are both an exceptional hostess and a talented writer."

"Oh, you are much too kind, Lord Phillip." She was blushing as she drew just inside the doorway.

"Not at all. You almost had me crying, and I hadn't even the pleasure of knowing the people in your story."

"It did bring out some emotion, didn't it? I was surprised myself."

"Tell me something," said Phillip, laying his book aside and motioning her to a chair. They both sat down, he settling comfortably into the leather cushions and she erect on the edge of hers. "Is it true that you have been managing Brookside for almost six years now by my calculation?"

"Yes."

"Incredible! You would have started as a mere child, then."

"You flatter me. A child in understanding, yes, but not in years. But indeed I have learned a great deal since then, largely through my mistakes."

"Haven't we all?"

"What have I interrupted?" she asked. "You were reading when I came in."

Phillip lifted the large, dark volume toward her.

"Ah, *Tales of the Arabian Nights*. You are an adventurer through and through, I believe," Agnes laughed softly.

"No more than you, I would wager." Phillip looked at her narrowly. "When do I get to hear your story?"

"I believe you did, an hour ago in the drawing room."

Phillip said nothing.

"A personal story, you mean? In which you get to hear about some of those mistakes I referred to?"

"With or without those."

Agnes touched her earrings and reflected. "Croquet is at eleven. I need to meet with Grandma Brown, as you know, tomorrow, hopefully in the morning while she is still fresh. She tires so quickly these days. Then the ladies are all going into town in the afternoon. I really can't say—"

"Of course," said Phillip apologetically. "I am selfish to want the hostess to myself. But I hope that one day you will honor me again with a personal audience and tell me about Agnes Eileen Somerset."

"You have found out my full name, I see."

Phillip's dark eyes twinkled. He opened the book where it lay on the table to the place he had left off. "You should get some sleep, you know. Croquet at eleven tomorrow. And I'm quite good."

"A challenge! Then I must be rested and ready!" Agnes declared, rising. "I have heard it said that I am quite good myself."

Phillip rose and, before she could move away, took her hand and kissed it gently. "Good night, Miss Somerset."

With heart pounding, she managed only, "I trust you will sleep well," and somehow left the room. Climbing the stairs, she realized that her fatigue had fled, replaced with an excitement that her body struggled to contain.

# Chapter 17

Irene Brown sat on the terrace, bundled in an old quilt against the cool morning air. Her small breakfast concluded, she watched the workers tramping through heavy dew as they prepared for the day's croquet tournament. The grass sparkled as the sun broke over the roof of the great house and lit up the west lawn.

Stepping out to test the day, Agnes found her grandmother sunk in a reverie. The old woman did not notice her granddaughter until Agnes stood fully before her. Grandma Brown raised her gentle face and smiled as Agnes placed a kiss on her soft cheek.

"Good morning, my dear! Aren't you a goddess in that dress. The pale green brings out the color in your eyes. You have your father's eyes, you know, with those little flecks of green."

"I feel like a goddess today, Grandma—or at least someone who wakes up in paradise. What a morning! But are you warm enough?"

"I'm fine. However, I do prefer eastern terraces—they get the sun in the morning, and then they're cool in the afternoon. Not that I expect you to do anything about that."

"I believe Phinnaeus built his terrace on the west to watch sunsets. From all accounts he was not an early riser." Agnes took a seat beside her grandmother.

"He was a profligate," frowned the old woman. "It was decent of you to leave that out of your history last night. Still, he was a successful profligate. Those are rare. Such habits usually lead to ruin." Grandma's face had darkened as she spoke, looking away from Agnes toward the bright lawn.

Agnes saw her opening. "Grandma, I want to thank you for all the help you have been to me lately. I know that we have you to thank that Brookside stays in the family. You have been so generous." Grandma squeezed her hand but said nothing.

"Grandma, something rather odd happened yesterday. May I tell you?"

Grandma Brown turned to her granddaughter. "Of course, my dear."

Agnes took Mrs. Brown's small hand in both of hers, feeling as she held it the swollen knuckles and the wedding band worn smooth

of all decoration. "Yesterday in the garden I overheard a
conversation. I wasn't trying to eavesdrop, but it couldn't be helped.
Wilbur and Eleanor seemed to be having a heated argument about
something. I learned that Eleanor had intended to write to me about a
serious matter, but Wilbur didn't let her. He told her that he should
tell me in person. They both indicated that you knew all about it,
whatever it is."

Mrs. Brown had not moved and hardly seemed to be breathing.
"Grandma?"

Gradually she drew a deep breath, her old eyes brimming with
uncertainty. She fumbled to pull a handkerchief out of her sleeve and
rubbed it nervously between her fingers. Isaiah approached with fresh
coffee, set down the tray, and withdrew discreetly. Agnes poured both
coffee and cream into a bright yellow cup and handed it to Grandma,
who sipped it intently and said, "Let us talk tomorrow, my dear. I do
need to discuss something with you. And bring along Mr. Rockwell
because I will want his opinion."

"Tomorrow? Are you sure, Grandma? I could certainly make
time today—"

"No, my dear, tomorrow will be soon enough," Mrs. Brown
assured her, patting Agnes's knee. She smiled at her granddaughter,
then turned back to the glittering lawn. "I was reflecting earlier on
how many mornings I have seen. A great many by now, I'm afraid.
As a child I would run through damp grass, delighted to start the day.
Now I sit and watch others. For so much of my life it felt like my
days might go on almost forever. You know I have married twice—I
question why I did it the second time—and have buried both my sons.
Life is so long, Agnes. Don't let people tell you it's short—that isn't
true. A dozen times, when things were dark, I almost wished to leave
it. But now . . ." She paused to set down her coffee. "Now I clutch
each moment that remains in this world. It's all swirled through with
the sweet and the bitter, you know, but still a world worth hanging on
to until the last possible hour."

The warming air coaxed Mrs. Brown to push back the faded quilt
from her shoulders. Agnes asked if she could get her anything, then
with a firm hug, left her to attend to final arrangements for the day's
activities. She dared offer up a quick prayer that her grandmother
might yet live to see a great-grandchild born into this world, a place

Agnes already knew well as "all swirled through with the sweet and the bitter."

# Chapter 18

By the middle of that sparkling morning, Wilbur and his bride had not exchanged a syllable since the day before. No sounds issued from the walnut room except routine noises of people dressing, opening windows, or clearing their throats in preparation to say something they decided against. Eleanor knew that her husband had no intention of joining in the croquet tournament, and she had so little interest in him at this point that she did not even consult him on his plans for the day. For her part, she resolved to play croquet with all the enthusiasm she could kindle, although on any other day she would have found this an excessively athletic activity and beneath her dignity. Wilbur watched his wife pin her hair and spray cologne around her regal neck as though she were alone in the room.

He straightened his cuffs and bent to wipe several flecks of dust from his gleaming boots. He had to talk with her, but she was a stone when she wanted to be.

"Look here, El," he finally blurted, "you can't go on like this in company. People will notice. I can tolerate your ridiculous silences when we are home, but in public this behavior is out of the question."

Eleanor added some powder to her imposing nose.

"You won't intimidate me like this, you know," he continued. "I do as I see fit. All you'll accomplish with this infantile display," he warned, coming closer, "is to arouse suspicion about our manners and our marriage. Is that what you want?"

With a last look at all sides of her perfected countenance, Eleanor left the mirror and picked up her hat, arranging its dull ribbon with perfect equanimity.

Unwilling to cede victory by losing his temper completely, Wilbur tugged at his waistcoat, straightened his narrow frame, and announced evenly that she could damn well do as she pleased, it was no concern of his. He would be taking Empress and Napoleon out for a run—whom, he took time to point out, she seemed to have forgotten all about in her self-indulgent tantrum of the last two days.

At this she shot him a burning look and pursed her lips tighter still. Her husband snatched up his hat and strode from the room, concentrating all his will to keep his hand from slamming the heavy door behind him. His long legs carried him quickly down the stairs, through the dining room, and out onto the terrace, where he bristled at seeing Grandma Brown, still sitting and watching the morning bustle. Seated beside her and looking like a great, dark monument by contrast was Mrs. Rockwell, accompanied by her insubstantial daughter. Wilbur did not hesitate but cut across the cool flagstones toward the kennel.

"Wilbur!" called Grandma Brown with a stern ring.

Wilbur halted and turned stiffly.

"We need to talk. Today."

"Of course, Grandma. I'll look for you this afternoon, eh?"

Mrs. Brown nodded without a smile and watched him scamper away.

"Your grandson is very devoted to his dogs, isn't he?" ventured Mrs. Rockwell.

"My grandson is a fool." The remark stood like a frozen sheet between the ladies, stark and unwieldy. Mrs. Rockwell searched for a way to continue the conversation around it, her daughter watching keenly to see what her mother would manage.

"I've known many men who could wear that title," she offered after a moment. "My own Abram tries me to the very limit at times— Sarah, you know this already—but he has a good heart. His problem is that he cannot see ahead, not in the grand scheme. He is wonderful with business, but there is much more to this world than business." She sighed.

"Your Abram," observed Mrs. Brown, "is a jewel. He has a heart of gold, just as you say, and that outweighs most faults in a man."

Sarah spoke up. "But courage is important, too, don't you think, Mrs. Brown? I can't abide a man who is not brave."

Both ladies looked at the young thing in surprise. "You make a good point, my girl," admitted her mother. "As long as you are not referring to silliness like duels or hunting grizzly bears with short knives or that sort of thing. But bravery of the soul, that is an admirable quality in a man as well as a woman."

"And harder and harder to find," observed Mrs. Brown. "My advice to you is, don't hurry"—pointing a cautionary finger at the girl—"take your time to find a worthy man. For it is true that kindness without bravery is useless, and bravery without kindness brings disaster."

The ladies watched Wilbur lead his dogs from the kennel and, to their surprise, head straight back toward them. He stepped up on the terrace, keeping the leashes short on his eager greyhounds, and smiled.

"I just want to ask your pardon, ladies, if I seemed rude a moment ago. It was not intended."

Grandma said nothing, so Mrs. Rockwell spoke up. "I am sure that a man in your situation has a great deal on his mind."

Wilbur's contrite smile fell away. "What do you mean?" he asked flatly, glancing at Grandma.

"Why," Mrs. Rockwell began uncertainly, "a gentleman of affairs such as yourself surely has much to keep track of even while taking some time away as we are. I know my Abram can never completely leave his work behind."

Wilbur looked unconvinced. He pulled the dogs closer with a short jerk and mumbled his appreciation for her understanding. With a short bow, he left them.

Mrs. Rockwell leaned toward Mrs. Brown. "Did I say something inconvenient?" she asked. She appealed to her daughter. "What did I say to him?"

"You said nothing improper, Mrs. Rockwell," Grandma assured her. "Pay no attention to my grandson. He is a bundle of nerves, and has every reason to be."

Mrs. Rockwell, confused, chose to simply observe that it was very decent of Wilbur to return and express his apology.

"You may think me an impossible old woman," replied Grandma, "but I can no longer abide illusions. Don't think too well of my grandson, please. He only came back because he wants something from me and can't afford to leave me irritated. However, since he is by nature and long habit unavoidably irritating, he would do better to simply keep his distance."

"Look," cried Sarah, "I believe they are starting the tournament! Are you coming, Mother?"

"Soon, my dear. I'll come along with Mrs. Brown as soon as we can convince ourselves to leave this pleasant spot."

Sarah grabbed her parasol and nearly ran across the lawn, her yellow hair bouncing in the bright sun.

"Oh," observed her mother, watching the girl go, "What truth in those words, 'A youth of frolics, an old age of cards.'"[1]

Grandma gave a soft snort of agreement, and the two women sat in silent reflection as the rapidly rising sun warmed their backs and chased away the morning's shadows.

---

[1] Alexander Pope.

# Chapter 19

A call went up from the croquet course, summoning the guests to the field of battle. The players were quickly converging to match skills and vie for the grand prize, which would be a rendering of the rose garden that Stella had agreed to paint for the occasion.

Fettles stood before the spirited congregation, struggling to get their attention in the open air. The butler clapped his thin hands together twice and launched into a thorough explanation. Players would draw from matching numbers from a hat, and the winner of each of these pairs would toss his number back into the hat to be paired with another winner, and so the competitors would be winnowed down to the last two standing. Referees were stationed along the course and would have the final word in all disputes. Those not participating in the tournament were asked to please refrain from entering the field of play or picking up any balls that went astray.

As he concluded, Mrs. Rockwell arrived helping Grandma to the chairs on the shady edge of the neat, sunny course. Mrs. Bairnaught was already seated and fanning herself, ready to cheer her husband to victory.

Agnes drew the same number as Eleanor, which she saw as a mixed blessing. While Wilbur's wife was the last person she would have chosen to play against, she hoped to pick up some clues about yesterday's conversation as they made their way through the wickets. The coveted position of playing against Phillip had gone to Mr. Schmidt, and Agnes told herself that she would just have to stay in the game as long as possible on the chance that she and the missionary might face each other eventually.

Eleanor's studied elegance worked against her on the croquet field, and Agnes surpassed her easily. Agnes slowed her progress at the fourth wicket in an attempt to decrease her partner's embarrassment. She had to admire the woman's concentration and honest effort at a game she clearly had never played. Added to this handicap was the presence of her husband standing silently in the shade, offering no encouragement, as the dogs panted on either side of him. Nearby players, seeing Eleanor's difficulty, offered comprehensive advice as to stance, swing, and aim, but although she nodded and applied herself with seemingly good intent, her ball moved only a few feet, and seldom in the desired direction.

Halfway through the course, Agnes cheerfully lied, "I think you are doing marvelously for your first time playing."

Eleanor dabbed her face. "Well, at least I am making an effort. Some people with no good excuse prefer to stand in the shade and smirk." She shot a narrow look to the sidelines.

"Wilbur, by chance?"

"Well, he's never one to join in any activities of a competitive nature when he's not sure to excel." She paused and seemed to reconsider. "Well, for the most part."

"He abstained from the hunt but made it clear that it was on philosophical grounds," Agnes recalled.

"Rubbish." Eleanor took a swing in the air, tried again, and sent her ball lolling just beside the wicket. "He didn't want me to participate in this game either, that was quite plain, but I know better how to conduct myself in company."

"I do appreciate your joining in, Eleanor," Agnes encouraged. "He does seem a bit more on edge than usual, if you don't mind my making an observation," she added, taking aim to move her ball around a small depression.

Eleanor glanced at her. "Does he? Well, he has always been high strung. Very capable, you understand, but high strung. That is often a trait among the elite, I understand, as in thoroughbreds. But you know, Agnes, you have done very well for yourself without a husband. They are a complication in life. Quite necessary if one is to really ascend through the layers of society. Still," she added in a low voice, "I do envy you sometimes."

Agnes stood staring at this impossible woman, wondering how to respond. A sudden commotion, however, removed all possibility of continuing the conversation.

Tearing across the lawn came Empress and Napoleon, their legs a blur, their necks outstretched, in single-minded pursuit of two rabbits that bounded over the croquet field in a mad effort to reach the shelter of the forsythia grove. In the pandemonium, Mrs. McMeed lost her balance and fell onto Mr. Schmidt, bringing them both down in a heap. At the very same time, his back to the chaos, Lord Phillip was in mid-swing, aiming to bring back his ball from a nasty knock-away by his opponent. On the upswing, his mallet caught Napoleon, who was just rounding Phillip in pursuit of his zigzagging prey. He struck the dog squarely in the chest and sent him flying backward several feet to land on his back. Phillip, thrown by the unexpected impact of his mallet upon the racing dog, staggered backward and only barely kept his feet.

Wilbur and Eleanor ran shouting to the dog's side and sank down beside him. Alone, Empress followed the rabbit into the thicket. Napoleon's breath came in short gasps, and except for his labored breathing, he lay completely still, his eyes wide open in surprise.

"What in God's name were you doing?" demanded Wilbur, glaring up at Phillip. He laid both hands on the dog's ribcage as though holding it together. The players formed a ring around the scene.

"I did not realize—" Phillip began. "I was not expecting your dog to be on the course."

"Everyone else saw what was happening! What's wrong with you, anyway, Your Lordship?" Wilbur sneered. "Not the sharpest knife," he muttered.

Agnes stepped forward, clutching her skirt. "Wilbur, how dare you!"

"No, no," said Phillip, putting a hand out, "it's quite all right, Agnes. Let me answer your cousin's question. 'What's wrong with me?' Well, let's see—apparently I expect to play croquet on a croquet course. I also, strange as it might seem, would not dream of bringing animals with me to visit the relatives, uninvited. I feel a good deal of gratitude to my hostess rather than an urge to embarrass her and condescend to decent people at every opportunity. I'd say that is what's wrong with me if you want to know."

Wilbur had risen and stepped forward, hands clenched, but Mr. Schmidt adeptly inserted himself. "Gentlemen, let us not try the patience of these good people with a scene we will, none of us, wish to recall. Wilbur, it's natural to feel concern for Napoleon, but one can't deny that Lord Phillip is quite blameless in this accident."

Meanwhile, Ned had been conducting his own examination of the dog, who was by now sitting up and breathing better, although shallowly. "Sir, your dog is well," he pronounced matter-of-factly. Everyone turned to look down at man and dog. "He's just had the wind knocked out of him. Now, he surely is bruised and will be hurting for a few days, but he's not damaged for long."

By now Empress was trotting back from her adventure holding one twitching rabbit in her pointed jaws, looking satisfied and quite unaware of the dozens of burs caught in her coat. Wilbur grabbed her trailing leash, handed it to Eleanor, and scooped up Napoleon. He stepped close to Phillip and breathed, "I don't know who you are really or what your game is—"

"I could say the same of you," Phillip whispered back.

Wilbur paused and squinted into Phillip's eyes. "There is no game," he said, and hesitated again as though waiting for something. "I'm willing to forget this for Agnes's sake."

"Then you should," Phillip counseled. "And I'd keep those hounds out of the way if I were you. For your sake."

With that Wilbur and Eleanor headed for the kennel to lavish their charges with tender care and a thorough grooming while Isaiah and Ned set to work quickly to reestablish the course. Lunch appeared, and everyone took a short break to calm their nerves over cold chicken, oysters, melon, and other delicacies suitable to a summer afternoon that had suddenly grown very hot indeed.

# Chapter 20

The tournament resumed with Sarah Rockwell challenging Agnes. Halfway through their game, Sarah knocked Agnes's ball aside with such gusto that the hostess was unable to recover, and the jubilant girl won by two strokes. This victory brought her to the championship round against Lord Philip himself. Agnes could predict the outcome and was hard-pressed to watch this final match from the shadow of the trees, as the young woman tiptoed and danced through the course, swinging her mallet idly and laughing at everything.

"She acts quite smitten, doesn't she?" murmured Vera. Agnes had not noticed her aunt standing beside her and dropping the last of the smoked oysters into her mouth. "Who knows, they might make a good pair."

"You can't be serious!"

Vera opened her eyes at Agnes. "Why not? He's available but without an occupation, she has loads of money, and old Abram could probably offer him a position in the firm."

Agnes crossed her hands and stared at her aunt. "That is so calculating for a romantic like yourself. What about the fact that she is a silly, inexperienced girl and he is a fascinating, deeply curious, man of the world?"

"Oh, don't you know a lot about his Lordship! I am here to tell you, my dear, that most men happen to prefer silly, inexperienced young ladies. They don't have to compete with them in wit or in stories to tell over dinner."

Agnes turned her gaze to the course. Lord Phillip was waving Sarah graciously on to the next shot, the sun shining on his tousled hair and white shirt, now opened at the neck.

"This one is not like most men."

"Why, because he was a missionary? Because he sniffs his food before eating? These things may make him odd, but not fundamentally different. But he is a good judge of character—he seems to detest our Wilbur."

"That was quite a scene, wasn't it?" returned Agnes. "And what about your Mr. Schmidt? Wasn't he gallant? Now surely you consider him a rare man."

"Frederick? He's absolutely one of a kind. The dearest man on earth, and not in the least threatened by your strutting cousin or a competent woman. I know you know how unusual that is."

"But why do you string him along as you do if he is such a treasure—which I agree that he is? You must know that he would marry you in a moment if you even hinted at the possibility."

Vera popped a grape into her beautiful mouth and thought. "I don't know. I suppose I'm afraid."

"Of what?"

"I don't know."

"He spoils you to tag along the way he does with no assurances. Have you ever considered that one day you might lose him?"

"It occurs to me every day, and how much I should hate myself if I let it happen. So what are we to make of it?" Vera shrugged. "Maybe I'll beg him to marry me tomorrow." Vera took Agnes's arm and pulled her back to the crowd gathered to cheer on the last competitors. Mrs. Rockwell stood anxiously with one arm through her husband's, giving her daughter advice of the most unworkable kind, while Abram kept reproaching her in good humor to let the child play the game. The Duke and most of the men were pulling for Phillip and doling out taunts about the honor of all the gentlemen riding on his performance, threatening him with shunning and a ruined reputation in the unthinkable event of his defeat.

Sarah sized up the positions of the brightly colored balls. She stood a good chance of finishing with one stroke. She had, however, already displayed an uncanny grip on the fact that this game was as much about strategy as skill, and not willing to invest all her chances of winning in one shot, she moved to the left and aimed for Lord Phillip's ball, which was only a yard from her own. Her ball hit his with a sharp clack, rocketing it neatly out of bounds. A great cry arose from the gentlemen, who threw up their arms and hung their heads, refusing to watch the young woman's final and perfect shot that drove her ball snug against the stake.

The Rockwells led their daughter off, exclaiming over the highlights of the tournament. The rest of the guests drifted away to relax and refresh themselves. Grandma Brown, uncharacteristically out of sorts and complaining of headache, had left the festivities just after lunch.

By now the sun sat high in a cloudless sky, and the time of day had arrived when the birds stopped flying and all the animals of the ground rested in the shadows. Even the insects took a few hours off from their activities, and a bright quiet settled over the grounds. Only the occasional bark of a hound, sent up as though to ask if he were alone in the world, troubled the stillness.

Agnes sat on her bed. Slowly she removed her shoes and tossed them aside. With apologies she had bowed out of the trip to town with Vera and Eleanor and lay down now to rest her head, which, as on most warm, bright afternoons, had begun to throb. Marie drew the drapes and laid a damp washcloth over her mistress's forehead. Agnes breathed deliberately, thankful for the hushed and darkened room and the chance to be alone. She tried to clear her mind and rest it from the colliding images of the last three days. Some things had gone splendidly; others had not. This was to be expected. Breathe in, breathe out.

What would Mother have done differently? Would father have been pleased? These questions lurked just below the surface of her mind. Sometimes she pulled them out and analyzed them openly. But when she had finished and put them away, her parents still hung close by like chaperones discreetly keeping watch. Breathe in, breathe out. She lay very still and gave herself over to the shifting kaleidoscope in her mind: his smile, his hair in the sun, the bright white shirt rippled by the breeze, his stepping back and laughing, the way he leaned on his mallet and observed almost everything . . .

# Part II. When Autumn's Fruit Does Fall

# Chapter 21

Agnes awoke with a start. How long have I slept, she wondered, snatching the washcloth, which had grown warm, off her forehead. She looked to the golden hands on the French mantel clock—only twenty minutes. Had she heard something? Strangely anxious, she sat up just as a knock sounded on her door.

"Agnes!" It was Wilbur's voice, urgent and restrained.

She went to the door in her stockinged feet and opened it. Wilbur stood there, ashen. "You must come. Something's wrong with Grandma." Without pausing to put on shoes, Agnes ran with him to her grandmother's room. She stopped short in the doorway. In the armchair where her grandmother had sat and talked with her just two nights ago an ancient woman now slumped. Though dressed like Grandma Brown, this woman looked shrunken and leaned heavily against the side of the chair. Her left arm hung limp toward the floor and the side of her face sagged frightfully. The poor creature raised her confused eyes to Agnes and moved her mouth, but no sound came out.

"Grandma!" The word caught in Agnes's throat. She ran to her grandmother and knelt beside her, stroking her face and bringing the useless arm into the matriarch's lap. She searched the old eyes questioningly, but found in them only frightened surprise as they moved from Agnes's face to Wilbur's, to the objects around the room.

"What happened, Wilbur?"

"I don't know," her cousin cried. "I came to see her as I'd promised, and I found her like this." Wilbur pulled out his handkerchief and dabbed at his grandmother's mouth.

"Have you called for a doctor?"Agnes asked.

"No, I came straight to you."

96

"Tell Fettles to get Doctor Bingham immediately. And tell Marie I need her. Find Mrs. Bairnaught and tell her what has happened. Oh, they are such old friends." Agnes squeezed her grandmother's useless hand.

"Should we lay her down first?" Wilbur asked.

"No, I don't think so. Hurry, Wilbur."

Wilbur hesitated, then ran from the room. Agnes took Grandma's face into her hands and stroked her fine, white hair. Tears rolled silently down Agnes's cheeks as she prayed in a whisper for a miracle to bring this beloved lady back to her. Marie hurried in, and the ladies pulled a light blanket from the bed and wrapped the old woman in it. Then Agnes sent Marie off for hot tea and brandy. As she dashed from the room the maid almost collided with Mr. and Mrs. Bairnaught, who were entering at a run.

Mrs. Bairnaught drew in her breath and, letting go of her husband's arm, crossed the room. She wrapped her arms carefully around the small, still body in the chair. "My dearest," she whispered into her friend's ear. Her husband drew up a chair for his wife, and she lowered herself into it. "Oh, what happens to us?" she asked, tipping her head to one side as she looked into Grandma's face. "What tricks does Nature play on us old women?" Mrs. Bairnaught rubbed Grandma's fingers in her own stiff hands. Grandma stared at her bosom companion, her confidant of forty years, with a fixed look of incomprehension.

Word spread quickly through the great house, and the guests began converging on the busy bedroom, talking in low tones with Mr. Bairnaught, who had stationed himself at the door. The drapes on the west windows had been closed against the harsh light of the late-afternoon sun. But the northern windows stood open, and a mild light filled the quiet room. Fettles arrived at last with Doctor Bingham and a nurse.

The doctor examined Grandma with a practiced hand and a knowing eye. After completing a short battery of observations, he straightened and sighed, placing his tools back into his bag. "Your grandmother is suffering from apoplexy—a stroke," he announced. "Her left side is paralyzed at the moment, but that could change. You might find that she improves shortly, or she may sink deeper still. The stroke probably occurred several hours ago. Did you notice anything wrong with her this morning? Did she have an emotional shock of any kind?"

Agnes reflected. "She seemed more tired than usual after breakfast. Her normal energy was gone, and she complained of a headache after lunch."

She turned to Wilbur, who shook his head and shrugged.

The doctor grunted. "We can't know what is happening in her brain. Strokes are mysterious things. Keep a close watch on her. Make her comfortable and see that she does not roll out of bed. Massage her limbs periodically to keep the blood flowing. The real challenge will be getting her to eat and drink in the next few days. Don't worry about that until tomorrow morning. For now, put her to bed with plenty of pillows and just let her rest."

A confusion of voices in the hall made everyone turn to see Vera entering, followed by Eleanor and Mr. Schmidt. Vera looked at Grandma, then the doctor, then Agnes. Mr. Schmidt took her arm and steadied her as a wailing Eleanor rushed past them to the old woman.

"Agnes," said Vera, "I'm so sorry I wasn't here." She turned to Doctor Bingham. "What can we do, Doctor?" She looked tenderly at Grandma Brown, now nearly lost beneath the folds of her blanket, slumping ever lower in the large chair. "We wait, don't we?"

"We wait," agreed the doctor. "I will leave Nurse Woolsey with you, and I'll return tomorrow to check on the patient." The stout man bent forward, three fingers tucked into his waistcoat pocket, and pressed grandmother's shoulder in his thick hand. "Mother, I will see you tomorrow."

The gentlemen followed the doctor out, and the ladies got Grandma into her nightgown and laid her in bed. Outside the still-open windows the birds had begun their evening songs. Gentle rays of sun lit the edges of the drawn curtains and snuck in to light a narrow path across the crimson rug.

Nurse Woolsey and Eleanor took the first shift, as Vera and Agnes tiptoed out and closed the door behind them. Vera followed Agnes to her room, where the weary hostess changed her dress and put on shoes. She told Vera everything that had happened since waking from her nap.

"This is unbelievable," she said, as Vera helped fasten a long row of buttons down the back of her dark evening dress. "I barely recognized her." Tears started up in her eyes again. "And who knows how long it will be before she can tell me what she had wanted to say to me!"

Vera hugged her niece from behind and rested her head against hers. "Don't worry about that now, dear. Our minds cannot handle so much at once. Whatever it is will come out in time."

Agnes put her face in her hands and stood still for several moments. Vera waited, lost in her own reflections. "This is a sad ending to our week," sighed Agnes.

"Now, Agnes, it isn't an ending yet," Vera reproved her. "Grandma may be better by morning. Don't start talking as though she's past all hope." But her optimism rattled dully in Agnes's ears— she knew enough to tell that her grandmother had slipped too far down a sheer slope to climb back up by morning.

A knock came at the door, and Vera went to open it. Phillip stood in the doorway, and Vera waved him in. He came to Agnes, took her hands in his, and raised them to his breast. He continued to hold them, looking into her face silently. In his dark eyes she saw a sympathy that surpassed words.

"What can I do?" he asked.

"Nothing, I'm afraid. I just need a little time to collect myself."

Phillip inclined his head. "Whatever I might do for you, tell me. Will you?"

Agnes nodded. He released her hands reluctantly and left.

Agnes looked at her aunt. "I feel I need a walk in the garden. I'll see you at dinner?"

"You certainly will."

Agnes clasped Vera's hand in parting and saw beyond her, out the window, how bright the sky was still. She remembered absently that it was the summer equinox, the longest day of the whole year—a day when the sun holds itself above the horizon and refuses to sink from view until the last possible moment.

# Chapter 22

Just before dawn Agnes and Stella took their turn by Grandma Brown's bedside, relieving Mrs. Bairnaught, who had been keeping watch since midnight.

"She's watching something," said Grandma's old friend. "Look how her eyes stare off that way. She has been like that all night. I wonder what she sees."

Agnes went to the big blue-and-white basin, soaked a fresh washcloth, and wrung the cool water out. Sitting down on the bed, she gently washed her grandmother's face and hands while the old woman's good hand played with the lacey edge of the sheet. Her wide, shifting eyes continued to watch the far corner of the ceiling.

Stella sat down in the padded rocker at the foot of the bed and watched her great-grandmother intently.

Agnes opened the book she had brought along. "Grandma, I am going to read you a story. Remember how you used to read *Aesop's Fables* to us in bed? Well, now it's my turn." Agnes thought for a moment that her grandmother was about to look at her, but she only moved her head on the pillow and continued to watch the invisible scene before her.

Agnes sat beside her and opened the frayed book to a loose page. "Let's begin with 'The Frog and the Mouse.' 'A young mouse in search of adventure was running along the bank of a pond where lived a Frog . . .'" And so she read to her grandmother several of the edifying tales that had many nights sent her and her sister off to sleep picturing sly wolves wearing sheepskins and golden eggs dropping from magical geese.

Doctor Bingham arrived as promised and made a short examination. Grandma's heart was racing and her blood pressure had sunk dangerously low. He gave her two days, no more. Agnes left Stella and Nurse Woolsey on duty and went to tell Vera the sad news. The two sat in Vera's room discussing church services and burial plots, when the nurse appeared at the door.

"Miss Somerset, your grandmother has passed on."

Agnes gasped. "Oh, why did I leave the room? But it was only for a few moments," she cried, now on her feet, looking from the nurse to Vera, "and the doctor said two days, but if only I had stayed—"

The nurse gently stopped her and said she must not blame herself. She had seen many a parent and grandparent wait until the family had left the room to give up their spirit.

"I think they see it as a final gift to those they love," she explained. "They spare them the memory of that moment of leaving." Agnes broke into unrestrained tears, and the nurse took her by the hand and led her like a child to her grandmother's room. The old saint lay under the cream-colored quilt, the sheet tucked below her round chin. Her features rested smooth and untroubled, and her hands lay calmly one upon the other.

Agnes stared at her grandmother, who looked for all the world like a woman merely asleep, as if she would wake if they spoke too loudly. Agnes sat down carefully on the bed and stroked once more the soft halo of white around the wrinkled face. She remembered with a rush the hours she had spent with Grandma in the garden looking for caterpillars and learning the names of all the flowers; the patient lessons on etiquette out on the terrace at a well-set table; Grandma's constant encouragement, even when Agnes had sunk below the surface from the death of both her parents and she felt powerless to carry on her own life, let alone take the family's entire estate in hand. Now Grandma was gone, too.

A hush settled on the household, replacing the gaiety of the previous days. Arrangements were quickly made, and they buried Grandma in the new cemetery at the edge of Chesterton, with its winding roads and young gardens. She was a pioneer here, one of the first graves dotting the lawns. The rest of the family lay in the tidy graveyard beside the Presbyterian church in town, but the county declared it full several years ago, shortly before Agnes's parents were entombed in the marble vault that her father had wisely purchased many years before. Grandma had made it clear long ago that she wanted to be buried with the Somersets, the noble family of her first husband, lost at sea without a marker. She wanted no association with her second husband, who had been buried at his family's insistence in a showy tomb in Philadelphia's best cemetery.

As the guests left the cemetery staff to their task on that gray burying day, more than one observed that it was fortunate, really, that they were all together to pay their last respects, and that Grandma had been fortunate to live her last days among the people dearest to her.

And so the celebration of Brookside ended. Trunks were packed, train schedules consulted, and guests were driven to the station over the next two days. The weather turned cool and a fine mist drifted down, further laying the festivities to rest.

Only one guest remained. Young Stella, comfortably installed in the mosaic room, would stay to restore her spirits and paint at her leisure the promised portrait of the rose garden. Vera left promising to return before the end of summer. Mr. Rockwell would return in a month or so to settle matters surrounding Grandma's will.

"We will all miss her," he sighed, putting on his hat to go. "But you should know that you stand to inherit a substantial sum, Agnes. This will be helpful, as the maintenance of Brookside has become somewhat more than your current reserves can handle. You pay the bills, so I know you have been aware of this."

Agnes remembered the talk she and Grandma had meant to have along with Mr. Rockwell. "Grandma had wanted to talk with me about some matter that was troubling her," Agnes said. "She died before I could mention it to you. Do you have any idea what it might have been?"

"None," admitted Mr. Rockwell. "She said nothing to me." He reflected a moment. "No, nothing comes to mind. It's possible that she wanted to make sure that her affairs were quite in order in case anything happened to her. Elderly people have a supernatural sense of these things, I've found. Well, take care, my girl."

With a warm embrace, Mr. Rockwell left Agnes in the foyer and joined his wife and daughter in the carriage. The firm rectangle of Mrs. Rockwell's face appeared in the window, and her darkly gloved hand waved good-bye. Agnes watched the black coach, shiny with water, rattle away beneath the long arch of dripping trees.

Her mind drifted back to the conversation she had with Wilbur a few days earlier. Amid the bustle of funeral arrangements, she had managed to talk with him privately. She would have preferred to have Vera with her, but she did not want Wilbur to feel like he sat before a panel of judges. She knew him: in that setting, he would clamp his mouth shut and wave her off as being nonsensical. Alone, she had hoped to coax some truth from him.

Once again, she had underestimated Wilbur's defenses. As they sat in Agnes's dim study discussing the disposition of Grandma's personal effects, Agnes carefully mentioned the conversation she had overheard in the garden. Wilbur's face drained of the smidgeon of color it normally held, and his jaw tightened as he stared at her.

"So what does it mean, Wilbur?" She held his gaze.

He rose, stuck both hands into his trouser pockets, and struck a pose that wavered between defiance and trust. "Eleanor is an emotional woman, Agnes. What you heard was part of a lovers' spat, nothing more." Wilbur looked at Agnes with a patronizing smile. Agnes found herself distracted, trying to picture the glacial couple as "lovers."

Agnes toyed with her tortoiseshell pen. "It seems that Grandma as well was concerned about something."

Wilbur inhaled. "You know, our grandmother was not an easy woman to live with. I'm sure you think me harsh, but beneath that sweet exterior was a very stubborn woman. Fussy, too, always twittering about this or that imaginary problem."

Agnes fixed him with a cold stare. "Isn't it a bit early to speak ill of the dead, cousin, even for you?"

Wilbur straightened and looked away. "Has it occurred to you that Grandma might have wanted to discuss with you the interests of this fellow Lord Phillip?" He sent a challenging look at his surprised cousin. "I've noticed the way he looks at you—I'm sure everyone has."

"What on earth are you talking about?" Agnes felt the blood rising to her face.

"Who is he? Does anyone really know him? This story about India, missionary work, smells like so much nonsense. And there are rumors about him, you know, that are not pleasant. I hope you are not considering his attention."

"Wilbur, I am quite capable of handling myself where Lord Phillip is concerned, or anyone else. I will thank you not to trouble yourself about my personal affairs." Agnes swallowed, almost at a loss for words. "And furthermore, I doubt—"

She was about to point out that Grandma would have had no reason to invite Mr. Rockwell to a discussion of her granddaughter's love affairs, but she was interrupted by Eleanor striding into the room. Clutching two silken leashes, she implored Wilbur's help with the dogs, who had gotten into the kitchen scraps and eaten, as she put it, "God only knows what." It occurred to Agnes to ask Eleanor about the mystery, but since relations had apparently thawed between her and her husband, it would be useless.

Agnes excused herself and hastened to the refuge of her own room. Wasn't it just like Wilbur to dodge the truth by pointing a finger at someone else? How dare he even talk about Phillip—he did not deserve to stand in the same room with the Duke's son, much less toss accusations against him. One thing was clear: Phillip made Wilbur uncomfortable. Was it just the silent reproach Wilbur felt from any God-fearing man? Or was it distinctly more than that? For the first time, Agnes wondered if the last thing her cousin might want was a new man in the family, a man to look after her, a man who might ask questions.

# Chapter 23

The afternoon that Phillip came to tea in Mrs. Thorne's parlor, he found the room filled with a deep red variety of her late-blooming lilacs. They stood in fat Chinese vases, their heads lolling together sleepily. Their perfume filled his nostrils and almost drove him to open a window for relief. For even on this warm day, Claudia kept all the windows fastened behind their heavy purple drapes.

Looking around the lavish room, Phillip remembered Agnes's recent words regarding Mrs. Thorne. As it happened, Claudia's new widowhood had left her free to entertain friends and occasional lovers to her heart's content. Her dalliances were no secret and somehow made her more popular at functions than not. Society ladies watched what she wore and followed suit. Gentlemen, both married and single, flirted openly with her, but most, if they were to tell the truth, would flee in terror if she ever turned her complete attention upon them.

The Wednesday afternoon had grown sullen. The day had started up fresh and sunny, but now the breeze had died and the sealed parlor felt close and moist. The table was set for tea, with plates of meringues, cakes, and tiny cucumber sandwiches. Phillip approached the impeccable display, raised a pink-iced petit four to his nose, and swallowed it nearly whole. He was contemplating a second when Claudia entered.

"Lord Phillip!" she enthused, holding out both hands with their perfect fingers unmarred by the gentlest toil. "How delightful of you to come see me."

Phillip, with a short bow, took the hands offered and smiled at her. Golden hair, garnet earrings—they go with the lilacs—perfectly carved face, a little dark under the large gray eyes—maybe we're not sleeping well—and an unnaturally wide smile. A hunter of exotic prey, he concluded.

"I hope the lilacs are not too much for you," she apologized. "They are particularly rich on a heavy day like this." Claudia assumed the usual compliments would follow.

"Not at all," he returned simply, and waited.

"Well," said Claudia after an almost imperceptible pause, "do sit down."

Phillip drew her chair back. As Claudia lowered herself into it, sweeping her luxurious gray silk to one side, he was confronted with the lustrous fullness of her hair, and he had to stop himself from reaching out to touch it. Instead he went around to sit opposite the beauty and folded his hands on the table. Claudia rang a silver bell at her elbow, bringing in a smartly dressed young man bearing a steaming pot under a quilted cover. He began to pour, but his mistress waved him away.

"Allow me," she smiled, pouring the perfectly steeped brew into Phillip's delicate blue cup. "Cream and sugar?"

"Both."

Claudia lifted a cube from a silver bowl with a tiny set of tongs and dropped it in without splashing, then poured an exact ration of cream. She did the same for herself and invited him to try the sweets.

"Thank you," he said, carefully selecting a miniature masterpiece . "Your petit fours are excellent." To her look of puzzlement, he explained that he had already sampled one before she joined him.

The tinkling laugh was released. "How refreshing! A man who sees what he wants and takes it."

"Well, I wouldn't generalize if I were you," he warned, carefully dunking a meringue as his hostess watched in well-managed amazement. "That might have been totally out of character—I might have succumbed to my urge only because of your cakes' utterly irresistible presentation and my having missed lunch."

Claudia rang for the servant again and ordered a cold lunch be brought in for her guest.

"You must know that you are all the talk, Lord Phillip," Claudia tossed out conspiratorially. "Handsome young missionary returns from India, eligible bachelor, son of the Duke. I feel quite giddy to have a private audience with you."

"I'm the newest thing around, I suppose, and that makes for conversation, doesn't it?" Phillip put two dainty sandwiches into his mouth, chewed them briefly, and swallowed. "Are they making up stories about me yet?" he asked innocently.

"Dozens. It seems you brought back a fortune in gems and are in the process of deciding on investments. Also you had three wives, served as translator to a tribal warlord, and you left the country ahead of a Hindu posse who was intent on having your head. To mention only a few."

"All true," replied Phillip, pouring himself more tea. "It grieved me to leave the wives behind, but time was precious. But I left them each a handsome dowry—those gems you mentioned—so I'm confident they will have no trouble finding another husband to take my place."

"I doubt that. You impress me as a man not easily replaced."

"No at all. India is teaming with pale-skinned Westerners hoping to marry a native and be treated like a king. Which is a situation not available to the average man on this side of the world." Phillip sat back and took in the room's furnishings, the bold colors, the oils in heavy frames. "Have you lived here many years, Mrs. Thorne?"

"Oh," she said, "my whole life. Mr. Thorne and I inherited Beaujour from my father. The place took a lot of freshening, I can tell you. Too many years in the hands of a widower, dear man, with other matters to tend to."

"So you have made it your own by now?"

"For the most part. There are a pair of dingy bedrooms still to address, and the gardens are a work in progress."

"I should like to see your gardens. I should like to see your house as well, if that would be possible. I find that a house says a great deal about its inhabitants."

Claudia shifted in her chair, uncertain how to respond. The cowed servant arrived with a plate of food, which Phillip finished off quickly while listening to Mrs. Thorne's theories on interior decorating. Names dropped from her lips, intimate friends, she noted, who had assisted her in resurrecting the house from the ashes of yesterday's fashions. Among them were several artists whose works now hung on the repapered walls only by virtue of her knowing them personally— their paintings were virtually impossible to procure.

Their tea concluded, Claudia led her guest through polished halls, parlors, library, music room, and finally climbed to the newly restored ballroom on the third floor. Phillip stood still, gazing slowly around at the gleaming floors, pale yellow walls, monstrous chandeliers, and marble statues tucked into niches. "Do you give many balls?"

"As many as I can," she replied, squeezing his arm in her enthusiasm. "I love nothing better than entertaining—well, almost nothing." He looked at her, but she was moving on. "A walk through the gardens now?"

As they descended, she observed, "I have done all the talking so far and have not yet heard your story of India. What can I get you to tell me?"

"It was hot. You tumble back and forth—now sopping wet, now dry as death. I made no converts to speak of. I failed to bring back a fortune in gems or anything else. And here I am, several years older and nothing to show for it."

"That's all?"

"I have some anecdotes, but most are not fit for a lady's ears."

They were passing outside onto a pebble path that led into a formal garden, strictly outlined by a low row of dense boxwoods. Overhead, heavy clouds in mixed hues of gray moved sluggishly on their long journey to somewhere. Claudia realized that she would not get any stories that day, but she knew how to wait.

"So now that you are back, what do you plan to do?"

"I've no idea," Phillip replied cheerfully.

"How was your stay at Brookside? Isn't Agnes a darling?"

"Miss Somerset is an admirable woman. I found that my father had been right about her in every way."

"Yes, I have always admired her myself. Such a strong woman, managing everything herself without a husband. And at her age, she may well stay single. That is a pity."

Phillip was silent.

"And what about you, Lord Phillip? Have any of our Chesterton ladies caught your eye?"

"Are there any you would recommend?"

As they walked, Claudia proceeded to enumerate the eligible daughters of the best local families with complete descriptions of their physical superlatives and financial standings, leaving out no detail whether good or bad, which was, as she said, the only responsible thing to do. By the time she finished her account of how the oldest daughter of the town banker had recently been jilted (made a public spectacle of when her fiancé turned out to be the only guest who failed to attend the engagement party), they had arrived back at the front of the house. A chill wind had picked up, blowing Phillip's hair about and filling Claudia's skirts.

"Rain coming in," predicted Phillip, looking up at the darkening sky. "I've enjoyed our visit very much."

"Then come back," said Claudia. "Any time. If I don't see you soon enough, I might just throw a ball to get you back. You do enjoy fancy dress balls, don't you?"

"An event I would not miss," he assured her. "Would you mind," he asked, looking approvingly at a nearby lilac bush heavy with blooms, "if I took a handful of these magnificent flowers with me?"

"Not at all," Claudia cooed. She broke off several twiggy stems and handed the luscious heads to him.

He took them carefully from her and bowed, watching her eyes. His coachman sprang forward to open the carriage door. Claudia began to say one thing more, but he was gone.

# Chapter 24

Agnes and Stella sat in the soft grass before the granite marker at Grandma's grave. The sky looked unfriendly, but Agnes seldom let the weather change her plans. She had brought an armful of red roses and arranged them in a pewter urn on the fresh earth in front of the stone. Stella sat with her sketchpad, making a study of the scene. She had promised Mrs. Bairnaught that she would paint a small canvas of Grandma's final resting place and send it to her.

Mrs. Bairnaught suffered a great blow with the passing of her friend. She clung more tightly to her husband and, in the days following Irene Brown's death, looked increasingly disbelieving, as though she had woken from a terrible dream and was looking for someone who could tell her that none of it was true. Tears rolled freely down her cheeks when she spoke and when she sat quietly and of course when she helped Agnes go through the few items Grandma had brought to Brookside for her stay. Agnes readily agreed to let her keep Grandma's Bible, whose pages were covered with notes in a neat, tiny hand. Mrs. Bairnaught had turned the thin pages to the place marked by a narrow brown ribbon. She read aloud, "The Lord is my shepherd, I shall not want . . .'" and looked up at Agnes. "This was the last thing I read to her," she said. "Isn't that wonderful?"

Today the cemetery was too quiet, even for a graveyard. Agnes broke the silence, her cross-stitch lying untouched in her lap. "I wonder how Mrs. Bairnaught is doing."

Stella frowned. "I feel so bad for her. They were friends forever, weren't they?"

"For about as long as you have been alive. Grandma told me that they wrote to each other every week. How terrible for Mrs. Bairnaught to find no more letters from her in the mailbox. When a woman like Grandma dies, it leaves so many holes."

"That's what I want," said Stella, pausing her pencil and looking around her. The wind was rising and bending the tall patches of unmowed grass. She took in the shadowless landscape, the young trees tethered to the ground in little groups, the sprinkling of headstones. "I want to leave holes when I go. Not permanent ones, of course, but I want to be missed. I hope everyone lying beneath those markers has people crying for them. What is sadder than a death unmourned?"

"Nothing," agreed Agnes, following her gaze. "Surely that is the worst of all."

"I wish Grandma could have been buried in the old churchyard," Stella reflected.

"I do too. But the war dead nearly filled it."

"Did you lose many people you knew?" asked Stella. At twenty-two, she was born during the war but was too young by its close to remember anything, and she had always felt somewhat cheated out of the drama.

"Two especially," said Agnes, remembering. "One was our groom who enlisted and was killed less than a month after marching off in his new uniform. The other was a boy I was very fond of as a child, a few years older than me. He was the son of one of Father's associates, and we would play together when they had meetings at our house. He fell at Gettysburg. His mother had sent him off with a coupon from that retrieving company, so when they found him on the battlefield they brought him home and the family buried him here by the church."

"I can't imagine searching through the pockets of dead men for embalming coupons," Stella shivered. "What a business to be in!"

"But it brought many a boy home for burial," Agnes reminded her. "His funeral was so sad. His mother came up from her seat and stood by his coffin as the service began. Her husband got up and stood beside her, and they remained there through the whole service. She didn't cry, she just stood there with her hands on her boy's coffin. At the gravesite she took hold of one of the handles and wouldn't let go—her husband had to pry her loose. I remember wondering if she was losing her mind, and I wouldn't have blamed her."

The ladies sat quietly for a moment. To their right, a fresh hole had been dug for a burial later that day. "Don't you wonder who it is?" asked Stella. "When I look at graves I always wonder what the person looked like as a girl or boy and how death must have surprised them, even if it came when they were ancient and bent over. Because I don't think anyone is ever ready to leave. I'm sure I won't be."

Agnes looked at her thoughtfully. "It's interesting that you mention that. The day of her stroke, one of the last things Grandma said to me in the morning was how she prized every day, how she wanted to stay in this life to the last possible minute."

"So do I," Stella admitted. "I really can't bear the idea of leaving. I don't understand why we all don't go around wide-eyed with terror over the whole, unavoidable fact."

"Have you been thinking much about that lately?"

"I don't know. They say that once you're a mother you fear death more because you worry for your children, you wonder who will look after them. But I've always thought about death. Doesn't everyone? Don't you, Aunt Agnes?"

"Sometimes. At night." She smiled at Stella. Should she admit that she fretted each orbit of the earth around the sun, bringing her another birthday but not a day closer to a husband or any great accomplishment? No, she would not be ready to leave either, because even if she found her destiny tomorrow it would not leave her the time she wanted to live it.

"Agnes? What do you think of the Duke's son?"

Agnes moved her legs and found that one had gone to sleep. Stretching them both out, she pulled off her shoes and felt the breeze freshen her warm feet. "Lord Phillip?"

"Yes. I think he's very unusual. I found him quite interesting."

"Did you?"

"He is so very pleasant, but he seems like a man with a secret."

"Really? What do you mean?"

"I can't say exactly. But I sense a certain mystery about him. That's quite attractive in a man."

"Indeed!" Agnes watched her niece return to her sketching and could not help admiring the insights of one so young.

"Did you notice how he observes everything so closely?" Stella resumed. "He's like an artist himself in that way. Wants to see something from every side, touch it, understand it. I wish my William were more like that."

"Ah, poor William," Agnes smiled.

"Well, yes, I wish he were more curious. He seems to think he already understands everything around him. The only thing he has an unlimited capacity to investigate is business—meat-packing methods and transportation options and partnerships. Agnes, when he talks about that to me it's all I can do to disguise my boredom. It's so horribly dull!" Stella exclaimed, looking at her aunt. "Why doesn't he want to talk about art or ideas or anything lively?"

"I suppose that's what you have female friends for, Stella. A husband can't ever be everything you want him to be. Father was much from the same mold as William. Absolutely irrepressible when it came to business and industry. But mother stopped even inviting him to the opera or exhibits in the City. He couldn't wait to leave and used any spare moment to work the acquaintances he ran into. She went with other ladies and amused herself far better that way."

Stella continued to draw silently, glancing at the headstone and penciling in the inscription, *Irene Lanham Brown. Widow of James Simon Somerset, lost at sea. Angels on earth now flown home.* Grandma had made it clear that she wanted no mention of Aloysius on her marker. She was sure that he, wretched soul, would spend his eternity where she and James need never run into him.

"You haven't told me your opinion of Lord Phillip," Stella reminded her aunt.

"My opinion is about the same as yours. He is a keen observer, a student of everything in his own way, especially people. Genuine, sincere. Handsome, you could say. Sometimes childlike. And, I agree, mysterious while giving the outward impression of being totally open."

"You say you can't expect everything in a husband," Stella repeated accusingly, "but the woman who gets him will have everything she could want, I imagine."

Agnes stopped Stella's hand from sketching. "Be careful, Stella. Be careful where your thoughts wander." Stella looked at her in surprise. "There's much we don't know about the Duke's son," Agnes continued. "What we do know is that he is at least my age and still has no occupation, no way to support a wife and children aside from his father's benevolence. No matter how fascinating a man is, he must be able to meet that responsibility or he is a poor match for any woman."

Stella looked straight at her aunt. "Are you saying that you would not be interested in pursuing a romance with Lord Phillip if you had the chance? That you would walk away from him and wait for some stuffy, fat, dry goods baron to propose?"

Agnes was silent.

"Aunt Agnes?"

Agnes sat back and clasped her hands.

"He is wonderful, isn't he?" prodded her niece.

"I will admit that he does possess some wonderful traits . . ."

"And you have your own money, so you don't have to worry about that end of it, if you don't mind my saying. Aunt Agnes, I hope you don't think me too bold, but he would be perfect for you."

Agnes laughed, a gay and fully alive sound that floated over the graveyard. "I appreciate your thinking about me, really, Stella! You are too dear. But you should know that I have competition."

"Who?" Stella's eyes opened wide.

"At this moment, our enigmatic friend is stirring sugar into his tea at Mrs. Thorne's."

The wind picked up several pages of Stella's sketchbook and flapped them crazily. Stella closed the book and tucked it beneath her skirt. She pulled her loosened hair from her face and held it from the wind. Looking up at the scudding clouds she asked, "Do you mean Claudia Thorne? The temptress?"

"The same. He accepted an invitation in my presence— practically invited himself."

"But she's not his type at all!" Stella thought a moment. "I think he's going as an observer—you know—wants to see everything, good or bad, and catalog it."

A gust, stronger than the others, snatched their hats, which they had set down on the grass, and sent them tumbling across the lawn. After a short chase the ladies captured them, and as their laughter subsided, they noticed Ned shouting from the carriage, waving them over and pointing at the sky. He had finished his errands in Chesterton just in time to save them from a good drenching, for no sooner had they grabbed up their things and climbed into the carriage than huge drops pelted the roof. Ned pulled his hat down hard and urged on the anxious horses. He squinted through the waterfall pouring from his hat and let the horses lead them home.

# Chapter 25

In the mail Ned had picked up in town were two more thank-you notes, from the Rockwells and Vera. Agnes stood the notes on her dresser beside the pile of gifts her guests had left in parting. Vera's gift was as perfect as she had let on: a pair of bookends cast in the likeness of Vulcan and Venus, which she had uncovered in a back-alley bookstore in Manhattan. There was a china serving bowl from the McMeeds, gaudy silver candlesticks from Wilbur and Eleanor, an ivory writing set from the Bairnaughts, a collection of fine teas from the Rockwells, and from the Duke three beautifully bound novels by Agnes's favorite English author, Charles Dickens. What dear friends I have, Agnes reflected, trailing her fingers over the carefully chosen objects.

Maria interrupted her reflections by announcing that she had a visitor downstairs.

Agnes looked warily at her maid. "Not the thorn, I hope,"

"No, ma'm. It's Lord Phillip."

"Oh!" This was indeed a strange time to call—well past tea and approaching the dinner hour. But it was, after all, the unconventional Phillip.

"He said it would only take a moment."

Agnes felt her heart fall just the tiniest bit, hoping for more. "How do I look?"

Maria looked her up and down. "That dress looks damp. Let's change it, and I'll fix your hair."

Agnes turned toward the mirror and laughed. The wind at the cemetery had made a new arrangement of her dark tresses, and she had forgotten to repair them. In five minutes she had changed into a sedate brown dress and Maria had deftly refastened her hair into a simple bun. A last look in the long mirror showed a well-dressed woman in the prime of her life, a well-shaped woman tense with an excitement that could not be hidden. With a nod to Maria and a look of "here we go," Agnes headed downstairs with measured steps.

Although the Duke and Phillip had left Brookside only a week earlier, it felt like a month since she had looked into his face. He must be on his way home from the thorn's, she imagined, and had decided to make a quick stop here. Maybe he was only asking after something he might have left behind. Maybe he was going to tell her that he was off to South America to join an archeological dig. Or maybe his father had put him up to visiting, and Phillip was simply obliging him.

She smelled lilacs as she rounded the landing of the main staircase. She found Phillip standing expectantly in the middle of the parlor, cradling in one arm a cascade of deep red lilacs. He smiled brilliantly when she appeared and held the flowers out like a little boy.

"Lord Phillip, what a wonderful surprise! And what heavenly flowers. Are they from your garden?"

"Oh, no, father hates anything with a strong scent. He's allergic. I poached these in a neighbor's yard. Aren't they splendid?"

Agnes took the bunch and called to Fettles to bring a vase with water, but he appeared magically with the same already in hand. Agnes arranged the bouquet on the center table and put her face into the deep aroma. "These look very much like Mrs. Thorne's prize-winning variety," she said rising.

"Really? Does she win prizes?"

"Every spring at the Lilac Festival. But she is zealously protective of her bushes and, as far as I know, has never given a sample of them to anyone. She probably fears that someone will graft it onto a shrub and produce a hybrid that will defeat hers. I can't believe you wrestled these from her."

"I simply asked. She tore them right off."

"Well, you are a man of uncommon influence, then."

They sat down beside a tall window flecked with water in the last light of the gray day. Agnes watched Phillip sitting easily opposite her and fought the urge to chatter at him. She waited for him to speak. His hair was windblown, and his boots had found some mud along the way. His clothes were well chosen but rumpled.

"Thank you for seeing me," he began. "I wanted to ask how you are getting along, now that the house is quiet, and you are no doubt remembering your grandmother. . . I thought it might have gotten sad."

"How kind of you. Yes, it is sad, but fortunately my niece Stella remains, and she is good company. We all need people younger than ourselves around, I think, to keep us from getting stiff and gloomy."

"Stiffness gradually falls upon all of us, but I cannot imagine you turning gloomy, no matter how the years may pass."

"Oh, you don't know me so well. I have a rather wide melancholic streak. I'd love to keep Stella here to brighten this whole house, but soon she must no doubt return to her husband in Chicago."

Isaiah entered quietly and lit some lamps.

"So how did you find Mrs. Thorne today—well, I trust?" Agnes ventured.

Phillip proceeded to give Agnes a full description of Mrs. Thorne's home (since Agnes herself had never gained admittance) and a summary on the status of the area's eligible maidens, as told to him.

"So, what do you think of our illustrious Mrs. Thorne?" Agnes asked cautiously. "You must admit, she is a remarkable beauty."

"She is similar to women I have met before. But my visit gave me an opportunity to make some interesting observations. I detected a poison in her more powerful than in most of her type. She is a woman to beware of."

"I agree entirely," Agnes assured him. "I have known her since I was a schoolgirl, and her treachery has only increased. I am always on my guard."

Agnes recounted her and Stella's visit to the cemetery (but not their topic of conversation) and Ned's timely rescue of them from the storm, and how much she loved a good rain. Fettles cleared his throat in the doorway, which meant that it was nearly time for dinner and would there be a guest.

"Would you join us for dinner, Lord Phillip?"

"I am hardly dressed for it," he laughed, and rose to go. "Another evening?"

"Tomorrow?"

"What time?"

"Eight sharp."

"May I bring the lonely Mrs. Thorne?" His eyes danced.

"No," Agnes smiled. "I doubt she dines alone. But do bring your father."

"He's away until Friday, I'm afraid. Should we postpone then?"

Agnes raced through the possible responses and their implications. "I'd rather not."

"Until tomorrow, then, Miss Somerset." Phillip took her hand, kissed it lightly, and walked away. She stood over the captured lilacs and breathed deeply. Fettles let their visitor out into the wet evening just as lightening began to dance across the sky and a long roll of thunder warned of a downpour to come.

Meanwhile, on the other side of the world, in the village of Rama Nagar, another storm raged.

# Chapter 26

Once again the village of Rama Nagar, like so many other middling towns dotting the vast expanse of India, was ankle-deep in water, and the nearby river was set to overrun its banks. Villagers ran splashing through the streets with clothing stretched over their heads as the water poured down without interruption. A man well into the second half of his life, dressed in a damp gray tunic and trousers rolled up to the knee, stood erect on a corner surveying the scene. A lopsided black umbrella, the only one in town, distinguished him as he held it importantly over his head. His face, known to everyone for its habitual cheer, was set into firm lines. These same lines had, in the course of recent months, worn themselves deep into the dark flesh of his face. A deep, vertical groove marked the space between his dark brows, now sprinkled with white, and furrows fell somberly from his nose to each corner of his mouth. His hair, too, was well mixed with white, hair that had kept its youthful black until this year.

Dhanesh looked up the waterlogged street with a mixture of sadness and contempt. For how many years had he urged the city council to build raised walkways along the main streets? Or pushed for them to dig proper drainage canals to carry away the rain that overwhelmed the business district every single year? It did not matter any more. Only one thing mattered. His mind had emptied itself of all his old ambitions, and these had been replaced by one consuming goal.

Two of his old colleagues on the council sloshed past and greeted him quickly, glancing up through the slanting rain, and walked on. So it always was these days. He would soon lose his seat on the council, but it did not matter. He would no longer even be consulted on special projects. He had become translucent, a man whom it was now in the nature of things to ignore. If not for his money, he would be altogether invisible.

Dhanesh straightened and began his march up the middle of the street. His wife needed curry and he had needed to get out of the grim prison his home had become. Her endless complaining and blaming were beyond bearing some days. The boys were leaving as soon as the rains ended. He would be left alone to absorb all of Neela's grief and rage. Sometimes he wondered if it would be better to put her out of her misery one night, deftly and mercifully, but he knew he never could. She had been so delightful when they first married, so perfectly beautiful, but the years and the fair-haired foreigner had stolen everything.

He was still stunned by the disappointment of yesterday's report from the British officials. The accused had been located in the United States and interviewed. There was no trace of Dhanesh's daughter and no grounds for further investigation. Nothing more to be accomplished in an official capacity, he was free to pursue by private means, with our sincere regrets, etcetera, etcetera. He had not even told Neela yet; let her continue to hope a while longer, at least until he decided on the next step. For he was not stopping here.

He stepped aside to make way for a rickety cart loaded with pottery that three men, all talking at once, were pushing through the mud. A fourth man led the dripping and reluctant donkey, who seemed to have given up pulling. Dhanesh looked into the animal's brown eyes as the noisy group passed, and he cringed with sympathy for the beast, burdened with a load he did not know how to move forward but could not free himself from. Involuntarily he put out a hand and ran it along the animal's wet fur. He watched them struggle on for a few moments, then continued on his way.

He would find the man, and his lost Rupa. After all he had done for that filthy Christian, to be repaid like this, stealing his daughter right out from under them, and on the eve of her wedding. He still shook remembering the morning when he found them both gone, the dawning realization of what had happened during the night, the impossibility of undoing it. And Manindra—Dhanesh had never seen such rage. He himself had done the right thing, had gone directly to the prince to inform him that the bride was missing (what horror had filled him at the prospect of saying the words, and how they had echoed in the marble receiving room.)

Manindra struck out immediately on a hunt of his own, with a dozen of his best men. They were gone for a week but returned empty-handed. So what chance did Dhanesh have now with the scent long cold?

It did not matter. The gods might be punishing him, but it was every man's responsibility to carry a thing as far as he was able to carry it. He would hire his own detective. He knew a good one in Hyderabad who was a bloodhound at finding missing wives. Or maybe he would just go himself and get away from Neela, away from everything. Once these abominable rains slowed, once he thought up a plan.

# Chapter 27

Dahlia could not have been happier. Her nephew had not only been vindicated, but had shown himself worthy of special commendation for his extraordinary efforts in keeping the wine cellar free of vermin. The Chateau Plessy had been found, all twelve bottles, by Fettles himself when he undertook a complete inventory of the remaining wine. He discovered the prized claret in a rack just around a brick pillar from the others. It turned out, upon investigation, that Dahlia's nephew had moved it there while pursuing a bold pair of rats who had made their home in the cellar. He had succeeded in trapping both and executing them without mercy, but had forgotten to replace the Plessy.

This was happy news for Agnes because she could now serve the fine vintage that night over dinner with Lord Phillip. She consulted Dahlia early in the morning regarding a menu, and they decided on veal in a light caper sauce, with asparagus and roasted potatoes. Agnes put in a special request for a batch of Dahlia's famous anise cookies to serve afterwards with coffee.

Stella was thrilled to hear who the evening's dinner guest would be and offered her aunt to let them dine alone. Agnes refused and insisted that Stella keep them company through dinner and coffee, too, if she was up to it. If Phillip felt like lingering still longer, they might take a turn in the garden alone.

"Aunt Agnes, you almost make me think you're frightened of his lordship," Stella teased, wiping a sleeve across her forehead as they pruned back the early-blooming roses. Both women possessed an industrious nature that forbid them to sit idle, even on a warm July morning, so they had put on their lightest dresses, leaving their corsets on the closet hooks, and asked Ned where he might use some help in the garden. After producing two pairs of pruning shears, leather gloves, and a wire bin, and after careful instruction on just where to cut and at what angle, Ned left the ladies to their work among the blooms and thorns.

Agnes explained that of course she was afraid of Lord Phillip, and what single woman would not be? She admitted to being taken in before by an irresistible scoundrel and did not want to ever let herself go through that again. Stella begged for details, but Agnes would share no more. She steered the conversation to lighter subjects, which occupied them happily until their exertions in the hot sun took their toll, and the ladies laid down their shears and strolled through the grass to the cool brook the estate was named for. There, behind a copse of old elms, they tied up their skirts, took off their stockings, and waded into the stream's little rapids, stepping carefully along its stony bottom while splashing cold water on their pink faces. When they were thoroughly refreshed, they wandered slowly up the hill to the house, ate a small lunch on the terrace, and went upstairs for a well-deserved nap.

As she began to doze, Agnes realized that she should not even have alluded to M. earlier in the garden. Just the mention kept him darting into her thoughts all afternoon. He looked back at her from mirrors and sat across from her at lunch. She felt his hands on her waist, his lips on her neck. Could anything be that good again, or would he haunt her forever?

She slept for only an hour, and when she woke evening was still a long way off. She passed the afternoon restlessly between reading and embroidery, and finding she could concentrate on neither one, she resorted to reorganizing her jewelry and letting her mind wander to how each piece had come to be hers. Somehow the hours went by, and at last it was time to dress. As Marie fastened the last pearly button on the back of Agnes's gown, she heard something through the open window and darted over to look down. Agnes's room overlooked the front drive, giving a full view of any approaching or departing guests. It had been her mother's room, and Agnes took it over a few months after her death since she, like her mother, had always loved its morning sun, the cool afternoons, and the ability to keep an eye on all comings and goings.

"He's here, Miss Agnes," Marie said, holding herself to the side of the drape. She watched for a moment. "He is a fine-looking gentleman, isn't he, ma'm?"

"Is he?" Agnes kept her voice even. Turning from the mirror, she caught Marie's look that told her they both knew it very well. "How do I look?"

"Prettier than a peach." There was a knock at the door and Stella entered, stunning in a deep blue gown that set off her red hair and pale skin.

"Stella, how lovely you are!" declared Agnes.

"It was all I could do to get this dress closed. Can you tell?"

"No, dear, you look perfect. We'll have to take you into Chesterton and get you some more comfortable dresses soon. That baby will just keep growing, you know."

Marie recalled that her mother sewed herself dresses out of tablecloths near the end of her confinements because nothing else was bearable. "Got big as you please, too, and that's what you need. Gives you a healthy baby if you don't squeeze the poor little thing into corsets."

Stella nodded. "My neighbor Mrs. Fielding has already lost two babies. The last one was a good way along, too. Mrs. Fielding doesn't ever want to look in a family way, though, so she keeps herself laced up into her regular clothes. I don't know how she did it. I feel like I'll barely be able to eat a forkful in this dress without bursting the seams."

"We can't have that!" exclaimed Agnes, "and you certainly must eat. Marie, what do we have for Stella? Maybe that Spanish jacket of mine? We could unbutton the dress and put on the jacket, and no one will ever know."

The item was located, and Stella was released from her torment. The jacket of dense black lace, a little long on her, perfectly hid the open back of the dress and was pronounced a success. Agnes took Stella's arm, and the ladies descended to greet their guest.

Stella managed to eat her fill at dinner, with second helpings of everything. In front of guests she would normally not indulge in such gluttony, but her appetite raged these days, and her two companions urged her to not hold back at the risk of depriving her child. Throughout the lively meal, Stella delighted in watching her aunt pretend nonchalance across the table from Lord Phillip. He presented himself relaxed and impeccably dressed except for his vest being misbuttoned by one, which gave him an oddly unbalanced look that failed to detract from his charm.

After cookies and coffee on the terrace, Stella announced that she was *a plat* and retired to her room. But before leaving, while Phillip was interviewing Fettles about the evening's wine, she whispered in Agnes's ear, "Are you still frightened?"

Agnes whispered back, "I have progressed to terrified."

She squeezed her aunt's hand. "Please don't disappoint me—" Her pale eyes were wide and urgent. "You must take him into the garden and tell me everything tomorrow. This night was made for you two." And she slipped away.

Stella was right. By now the night fully enveloped them, and stars twinkled in the blackness above. The breeze had died with the setting sun, but the soft, humid air felt delicious. It was a night bursting with potential, a night when you felt anything could happen.

I hope he doesn't run off now that Stella's gone, thought Agnes. Phillip returned and sat lightly on the edge of his chair. His face glowed in the light from the table lamp.

"Are you tired too?" he asked.

"No, not particularly."

"My father accuses me of tending to overstay my welcome. If that's so, I rely on you to point me toward the door."

"Very well," Agnes laughed, unable to imagine ever wanting him to leave. "This might be rather scandalous, but what do you think of a nighttime tour of my garden?"

"I love a garden at night," said Phillip, looking toward the darkened path and the black silhouettes of sculpted shrubs. "The smells really come out after dark." Phillip rose and put out his arm. Agnes called to Fettles not to worry, they would be in the garden, and together they stepped off the terrace and away from the light. They passed beneath a series of trellises draped in honeysuckle, whose creamy blooms could still be seen in the gloom. Their fragrance was intoxicating. Agnes stopped and plucked one. She snapped off the tiny end and carefully drew out the stamen for the tiny drop of nectar clinging to it. She held it up to show Phillip.

"I used to pick apart dozens of these as a child to taste the one sweet drop inside each one. Did you?"

"Oh, yes," he replied. "I tried to make a goblet of it one day for my mother. I was knee-deep in ransacked blooms by the time I gave up. Naturally, I licked up the tiny bit of nectar I had and went off to play, knowing that Mother would understand."

"What was your mother like?"

Phillip thought for a moment. "She was a wonderful storyteller and a genius with languages. But most of all she was a daring woman. You would have liked her. Not daring in a showy, obtrusive way, flinging her adventures in your face the way some women do. She was daring in a considered, intelligent way. And she let all of us children be who we were. She and my father got into more than one argument over that."

"About you maybe?"

"About me and my sisters, both older. My father wanted to protect us from idiotic mistakes, like most parents do, and my mother wanted us to find out what truly suited us. I have taken the longest time to find that out. Still looking, still chafing my father's poor nerves."

"You have two sisters?"

"Yes, as different as earth and water, but wonderful girls. Both married and living in the City."

"You alone have escaped matrimony."

"Not so much escaped as failed to locate. I'm beginning to think my compass is a few degrees off. I never seem to quite arrive where I meant to."

A frog, hidden beneath the asters, croaked out a simple but impenetrable message as they passed. Two mice darted across the path, then peeked from under the leaves as though to reassure themselves of what they had just seen—two humans at night, trespassing on their playground.

By now Agnes and Phillip had reached the hedge that separated the garden from Agnes's private bench. As of one accord, their feet took them around it and stopped. Beneath them stretched the dark landscape, its farms fast asleep. Stars spread across the sky like tiny sequins spilled from a seamstress's lap. Beside them the marble bench and its two guardians glowed softly in the dark.

Phillip turned to Agnes, and she looked up at him. "Now I want to hear your story," he murmured.

# Chapter 28

Sitting once more between the yearning statues, Agnes summed up her life for Phillip as neatly as possible. She was born at Brookside three years after her sister, now dead. Her mother and father were wonderful people who died in quick succession, leaving her to manage the estate. She was a college graduate. She had seen Paris and London and Hamburg but traveled little since assuming care of the family home. Her French was fluent, and she, like all her family before her, was a Presbyterian. She hoped one day to visit the Greek ruins and ride a gondola through Venice.

"Well, that's about all. I'm not as interesting as Aunt Vera or probably your mother, I'm afraid."

Phillip leaned back and studied her narrowly in the light of the rising moon.

"I suspect," said Agnes, "that I have not satisfied your curiosity."

"I'd like to know what you love. Also what has disappointed you. Maybe even what you hope for, beyond a gondola ride."

Agnes gathered her skirt absently into a loose fist. "A woman is not accustomed to sharing intimate feelings with someone so early in their acquaintance," she demurred.

"Was I being intimate?" rejoined Phillip with a look of surprise. "I didn't realize. I just wanted to know something real about you, not a family tree."

No man had ever wanted to know this much about her. Although she was sitting, she felt almost dizzy. She gripped the edge of the cool marble.

"Very well. But you will need to ask questions. I can't just ramble on about myself. You might as well know that I've been accused of thinking in lists, so please don't criticize if my answers are spare."

"Agreed. Let's begin with disappointments and get those out of the way. Of course I don't expect you to tell me anything you don't want to," he assured her.

Disappointments. Where should she start? A cartoon popped into her mind, one she had seen years ago in the newspaper. A little old man sat behind a desk with two books on it. One slim volume was

127

labeled *Appointments*. The other, a massive tome at least five times as big, was titled *Disappointments*.

"All right. I wish I were more like my mother. I am disappointed that I don't have her grace, her easy sophistication, her equanimity in the face of trouble. She made life look easy, but I seem to churn over the smallest things."

"I'm certain that you have many qualities she found lacking in herself."

"Oh, I don't think so. Yes, I have my strengths, but Mother was completely sufficient. And sure of herself. But there's more. I'm disappointed that I don't get to travel anymore as I did. Even if I managed to break away from my duties for a few weeks, all my friends and relations seem to be busy with their own lives and I would have to travel alone, which sounds dreadful. Sitting on the Champs Elysée at a table for one—hardly worth the voyage."

"These things are difficult," said Phillip, watching her. "To be a woman alone with the responsibility you carry. How do you get through, if I may ask such a question?"

Agnes looked at him. "How do you get through? You are also alone."

"I have no responsibilities," returned Phillip. "I should, but I somehow, even at my advanced age, do not. You are different."

"Well, I don't really know. Of course I pray, but that doesn't always pull one all the way along, does it?" She reflected a moment, then plunged ahead. "You may have noticed that I do not take wine at dinner."

"I assumed you were one of our temperate sisters."

"I used to take too much wine. The warm comfort of a good red helped me through dark times, starting with my sister's death, really, until it brought me down altogether—leaving me with the punishment of never enjoying a glass again."

"Is such strictness truly necessary?"

"I found that for me there is no such thing as 'just one glass.'"

"I understand."

"Do you?"

Phillip leaned back and watched her a moment. "Yes. I imagine it's rather like opium, but people do not sit around the dinner table smoking opium, so it's not so hard to avoid as alcohol."

"Are you telling me that you have frequented opium dens?"

"No. But I have tried it and know its allure. It was during the famine. Everything around me was so terrible—there was no relief, almost nothing to lose. Someone gave me a little and it quieted the pain beautifully. Until it wore off, of course."

"Ah, that is the hard part. All the pain is still there, waiting."

"Yes, and it frightened me. I knew I would not have the strength to resist the drug's sweet oblivion."

They sat silent for a while. Then Phillip asked, "What do you love?"

Agnes thought for a moment. "I love Brookside. I don't know how I would live anywhere else. I love roses, especially the complex, thorny ones. I love good, hot tea in the morning with cream and coffee after dinner. I love the symphony and the opera, especially Bach and Verdi—that huge, rising sound that goes straight to your heart. I love thunderstorms and the wind at night. This list could get very long, you know."

"Have you been in love?"

"Of course."

"Did he know you loved him?"

"Yes."

"But he ran away?"

"Something like that. Yes, he did run away. For a long time it felt like he took the better part of me with him. But we eventually heal, don't we?"

"Most of the time."

"And you, have you ever been in love?"

"Oh, yes. That riotous affliction of the senses! It has taken hold of me more than once."

"And yet?"

"Turned down, I regret to admit. The ladies like me, but I don't seem to be marrying material. Father says I tend to be a bonfire where what's wanted is only a good lamp with an obedient wick."

"I'm very fond of bonfires. I like their intensity."

"As long as they are not in the parlor."

"They need the right setting, of course. And one needs to keep an eye on them."

"They don't frighten you?"

"Not at all."

They were looking directly at one another. Phillip put out a hand and traced Agnes's cheek with his fingertips. She felt his hand slide behind her head and saw his face draw close, then his lips were upon hers, and she smelled him and felt him and wanted to walk bodily into the roaring fire that was Phillip.

* * *

Stella had been asleep for hours by the time Agnes tiptoed past her room. Undoing her dress with some difficulty, Agnes hung it over a chair, pulled open the drapes, and lay down to stare at the bewitching night. She listened to the frogs and nocturnal insects and let the adrenaline course through her body. Did tonight really happen? Over and over as she lay on the cool sheet she felt his hand on the nape of her neck, his moustache so much softer than she had imagined against her face, his lips pressing against hers, his hair between her fingers. Two hours had slid away like minutes as they embraced, clinging to each other and wishing that the world would slow its turning toward the waiting sun. Periodically they pulled back to look at one another in wonder or gaze out at the magical night landscape. Agnes wanted to seal the image in her mind: the immense sky, the stars, the blue-black fields stretching away luxuriously, the heavy scent of honeysuckle, the look of her hand in his. Shortly before dawn a brief sleep overtook her, swirled with dreams in brilliant colors.

# Chapter 29

At ten o'clock in the morning Stella crept to Agnes's room and put her ear to the door. Hearing nothing, she rapped softly, then again. A muffled voice told her to come in, so she opened and stepped into the sunny room. Agnes was pulling herself up in bed with the filmy look of one who has just awoken. A warm breeze lazily swelled the open drapes.

"Did I wake you up?" asked Stella, approaching softly.

"Yes, but that's all right."

"I couldn't wait any longer to hear about last night." Stella perched on a velvety chair beside the bed.

Agnes stared at her niece for a moment, then let a smile creep across her face. Stella sprang to the rumpled bed. "What happened? Oh, you must tell me everything!" she ordered, grabbing Agnes's hands.

"My dear, everything feels new this morning," Agnes said slowly. "I know this is the same room I woke up in yesterday and that's the same sun outside the window, but it's all different."

"Did he kiss you?"

"Stella!"

"He did, didn't he? I hope you kissed him back. I think it's silly to play the coquette when a man makes his intentions clear. So tell me!"

Agnes straightened against her pillows and sighed. "Well, we took a walk through the garden. I don't remember when I was last in the garden at night. It felt positively magical. The air was warm and heavy. All the little creatures were croaking and singing and everything felt alive. *I* felt alive—almost too alive, do you know? Anyway, we walked and chatted and then sat on my bench beyond the hedge."

"Oh, you are wild! Did Fettles come looking for you and try to spoil everything?"

"For once he left me alone. He must like Lord Phillip."

"And then what happened?"

"All right, yes, he kissed me. And don't worry, I did not push him away."

Stella threw her arms around her aunt and squeezed hard. "I am so happy for you. How long were you out?"

"It felt like half an hour, but when I got back in I saw that two hours had passed."

"He seems like a wonderful man, Aunt Agnes. You deserve this."

"Do I? Well, I don't want to rush into something willy nilly. Mother always said, 'The right match is not a summer bloom; let it wait a season to see if it lasts.' But this is so exciting, Stella, I can't lie." Agnes looked intently at her niece. "I am afraid that I am going to run headlong into this and there's nothing I can do to stop myself."

Stella slid off the bed and stood with her chin in the air, her hands gently clasped. "A lady maintains her decorum. A lady does not show her hand. A lady bides her time and controls her passion, if she has any, giving the gentleman ample time to appreciate her character before any demonstration of affection is exchanged."

"Well spoken," Agnes cheered. "But too late. Anyway—" she threw back the sheet and sprang out of bed, "I had better put myself together and get downstairs before Fettles thinks I caught pneumonia in the night air. I don't know if you know, but the dear man worries more than three old women put together."

Just then Marie entered with coffee on a tray. Together the three ladies worked merrily to prepare Agnes for a new day.

# Chapter 30

Living with one's father long after outgrowing the nursery is seldom easy for a young man. And rare is that father who can co-exist peacefully with the man he himself produced, especially one who has not found his path in life. The father wants more for his son, he is anxious for him, and—most difficult of all—he finds through such close association that his son has become a man who views the world differently than he. Each generation that tumbles out of the one before thinks itself a new breed, unbounded by the limitations of its parents, destined to split the future in two with its bare hands and walk triumphantly through the middle.

And so it was the most natural thing that Phillip should return from India to his father's house knowing that it would be a difficult season for both of them. Never has a son loved his father more, nor a father his son. Nevertheless, Phillip intended to make his stay at Fellcrest as short as possible, taking just as much time as necessary to discern his next move. But he was tired. And he had not the smallest fragment of an idea what he should do next or where he might go.

After the exhilarating week at Brookside, the days in his father's house felt especially long. They were at the same time perfectly pleasant and consistently nerve-wracking. The Duke brought him into his affairs and tried to make him feel needed, but Phillip found it difficult to concentrate on the political goings-on and business strategies of his father's circle. Just like when he was a boy, once he understood the principle and pattern of the game, he was ready to play something else.

The Duke introduced him to innumerable worthies in the best social spheres and did not hesitate to ask that they consider his son for a part in their firms. A few, out of deference to his father and a genuine wish to help the young man, offered him positions of one sort or another, some of substance and others merely titular; but Phillip had so far declined them all.

One brilliant July afternoon, riding home from Albany, father and son sat looking out at the glowing countryside in silence. The Duke sat across from Phillip and studied his face. The boy's features were placid and not in keeping with one who should be turning over in his mind the promising events of the day. The Duke adjusted his cravat, glanced at his watch, and back at his son. Finally he spoke, his words carrying an unmistakable edge.

"So, what do you think? Can you see yourself working with Messrs. Hodge and Blest? They are capital fellows, I assure you. Excellent reputation, solid firm. And they have offered a most interesting position, you must admit."

"I liked them very much," Phillip smiled. "Especially Mr. Blest. So affable. He demonstrated the highest regard for my abilities when he couldn't have the faintest idea what I would do for his company."

"He's a good judge of character, Joseph Blest. A house cannot succeed like theirs unless they engage only the best people. You impressed him."

Phillip uttered a laugh. "I didn't say ten words."

"All the better! 'A prudent man keeps his knowledge to himself, but the heart of fools blurts out folly.'[2] You did well, Phillip."

Phillip stared out the window at a farm sliding by. The stern white house, softening in aspect beneath its gently peeling paint, sat just off the road, with a dirt yard and a tumble of outbuildings beside it. Off in a green field two figures, possibly the farmer and his son, walked slowly toward a weathered barn with tools over their lean shoulders. A sparse herd of cows came into view, lying on their knees in the shade of scant trees, moving their jaws lazily from side to side and watching the road.

"So, what do you think?" the Duke repeated.

"I think," sighed his son, "that it's a fine position with the very best company a fellow could hope to join, but I don't know if I am the man for the job."

"Why?" exploded his father, waving his arms as far as the confines of the carriage allowed. "Why do you doubt yourself? I don't know what else I can do—"

"Nothing, father. You have been heroic in trying to help me since I've been back. Your associates have offered me more than I could possibly have expected, and I'm very grateful to them and to you."

"Then why do you drag your heels this way? Why not say yes to something and get on with your life?"

---

[2] *Proverbs* 12:23.

Why indeed. Phillip could not explain why the prospect of working in a respectable office with serious men of business backed by piles of ledgers and books on taxation and exchange rates froze the blood in his veins. He needed to ply some trade that took him outdoors or kept him on the move. He looked out at another farm, much larger and tidier than the last. A half-grown crop of bright green corn stretched across a vast field, and after that came alfalfa, then beets.

"What do you think of agriculture?" he asked his father.

The Duke hesitated. "What do you mean?"

"None of our family, as far as I know, has ever dabbled in agriculture, have we?"

"Not that I know of. Not our business. My uncle was a master with roses—even developed his own hybrid. Did you know that? The Queen's Veil. It was almost black, very unusual, rather foreboding, but it made quite a sensation among the horticulturalists."

They rode a mile in silence and Phillip began again. "Father, I've been thinking that I might like to give farming a try. In a small way, of course, not hundreds of acres. But it looks satisfying. It produces something real, you understand?"

He looked intently at his father, who sat back with his hands on his knees and asked, "What do you know about farming?"

"Very little, but I've been reading up on it and talking to our neighbors. From what I've gathered, potatoes would be a good idea. We really don't have enough of them, they store well, and they don't need as much water as corn, which can be tricky. Alfalfa is very good, too."

"Are you making a proposal, son?"

"What would you think, Father, if we bought a few acres and tried our hand? There's a piece for sale about 15 miles north of us, just under 100 acres. He'll sell the whole thing or halves. He's an elderly man with no one to leave it to. His children have all gone into the trades of one kind or another."

"Is there water?"

"Yes, two fine brooks that he says run all year."

"We don't know anything about farming, Phillip," the Duke reminded him, as though realizing it anew.

"Not now," admitted Phillip, sitting up straight, "but by next year I could have studied a great deal, and the old man was willing to show me. I visited the property two weeks ago. I didn't want to mention anything to you then, but I wish you had seen it: The old man stood at the gate before I left and talked a good while. He told me he had no one to teach everything he knows to. Everything that he learned the hard way, it all goes with him. He looked destitute, although he owns this marvelous piece of property. It was very sad."

"So you have been thinking this over for a while? Well, it's not the worst idea you've had." The Duke thought for a few moments, recalling a proverb about he who works his land will have abundant food, while one who chases fantasies lacks judgment. He had surely seen his dear boy chase plenty of fantasies.

He looked at Phillip and saw an eagerness that had been absent. "I suppose I could take it under consideration." Father and son sat in silence the rest of the way home, and the Duke watched the rolling, green properties pass by as though he had just been given a new pair of eyes.

# Chapter 31

Abram Rockwell was getting stiff. The train for Philadelphia arrived late to pick up its passengers in New York, which meant that he had sat an extra hour on a hard wooden bench in Grand Central Depot before boarding. He resented this trip anyway. If people conducted their affairs properly, everything ran smoothly and details could be handled by correspondence. Poor judgment and procrastination led to a great deal of bother for people who should not be inconvenienced but inevitably were in order to get the job done. If Benjamin Somerset were alive, none of this would be necessary. He had a way of handling his family, even those not in his household. But with his death the rope began to fray in various directions, and Mr. Rockwell could not keep his eye on everyone.

He did not dismiss Agnes's concerns about Wilbur as easily as he pretended upon leaving Brookside. He had kept his ear to the ground and made discrete inquiries regarding Wilbur and Eleanor's acquaintances in Philadelphia. He did not like what he heard. Most of all, he was alarmed to see the balance of Grandma Brown's accounts as he proceeded with the disposition of her property according to her will. Repeated letters to Wilbur had gone unanswered until he received one that claimed the situation was complicated and would require Mr. Rockwell's presence to fully explain. Convinced that Wilbur was using this as a dodge, thinking the venerable accountant would not make the trip, Mr. Rockwell fired back a telegraph to let Wilbur know of his arrival in two days' time. He received in answer two cryptic lines, "Will meet in town. Carriage on Market."

The train pulled into the Philadelphia station in a driving rain. Mr. Rockwell stood up and stretched his aching back, looking up and down the railway car. Never a porter when you need one, he reflected. He pulled his one bag down from the luggage rack with some difficulty, he being a small man, the rack being high, and his bag being over packed by a careful wife. He set it on the seat and pulled out a small umbrella, settled his hat firmly on his head, and stepped from the car.

The late-July afternoon was suffocating, and the new Broad Street Station roared with the hiss of steam and flocks of damp people hurrying left and right. Smartly dressed travelers wove between confused huddles of foreigners and ragged boys running with boxes on their backs, tied together as were their shoes with lengths of string. Mothers patted their crying babies, and young men in cheap suits leapt aboard westbound trains to find their fortune in Denver or San Francisco. Vendors added to the din, shouting out their offerings of candy, lemonade, newspapers, and shoe shines.

Mr. Rockwell caught the attention of a porter who shouldered his bag and led him nimbly to the great doors of the Market Street exit. The rain had slackened but not stopped. Black carriages waited in a long row up and down the street and, beyond them, trolleys trundled along the steaming pavement. A hungry-looking man in a sodden cap ran up to them and asked in a thick Irish accent if the gentleman might be Mr. "Abraham Rockell," which was close enough to convince the accountant to have his bag handed over and follow the lean driver to a nearby carriage. Mr. Rockwell was happy to pull himself into the cab and settle into the soft, burgundy cushion. The cab picked its way through the hubbub of Market Street for two blocks, then turned north. Mr. Rockwell had never visited Wilbur's offices and hoped they were not far off. He badly wanted a stationary seat, a sandwich, and a cup of coffee.

He opened his bag and took out a notebook. Absently he reviewed the numbers he had already checked three times. For years Grandma Brown's estate had been worth some six million dollars. It had grown to nearly eight recently when an investment he had made on her behalf had returned a handsome profit. But that was in February, and he knew of no activity on her accounts since then. Naturally he was shocked to find three weeks ago that her accounts held just under one million. After assuring himself that the banks had made no errors, he turned to Wilbur, who had thrown up a wall of silence. Mr. Rockwell had said nothing yet to Agnes. He wanted to know the whole story before making any report to her. And if there was some explanation, why disturb the woman unnecessarily?

Looking out the window, he noticed that they were in a very select end of town. Tidy brick buildings lined the street, all with black shutters and shiny hardware. The cab pulled up in front of one, well situated on a corner, displaying beside the door a brass plate inscribed with *Brown and Associates, Ltd.* The driver helped Mr. Rockwell down and handed him his bag. The sun was pushing its way through the clouds, pulling up waves of hot vapor from the cobbled street. Mr. Rockwell took a labored breath, stepped up to the freshly painted door, and pulled at the handle. To his surprise, he found it locked, so he knocked smartly.

In Mr. Rockwell's many years of travel in and out of hundreds of offices, those of lawyers and accountants and merchants in both low and high stations, he had never laid eyes on a less desirable specimen of an employee than the one that opened the door to him now. A lad of not more than fourteen years, small-eyed and smudged, in dirty dungarees and ill-fitting shoes, stood squinting at him in the doorway. His vest was too small by several sizes and kept itself closed through the heroic work of two cracked buttons. His hair gave Mr. Rockwell the impression of having been cut in the dark of night and had not enjoyed the benefit of a bucket of water for a very long time. As unfortunate as the young man's appearance was, it impressed the visitor less than did his attitude, which fell somewhere between extreme apathy and hostility.

The boy was just finishing pulling his sleeve across his pale nose when he opened, and looking at his guest without any trace of curiosity, demanded flatly whom he was there to see. He grudgingly admitted Mr. Rockwell, closed the door, and tromped to the back in search of his employer. Mr. Rockwell was left still holding his hat and umbrella in a spare but attractively furnished reception room. Various maps hung on the walls, and a mahogany bookcase held a few volumes of standard business texts. In a moment the dreary young man returned, the heels of his too-large shoes clattering against the bare floor.

"Mr. Brown asks that you wait a bit as he's engaged with a client." The boy then held out his grimy hands for Mr. Rockwell's things, hung them carelessly on a wall rack, and sat down to gaze glumly out the window. Mr. Rockwell took the liberty to sit down. His stomach reminded him that he had not eaten since breakfast, and he decided that he needed food one way or another.

"Young man." His voice echoed in the quiet room. The boy turned his head toward him. "What is your name?"

"Jenkins."

"Mr. Jenkins, is there by chance an eatery nearby where you could pick up some lunch for me?"

"There's the Liberty, but it's not very good. If you want to pay more, the Black Bell's got good corned beef and chicken pie."

Impressed by the young man's knowledge of nearby comestibles, Mr. Rockwell reached into his pocket and pulled out a bill. "Bring me back a chicken pie and coffee if they have it. And I'll want a receipt and the change. If you return promptly I'll make it worth your while." Mr. Rockwell looked at the boy seriously, with no hint of smile beneath his heavy gray moustache. He knew better than to confuse the urchin with kindness.

The boy sat in the window a moment as though considering whether or not to accept the assignment. Gradually he pulled himself to his feet, took the money, grabbed his limp cap from its hook, and left. He had not been gone a full minute when low voices approached from the back rooms, and Wilbur entered accompanied by a heavily starched man with a waxed moustache.

Wilbur broke away from his client, extending a hand to Mr. Rockwell. "Abram! Thank you for coming. You picked a steamy day, didn't you?"

Mr. Rockwell bit his tongue. Coming was not my first choice, he thought, and should not have been necessary. Instead he simply shook Wilbur's hand silently. Wilbur made no introductions but began a hurried goodbye to the starched man. The gentleman gave every appearance of being thoroughly unhappy with the outcome of their meeting, and Wilbur propelled him out the door with assurances that they would talk again tomorrow.

"An unhappy client?" asked Mr. Rockwell.

"Oh," replied Wilbur, creasing up his face, "a fellow who wanted to make some changes in investments. Doesn't like the way the market's going. Nervous sort. They'd be better off putting their money in an iron box under the bed."

"Sometimes that's the wisest course," concurred Mr. Rockwell.

"You must be hungry. Let's take you out for a bite of food. What do you think of our new station?"

"It seems to serve the purpose. And I just sent your boy to get me a chicken pie, so that will do just fine. I'd like to get started immediately with the business at hand, Wilbur. I plan to take the night train back. Can't sleep anymore if I'm not in my own bed. By the way, how did you come to hire such an unlikely office boy? You could do better, I'd think, and a well-groomed assistant would more respectably represent Brown and Associates, don't you think?"

"Oh, Jenkins? He's a stray dog," laughed Wilbur uneasily, leading his guest back to his office.

"A stray dog?"

"Yes, he's always coming around sniffing for a tip. I let him get what he can. It's all harmless."

"What you mean is that you don't pay him."

"Of course not! Would you? But it keeps me from having to hire someone, which makes good sense to me. Well, where do you want to start with all this? Can I pour you a drink?"

"No, thank you."

It was only three-thirty in the afternoon, but Wilbur poured himself a half-glass of bourbon from a handsome decanter, swallowed it, and poured another. Mr. Rockwell watched all of this frowning, and with deepening concern for whatever he was about to learn.

# Chapter 32

"So where shall we begin," asked Wilbur brightly, indicating a chair. Mr. Rockwell sat, opened his bag, and removed his notebook.

"As you know," began the accountant, "It is my responsibility to conduct the final disposition of your grandmother's estate according to her will. As Agnes is a single woman without substantial income, Mrs. Brown intended, as you were aware, to leave the lion's share of her liquid assets to her. A will to this effect has been in place for many years. Agnes was, as a result, looking forward to an absence of worry regarding the upkeep of Brookside."

"The balance of your grandmother's accounts as of February 28 was nearly $8 million. No transactions came across my desk since that time. However, when I checked the balances in preparation for making the proper distributions, I found that they totaled only $748,000. Since you and Eleanor were her daily companions, and I can only assume were privy to some discussions of her finances, I am looking to you for help in explaining this."

Wilbur had seated himself behind his desk while listening. Now, downing the last of his glass, he rose and began a thoughtful pacing.

"Abram, as a man of business and considerable assets yourself, I know that you know the importance—no, the necessity—of continuing to make one's money work for one's family. A dormant fortune is a shrinking fortune."

"I am well aware of this principle. And you have always been free to invest your wealth where you saw fit, I am sure."

Wilbur cleared his throat and tugged at his vest. "You may not know that my assets have been committed for some time now to improvements at my estate, Montefiore, and a small number of long-term investments abroad."

Mr. Rockwell interrupted, his color rising. "You have made use then of your grandmother's funds without consulting me? Is that what you are saying?"

"Some opportunities require immediate action," Wilbur returned sharply. "I have taken advantage of chances that could not wait."

"Such as?" Mr. Rockwell was clearly struggling to control himself.

"Principally real estate."

"All since February?"

Wilbur was silent for a moment, then poured himself another dose of dark orange whiskey.

"And by what means? With the exception of your grandmother, I am the only one authorized to access these accounts."

"Grandma Brown saw the wisdom of the purchases and was amenable to offering me power of attorney to make use of additional resources."

"What?" Mr. Rockwell exploded from his chair. "Without asking me? Without even notifying me?"

Just then both men noticed Jenkins standing in the doorway with a bundle and a tall mug.

"Well?" Wilbur snapped at the wide-eyed boy.

The youth mumbled that he had the gentleman's chicken pie and his coffee and could he keep the change as he had run all the way back with it. Mr. Rockwell, like a man in a daze, said he could keep the change and the food for that matter. At this the boy, after a moment's confusion, darted back out the front door to eat his dinner before the strange gentleman changed his mind.

Wilbur proceeded to assure Mr. Rockwell that he had the situation under firm control. When asked for receipts and ledger books, he raised his arms helplessly and said that his associate had been called away to Washington that very morning on an errand of the greatest importance that had required him to take those items with him. He should be back next week, though, and they could sort it all out then.

"Do you mean to tell me, sir, that you have nothing to show me at this time?"

"Sadly that is true. I do regret the great inconvenience, Abram. But you are more than welcome to spend the night."

As the weight of Wilbur's words registered with him, Mr. Rockwell dropped into his chair like one whose legs had been knocked from under him. His mind whirled. At length he demanded, "I should like to see this power of attorney you mention."

"Of course." Wilbur pulled out a desk drawer and produced the document, duly signed and witnessed and dated March of the same year.

"Why wasn't I advised? It is not like your grandmother to not communicate with me on such a matter."

"She had confidence in our plan and was afraid you would not approve. After all, Grandma was entitled to make her own decisions, was she not? She was a sharp old woman to the last." Wilbur tried to smile, but the effect was ghoulish.

Mr. Rockwell tucked the document into his bag. "I'll take this. I'm sure you have another copy." He rose and stood squarely in front of Wilbur. "You have much to answer for, Wilbur. There could be a challenge. You might have to liquidate these recent investments to give the family its due, and soon. I hope you invested very wisely." He picked up his bag. "As for spending the night, no. If your boy will get me a cab, I will return to the station directly. As soon as your associate is returned, so shall I, and we will have a full accounting of all this. Make sure your papers are in order. I will not come alone."

Mr. Rockwell headed to the door, grabbed his hat and umbrella on the way, and walked out. Wilbur, just behind him, whistled for Jenkins, who set out to find a cab while chewing the last mouthful of pie. Wilbur said an awkward good-bye and closed the black door behind his visitor. A carriage, which had been parked half a block away, pulled out and came to a stop a few yards from where Mr. Rockwell stood. A head projected from the window, and a hand beckoned, and Mr. Rockwell recognized the imposing countenance of Mrs. Eleanor Brown.

# Chapter 33

Eleanor's carriage, with Mr. Rockwell inside, pulled away at a brisk clip just as Jenkins, already planning how to spend his next tip, appeared with a cab for the gentleman. Mr. Rockwell looked through the rear window to see the young man crane his neck one way and the other, then run into Brown and Associates in search of his fare.

Meanwhile, the puzzled passenger turned his attention to Eleanor and waited for her to speak. The shock he had just been dealt had robbed him of his usual manners.

"I know you have just met with my husband," Eleanor began. She clearly saw no need for polite preamble. A Persian cat dozed in her lap as she absently stroked its luxurious head. "What did he tell you?"

"He told me things my ears could barely take in, madam. That he had secured power of attorney over his grandmother for the purpose of using her money to make certain real estate investments, none of which I was consulted about. When I asked for receipts he told me that they were all with his associate who happens to be in Washington this week, and if I would be so kind as to return next week, he will provide a full account of this shocking situation." Mr. Rockwell's voice swelled as he finished, and Eleanor shrank inwardly at the fury she and her husband would now face. "Can you tell me anything further?" the old man asked, raising his eyebrows.

"I can tell you that I had nothing to do with all this. I warned him many times, and I urged him to talk to you and to Agnes, but he refused, kept putting it off."

"Why didn't Mrs. Brown contact me?"

Eleanor looked away. "She did. That is, she wrote letters and Wilbur always took them to town to send. I suspected you might never receive them." She paused and glanced at her visitor with a dark mixture of fear and hesitation. "I have reason to believe that he led her to think you replied . . . approvingly, and even concealed the actual amounts."

"Infamy! And what do you know about these investments?"

"What investments?"

"The $7 million of investments your husband says are in real estate opportunities."

Eleanor stroked the sleepy cat. "I'll only say this. Do not expect to return next week for a full accounting. If I were you, I would take whatever money remains and safeguard it. That may be all Agnes will ever see."

Mr. Rockwell's face blanched and his hands went cold. "What are you telling me, Mrs. Brown?"

"I had nothing to do with it. It can't be helped now. I'm sorry." She raised her chin and the muscles in her neck tensed.

The carriage door swung open. Mr. Rockwell had not even noticed that they had stopped. Mechanically he looked out and saw that they were at the station. Understanding that their conversation was over, he descended to the street, shuffled into the great train station, and found Western Union. He sent a telegraph to his office to freeze what remained of Grandma's assets and request the current balances. "Urgent. Will explain upon immediate return."

The air in the station hung gray and stifling as outside a steady drizzle resumed. The old accountant realized that his clothes were sticking to his body and that he had not eaten for many hours. He bought a sausage and coffee, downed both without tasting them, and boarded the next train to New York.

How could he have let this happen? He had let down the family, he had let down Benjamin. He should have been more vigilant. He would press a lawsuit. If necessary, Wilbur could sell his mansion to recover the money due Agnes. There would be a solution, it would just take time. But what did Eleanor mean about there being no accounting? Was there no property purchased? If not, how had Wilbur spent $7 million in only a few months?

These and a hundred other questions swirled in the old man's head. But emerging above them all was a fear that gripped him more with each mile that separated him from Philadelphia: What if Wilbur disappeared? Would he dare? Mr. Rockwell had heard enough that afternoon to know that the man was capable of anything to save his skin and not face whatever it was he had done. He felt it in his bones.

And what in the world was he going to tell Agnes?

# Chapter 34

Agnes was a new woman. All the staff at Brookside agreed. While still the vigilant mistress of the manor, she displayed a healthy distraction. Something larger inhabited her now, and the affairs of the estate were details that she faithfully tended rather than the axis on which her world turned.

She and Phillip saw each other several times a week. He would stop in on his way to one place or another and often drop in again on the way home to deposit an offering. One day it was a bouquet of small white roses; another time, smoked clams that he insisted they sit down and eat immediately. Two days later, silk handkerchiefs for both Agnes and Stella, each embroidered with a small cross in gold thread. He became a regular guest at dinner, and the evenings he did not come took on a length and dullness that drove Agnes to put an ear to the clocks to make sure they were still running.

The lovers did not allow themselves again the intimacy of that night on the marble bench. This did not mean that their feelings for one another were cooling, but rather the opposite. The growing intensity of their relationship convinced both of them that to be alone, in each other's arms, might provoke a temptation too strong to resist. So they restricted themselves to open places and quick embraces. On Fridays they made a habit of going into town together for lunch and then ambling along the main street to window-shop. Everything on display had become interesting, from boot-blacking supplies to children's bonnets.

Of course, the two became Chesterton's favorite topic of speculation. Most of the local dowagers had decided that Agnes was consigned to spinsterhood at her advanced age of thirty-some years and were confused by Lord Phillip's lack of interest in Chesterton's brilliant young crop of eligible ladies. Some accused him privately of pursuing her for the Somerset fortune, soon to be hers in the wake of her grandmother's death. Others worried, not without relish, that he was a confirmed bachelor who was toying with the mistress of Brookside, and that Agnes would add another sorrow to her life story when he scampered off to his next adventure. And some subscribed to the foggy but salacious rumor of his ill conduct while abroad posing as a missionary and shook their heads at a woman of Agnes's standing taking up with such a character.

Then there were those few who actually rejoiced to see two people happy together and so natural in every affection. These admirers noticed how Phillip held open the carriage door whenever Agnes climbed in and then tucked her skirt carefully around her feet. They saw how she studied his face while he talked, how he listened gravely to all she said. Those who noticed these things nodded to themselves saying "That is a match for sure," and their hearts swelled to see the marvel of true love. These were people happy enough in their own lives to want happiness for others. Such people, sadly, have always been in short supply and are barely sufficient to lighten the world's dark load of envy.

So August came, and the weekend Agnes had promised to visit Vera in New York City. She hated to leave Phillip because one day without seeing him felt like a fortnight. Still she had promised, and she was bursting to tell Vera about her bliss. And Vera had pledged to take Agnes to Central Park, where all of New York came together to play and promenade. Agnes usually visited her aunt during the theater season—just last winter they had seen Mozart's *The Marriage of Figaro*, bringing more whispered assurances from Vera that marriage was not for her. So it had been many years since Agnes had seen the grand park in its summer glory.

Her first morning in the city was a Sunday. It dawned bright and blue, so after church the ladies lost no time in breakfasting and boarding a cab for the park. Vera had a hundred questions for her niece that she had not had the patience to write out in letters.

Agnes and Vera stepped off the cab and into the bustle of Central Park. They paused to take in the scene. Men in summer suits walked arm-in-arm with their young ladies in pale, ruffled dresses, tilting parasols against the late-morning sun. Mothers and nannies pushed baby carriages while scolding older children to watch where they were going and stop throwing stones. Older men filled the benches, some with their faces hidden in the day's paper while others smiled at the energy of little boys running by. A large clan of Germans was setting up for a picnic under a spreading oak. Two of their men sat plying red-and-white accordions in their laps, serenading the group with native tunes.

"What a wonderful place!" declared Agnes. "In winter it's impossible to picture this. If I were you, I think I would be here every day."

"No you would not," replied her aunt. "Everyone thinks that, but you get busy no matter what. Pastoral walks or tea with friends get pushed to the back until visitors come to town to drag us to the things we should have been doing all along."

Agnes looked around her more closely. "There seem to be more people—different kinds of people—than I remember."

Vera smiled. "Oh yes, we have gotten more democratic in the use of our park these days. Those Germans over there? Such a large group was not allowed before. The working class has even gotten the park commission to move the summer concerts from Saturday to Sunday since it's their only day off."

"That sounds sensible," observed Agnes.

"Yes, I'm sure it is, but still . . . it changes the flavor. I haven't been to one in years now."

As they walked on, Vera put her questions to Agnes, who answered them as fully as possible, not scrimping on peripheral details that she felt might perfect her aunt's understanding of the situation with Phillip. They stopped at the top of a broad set of steps that led down to a grand fountain, where sheets of water fell into a sparkling round pool.

"So what do you think?" Agnes asked at last.

Vera looked keenly at Agnes and folded her hands. "I think this is the happiest summer of your life. You are in the middle of an exquisite memory, my dear, that you will look back on with great fondness, whatever might happen."

Agnes paled. "It sounds like you do not see a future for us."

Vera looked at her earnestly. "Have you thought that many of the qualities that make your Lord Phillip so exciting, so novel, so lovable, are precisely those that might make him a poor choice for a husband?"

"Such as?"

"He is available to spend lots of time with you because he is not employed. And you know the Duke has made no secret of wanting Phillip to make his way in the world rather than living off the family's money. Also, he is unpredictable. His manners are refreshingly unorthodox, which may keep you two from receiving the better invitations, or any at all. He has all kinds of fascinating experiences to talk about because he has specialized in nothing. And, you have no way of knowing the truth of his adventures in India. This, too—the rumors that follow him on this account—may lead respectable people to keep you at arm's length. Have you considered all this?"

"A hundred times over."

"And you are undaunted?"

Agnes looked intently at her aunt. "If I had to live in a lonely cottage with Phillip and eat turnips at every meal, I see it as far, far better than marrying a dull pillar of society and becoming the first couple on everyone's list. But remember," she cautioned, straightening again, "he has made no proposal or given any indication that he means to marry one day. I must admit," she added, "I thought you would be happier for me."

"I'm sorry, Agnes. I've spoken as though you did not know the snares of this world. I feel I still have to warn you about the ugly things that lurk inside pretty pink seashells. I am thrilled to see you so happy. I adore Lord Phillip and, if I were only twenty years younger, I would be head over heels for him if he paid me the slightest attention. I know I seem to be turning into an old prune, but it was my duty to point these things out."

Agnes smiled and put an arm around her aunt's small shoulders. "Nonsense! I understand that you are looking out for me. You know I depend on you to be honest with me, Vera. You have done your duty!" Agnes adjusted her hat against the sun. "And now tell me your news. How is our beloved Mr. Schmidt?"

They descended the stairs and took advantage of the first empty bench they came to. Vera confessed that Mr. Schmidt was as loyal and stainless as ever. He was in Richmond at present, tending to his father who was near death. Frederick was trying to sort out the old man's tangled finances before he breathed his last. His mother had died years ago and there were no other children, so everything, for good or ill, was falling upon Frederick.

"But that man never complains," observed Vera. "He is stoic in all situations. I am up and down like a jack-in-the-box, but he is steady as a barge. I really don't know what I would do without him anymore. He has become my anchor." Vera had removed her hat to feel the breeze blowing their way. The midday sun shone brightly on her face as she watched a team of bicyclists circling the fountain. Agnes noticed in the bright light the fine lines around her aunt's eyes and mouth, and reflected how they did not in any way detract from her beauty.

"That's why," Vera continued, "I have agreed to marry my dear Frederick come Christmas."

Agnes gasped and half rose from her seat. "We could have a double wedding!" She clapped a hand over her mouth, realizing the rashness of her comment and how it had betrayed what churned in her heart. But Vera simply admitted that they just might, so the two ladies spent the rest of the day in the most excellent spirits possible, taking a short tour of the zoo and even riding the park's wildly painted carousel three times. They planned Vera's winter wedding down to the menu and the bride's bouquet and indulged in a bottle of champagne over dinner to celebrate the rosiness of their twin horizons.

# Chapter 35

Mrs. Thorne waited several weeks for Phillip to return to Beaujour, but in vain. So, true to her promise, she issued invitations for a summer ball to every local luminary not traveling abroad in August or hiding in their Adirondack retreats.

Word had reached her that Lord Phillip was spending his leisure time at Brookside. She had seen him and Agnes in town, taking tea and walking close. They gave every appearance of a carefree couple in the early throws of romance. Agnes always thought herself so far above, Claudia reflected, even in school. Miss Virtue herself of the lofty Somerset clan, reigning supreme over the legendary Brookside. Now she thinks she'll get the grand prize after all, the son of British aristocracy. Claudia's heart beat faster and her breath grew shallow as she thought about it.

She had not forgotten how that woman had stolen M. from her. The years had not dimmed her rage. He could have been hers, should have been hers, and she could have held him. But Agnes had to get in the middle of everything and pull him away—then she couldn't even make him stay. But by then Claudia had accepted Sherman's proposal (more from spite than love), and by the time M. lost interest in the golden girl, Claudia had a ring on her finger. She had, plain and simply, been robbed.

However, not all the news reaching Claudia these days about Agnes was good. Miss Somerset's great catch had a shadow over him. Claudia had heard from more than one source that he had been embroiled in a sordid affair with a mere girl, an Indian beauty. He had apparently left India with her and then hidden her away. It was not hard to guess why he would have needed to do that, and a few well-placed inquires had told her just what she had hoped for. Agnes probably knew nothing about the whole thing, or if she did, had dismissed it. The ball would be the perfect setting for pressing home the real story of why her beau left his sacred work among the Hindus.

It had taken Claudia no time at all to think up a theme for the evening: The Secrets of India. She had ordered yards and yards of brilliant cotton and silk to drape the doorways. She brought in tropical plants of every description and even a life-size papier-mâché elephant with onyx eyes for the ballroom. For herself she had commissioned a lavish sari with a low, tight bodice and a length of deep emerald silk to wrap around her exquisite body. A saffron veil and exotic makeup would complete the effect.

Claudia had issued invitations to absolutely everyone in Dutchess County who mattered at all. Most had already returned their acceptances. The wealthy, the political, the powerful would be well represented at her little *coup de foudre*, ensuring that a blanket of gossip would start spreading over the surrounding counties as soon as her guests returned home. She could not help congratulating herself on her truly astonishing ingenuity and unrivaled capacity for deception.

* * *

Agnes had only been back from New York City a few hours when the invitation arrived, hand-delivered by Claudia's man. Fettles decided not to interrupt his mistress but left it on the foyer table for her to find. Agnes was upstairs with Stella and Marie, unpacking her trunk, putting away the lovely summer dress Vera had insisted on buying her. Stella urged her aunt to tell every detail of the visit, and Agnes obliged, keeping just a few reflections to herself. (She remembered hugging Vera goodbye, looking into the shining eyes of the engaged woman, and shouting inwardly, "Yes! This is what I want.")

It was well toward evening when Agnes noticed Claudia's invitation lying on the table. She read it with mixed emotion. On the one hand, she dreaded any contact with the invidious Mrs. Thorne. On the other, she was thrilled at the prospect of showing off Lord Phillip and waltzing the night away in his arms. The ball's theme troubled her—surely the woman was up to something, or maybe she was simply trying to impress Phillip and his father with her zeal for the exotic. Agnes conferred with Phillip at dinner, and he told her that sheer, mad curiosity prevented him from even considering not attending. Agnes rebelled at the idea of his appearing unescorted, so her decision was mostly made.

Still, Agnes knew she should consult her butler on this matter, a man of such perspicacity and up-to-the-minute knowledge of all the area households that he was indispensable in such dilemmas. Agnes found him the next morning seated at the great table in the library, cataloguing a pile of unusually tall, dark blue books that had just arrived from her New York agent.

"What have we here? Oh," she cried, coming closer, "the Audubons! Aren't they huge? And look at the illustrations." She had opened one volume to a full-page rendering of a long-legged bird with delicate white feathers, posing aristocratically. "The Snowy Egret," she read. "Are there still any of those left?"

"A few," responded Fettles. "Protected now, I understand."

"I wonder how he drew them with such detail. I'm sure they did not stand still for long."

Fettles looked at his mistress and blinked. This was always his way of saying "I know something I could say, but it might embarrass you."

"Well? Did you want to say something?"

"Madam, he shot the birds. Then he inserted wires to create a lifelike pose."

"These are all pictures of dead birds?"

"That is my understanding."

Agnes closed the magnificent book. "Somehow they lose something, don't you think?"

"I can't imagine any other way Mr. Audubon could have drawn his pictures. And taking one to preserve its likeness for generations to come is surely nothing compared to all those sacrificed for hat feathers."

"Well, still . . . Fettles, I need your advice."

The butler replaced his pen in its well and folded his hands on the gleaming table. Agnes explained the difficulty in her attending Claudia's ball, an event about which Fettles already knew a measure more than she did. He advised her unequivocally that she had made the right decision—she simply had to attend or speculation would run wild about the reason for her absence, and this was an opportunity to make a public statement about her connection to Lord Phillip.

"I say this," cautioned Fettles, "knowing how cunning Mrs. Thorne is. You must be on your guard in all you say. Remember that her servants are often put up to spying for her and will recount to their mistress anything they hear. She's a bully and a serpent all in one,

Agnes"—in his concern he slipped into using her given name. "The only way I've found to handle a bully is to adopt a guarded position of attack yourself. Retreat never works. As for the serpent, well, that is harder to defend against."

Agnes sat against the table and gathered her skirt fabric into her hands. "I'm sure you are right. I do feel like I am walking into a trap."

"Possibly. But you are up to it, I dare say. And you will have Lord Phillip as reinforcement and shield."

Agnes smiled vaguely and thanked her butler. She went away with a troubled spirit to tackle the easier challenge of a ball gown for the beautifully expanding Stella.

# Chapter 36

In the whole history of that strange phenomenon known as fancy dress balls, no one has enjoyed the sport more than young Stella Moll. So it never entered her mind to decline Claudia's invitation just because she was in a family way, even if it did raise some eyebrows. A gifted seamstress as well as an artist, Stella had made several of her own costumes from the age of thirteen, including a pirate queen, a Russian gypsy, and a wood nymph. She had advised her aunt that their costumes for Mrs. Thorne's ball should be lightweight, given the season, and colorful. She felt confident that she could gracefully drape her own widening figure, given enough chiffon, as well as devise something suitable for her aunt.

Agnes's enthusiasm did not go as far as her niece's. She had accepted Claudia's invitation but did not feel like extending herself to procure an elaborate gown or run the risk of appearing foolish in an attempt to fulfill the night's theme. Even Stella's pouting could not sway Agnes from her position.

"So what *are* you planning?" asked Stella, rising from her seat at the easel and bracing her lower back. She had been painting a spectacular arrangement of rhododendron as it stood on the old piano, washed by the morning sun. The supply of art paper she had brought along was nearly exhausted since all around her she found subjects begging to be painted—a corner of the garden after a good rain, the terrace at sunset, the splashing fountain surrounded by velvet roses.

"My dark blue gown from the big dinner should do quite nicely," replied her aunt, randomly pushing down some ivory keys. "I haven't worn it in public before."

"But it's a costume ball—you'll need to do something to it, you know."

"Who says I must play along with Claudia's 'Secrets of India'?"

"If you don't make any effort you might be seen as a humbug," cautioned her niece.

"Nothing to fear, that word has already gone out."

"Really, Aunt Agnes, won't you let me create something for you?"

"Stella, you will have your hands full creating your own gown."

By the end of the conversation, Agnes had agreed to let Stella sew a moon and stars from silvery damask and attach them to her dark gown, allowing her to be technically in costume using the tried-and-true allegory of Night. "After all," observed Stella, "India has her nights, and night is everywhere the perfect place for secrets to be born."

That evening the ladies revealed their costume plans to Lord Phillip and his father over dinner. Agnes observed that gentlemen had the easy end of dress balls, being obliged to appear in nothing more imaginative than their regular good clothes and a small mask. Stella felt that the gentlemen should make some effort at decoration so as to be in keeping with their female partners. (With Phillip pledged as Agnes's partner, the Duke had offered to accompany Stella. Although he told his son that it was simply right that he spare the lady from attending unescorted, he had become increasingly absorbed in preparations for the evening, sending out for a tailor and consulting illustrations in historical journals.)

"Who says that I am not honoring the spirit of the evening?" asked Phillip. "I shall appear in a black silk domino from head to foot—I found an exceptionally nice one in father's trunk yesterday. And I've picked up a dark blue mask to complete the mystery."

Stella stared, then glanced at Agnes. "A domino? I don't think I've seen one of those since I was a little girl."

"Yes, they were all the rage forty years ago," said the Duke. "I wore that cape as a young man to the first ball I attended with Phillip's mother. Never could bring myself to throw it away. And here it comes, pressed into service again. Capital idea!" he cried, waving his dinner roll at them.

Stella tried again. "But as this is fancy dress, do you think that the plainness of a domino—" She was cut short by a look from Agnes, which sent her stumbling in a new direction. "I'm sure, Lord Phillip, that you will be striking, and a wonderful complement to Agnes's starry Night."

As dinner concluded, the Duke urged Stella to show him her recent paintings, and the two graciously left Phillip and Agnes alone in the dining room. The two sweethearts walked out onto the terrace and stood on the far edge looking at the night sky, each with an arm around the other. Agnes confessed that she was increasingly nervous about the ball. Phillip squeezed her tighter and murmured that he would be there to protect her, and this filled her with a calm and a gratitude that she could not remember feeling. To have a man protecting you—what a delicious position for a woman to be in. And she knew Phillip said it without condescension but only from devotion. She gave in to the sweet feeling and looked up into his eyes, so soft yet so sharply awake. Closing her eyes, she let him kiss her long and tenderly on the lips.

Phillip pulled back at last and gazed at her, running one finger around her moonlit face. "Agnes Eileen Somerset."

"Yes, Phillip George Aspen."

"May I call on you tomorrow morning?"

"Whatever for?" she asked limply, still holding his gaze.

"I have a question you may have the answer to."

"Well, why don't you ask me now?"

"I cannot. I am not . . . completely prepared." His lips brushed her ear.

"I wish you would try." Their voices were no more than whispers. "Otherwise how will I sleep, wondering all night through what your question could be?"

Phillip drank in a long draught of the rich evening air. "Come along." He pulled her behind him and the two broke into a run toward the dark garden. They did not stop until he had led them clear to the other end and around the hedge, to the special bench between the lovelorn gods. They sat down facing each other and he took both her hands in his.

Agnes studied Phillip's face while her heart beat like the hammer of a blacksmith in her chest. She felt lightheaded and struggled to catch her breath. Phillip was perched on the edge of the seat like one ready to spring up at any moment. She waited for him to speak. With an impatient sigh he let go of her hands, rose, and began walking back and forth in front of her.

"Agnes, I have had many false starts in life. You know that. I have hidden nothing from you. I stand to inherit my father's estate, but God willing, that is a long way off. We have bought land a few miles north—I told you about it, to farm, and I intend to make a comfortable profit from that, although surely nothing extravagant. I cannot pretend that I deserve you in any way, either by virtue of fortune or character. But I love you like nothing I have ever imagined." He sat back down and ran his hands down both sides of her neck and shoulders, then took her hands again and studied them. "I can barely breathe when I am near you." He raised his eyes to hers. "I admire you more than I can tell you. Of course, if your father were alive, I would be asking him, but as things are, I come to you directly. My father and I have discussed it, and he has the very highest regard for you, so he is completely behind us."

Phillip paused and watched the face of his beloved. "I don't need your answer now, but I beg you to consider my offer."

Agnes reached up and smoothed his forehead. "But my dear Phillip, what is the offer?"

"What is it? I thought I said."

Agnes shook her head.

"Good Lord. My dear Agnes, here it is: I want to be your husband. I want you to be my wife. We have not known each other long, I admit that, only a few weeks, really, but it seems I have known you for years. And time is not standing still for us, is it? Every day away from you seems wasted." He got to his feet and spoke to the fields below them. "I want to wake every morning and see you even before the sunlight. I want to hold your hands and look at you any time for as long as I like. . . and hear your voice before I close my eyes at night . . . I want to ask your advice and eat with you and make your bath and, if God blesses us, give you children—you would be a wonderful mother," he added warmly, taking his seat once more. "Agnes, my question is, will you be my bride and live with me every day for as long as we are on this earth? Would you?"

Agnes's tears shone in twin lines down her cheeks. She put her arms around Phillip's neck and gathered him to her. For several minutes she could not find the breath to speak, but let herself cry quietly against him. He encircled her with his arms and rested his face against her hair. At last she straightened and began to dry her eyes on her sleeve. Phillip searched his pockets for a handkerchief but, finding none, braced himself and waited.

Agnes sighed and sniffled. "You must understand," she said, pinching the pleats of her skirt, "that you don't really know me. I am given to spells of gloom that turn me quite ugly at least once a month. I haven't as much money as you may think. And my time for having children draws short, I'm afraid. You need to understand this." She raised her eyes to his.

Phillip leaned back as a perplexed smile lit his face. "Are you trying to talk me out of it? That job is usually left to well-meaning friends."

Agnes uttered a short, gasping laugh. "No, I am not trying to talk you out of it. I don't know what I should do if you changed your mind. But are you sure, Phillip?"

Phillip took her face in his hands and drew closer, then closer, and pressed his mouth to hers in a way that left no fragment of doubt. When he released her, she put her lips to his ear and whispered over and over the word he had prayed to hear: yes, I will marry you—yes, yes, yes.

# Chapter 37

Of course, no one must know. One summer was a scandalously short time to be acquainted before a betrothal. Agnes and Phillip agreed to keep their promise a secret until spring. They would attend the ball as interested friends—even romantically inclined friends—but with nothing more than the usual affection they displayed in public. But the excitement was almost more than Agnes could bear, and she imagined that everyone would see the beautiful words *bride to be* written across her shining features. She must not even tell Stella or Vera, which would be hard indeed.

Ten dizzying days passed, and the date of the ball arrived. The weather fit Claudia's theme perfectly. They might well be in Hyderabad, with the mercury at eighty-nine degrees and a stifling humidity dampening everything. Throughout the afternoon most of Brookside's rooms stood deserted as staff, having dispatched their most necessary duties, were allowed to sit languidly under shade trees or play cards in the cool of the cellar. Dahlia served a simple dinner of cold meats, boiled eggs, and potato salad, which Agnes, Stella, Phillip, and the Duke ate on the terrace.

"Terrible luck," observed the Duke, "to have this miserable heat the night of the festivities. One hardly feels like putting on a costume or dancing."

"We may be relieved by rain," said his son, observing the sky. "Those clouds to the north look like they shall do something before the night is out. I smell a storm coming."

Stella shifted in her chair. "The only thing worse than a warm costume is a wet costume."

"We shall not let that happen to you, my lady," the Duke assured her, brandishing a forkful of potato. "Phillip and I will shelter both you ladies under umbrellas, one in each hand, if needed."

As the red sun sank, the foursome pushed back their chairs and went in to put on their costumes. Marie helped Agnes into her magnificent starry gown, dusting her mistress generously with powder before closing her into it. Mrs. Williams tucked Stella into the dark orange dress the young artist had fashioned from yards of misty chiffon, which molded lightly around her young bosom and fell in airy folds to her slippers. With a short veil and satin vest, she was transformed into an Afghan princess ready to invade her neighbor to the south. She was the perfect accompaniment to the Duke, who had agreed to become the legendary Lion of Punjab, complete with a curving tin sword hanging at his side. Phillip wrapped his father's head in a black turban below which his gray side whiskers bristled impressively. For his own part, Phillip combed his hair and grabbed his domino and mask; he was ready for the ball.

The Duke's carriage stood waiting for them as they emerged into the tropical dusk. The trees etched their dark outline against the violet and orange sky, and the insects of the night began to intone their habitual warnings. With minor difficulties the party hoisted themselves into the conveyance, being careful with the ladies' generous skirts and making allowances for the Duke's sword. Despite her misgivings, Agnes felt a delicious thrill as she rode through the warm night, seated across from the most fascinating man in the world, a man who loved her, a man who made her heart stop as she looked at him, and she could not help squeezing Stella's hand.

"My dear," she said, looking at her niece with a smile, "this ball will put you well past your usual bedtime. I'm afraid you'll tire yourself terribly."

"Then simply lay me on a divan until you are all ready to leave," returned Stella. "I will not be the cause of anyone's going home early!"

The Duke patted Stella's knee. "This princess will surely tire no sooner than I. These two," he waved a finger toward the fiancés, "can gambol about all night, I'll wager, dancing until dawn. You and I can take the carriage home when we're spent and send it back for them. Though I don't envy the driver his wait."

In no time it seemed they had covered the three miles between the two homes and turned up the drive to Beaujour. Red lanterns lit their way to the house that sat throbbing with irresistible danger, ablaze against the black sky. Carriages choked the driveway as they discharged their passengers. The guests stepped out gingerly in glittering costumes, calling to acquaintances, laughing, shaking hands, and kissing powdered cheeks. Music drifted down from the third floor ballroom, and Agnes felt her heart quicken as she imagined dancing with her escort. Then her breath stopped. In the wide-open doorway, silhouetted against the yellow glare, stood what had to be Claudia. Her outline alone could rob a man of his senses. She advanced to meet Agnes's party as they came up the broad steps, and Agnes could see the shocking beauty of her silk costume and boldly made-up face. Phillip squeezed Agnes's hand in either sympathy or fear, she could not guess which, as their hostess broke into a luxurious smile.

"Oh, don't you look festive," exclaimed Mrs. Thorne, taking them all in with her gaze. "A domino, Lord Phillip," she went on, looking at him slyly. "How charmingly sentimental. And this lovely young lady must be the niece." She looked so intensely at Stella that the poor thing blushed a deep pink.

"Claudia, this is my niece Stella Moll from Chicago," Agnes explained. "She is the wife of William Moll."

"Moll of the stockyard fame?" asked Claudia, widening her black-lined eyes and extending a limp hand.

"Yes," Stella spoke up with a challenge in her voice and gave the extended hand a brief but certain shake. "I am flattered that you know of my family and very grateful that you included me in your invitation. It's so nice to meet the woman I have heard so much about."

"Indeed," returned Claudia, with a short, lifeless shake of Stella's hand. "Well, I like to keep up with who's who. You and the Duke make quite a pair tonight. This is the most darling dress! My dear Duke, you look devastating in that turban. And you are …?

"The Lion of Punjab, Madam," declared the Duke, drawing his sword to everyone's alarm. Claudia darted an inquiring glance at the others.

"Maharajah, Madam," the Duke explained, "and conqueror, ruler of the independent state of Punjab. Accompanied by her highness, the Princess of Afghanistan, lately acquired."

"And Agnes is the Night Sky," put in Stella, unasked.

"Of course," said Claudia, taking Phillip's free arm and leading them the rest of the way up the steps. "She can join the other Night Skies already inside."

It was true. Before they reached the third floor and Claudia drifted away, they crossed a pale young woman in a black dress wearing a halo of silver stars as well as a stout woman in deep violet

163

whose tiara supported a teetering crescent moon. The Duke took a moment to observe in a low tone to both Stella and Agnes that neither of the other Nights could compare to Agnes's magnificent gown with its application of celestial bodies. He also assured them that the decision to forego a headdress had clearly been a sound one.

Stella whispered back that she did not much like Mrs. Thorne or her comments on their costumes and understood now her aunt's warnings. But Stella was at that moment startled out of any further observations.

# Chapter 38

A small, dark man stepped in front of the foursome, extending the head of a massive snake as though for approval. The serpent lay motionless across the man's bare shoulders and hung almost to the floor. Without opening its jaws, it shot out a crimson tongue. Both ladies recoiled, clutching their escorts, and the little man smiled. Lord Phillip said something in Hindi, which caused the man to lose his smile and wander away toward another group of new arrivals.

"How hideous! What did you say to him?" asked Stella.

"I told him that the serpent will be crushed beneath the heel."

"Good show," put in the Duke, adjusting his turban. "I didn't think she was going to bring in a bunch of natives with their menageries. Questionable taste, I feel, especially with the ladies present."

"You will find," explained Agnes, "that Claudia likes to shock more than anything. Good taste is a halter she has never worn."

The group pondered these words as they took in the ballroom. Phillip hardly recognized the space he had been shown just a few weeks before. Tonight, the three chandeliers dripping with prisms blazed above their heads. Every statue in its niche wore a rich silk wrap and was hung with garish flowers. The papier-mâché elephant towered over guests at the far end of the room, and tall potted plants created tropical islands where caged birds hung, brilliant specimens unknown in North America.

The two couples separated to make their rounds of the guests and greet acquaintances. Phillip lost no time pushing his cape behind his shoulders and pulling his mask down to hang at his collar. Agnes looked him up and down, shivered inside, and said simply, "I am so happy to be with you." Phillip walked her forward murmuring at her ear "You honor me, madam."

Agnes was glad they had come. What could Claudia do to her in front of so many people? Why, they had greeted the governor and his wife on their way in and had already talked with several members of the state legislature and kingpins of local industry. Surely this was a night for Claudia to show off, nothing more. The small orchestra struck up a new Tchaikovsky waltz, and Phillip and Agnes lightly took hold of each other and stepped into the dance. They moved as one, barely touching the polished floor, unconscious of the couples twirling around them. They emerged from their reverie only once, when Phillip's father collided with them as he led the patient Stella through this dance he had never quite mastered.

From time to time from the corner of her eye, Agnes thought she caught Claudia watching her. But before she could direct a look toward the mysterious woman, the hostess had moved her attention elsewhere, now laughing gaily, now slipping from sight, now showing her gleaming bangles to admirers.

The evening flew by, and midnight approached. Stella and the Duke prepared to leave, having pushed their fatigue aside for as long as possible. It was agreed that they would depart after the Indian tumblers performed on the front lawn, scheduled for the stroke of twelve. Claudia threaded her way through the guests, reminding them to congregate on the front terraces to watch the performance. By five minutes to the hour, the ballroom was empty. Ladies took up their positions outside at the marble railings with their gentlemen behind, the smaller men shifting between the great hairdos and hats as best they could. Agnes, Phillip, Stella, and the Duke maneuvered their way to the top of the stairs that led down in a graceful curve to the drive, gaining a good view of the improvised stage beyond. To the north, lightening flashed high and silent but brought no rain, and the day's heat continued to hang over the costumed crowd.

Out on the lawn, just outside a ring of torches, seven lithe men stretched their limbs and hopped about in preparation for the feats they were on the verge of demonstrating. Others sat in a small huddle with instruments in their laps. They all wore loose pants, gathered above the ankle, and bright-colored vests with no shirts. Their hair hid itself under tightly wrapped green turbans.

"She certainly went to great lengths, didn't she?" remarked the Duke. "Where do you imagine she found these chaps?"

"I overheard that she ordered them from the City," put in Stella. "You can get anything in Manhattan, I understand."

"Claudia has lots of connections, some rather unconventional," added Agnes. "Clearly money was no object tonight."

All talk quieted as Claudia emerged into the ring of firelight, faced her guests, and raised her arms. Her sari glistened in the light of the torches, and no one looking on could be insensible to her outrageous beauty. Every line of her face, every gesture, reflected her certain knowledge of this fact.

"Mesdames et Messieurs," she called out. "A thousand thanks for joining us tonight for a journey through the Secrets of India. I hope you have enjoyed our special performers tonight."

At this point she waved her arm once and the snake-bearer emerged from the shadows and paraded before the crowd, holding out his reptilian companion to best advantage. A contortionist followed, who propelled himself in indescribable ways along the same route, inciting both fascination and revulsion. Behind him danced three ladies in exotic and revealing costumes, who throughout the evening had met with favor from all the gentlemen and with enmity from their wives. Last of all came the magician, who had stunned Agnes earlier with the implausible objects he could make appear and disappear from his hands and mouth. The guests applauded the procession enthusiastically, twittering with anticipation for the main attraction.

"Thank you," Claudia shouted. "Now, I hope you will enjoy the Troupe of Seven Wonders, here to entertain you from their home in Bombay, a group that has amazed audiences around the world. Gentlemen . . ." With a gesture toward the performers, Claudia glided out of the circle of light and two drums began an urgent beat. Into the brilliant glow ran the seven tumblers, who, as they moved, gave the appearance of weighing nothing. They ran around in a sort of dance, weaving this way and that, jumping over one another or using each other as human springboards into impossibly high somersaults. An Asian flute started up, then a mournful sitar.

The Seven Wonders formed a line and, as one, sprang into a back flip, then a front flip, then became a tumbling chaos of color like a fast-turning kaleidoscope in the wildly dancing light.

So rapt was the crowd that no one noticed a carriage trundling up the drive until it pulled in front of the house, halting between the audience on the terraces and the performers whirling on the lawn. The Seven Wonders gradually came to a stop, unsure whether to continue, and looked to their client for direction, but she had vanished. They stood breathing heavily and looking at one another while the music sputtered out. The guests murmured in puzzlement.

In truth, the main attraction had just now arrived.

# Chapter 39

The carriage door was thrown open from within, revealing a man's arm, berry brown below the edge of his sleeve. Then the arm's owner appeared, wild-eyed, crouching in the opening. The man jumped to the ground and straightened, showing himself to be of middle age, stout but erect, with a confusion of gray hair about his head. He wore a rumpled tunic, loose pants, and sandals. As he stood there, his eyes scanned the gathering intently. A thin female stepped down carefully behind him and lifted out a small child about six months old. In her dingy sari, she cringed against the carriage, holding the child close. The three travelers stood on the drive of Beaujour, facing the crowd, as though transported magically between worlds.

In the great arch of the mansion's front door, tucked between the two raised terraces, Claudia stood with her butler. An honest man not long in her employ, he had seen enough things in the last few weeks to make him already regret accepting the position. Now seeing the bizarre disruption going on in the driveway, he started forward to demand an explanation from the interlopers. But Mrs. Thorne put a firm hand on his arm and held him back.

Meanwhile, at the top of the steps, one man's heart had frozen as the disheveled man emerged from the carriage. Agnes felt Phillip clutch her shoulder and pull her against himself with a sharp intake of breath.

"What is it?" whispered Agnes, looking up into his stricken face. Her slight movement attracted the traveler's attention, who cried out from below, "There he is!" Then pointing in fury toward Phillip, the man nearly screamed, "Come here and tell me where my daughter is!"

Stunned silence gripped the assemblage. The Seven Wonders and their musicians drifted around the carriage, keeping their distance, to see what was happening. All eyes turned upon Phillip and Agnes. She held his hand and searched his face, but he pulled away. Slowly, maneuvering through the crowd, he descended the stairs.

"Where are you going?" demanded the Duke, but Phillip ignored him. He stared fixedly at the wild man as the onlookers pulled back to let him pass, too intrigued to even whisper. He walked toward the man, and the only sound was the crunch of gravel beneath his measured steps. He stopped within a few feet of the visitor.

"Where is my daughter?" demanded the man. "Give her to me. I found you at last, you see? For a year I am looking for you—now I found you."

Phillip spoke in a low, even voice carried by the warm night breeze. "I cannot help you, Dhanesh. I left Rupa with the nuns."

"The nuns! We went to Rheims. This is all that was left from my daughter at Rheims." Rupa's father grabbed the arm of the attendant and pulled her and the boy close. "Look at him. She left him behind. I know she came here to be with you, you scoundrel. Where is she? Where do you hide her?" Dhanesh's face was by now only inches from Phillip's. Phillip stood planted like a stake.

"She is not here. I left her at Rheims and have not seen her since, I swear to you. When did she leave the convent?"

"Half a year ago."

"And she told no one where she was going?"

"Here, she came here!"

"Did the nuns tell you that?"

"They don't have to tell me. I know."

"Nonsense! She is not here. But even if I knew where she was, I would not tell you."

Dhanesh grabbed fistfuls of Phillip's shirtfront and stared madly into his eyes. At this the Duke, who had until now stayed with the ladies and strained to hear the dialog below, put a hand on his sword hilt and pushed his way down the stairs. Dhanesh saw him coming, a middle-aged maharajah with a tin sword banging against one leg, and for a moment the puzzled Indian froze. The duke halted beside his son and glowered at the stranger, whose face had gone from rage to wonder. Suddenly aware of his costume, the Duke snatched the turban from his head and tucked it under his arm.

"Who are you?" he demanded. "What's the meaning of this?"

Dhanesh looked from the father to the son, still holding Phillip fast. "Father," said Phillip, "this is Dhanesh, the man I stayed with in India before returning home. He thinks I have abducted his daughter."

"Abducted his daughter? Rubbish! What would we want with his daughter?"

Somehow, from beyond his fury, an understanding began to creep over Dhanesh that his daughter might not be here. No, she would not be good enough for these men to keep—only to use up and leave behind. He had traveled thousands of miles over land and water and come to a dead end in this strange place, on this night, even with the hunted man now in his grasp. He stared up at the glistening faces, the gaudy costumes, the glowing house, all wrapped in stunned silence. Tears began to fill his dark eyes and spill down his cheeks.

The Duke shifted his weight. Whoever this man was, he had lost his daughter. Embarrassed and pained for him, he slipped a hand inside his jacket and produced a handkerchief. Dhanesh looked stupidly at the neatly folded square of white linen, then turned his gaze on Phillip. He spoke haltingly as he slowly loosened his grip and dropped his arms. "At first, I thought I must kill this bastard child. But he is my blood. What can I do?" He looked to the Duke as though for an answer, then back to the young man. "You have ruined my family. You have disgraced us." The words came out more pleadingly than angry.

"You ruined your family," Phillip replied sternly. "You allowed your wife and sons to abuse that girl mercilessly. Then, Dhanesh, then you used her to connect yourself with a royal family—even if she had to marry the devil to do it."

"You have dishonored us!" Dhanesh cried with renewed fury.

"I did not! I swear by all that's holy, I never trespassed on your daughter's honor."

"She was almost married—only two weeks until the ceremony and you kidnapped her."

"I only tried to save her from the fate you had arranged. And it was she who came to me for help, Dhanesh. There was no kidnapping."

Confused, Dhanesh grabbed the wide-eyed baby and held him up to Phillip. "Look at this. This is yours. I see you in his eyes, his skin, his soul. I curse this child and I give him to you. I am finished!" The words rang out in a wail, and he pushed the child into Phillips' arms. "I will go home now, but I have no home. My house has fallen and my sons hang their heads in shame." Dhanesh looked around like a man surveying the field of battle, where his cause is lost and he is the last man, barely standing. He had come to the end of his mission, this quest that had driven him for over a year, and now, with nothing left to do and no road ahead, he could only turn back the way he had come.

Phillip patted the frightened child and extended him to the woman, who stepped forward to take him. But Dhanesh stopped her.

Phillip transferred the tiny boy to the crook of one arm, where the child grabbed the hanging mask and pulled it to his little mouth. Phillip put a hand on his accuser's shoulder. "I am sorry, Dhanesh." The spent man did not pull back. "You were good to me. I am sorry you have lost your daughter, I truly am. But my friend, you have only yourself to blame. This is not my child, though. You must believe me." He untied his mask with one hand, surrendering it to the baby, and gently held the boy out to his grandfather.

Dhanesh, strangely calm, looked past the baby and into Phillip's eyes. "What have I done for this to happen to me? How do I anger Vishnu to punish me this way?" Slowly he wiped his eyes with a sleeve and looked at the baby. "The nuns named him Henri. Call him what you want."

Dhanesh turned and climbed into the carriage. The attendant tugged his sleeve and indicated the child, but he waved his hand impatiently and pulled her inside. The coachman shut the door, exchanged a quick word with his passengers, and climbed up to his seat. Phillip, still holding the child, watched the driver slap the reins and direct the carriage back down the long drive, its shiny black sides glinting ominously between the rows of red lanterns. He looked down with wonder at the baby in his arms, who held the soggy mask in one hand while fingering Phillip's pearly buttons with the other.

In the grand doorway, Claudia let out a long, slow breath. Her ball had achieved perfection.

# Chapter 40

Phillip stood distractedly smoothing the child's silken hair, uncertain what to do next. Turning, he saw that Agnes and Stella had joined his father, and all three stood staring at him. Behind them the crowd began slowly to disperse. Some guests returned to the ballroom, some called immediately for their carriages. Agnes and her friends withdrew from the now busy drive to the edge of the circle of torches, where she examined the child, looking from his round face to Phillip's and back again. This was a mixed baby, clearly the product of one fair parent and one dark. His large eyes, rimmed in thick lashes, shone hazel, and his hair and tiny eyebrows were deep brown. His skin was the gentle color of tea with too much cream.

"He is not mine, Agnes." Phillip's voice was decisive, but she did not know what to say.

The Duke, with a face of stone, declared simply, "It's time to go home."

No one suggested they say goodnight to their hostess. They found their coach and rode to Brookside in silence except for the baby who, once tired of playing with Phillip's shirtfront, whimpered and squirmed in his lap. A thousand questions collided in Agnes's mind, but none found its way to her lips. As they pulled up to her home, she chose hurriedly to ask one.

"What do you plan to do with him? He'll have to be fed, you know."

"And he must be soaking by now," put in Stella.

"Mrs. Morgan will know what to do," replied the Duke gravely. His housekeeper, a no-nonsense Irish woman, had been with the family since their early days in England. And the Duke knew her well enough to know that she would not quietly accept a baby suddenly falling into her basket of responsibilities.

Agnes put a hand on Phillip's as the Duke helped her down. "Now we know the purpose for the ball, don't we?"

Phillip raised his eyes to hers. In that moment, the shipwreck that Mrs. Thorne had engineered became clear to him. Their promise to each other, their shining future, had been dashed against the rocks in a single, violent surge. Agnes stroked his cheek once with her gloved hand and said no more, disappearing inside the dark house with Stella.

Phillip and his father sat numb as the carriage rolled toward home. The crying child made the ride three times its normal length. Upon arriving, the Duke got Mrs. Morgan out of bed and gave her a short description of their situation. The head housekeeper grudgingly took the now sleeping child from Phillip and woke the youngest servant girl. She sent her to the old nursery to get it ready for a new occupant while she herself shuffled to the kitchen to find something to feed the child.

Phillip and his father faced each other. Phillip could hardly look at the deep disappointment in his father's face. "We will talk tomorrow," said the Duke. And the two repaired to their rooms to spend what remained of the terrible night.

* * *

After kissing Stella goodnight, Agnes stole through the garden to her secret bench and sat stricken, looking blindly out at the dark fields. Over and over she replayed the night's scenes: the costumes, the gay walzes, the snake, the Seven Wonders, a grinning Claudia. But mostly she watched again a desperate man jump out of a carriage and accuse her beloved of seducing his daughter, then handing him the baby that proved it.

One moment she and Stella were enjoying a splendid evening with two charming men and the next—scandal. And in front of dozens of society's very best, who would spread the word to dozens more before a day went by. No respectable woman would have anything to do with the Duke's family now. They were ruined socially, just like Dhanesh's family, unless Phillip could somehow undo this ugly knot. And what on earth were they to do with this baby? To keep it would mean Phillip fathered it. To abandon it to an orphanage would be despicable.

So here she was again, deceived. How could she have been so thoroughly wrong about Phillip? She thought she had gotten smarter since M. He said the child was not his, but everything pointed to him. What if it were his son and he had lied to everyone, including her— could she still love him? If she forgave him, could she brave the world's scorn and stay by his side? Even if he had told her the truth, who else would believe it? They would be alone in the world.

She thought of her mother. What would she say if she were here? Of course, Mother would never have considered Phillip a serious suitor for her daughter. She would have found him amusing and in some ways admirable, but never a candidate to join the Somerset family. Father probably would have understood more, but Phillip's doleful employment history would have eliminated him from any possibility with Father.

And so she sat for hours, clenching and unclenching her skirt, looking for answers in the starry sky, too stunned to even cry, which might have given some relief. The sky lightened, and the horizon turned pink, then pale blue. Agnes saw another day coming up whether she was ready or not. She forced herself to her feet and walked slowly back to the awakening house, where she lay down on her bed without undressing and fell asleep.

\* \* \*

Down the road at Beaujour, the day was also dawning. Most of Claudia's servants were sleeping later than usual, having been up into the wee hours assisting guests, extinguishing lamps, and storing away the remaining food. Their mistress slept far into the morning, enjoying that deep, dreamless rest of one who has accomplished a long-sought goal. She had gone to bed with a smile on her magnificent lips shortly after the last guest left, after agreeing with everyone that it was a terrible shock how the Indian had disrupted her ball and so very strange that he had caught up with Lord Phillip tonight of all nights, and how damaging this must prove for the Duke's family, who were such very nice people, really.

Of course no one should ever find out how she had herself meticulously built the night's climax. Her connection to remnants of the East India Company was not well known, and her good fortune— finding that her man in Bombay was back in New York City, that he knew the whole story, and that Dhanesh was already careening around the state searching for the runaway father—could hardly be believed. It had required so little to bring the whole beautiful tragedy together that it would take her some time to understand that she had indeed trampled her foe, along with the foolish man who was so fond of her.

# Chapter 41

Misfortunes travel in groups, or so it is said; if one wanders in, his companions are not far behind. Agnes's life was forming itself into a testament to this truth. Grandma had been buried only a few weeks ago, followed by the debacle in Claudia's front yard. And now, a third catastrophe was quickening its steps toward Brookside.

It was lunchtime on the day following Abram Rockwell's trip to Philadelphia. He had by now assembled the replies to his office's inquires of the previous evening, and he had to face the shocking picture of what remained of Grandma Brown's millions. At the Bank of Philadelphia: seven dollars. At the First National Bank of the East: twenty-two dollars. At the First Union Bank: fourteen dollars. Even her interest in the railroad and several smaller but thriving companies had been liquidated. Abram sat at his desk with his head in his hands, staring dumbly at the telegrams spread before him. Two old associates stood in the room, lost in thought, their brows contracted in a mighty effort to find some way around the financial carnage piled before them.

At length one of them spoke, turning partially from his position at the window. He was a short, wide man, fastidiously dressed, with a few remnants of hair carefully oiled and combed behind his ears. "There's no way around going to court. Especially if what the wife says is true. It all smacks of outright theft, not investment—not even bad investment."

"Of course," put in his colleague from across the room where he had been leaning against a very full set of bookshelves and absently stroking an unlit pipe. "If it were invested he would have had something to show you. Receipts don't go traveling, we know that. It's a bad business, Abram, and the sooner you file the better. You'll surely get no more information from that villain or his mysterious wife."

Mr. Rockwell raised his eyes in a dull stare. "You're absolutely right, both of you. And I blame myself. How could I not?"

The two men disagreed strongly. One exclaimed that no one could have foreseen such conduct, and the other pointed out that an embezzler could strike like a snake, and if he's clever enough, rob a millionaire blind in a matter of days.

"The essential thing is to get a lien on that house of his immediately," urged the wide man.

"Quite right," said the other.

Mr. Rockwell, like one emerging from a strongman's hold, pushed himself to his feet and reached for his hat. He gathered the papers together and added them to his bag. "Gentlemen, there is no time to lose. Mr. Swank"—he turned to the wide man—"would you be willing to accompany me to our legal counsel? I find myself in such a daze, as though I'd had a boxcar dropped on me. I need someone to make sure I am talking sense to our lawyer. Babbidge," he continued, putting a hand on the arm of the man with the pipe, "Get in touch with our people in Philadelphia and find out anything you can. Make sure they know that I am willing to pay for information."

And so two of the senior accountants at Rockwell, Swank, and Babbidge set off for the law offices of Gray, Heinrich, Stubbins to start the ugly process of declaring a possible crime and taking measures to safeguard any of the perpetrator's goods that they might lay claim to. Two questions haunted the men as they made their way to the attorneys' offices situated in the bustling streets around city hall: Was this indeed a crime if Wilbur had done everything legally, and had his house already been surrendered to other creditors?

By evening of the following day, the men had their answers, thanks to the excellent work of Mr. Babbidge and the arrival of a small package by special delivery. The package came in the late afternoon, wrapped in brown paper and addressed to Mr. Rockwell. It bore no return address and looked like something hastily assembled. The address was written in a large, hurried hand, probably female. As soon as the office boy delivered it into Mr. Rockwell's hands, the old gentleman suspected somehow that it must relate to the case. Taking it to his desk, followed closely by Messrs. Swank and Babbidge, he took a sharp scissors to one end and carefully cut it open. Reaching inside, he pulled out the contents.

In his hand were a stack of what appeared to be receipts, some formal, others just scribbled notes. As the accountants spread them out, they realized that they were not looking at receipts but rather promises of payment. Some bore the stamp of casinos as far away as Geneva. Others were scrawled reminders from individuals of debts owed. Some included the name of the debtor: Wilbur Brown. Mr. Rockwell stared at the collage of papers with uncomprehending eyes. He looked back in the packing to see if he had missed anything and extracted a single sheet of fine stationery, written in the same urgent hand as the address. He read aloud in a low voice:

*August 188__*

*Mr. Rockwell,*

*You must be told the truth now or else waste a great deal of time and effort in finding it out yourself.*

*There are no investments. There was one, of a very unsavory nature, that I shall not reveal, but as my husband was dealing with unscrupulous foreigners in that venture, it is not surprising that they took his portion and disappeared.*

*Again, I had nothing to do with that or what you see before you now. W. developed a taste for gambling in France, and for a while he was able to cover his debts. Then he managed to hold his creditors at bay as only he can. However, several months ago he was obliged to start paying them to avoid outright scandal, which would have been unfortunate for the family, as I am sure you would agree. His debts had grown so large that* [here the writer had crossed out a word and started again] *steps had to be taken.*

*As far as I know, all of Grandma's money is gone, and the house as well. If I believed in God, I would pray for forgiveness for my husband and wish some sort of providential care for the family. As it is, I can simply send you and Agnes my regrets that things turned out as they did.*

*E. B.*

Mr. Swank hurried to a side cabinet and poured a tall glass of brandy and water for his colleague, who was sinking into his chair. Babbidge spoke first.

"Abram, I was just going to tell you when I was interrupted by the arrival of this parcel. I received a telegram from one of my people in Philadelphia not an hour ago. The Brown's house is now the property of First National. It was signed over only two weeks ago for payment of debt. Moreover, the Wilbur Browns seem to have sailed for other shores yesterday afternoon. Someone was dispatched to the house to check the story, and it was true. The servants said they had packed and loaded several trunks into a carriage and the two brigands left, telling no one where they were headed. I'm told they left without paying the staff their wages due, and our man saw several of them putting silver into bags and carrying away paintings. It was chaos." Mr. Babbidge paused for his friend to absorb this news. He wished there was some way to soften it, to make something better of it. Instead he could only conclude, "It seems they have gotten away, Abram."

Mr. Rockwell looked up. "And their lawyer? Their accountant?"

"One and the same, and he has disappeared as well."

"They could be headed anywhere," reflected Mr. Swank. "Europe, South America, even India. They must have kept enough cash on hand to pay for steamer tickets and living expenses. Might even be traveling under assumed names. They're needles in a haystack now."

Mr. Babbidge sat down across from his beleaguered colleague. "To make this tragedy complete," he went on quietly, "our attorneys have determined that the documents Wilbur used to extract money from his grandmother are quite legal—dastardly but legal. We probably have no recourse there."

The gentlemen were silent. On the mantle a very old clock ticked away the seconds. From down on the street, floating into the still room from an open window, the clatter of horses and shouts from rowdy cabbies seemed part of another world entirely.

"Who could have imagined?" sighed Mr. Rockwell, sitting back in his softly creaking chair. He took a slow sip of the ruddy brandy and raised his eyebrows as though about to make an observation, but only stared mutely at his littered desktop.

Close by, the great bell of St. Martin's tolled six. The dolorous sound spoke of more than the hour to the three men, who heard in it a reminder of the timeless struggle between virtue and vice. Deep in its solemn voice the bell spoke also of that final day of victory, which to these defeated men felt very far away.

* * *

Mrs. Rockwell took in the news of the Somerset family's financial ruin like a Buddha, her face immutable, her figure motionless on the velvet divan. In all matters, she was her husband's most respected counselor, but he had put her off for two days before sharing the tale. He wanted to get it all out at once, not just one ugly piece at a time. Tonight, he had come home and asked to delay dinner. He led his wife into the parlor saying that he had a story to tell, which he recounted in a clear and dispassionate manner. But the hunch in his shoulders, his slow pacing back and forth as the words came out, the fixed expression of wonder in his eyes, betrayed that he was at the very limit of what he knew how to bear. When he had told everything, including a description of the packet from Eleanor followed by Babbidge's news that all of Wilbur's crimes were done within the law, his voice stopped, but he continued to walk absently about the room.

Mrs. Rockwell sat quietly for a few moments, her hands folded across her generous lap. One could almost hear her mentally cataloguing the facts, considering the repercussions, and arranging in order of practicality the possibilities for action. When she was satisfied, she put a hand on the cushion beside her and asked, "My dear, can you sit?"

Abram Rockwell sat down beside his wife. She rested a hand on his leg and asked, "What do you intend to do?"

Mr. Rockwell sighed deeply, his gaze resting on the dark fire grate across from them. "I must go to Brookside and tell Agnes in person. Immediately. First I'll check what remains in her own accounts so I can give her a full report all around. But we both know that she needed Irene Brown's money. It was she who paid the taxes on the estate each year. They come due next month. That alone will wipe out much of Agnes's reserve. Even if Agnes trims her staff to a minimum, there will be enough left to keep the house running for, at best, six months—maybe less."

"She will have to sell?"

"I see no other course."

Mrs. Rockwell frowned and considered. Then she straightened her shoulders and announced, "I am going with you. She will need a woman at a time like this. We will tell her together, then you can arrange the legal matters. I might stay a few days to help her think. And we should bring Vera along, if the woman isn't off exploring the western frontier."

Abram turned his eyes directly on his wife for the first time that evening. "You are a singular woman," he observed with a touch of amazement in his voice. "I know you will be a great help to her." His gaze shifted and his eyes welled up. "I feel this is my fault, Doris. I should have noticed somehow, taken more precautions, checked more frequently—"

"Abram!" Doris Rockwell took her husband's face in her hands. "You are a competent and conscientious man. This is Wilbur's fault, and Eleanor's. They did the thieving. Don't let me hear you say that again."

Abram Rockwell slumped against his wife, who enclosed him in the protection of her arms, and they remained that way as the room darkened into late evening. At last a servant tapped gently on the parlor door and, hearing nothing, carefully opened it to inquire if they would be wanting dinner. Mrs. Rockwell asked that a plate of food be brought up to their rooms and stated that they would be leaving the next day for Brookside.

# Part III. *La Donna Sola*

# Chapter 42

As the sun rose toward its zenith in the perfectly blue sky, Agnes slept on until nearly noon. In this week following the ball, she found it harder each morning to get out of bed. When she opened her eyes on this fair day, she beheld Marie and Stella sitting across the room. Stella was embroidering a tiny cap held fast in a wooden hoop, and Marie was reading her mother's book of prayers. Their faces wore a concerned look, and they had started keeping a close eye on Agnes, which grated mercilessly on her nerves and violated the solitude she now sought. One or the other of them had surely removed the half-full bottle of Abbé sur Rhône from under the mattress, but she had been too ashamed to ask them when she found it missing. The wine had been a pathetic attempt, she knew, to treat a pain this consuming, and she felt the futility of procuring any more.

Neither attendant noticed that their patient was awake, so Agnes lay still and waited, letting the new day's realities gradually line up for review. When she had taken a long look at their full and ghastly measure, she turned her attention, as though for refuge, to a piece of errant lace that dangled from her canopy. I must mention that to Marie, she thought; I keep forgetting, and it's so bothersome to look at every morning.

Presently her companions noticed that she was awake and began humming around her, making her get up and wash and put on fresh clothes. Refusing any breakfast, Agnes took a cup of tea and wandered into the garden. Stella tried to talk with her, but Agnes said she felt like poor company, so the young woman quietly went back to a canvas of morning glories that somehow had not advanced past a middling state since the week before.

From the dining room windows, Fettles watched Agnes stroll languidly through the garden paths. Having been provided with a complete description of Claudia's spectacle by the coachman the morning after, he had been beside himself ever since. Although a bachelor, Fettles was a romantic who had thrilled at the sight of Agnes and Phillip together, and more than once made sure they were undisturbed in the garden during the young man's visits. Love, he told the servants, is a delicate plant that thrives in the shade of seclusion.

Now he watched the face of his mistress drain of love's blush, the bloom that was just there yesterday, faded overnight. She looked empty and ate little. At teatime, Dahlia baked a batch of orange biscuits she knew were Agnes's weakness, and Fettles arranged them beside two white roses on her tray. Leaving the kitchen with these temptations in hand, he overheard two servants in the pantry speculating on Phillip's fatherhood. Fettles set down the tray and, seizing a nearby rolling pin, strode to their dark nook and brandished it at them. He asked how they thought their mistress would feel if she heard them. If they wanted to lose their positions, they might let him catch them again discussing the matter. The frightened girls returned speedily and silently to their work.

Claudia had of course sent a card, expressing deepest regret at the appalling events of that evening, which she was powerless to forestall. The timing could not have been more unfortunate, she wrote, and she was miserable at the thought that her gala had been the setting for such an unhappy scene. She begged Agnes to please send word if there was anything she could do to be of help or solace. Agnes tore the scented message into tiny pieces, sprinkled them into the fountain, and watched the splashing water churn them under.

Each sparkling late summer day dragged on. Agnes longed for night, for the blanket of darkness to hide in. She picked at dinner and retired early with no lamp, usually falling asleep before the sky lost its color. So it was that she was sound asleep the evening the Rockwells came through the front door with their few bags and terrible knowledge. Upon learning that Agnes had retired for the evening, they were relieved that they could also get a night's sleep before sharing what they had come to tell. Vera arrived an hour behind them, with the faithful Mr. Schmidt. The four took a light supper together, during which Mr. Rockwell indicated only that he had a matter of the utmost importance to the family to discuss, but it would wait until morning when they could all meet with Agnes. Fettles found four bottles of wine left from the celebration earlier in the summer, and the small party finished them off (Mrs. Rockwell abstaining), which was a good deal more than any of them was in the habit of drinking. However, it ensured a sound slumber, mercifully dulling their anticipation of the next day.

Agnes herself slept deeply until morning. When she opened her eyes, the sun's first rays had snuck between the curtains and lit up a note left beside her bed sometime during the night. She reached for it and read: *Miss Agnes, guests arrived after you retired. Mr. and Mrs. Rockwell, Vera and Mr. Schmidt. Breakfast at 8:30. I will be up to see you at 8:00. –Marie*

The golden hands on the mantel clock read 7:30. What happened? Had she forgotten that they were coming? She threw off the sheet, put her feet into slippers, and rang for Marie. Within moments there came a knock at the door, but to Agnes's surprise Vera entered. She was dressed in dark trousers, a fitted lace jacket, and an emerald ascot. Agnes stood in her nightdress and stared. "Vera, my dearest, you are getting less conventional every time I see you."

Vera strode forward, hugged her niece, and stepped back to look at her. "You don't look well," she observed.

"I'm alright. I'm just surprised to have a visit that I seem to have forgotten about. I'm—I'm not prepared," she stammered.

Vera led Agnes to the chaise longue and sat down beside her. "You didn't forget anything. Abram sent me a message yesterday to be here. I don't know any more about it than that. Do you?"

Agnes's eyes were wide. "I don't know anything."

Vera scrutinized her. "What's going on?" she asked. "You've changed. It's like—" she searched her niece's eyes. "Almost like the life has gone out of you." Vera stroked the pale face. "And you feel warm," she said, her eyes darkening.

Marie appeared at the door. Agnes turned back to her aunt and observed slowly, "Oh, I'll be fine. I must get dressed now." She rose to her feet. Looking back at Vera, she continued, "Well, I suppose I must tell you a very strange story." As Marie helped her mistress into a pale blue morning dress, Agnes told Vera about the ball, Dhanesh, and baby Henri. As the tale concluded, Vera for once seemed at a loss for words except to say finally, "Why didn't you tell me all this? Why didn't you write to me?"

Agnes shook her head. "I considered it. But I could not bring myself to write it out. Besides," Agnes continued with a wan smile, "I imagined you would hear about it soon enough with the story no doubt buzzing from one social hive to another." She drew a breath. "But it seems we must put the whole intrigue aside for the moment as Mr. Rockwell must be bringing us something much bigger to think about."

Downstairs, Agnes greeted the Rockwells and Mr. Schmidt, already at breakfast. She noted Abram's drawn face, so changed from the last time she had seen him. Mrs. Rockwell patted the chair beside her as Fettles drew it back, apologized for the surprise visit, and assured her that they would explain things after breakfast.

Agnes attempted a cheerful face and, while breaking off crumbs from her muffin, congratulated Mr. Schmidt on his accomplishment in winning Vera's hand. Vera explained that he had worn her down and that's all there was to it. Frederick could not keep from beaming. Stella came down, and the meal passed with pleasant talk of plans for Vera's Christmas wedding. Agnes felt a knife turn within her as she remembered her joy just a few weeks ago when she shared with Vera the happy prospect of a wedding of her own.

After breakfast, the party arranged themselves in the drawing room. Stella had offered to withdraw, but Agnes held her hand and insisted that she sit with her. Stella felt the warmth of the hand in hers and only then noticed the new tinge of pink that colored her aunt's cheeks.

Agnes sat loosely beside Stella, leaning against the back of the sofa and feeling a wave of deep fatigue wash over her. How she wished Phillip were there to help her hear whatever Mr. Rockwell was about to tell them. But no, she was back to managing by herself, *la donna sola*, an independent woman. Tears rose in her eyes but she fought them back with the little strength she had. There would probably be some better reason to cry soon enough.

# Chapter 43

Mr. Rockwell stationed himself in front of the white marble fireplace and cleared his throat. How small he looks, thought Agnes, and how old. I don't remember him like this, and only two months have passed since I last saw him. In contrast, Agnes saw his wife as stronger than ever, seated a few feet from him, her large hands folded firmly, her keen eyes training a determined look upon her husband.

After dabbing his forehead with a handkerchief—the late August day was bright and already warm—Mr. Rockwell began. He started by summing up the previous condition of the Somerset finances and what support Grandma Brown had been providing. He proceeded from this robust portrait to recount his recent discoveries, beginning with the trip to Philadelphia and ending with the packet from Eleanor that revealed the finality of their new situation.

"To conclude, then," said Mr. Rockwell, "your money, Agnes, can only keep Brookside running for, at best, six months, and only that long if you trim expenses. Barring an influx of capital from some unforeseen source, that is where we are." He cleared his throat again and looked at his wife. "This means that I see no alternative at this time but to advise you to put the estate up for sale as soon as possible, as finding a buyer may take some time."

His audience sat frozen. Mr. Rockwell put his hands in his coat pockets and waited for the reactions, the angry questions. He could certainly guess their thoughts. They would be the same thoughts that had been tumbling over and over through his own mind. Could this all be true? How could they sell Brookside? It would be like selling a limb, an organ. Who would this family be without this home where so many had been married, where children had been born and parents had died; where holly had been hung and songs sung every Christmas; where each spring the gardens had welcomed life back and the sparkling fountain told them another winter was over; where they had thrilled to the sound of carriages on the drive, bringing friends and relations to fill the guest rooms with a happy hubbub; where Grandma Brown held class on the terrace, teaching little Somersets to curtsy and use their silverware; where the sun had risen and gone back down upon this family every day for a hundred years?

When no one spoke, Mr. Rockwell walked over to Agnes and took her hand. His old eyes glistened. "My dear girl, I am wholly unable to express the depth of my regret at this terrible turn in our fortune. I say 'our' because I love your family as my own." Mrs. Rockwell quietly came up and put a hand on her husband's back. "Your father," Mr. Rockwell continued, "was much more than a partner to me, and I feel you are another daughter to us. I blame myself even though there may have been no way to prevent what your cousin did. We can only offer now to help in every way possible. But I know that is little comfort, little comfort indeed."

Mrs. Rockwell gently handed her husband off to Mr. Schmidt, who led him away hoping to find some brandy to salve the accountant's breaking heart. Mrs. Rockwell lowered herself onto the sofa and wrapped a sturdy arm around Agnes. Agnes continued to sit motionless, her cheeks glowing with a bright flush. On her other side, Stella held her hand fast as tears began to trickle down her own face.

"This is a great shock, my dear," began Mrs. Rockwell. "Don't try to make sense of it all at once. I am prepared to stay, if you wish, to help sort out what's to be done. I hope you will let me do at least that."

Stella leaned forward. "Mrs. Rockwell, isn't there some way to avoid selling Brookside? I can hardly even say it, it's so—it's so—unthinkable."

"Mr. Rockwell will be investigating every possible idea," she replied. "But we must look for an interested buyer in the meantime and do what seems necessary at the moment."

Vera had begun pacing the floor, her arms folded tightly across her chest. "The scoundrels! Brigands! I can't believe he had the audacity to use Agnes's inheritance—or that Grandma Brown went along with it. How could she?"

"Grandma had a story to tell." Agnes spoke up in a hollow voice. "But she never got to tell me. Now I know what it was. I cannot blame her for what happened—she is not here to tell us her side."

"We could go to Europe, Agnes, and look for them," Vera proposed, her eyes flashing. "They're not that bright, either one of them—they've probably left a trail a blind man could follow."

"Aunt Vera, they might not be in Europe," Stella put in. "You heard Mr. Rockwell: they could be in South America or India or anywhere."

"Well, I'm not ready to give up," replied Vera. "Or to let anyone put Brookside up for sale."

Agnes looked around her. Looming over them was the portrait of her father dressed in a black coat that nearly merged with the painting's background, a more serious cast to his features than they ever wore in life. Her gaze ran over the finely chiseled mantel and black marble hearth. Above their heads hung a golden chandelier rich with prisms. She saw the yellow drapes heavy upon the windows, and beyond them, the bright, hazy morning, and she said in a whisper, "I have lost it, Father. Everything you worked for." The thought filled her mind, turned her stomach, and she felt hot all over. She pictured Wilbur as he lectured her on the necessity of investment, his face twisted into a condescending smile. Her mind shot to Claudia wrapped in a silken sari and smiling, always smiling. She saw Phillip standing like a fool in front of a silent crowd with a bastard child in his arms.

Agnes sat up with a strange look on her face. "It's all right." She rose to her feet and looked at her listeners, brightening. "Of course there's no money. Why should I get an inheritance? Why should we have any happy endings here?" Her voice changed as she walked about the room, twisting her handkerchief between her hands. "None of this is supposed to matter after all, is it?" she asked, waving a hand at the grandeur that surrounded them. "The rich man and the eye of the needle. Maybe I should have sold this millstone years ago and joined the convent—that's what I should have done if I'd any sense at all!" She was nearly screaming now. "What did I think I was doing, perpetuating this place single-handedly, and for what?"

She looked one by one at the women who surrounded her; they all had a mate, someone to share the burden of life with, even if not perfectly. They did not understand what it meant to carry on the affairs of the great Somerset family alone, including the house they sat in now; to have no prospects, no hope of not being alone, while the years slid by and left their mark. Hot tears filled her eyes. She grabbed a Bavarian candlestick and tossed it to Vera, who caught it easily. A Wedgewood vase sailed toward Mrs. Rockwell, who fumbled it, but deflected it undamaged onto the sofa.

"Take what you want," Agnes cried. "We'll sell the rest or give it to charity."

"Agnes!" scolded Mrs. Rockwell.

"What?" The challenge cut the air. By now everyone could see the red flame that burned on her cheeks and the wild, glassy eyes. "What do I need with these things, with a house like this? Has anyone noticed that there are no children running through these halls, no man to sit down to dinner with—"

She grabbed a pink-flowered candy dish, and Stella raised her hands. But Agnes threw it wide. It sailed incongruously through the air until it met the stone mantelpiece, which transformed the dainty dish into a spray of chalky fragments. Stella began to cry outright, but the crisp sound of shattering china served to bring her aunt back to herself. Agnes bowed her head, and Vera stepped toward her, but Agnes held out a stiff hand. Carefully she picked up a Venetian paperweight and polished it against her skirt, then raised her head to look out the tall window where the lush lawn spread beneath ancient oaks. "'*Le destin est railleur*.'[3] Fate mocks us, my friends." She stood quiet for a moment and motionless. The women waited. "Still," she said at last, "I will miss the garden."

Saying this, she swayed slightly. Mrs. Rockwell, who was closest, stepped forward and put both arms around her. Vera removed the precious paperweight from her hands, and they took Agnes up to bed, where she fell into a fever that made Ned run for Doctor Bingham and sent Fettles into a near panic. He ordered Dahlia to boil up a gallon of her best chicken broth as well as a variety of herbal teas against whose salubrious effects no illness had yet prevailed.

"A person can only take so much," he was heard to mutter as he flew up the stairs. "What does He expect of her? What did we all expect?"

---

[3] From *Cyrano de Bergerac* by Edmond Rostand.

# Chapter 44

A baby is a demanding houseguest. Phillip's life so far had not brought him in touch with young children except for the urchins who had drifted into his mission to listen to stories and get a lump of sugar. So the degree to which his entire household was turned inside out at the arrival of the six-month-old infant made him stand back in awe.

The child proved to be a fussy one, and Mrs. Morgan announced that he was undernourished and in poor health. The first priority was to secure a wet nurse for the child, which position was filled quickly by a robust young woman whose infant had died just a week earlier. On seeing her new charge, however, the lady hesitated, frightened that "the little heathen" might have a dread disease that he would make it his business to pass on to her. Doctor Bingham was brought in to inspect the child and, aside from being underweight, pronounced him as fit as any baby in the county.

On this visit, the doctor took Phillip aside and asked if he had been to Brookside in the last day or two. Hearing that he had not, the doctor advised him of Agnes's poor health, having just come from her bedside. Doctor Bingham acknowledged that he was aware of a certain fondness between them, and it might be wise for Phillip to find time to visit the patient to the extent the ladies of that household might allow.

Phillip's face blanched at the news. "Are you going back that way?" he asked, grabbing the doctor's sleeve. "May I ride with you?"

Phillip knew of the doctor's reputation as a man of sagacity and unimpeachable discretion. So during their ride to Brookside, Phillip confided the events at the ball, most of which the doctor had already heard from every one of his patients in the last week, with fantastic variations.

"So you see," Phillip concluded, "this has all been a great shock to her, surely. What is she to make of it? I would have gone to see her but I did not know what to say."

"My friend," replied the doctor, training a keen eye on the young man, "take the advice of a man who has made many mistakes himself with the fair sex. In a case like this, saying almost anything to her is better than saying nothing. It's the terrible silence that can crush them, as they imagine the worst, with nothing to contradict their wild ravings. Don't leave her alone with this, whatever you do. She may reject you. That is her right. But then again, she might not."

By now they had arrived at Brookside. Phillip thanked the doctor quickly and jumped out to untie his horse from behind the carriage.

"One more thing," called the doctor after him. "Demand nothing. Don't ask her to believe you. Give her time."

Phillip knocked at the great black door and waited what felt like days for it to open. When it did, Fettles stood blocking the entrance.

"She's not well," he announced.

"I've heard. Doctor Bingham dropped me by. May I see her?"

Fettles paused. He was furious with this man and the rest of the pack who had brought his favorite girl in the entire world to her knees. "Why have you come?" he sputtered, fighting to keep his voice low. "Why should I let you disturb her further?" His eyes bulged and the veins in his lean neck stood out with the effort to control the anger pushing hard within him.

"Because, Fettles, by the grace of God, she may still tolerate me. And I love her." He looked directly into Fettles' eyes, unafraid of his rage. "I love her," Phillip pleaded, "almost as much as you do."

Fettles' mouth twitched, and water filled his eyes. Stepping slowly aside, he admitted the young man, softly closed the door, and led the way upstairs. They found Vera at the bedside, applying a freshly soaked cloth to Agnes's forehead. Vera looked at them without speaking and turned back to her patient.

"Lord Phillip wishes to see Miss Agnes. I told him it would be up to you."

Vera looked down at her niece, whose eyes moved fitfully beneath the closed lids. "I can't see that it matters. She'll be as unaware of you as she is of the rest of us."

Phillip stepped forward, "Just let me sit next to her and hold her hand. She'll know I'm here. I won't make her speak."

Vera and Fettles exchanged uncertain looks. "Very well," Vera decided. "Sit here. I'll be right outside, and I shall leave the door open. If you trouble her in the slightest way I will throw you out in an instant."

Phillip sat lightly on the edge of the bed and caught up Agnes's hot hand in his. He took the cloth off her head, rinsed it in the basin of cold water at his elbow, and dabbed at her neck and wrists. Vera peeked in at him as he half sat, half knelt beside the unconscious woman. The scene brought back suddenly her days in the field hospital, where the occasional sweetheart would find her man and hold him for the few days it took for his life to run out.

"When did you eat last?" she called to Phillip.

Without taking his eyes off Agnes, Phillip replied that it was sometime the day before. Vera slipped away to find a plate of food.

Phillip spent most the following days sitting quietly in a corner of Agnes's room as her fever rose, dipped, hovered, and rose again. Now and then Agnes would wake for a few minutes, and her attendants would ply her with sips of water and broth. Then she would close her eyes and fall back into a restless, mumbling sleep. Occasionally Phillip took a short break to walk through the gardens and gather an odd arrangement of flowers and honeysuckle vine for her room, always hoping to see some improvement when he returned. Each night he left for his father's home, only to return early the next morning. The Duke stopped by several times to inquire after the patient and stay to tea, afterwards forcing the ladies into a game of cards that provided them all a brief relief from their worry over the patient upstairs.

By virtue of Phillip's constancy, on the fourth day of Agnes's sickness Vera and Stella shared with him the dark news the Rockwells had brought them. Upon hearing it, he brought the flat of his hand down violently on the parlor table.

"I knew there was something!" he exclaimed. "I knew that man was about the devil's work—but I could not tell what, of course. Damnation!"

"Uncle Wilbur has always been bad," explained Stella. "I personally have always detested him."

"But none of us could have anticipated this," put in Vera, "not even Mr. Rockwell, who is the closest to the family's financial affairs. No one could have guessed . . ." Vera's voice trailed off as though she had run out of words. Her face wore the blank look of extreme fatigue.

While Phillip seethed at Wilbur's villainy, he somehow took upon himself a measure of blame, feeling like a carrier of disaster since entering Agnes's life. It seemed he harbored within him the seeds of plague, which he had unwittingly spilled upon her and her entire home. He left the ladies and went out, riding through the countryside all afternoon, dismounting now and then to tramp through fields and scream at the sky. Everything he touched turned to ruin. As soon as she was well he would leave her alone for good, he resolved. He must let her rebuild her life in whatever way God in his mercy might grant. But would she recover, he wondered, reflecting on the pale, damp face on the pillow, the sweet mouth that muttered nonsense and refused anything that might strengthen her.

Heavy with a grim resolve, Phillip returned to Brookside the next day and the next. On the seventh day, he had fallen asleep on the rug at the foot of Agnes's bed. Stella had left the room for a moment to get a finer brush for the miniature she was painting. A deep stillness lay upon the house, and only the repeated chirp of a cardinal looking for his mate broke the silence of the afternoon. Suddenly a faint voice startled Phillip from his light sleep. It came again: "That silly lace . . . still hanging there." He leapt to his feet and found Agnes awake and clear-eyed. He leaned over her and put a hand on her head. It was cool to his touch. The young man uttered a cry and collapsed, taking her into his arms in a grip that threatened to crush her. Presently he unwrapped her and held her at arms' length, staring. Agnes looked back at him and tried to smile but managed only to twist her lips weakly and lean against him. Stella returned, screamed with delight, and ran to tell the household.

Agnes spent two weeks recovering her strength. Phillip stopped by every few days to discreetly ask Fettles for a report on her progress, but refused to go inside the house. During her convalescence, Agnes spent long, desultory hours in the garden doing nothing more than watching Stella sketch or listening to the birds chatter. The great troubles that had crushed her now seemed to belong to another world, one she could look at but not feel. Without the strength yet to step into that world, she knew reality would simply have to wait for her.

It has been said that never is one more comfortable or content than in the sweet, powerless days following an illness. The patient has the world's permission to do nothing and can sit idly with the happy thought that health is on its way back and all she has to do is wait. Afternoon naps, people plumping your pillows and bringing you frivolous books to read (not the serious ones they suggest the rest of the time), hot soup and your favorite puddings, all these special attentions put a glow upon such days that one remembers fondly long after resuming the regular pace of life.

The other ladies of the household, by contrast, had busied themselves these three weeks with a great task. While Agnes lay tossing upon her sickbed, Mrs. Rockwell and Vera had begun a comprehensive inventory of Brookside. When Agnes was strong enough, they sat with her and added notes on what she wanted to keep for herself and what she would consider giving to family and friends. The rest, painful as it was to consider, could be auctioned off if Brookside were sold.

Messrs. Schmidt and Rockwell had stayed three days to walk the grounds with Ned and write down all the particulars regarding the stable and kennel as well as topographical features that could be included to good advantage in a description of the property.

After four weeks Mrs. Rockwell returned home, leaving Agnes and Vera to resolve the last and most distressing matter, reducing the number of staff. Agnes, being of an efficient and frugal nature, had kept the Brookside staff fairly small, although large enough to keep any one person from being overburdened in his duties. Most had been with the family for years, and some for decades. Now, behind closed doors, the two women pondered a list of names, weighing each one's ability to secure new employment and the possibility of getting along without them.

In the years that Agnes had managed the estate, she had only had to fire two people. One was a scullery maid who failed to curb her profane language; the other was a butler's assistant who napped more than he worked and was suspected of being behind the attrition of teaspoons from the silver chest. But now she was faced with letting perfectly good workers go, putting them out of a position with nothing more than a few dollars, an apology, and a letter of reference.

And so the two women made the difficult decisions, with many tearful retreats into reminiscences and wishing things were different. Seven servants had lines through their names. To manage with such a reduced staff, all rooms not used daily would be closed off and not cleaned. Entertaining beyond a half-dozen dinner guests was at an end. The stables would be winnowed to three horses from six; and only those gardens closest to the house would be maintained. Philanthropic donations ceased (this despite Agnes's misgivings, remembering always the story of the widow who gave away her only coin).

So absorbed were the women in stripping down Brookside and laying bare all of its workings that they were able to put aside the question of Phillip and the baby. However, the day dawned when Agnes could no longer avoid the unsettled affairs of her heart and must, as Vera reminded her, sift through that "pile of dry cuttings."

# Chapter 45

One morning brought a chill with it and the distinct feeling that autumn was close by. The sky stretched above Brookside like a canvas sloppily painted, with patches of dull white showing through the steely gray. Pallid daylight hung at the windows, too weak to enter the dining room where Vera and Agnes sat at breakfast wrapped in thin shawls. The last few weeks had taken a toll on both of them, and Stella was talking about getting back to her home and husband.

"So how are you doing?" asked Vera, absently spreading a spare coat of blueberry jam onto her toast.

"In what way?" replied her niece without looking up from the slice of ham she had begun cutting into unnecessarily small bites.

"It was a general question. But to begin, what are you thinking these days about his lordship?"

"I've been rather too busy to give him much thought," Agnes half lied. "I'm sure that once I do I won't know what to think any more than I did the morning after that diabolical ball. He's not stopping by any more, is he?"

"No," replied Vera. "I understand that after you woke up finally he came every couple of days for about a week and then stopped. He probably realized you were stable and otherwise occupied. "

"Do you think everyone knows about our situation by now—I mean, about the house and all?"

"If the servants talked—especially those we let go—then yes. But I haven't heard any gossip in town yet. As soon as the house goes up for sale, though, speculation will run wild."

Agnes poured herself some coffee. "I had Mr. Rockwell promise that he would not list the house until I said so."

"The reason for that?"

Agnes waved her fork. "I'm expecting a miracle, I suppose. No, I'm not. I just need time to get used to the idea."

"When you first came back to us you talked as if selling Brookside would be a relief. Do you remember?"

In Agnes's first exhausted days after awakening from her fever, she had in her ruminations begun to feel that the collected disasters might be pushing open a door for her. She pictured the weight like that of the great mansion itself being lifted from her tired frame. Propped against a bank of pillows one morning she had admitted to Vera that maybe the time had come to surrender the reins.

"Yes, I remember," Agnes admitted. "But it was a passing feeling. Much of it is true, of course—letting go of this whole responsibility is very appealing. But it means losing my home, Vera, our family home. You don't get that back. It is a huge decision."

"I know, my dear. I know. But you understand that you probably won't be making that decision, don't you—rather, the circumstances will."

Agnes continued eating and said nothing. She still had not gained back the weight she had lost in her illness, and her color had never completely returned.

"How about a walk in the garden?" Vera proposed a little too brightly.

"It's cold."

"It will be good for us. It will put some color in our cheeks." Grudgingly, Agnes agreed. They each fetched another shawl, and the two walked down the familiar garden paths. Already the weeds were beginning to clutter the beds, and Agnes had never seen the shrubs so untidy. It reminded her how quickly two gardeners are missed. Agnes bent to unwind a thin vine from the creamy bells of a late-blooming foxglove.

"They don't know what's coming," she mused. "The foxgloves and the roses and the lilies. Choke-weed and violets will overrun them in no time. Do you know what gardening is, Vera? It is man's attempt to keep Nature from doing what she is determined to do. How could we hope to win in the long run?"

Vera gave Agnes a long, frank look. "I think it's time to talk about him—about the two of you."

They resumed their walk. Agnes watched her feet as she put one in front of the other. They looked so far away, as though they did not belong to her. What was there to talk about? They had no new facts. Maybe the child was Phillip's son, maybe he wasn't. Either way Phillip was now a social outcast—everyone would believe the story Dhanesh told. How could they marry? Besides, his absence could only mean that he had lost interest in her. Maybe she was not as attractive without the Somerset fortune after all.

"Do you think it's his child?" asked Vera pointedly.

"I don't know. I want to say no, and deep down I don't believe it is, especially since he was so adamant about it. But I have been fooled before, as you know. And there is a certain resemblance. Of course everyone else must think it is."

"True," Vera reflected, "If you did decide to join him you would be out of any social circle for a very long time. Until he did something profitable, that is, and got readmitted."

Agnes smiled. "That's unlikely, as you observed yourself. He is not gifted with a profession or any money-making talents. And with my new situation, I cannot make him a kept man. Maybe that's why we don't see him anymore."

Vera stopped. "Agnes, did you have any understanding with Lord Phillip?"

There was no point in keeping the secret. Exhaustion spread over her suddenly, along with the now familiar feeling that nothing much mattered. "We had agreed to marry. But we told no one because we knew that everyone would be shocked at an engagement after so short a time. It doesn't matter now."

Vera's heart melted as she looked at her niece, so diminished from the girl she knew. "Do you still love him?" she asked.

"Of course."

Vera thought for a moment. Then, turning Agnes around and pulling her gently along, she announced, "My dear, we are going to pay a visit."

"Vera, I'm not—"

"Not a word! We will get our hats and gloves and take a little ride up the road."

"To where?"

"To see our good friends, the Duke and his son. After all, Agnes, if we do not visit them, who in the world will?"

# Chapter 46

Agnes did not protest, but allowed her aunt to lead her back toward the house. She turned over in her mind what it would be like to see Phillip again and felt a swarm of conflicting emotions fill her whole body. But as they neared the house, she was distracted from her reflections by a cab parked in the porte-cochère. Coming closer, they heard Fettles' voice rising in pitch. As they rounded the cab they found the butler standing in the drive, facing a cabdriver. The driver was a crude-looking lump of a man, who stood in an immovable stance with his chin thrust out. More important, the driver held in one dirty hand the leashes that led to the thin necks of two dogs in matching black jackets—two greyhounds, in fact, one with a jeweled collar.

Vera and Agnes looked at each other. Surely not, their eyes said.

"But it's Empress and Napoleon!" cried Vera. At this the dogs raised their heads and looked expectantly at her.

"Fettles, what is going on?" demanded Agnes, stepping forward.

"Madam, it's incredible. Incredible! The dogs—this man insists that they were sent here and he's delivering them from the train. And he is asking for payment. I told him that this is impossible, but he will not budge."

Agnes addressed the taciturn driver. "Where did these animals come from?"

The man unfolded a limp piece of paper. "Says here Philadelphia. Going here. This is Brookside estate, ain't it?"

"It is."

"Well then my job is done. And that'll be two dollars for bringing 'em up from the station—nobody's paid for that. I should charge more for animals, but they was well behaved, so I'll leave it at two dollars."

The three recipients looked at one another, at the dogs, at the driver. Finally Agnes said, "Fettles, please pay the man. This is not his problem."

"But, madam, we can't accept these animals! Why did we sell three excellent horses if we are going to start taking in homeless dogs? Dogs which are being forced upon us?"

"We'll find another home for them. For now, just pay him the fare," Agnes said testily. "We can't stand here the rest of the day."

Fettles produced the money, and the driver handed the leashes to Agnes. As he climbed onto his cab he paused. "Oh, I almost forgot." He pulled another rumpled note from his pocket and handed it to her. "This came with 'em." Then he fell into his seat, slapped the reins, and rode away, leaving behind his distinctive scent. Fettles and Vera drew close to Agnes and looked intently at the paper as she unfolded it. In a tight, masculine hand was written simply,

*To Brookside Estate, Dutchess County, New York*

*Agnes,*

*If you get this message it means that Montefiore is in other hands now, and my butler was unable to keep the animals himself. I cannot take them with me, although they are probably the only living things I care much about. Please take care of them one way or another. I would not add this to your burdens but, cousin, you are after all one of the only decent people I know.*

*Wilbur*

How interesting, Agnes reflected, that a cretin like Wilbur actually did esteem her. Somewhere in him he knew right from wrong, good from bad. He recognized in her a decent person, but this did not stop him from squandering her entire inheritance and leaving her without a roof over her head. How did he become what he was, a man with no heart for even his own family, who stopped at nothing to save his miserable skin, whose sense of duty warmed only toward these dimwitted dogs?

Agnes handed the animals over to Fettles with instructions to have Isaiah give them something to eat and take them for a walk. They had, after all, probably been cooped up in crates for some time. They would take up residence in the kennel until a home could be found. Fettles led them away, muttering uncontrollably.

Agnes went inside and checked her hair, exchanged her shawls for a heavy silk jacket, and pulled on a pair of gloves. Marie pinned a sober black hat on her, and the ladies were ready. Ned had hitched up the horses to the open buggy as Vera had requested, feeling that the cool air would do Agnes good. As they rolled up the road to Fellcrest, Agnes thought of asking her aunt why exactly they were making this trip. The thought of seeing Phillip frightened her, but at the same time she thrilled at the idea. She said nothing and watched the countryside instead: the patches of wild woods, the farmers' fields tall with sturdy corn ready for harvest, here and there a fallow field waiting its turn to grow another crop. She recalled Phillip talking about buying land and trying his hand at agriculture. She had no trouble picturing him plowing fields like those they were passing, reveling in the scent of freshly turned earth and dancing at the sight of emerging barley shoots.

Fellcrest was set unusually close to the road. Just a few yards up the driveway a pair of tall iron gates obliged visitors to stop, open, and reclose them. Ned, a man not usually given to grumbling, found this procedure irritating and unnecessary and let his feelings be known. Agnes knew that the gates were put up by the previous owners, but did wonder why the Duke kept them in place despite repeated promises to remove them for being singularly "undemocratic."

A buggy was parked in front of the house, and some sort of activity that sounded not altogether agreeable was going on around it. Agnes and Vera leaned forward as they approached. "It seems to be our day," Vera murmured to Agnes, "for witnessing dramatic arrivals or departures!"

They watched as Lord Phillip held the buggy's door open for a young woman who climbed in roughly and sat herself down in a defensive posture, clutching a small bag in her lap. Mrs. Morgan, her face a collection of anxious lines, stood to one side with the baby on her narrow hip.

". . . have already been paid more than you deserve," was the first fragment the ladies could distinguish, uttered by Lord Phillip as he slammed the buggy door shut.

"Your little bastard doesn't deserve a decent nurse like me," sputtered the woman. "You took advantage of a girl in need of a position. I quit, you understand, I quit!"

Phillip noticed the visitors. "Take her back," he shouted to his driver. "Take her back where she came from."

As the indignant girl was driven away, Mrs. Morgan turned to Phillip. "She won't be easy to replace, you know. Nurses are hard to find."

"I don't care," Phillip cried, leaning toward the startled housekeeper. "I won't have this child mistreated. I'll feed him goat's milk first. I am surprised that you could let this go on, Mrs. Morgan."

"This child has no business being here—either in this house or in this world," snapped the housekeeper.

Phillip, clearly stunned, stood staring at her for a moment. Then he reached out and took the child from her. "We may not know this child's earthly parents, Mrs. Morgan, but we know one thing. God made him, and with some purpose. Now that I understand your feelings, I relieve you of any responsibility toward him."

Mrs. Morgan clenched and unclenched her hands, but having no defense, she pressed her thin lips together and walked briskly into the house.

A warm rush of admiration washed over Agnes as she remembered why she loved this man.

# Chapter 47

With his one free hand, Phillip helped the ladies down. He smiled politely at Agnes, then turned to Vera. Vera took the lead, and avoiding any reference to the unpleasant scene they had just observed, chattered about how long it had been since she had visited Fellcrest and what a handsome home it was. Phillip glanced periodically at Agnes, but she was not ready to speak. She stood with her hands clasped—tightly, she suddenly realized—observing the natural way Phillip held the child. He took on a different light with this baby in his arms. It was as though another Phillip had joined the one she knew, making him doubly attractive. This is what being a father looks like, she mused. And does a man, when he sees his wife with their new baby, observe the same thing? Does she shine in a wholly new way? Agnes glimpsed for the first time how a couple magically expands, in a way she never imagined, when they become parents.

She stepped closer to Phillip and extended her arms toward Henri. She saw the surprise on Phillip's face, but he handed him to her. Agnes marveled at the baby's flawless skin, so dark and creamy. She took his smooth little arm in her hand and let him grip her fingers. His shiny hair was already waving about his neck and forehead. He looked up at Agnes and stretched out a hand to pull at the netting of her hat. Phillip stepped in to loosen his grip, while Vera unpinned her niece's hat to remove it from danger. Agnes thought she saw Phillip in the child's brow and nose but, after all, this was a baby's face and subject to change.

"I have been negligent," Phillip was saying. "I have not come by to check on you in some time." He observed her thin face and the dark patches below her eyes. "You look very well, though."

"You are being kind," Agnes replied, combing the baby's hair with her fingers. "I am quite well, but I have looked better. These last few weeks have been rather difficult."

Vera and Agnes accepted Phillip's invitation to lunch. Phillip handed Henri to a young servant with instructions that he was not to be given into Mrs. Morgan's care under any circumstances. The girl beamed with the baby in her arms and hurried off toward the kitchen.

Phillip showed the ladies into the front parlor, a room whose tasteful decoration could not disguise the fact that a woman did not manage the home. The gold wallpaper was growing dingy, the furniture had been arranged in a practical but unappealing way, and the room had a lifeless quality unrelieved by even a vase of flowers or pictures of family.

The Duke was in Albany for the week, and Phillip was managing the newly complicated household without him. It took little urging to get from him the story of the dismissed wet nurse. Phillip had noticed the small bruises on Henri's tender legs just that morning, and Mrs. Morgan had informed him when questioned that she had seen the nurse "encouraging" the child to feed more steadily with "gentle" pinching. A quick survey of the other servants revealed that the nurse had several times left the child unattended while she went down to stuff herself in the kitchen and was seldom known to change his diapers.

"What will you do now?" asked Agnes.

"I've been asking myself that all morning," replied Phillip, moving a crepe to his plate. He had taken advantage of his father's absence to request French crepes of their cook. They were among her specialties, but the Duke forbid them on the grounds of their Frankish origins. Phillip also took the liberty of having their meal served in the parlor because, as he explained it, the dining room wallpaper—a dark, peacock-laden pattern selected a few years earlier by Mrs. Morgan— robbed him of his appetite.

"It crossed my mind that your visit is no coincidence, and I dared hope that you both might help me think of something. Of course, there is the orphanage at Newbury but I know nothing about it."

"Could you do that?" Agnes wondered aloud.

"Well, I assume they must take in any child who has no parents."

Vera stirred her lemonade. "Of course, since the child is not yours, you have no actual responsibility toward him. But we might wonder if the orphanage is the right place for him."

Phillip put down his food and waved his arms. "I have no other resource! I trust no one here to look after him properly. I wish there were someone I could give him to, but whom? He is of unknown but obviously mixed parentage. Not much of a pedigree there, poor little devil."

"Speaking of pedigree," put in Vera, changing direction, "we have our own unexpected charges just arrived at Brookside." She told about the delivery of Empress and Napoleon that morning, which led to (with a nod from Agnes) a summary of where they stood with the disposition of Brookside, its contents, and its staff. As Vera talked, Phillip reached for Agnes's hand. Feeling the pressure of his consoling grip, tears formed in her eyes. How often it happens that strong people can trudge through terrible trials dry-eyed, but let someone squeeze their hand or enclose them in a simple embrace, and the sorrow spills out. Phillip wrapped an arm around Agnes's shoulder as she cried quietly.

"It seems," he observed as Vera concluded, "that we are both of us mired in crisis."

"But yours," Agnes managed, struggling to recover herself, "is more immediate than ours. The child needs to be fed today."

"I see only one solution, although it is a temporary one," Vera said boldly. "You say there is no one you trust him with in your household. Well, would you trust us? Just until you can make proper arrangements for him, of course."

Agnes looked at Vera with a mixture of joy and terror. Phillip looked from one to the other.

"Are you sure?"

"Well, I've given this no thought. It simply struck me that little Henri needs someone and we are here. It might not work at all. Neither Agnes nor I have any first-hand experience with babies, and neither does Stella. However, I am sure we can count on someone at our house who will know just what to do, and that is the indomitable Mrs. Williams." Vera looked triumphantly at Agnes.

Brookside's head housekeeper possessed knowledge that stretched beyond the boundary of keeping a mansion clean and beautiful. She had lost her husband in the war after only two years of marriage and no children. Her grief drove her to action, and she poured herself into ministering to mothers struggling through those years without their husbands. After a brief course in home nursing, she busied herself making the rounds of households run by overwhelmed women, dispensing instruction on efficient household management and proper hygiene and rocking fussy babies while their exhausted mothers slept. After the war ended, she accepted the position at Brookside, but Mrs. Somerset encouraged her to continue her home visits to struggling families every Saturday. Only recently had she given up this mission as her aging back made it too difficult to ride around the countryside in all weather, climbing in and out of carriages and picking up sturdy children.

"This would be magnificent," beamed Phillip. "I did not dare ask such a thing of you. It will put you in a delicate situation to take this child in. You know how people are."

"At this point," smiled Agnes, rising, "we haven't much to lose, have we? Let's take the little thing with us and see what we can do."

And so Agnes and Vera left Fellcrest with baby Henri, a pile of cottons that the staff had cut for diapers, and the few gowns they had so far been able to sew for him. The cook provided a hard biscuit dipped in molasses for the baby to suck on and, bundled in a light blanket, he took his place on Agnes's lap for the ride to Brookside.

"God bless you both," said Phillip. "I will come to see you tomorrow." The ladies left with full hearts and a rush of purpose, so different from their faltering spirits of only that morning. As for Phillip, it did not strike him until he was waving goodbye that he had already broken his promise to himself to stay clear of Agnes and not burden her a moment longer with himself or his trouble.

It was nearly three o'clock when the ladies got home with their new acquisition, found Mrs. Williams, and told her what had happened. "I'm going into town!" cried the housekeeper. "Get the carriage ready, and don't lose any time," she barked to Fettles. While bustling to fetch her hat, gloves, and purse, she explained that she meant to find in the Chesterton shops some of the new infant formula they had started making. "Not as good as mother's milk, of course, but he's not ready for cow's milk. I believe we still have a baby bed?"

"Oh, yes, mine is in the attic," said Agnes, letting the baby chew on her finger. The biscuit had not lasted long. "We can set up the nursery again, but we'll need bed sheets."

Mrs. Williams promised to get everything necessary. She left them with instructions to take an old handkerchief, fill a narrow bit of it with chopped apple, tie it off, and let the child chew on that. "And for heaven's sake," she ordered over her shoulder, "change that diaper and oil his bottom!"

# Part IV.  A La Coquette

# Chapter 48

Wilbur wanted one more chance. It was still possible, with a short run of luck, to win back part of what he had lost. Not enough to save Brookside or his own Montefiore at this point, but enough to stand Eleanor and him in good stead for a few years if they lived modestly.

Staying in Paris was too risky. Some Somerset acquaintance might be there, taking in the sights, and he might just stumble across them at a carriage stop or bistro. Marseilles, on the other hand—hot, raucous, smelly Marseilles—should be quite safe from tourists of their class. It stood at a manageable distance from his preferred casinos, and would be cheaper as well.

Eleanor could stay in her room and pout; it did not bother him any more what she thought. They no longer spoke, anyway, except when necessary. And this would be a good place to get rid of Morel, Wilbur's solicitor, who had been tagging along across the Atlantic, looking over his shoulder the entire way. The man could no doubt take up some sort of trade in this port city, fleecing sailors and fishwives in some new and rewarding way.

The Wilbur Browns checked in to a small but snobbish hotel that managed to fall short of expectations in every way. For once, Wilbur did not fuss, knowing that their stay would be brief. After they had rested for a few days, they would swing through the south of France and on to Italy, where one could live a long time on next to nothing. For now the couple made themselves as comfortable as possible in their second-floor *chamber à deux* with two sagging beds, a large cracked window, and a thick layer of dust protecting every surface.

Eleanor closed the thin drapes, wetted a washcloth, and stretched herself out on one of the beds. Placing the cloth over her eyes, she said flatly, "Bring me the headache powder from my gray bag and a glass of something, if you can manage it."

Her husband chose to ignore the condescension and placed the requested items on the gritty table beside her. "A big one?" he asked.

"They are the only kind I get any more."

Wilbur's question, far from being one of solicitude, sprang from practicality. If Eleanor was having one of her small headaches, she would be up and around (and possibly in the way) in about an hour. If, on the other hand, she was suffering a major attack involving a full complement of artillery, she might lie low for an entire day and night, sometimes two. In this way, he would be able to pursue his pleasures unimpeded and unquestioned.

Wilbur looked down at his motionless wife, his thumbs tucked into his vest pockets. After so many long days of confinement with her on the ship and then the train, he could now stretch his legs and escape her beady eye. "I'll have them send supper up in a bit," he told her. "I am going out exploring. Don't wait up for me."

"Why on earth would I do that?" she returned in a monotone.

"That's my Eleanor." He splashed some water on his face, combed his hair, and went downstairs, telling the concierge to send up dinner for one at suppertime with no frills. Wilbur had passed through Marseilles once before, as a young man. The brutality of the place attracted him, but the heat and the color confounded his senses. After taking a short tour of the docks he wandered up and down a few streets where people were beginning to reemerge as the sun retreated. He stopped at a small shop to buy a map of the city—he liked maps very much—and a pocketknife. (He had lost his knife, a beautiful little weapon that Eleanor had bought him years ago, in a game of after-dinner blackjack just the day before on the train.) The stocky merchant polished the folding blade on his shirttail before handing the knife to Wilbur.

"Monsieur would like the tobacco maybe? Some whisky?"

"No, thank you."

The man counted Wilbur's change slowly into his hand. "Monsieur likes the ladies?"

Wilbur looked at the shopkeeper for the first time. The merchant's pale eyes were veiled in cataracts and surrounded by sun-toughened skin. His smile revealed three teeth, all of them brown.

"Why do you ask?" Wilbur asked. He was stalling. To answer the man's simple question—*do you like ladies?*—would have required the explanations of several men learned in the mental sciences and familiar with Mr. Brown's numerous peccadilloes.

"We have many nice women here in Marseilles." The man continued to smile.

The basic truth was that Wilbur did not like ladies much at all. He found them "too frothy" and quite suffocating. They were always wanting some demonstration of affection, pulling on your hand, asking where you were going, or making some silly comment that betrayed their low intelligence. Eleanor had been a rare find—serious, a woman who kept to herself for the most part and demanded no romance or petting. Still, Wilbur liked to look at women. He even enjoyed, for reasons he could not explain, indulging in brief physical contact now and then.

He pocketed his change. "Whom do you recommend?"

The merchant waved his stiff hand in a circular motion. "*Ah, il y en a beaucoup*. There are many to recommend. Maybe you start at La Coquette for a dinner and the show. His ladies dance very nice, and the best of them all is his new girl, La Violette."

"Indeed," replied Wilbur. "And where would I find this establishment?"

The merchant gave Wilbur directions. "You tell Monsieur Vaudin that Emile sent you, yes?"

"Of course," returned Wilbur, pausing at the door. "You receive a commission, no doubt. I would not expect you to make do on what you get overcharging travelers for maps and tobacco." Wilbur smiled at the confusion on the merchant's face before he turned sharply and exited.

Wilbur did not need to consult his pocket watch to know that it was nearly time for dinner. The long shadows in the square told him that the day was drawing down. After a quick look at the map, he directed his steps toward the dance hall. This will probably be a disappointment, he thought, both visually and gastronomically, but it will at least be something new. On the way, he amused himself by picturing the famous La Violette, building her into a lithe, towering creature whose beauty might be irresistible were it not for some critical flaw that the locals were willing to overlook. Turning a corner, he spied the telltale sign hanging just a few yards ahead, the white wooden half-leg painted with the words *La Coquette* in deep red. His heart quickened, and with his habitual glance right and left, he entered.

The place was already filling up. Sailors stood in knots drinking at the polished bar that ran along one side of the room. The bottled-up smell of seamen nearly drove Wilbur back outside, but he wiped a scented handkerchief across his nose and stood his ground. To the right was a scatter of tables where some were eating in silence and others played cards. Wilbur noticed the large pile of coins in the middle of one table and made a note to come back the next night with some cash. A dark urchin approached him and offered to take his hat. Wilbur looked down on him, confident that the child did not speak English.

"You'd like to take this, wouldn't you, and give me back some pauper's broken derby. *No, merci.*"

The child's large brown eyes searched Wilbur's face, unsure what to do. He looked to the barkeep for help, who snapped something in Arabic, causing the boy to dive into the background. Wilbur walked to the rear of the room where a heavy red curtain hung, and parted it with a finger. Tables and chairs cluttered the floor in front of a low stage. He felt a tap on his back.

"Monsieur would like to see the show?" A capable-looking man, clear-eyed and soberly dressed, was asking in English.

"Possibly. What does it consist of?"

"Monsieur will enjoy the most beautiful girls in Marseilles, dancing in a most pleasing way. And, of course, you may take your dinner and drinks while you watch. Our food is excellent."

"I doubt that." Wilbur looked back at the dim stage. "How long until the show starts?"

"In one hour. If I may ask, did someone recommend us to Monsieur?"

Wilbur smiled. "No, I was just passing by."

"Very good. Monsieur might like some *rouge* and a game of chance while he waits?" The man, who was none other than Monsieur Vaudin himself, proprietor, pointed with a glance toward the card players.

Suddenly remembering the new knife in his pocket, Wilbur realized that a game might not be out of the question. He joined a table of decently dressed men eating sardines with one hand while holding their cards in the other. A serving girl was just delivering another bottle of wine. She put a glass in front of him and poured, smiling in that empty way that saloon girls do. Wilbur anted in with small coins and was dealt an outstanding hand. He bet low, matching the others, exchanged one card that magically gave him a full house, and threw in the pocket knife when his turn came around. Its value declared and proven by the bill of sale he displayed, two players chose to see his bet. Wilbur spread his hand on the dark wooden tabletop. The gamblers leaned in to examine it, three kings and two tens, then turned their cards face down and pushed them to the middle. Thus began a lucky evening of cards for Mr. Brown during which he not only kept his new knife but won enough to buy dinner, two bottles of wine, admission to the show, and a return to La Coquette the next day for another go.

Before he knew it, an hour had elapsed. Monsieur Vaudin announced that the show was about to begin and collected the small fee required from each customer as they passed through the red curtain. Wilbur ordered lamb and potatoes and, for the sake of adventure, a glass of rum along with a bottle of decent wine, and took a seat at the foot of the stage. As he waited he remembered Eleanor alone in their hotel room and hoped her headache was continuing in full force.

# Chapter 49

The tobacco seller and the Monsieur Vaudin proved equally correct: Wilbur was not disappointed. The ladies were all acceptably pretty with their makeup, and they revealed enough of their persons to keep his interest. But the six girls kicking up their legs through the warm-up paled beside the main attraction, La Violette. Although much smaller than he had expected, she was as beautiful as she was exotic, mysterious but at the same time intimate. Wilbur felt himself darkly drawn to her as she performed her restrained yet suggestive dance, and when the show concluded, he signaled Monsieur Vaudin with a finger. The owner informed him that yes, he could invite Mademoiselle Violette to his table for a drink and conversation, but they had another show in thirty minutes. Wilbur pressed a bill into his hand, which the owner did not refuse.

Presently the girl emerged from backstage and walked self-consciously among scattered cheers to Mr. Brown's table. He drew back a chair for her and she sat with her hands in her lap, looking down. Wilbur studied her face, framed in a sheer orange scarf, and thought how much more beautiful she would be without the paint. He liked especially her full mouth and luxurious black lashes.

"Mademoiselle, your dance was marvelous. Some wine?" Wilbur asked her in French.

La Violette raised her eyes slightly and smiled, and he poured her a half-glass from the open bottle. She made no move toward it.

"Where are you from?" he pursued.

"From India." Her voice was a high and delicate, like the song of a small bird.

"From the south, I assume," Wilbur ventured, judging by her dark skin.

"Hyderabad." On this one point, she always told the truth. Hyderabad was a large region, and she felt no risk in naming the place of her birth, a hot, colorful world she sometimes missed with a longing that pierced her heart.

Wilbur turned the word over in his mind. It was familiar. Suddenly he remembered.

"Hyderabad. Quite a famine you had there a while back, eh? Drove you out, I suppose."

She took a sip of the wine, barely wetting her lips. "Monsieur knows much about my country."

"Not really." Wilbur sat back, his arm stretched across the table and his hand wrapped around his glass. "I happen to know a fellow who came back from your area not long ago. Failed missionary. Told about the famine and the heartless Brits and all that sort of thing. Don't suppose you know him." Wilbur laughed as the wine and rum began to loosen him, enjoying the absurd idea of her knowing the one man he knew who had traipsed briefly through India.

She glanced at him for the first time. "It is unlikely."

"It's preposterous," Wilbur returned gaily. "Lord Phillip, vagrant extraordinaire."

La Violette looked up at him, her brilliantly painted lips falling open. Wilbur, however, was too caught up in his own amusing reflections to notice.

"He is a friend of yours?" she managed to ask.

"Good Lord, no. Met him at a party. Lives near my cousin with his doting father. Poor devil—things seem to be turning out rather badly for him. I heard just before departing for this charming shore that he made a false move while trying to convert the heathens, got a bit too close to one. The girl's father tracked him down and showed up in a most embarrassing way with a child for him. Great scandal. Who cares?"

Wilbur emptied the wine bottle into his glass. "I should like to spend more time with you, La Violette." He enunciated her name precisely. "Shall I talk with your employer?"

When she did not answer, he noticed finally that she was gripping the edge of the table.

"What's wrong?" he asked shortly. There was no reason he should understand why, for Violette, the room was tilting crazily while a hundred sensations rushed upon her.

The girl drew a breath and looked at him. "The wine is not good for me, I think. May I ask, what happened to the missionary man and the baby?"

"You women always want to know how the story ends, don't you? I've no idea. He's probably looking for some softhearted woman, like my dear cousin, who will take it off his hands. Or he's dropping it at the nearest orphanage, if he has any sense."

La Violette got to her feet and excused herself, stammering that it was almost time for the next show, and nearly ran from the room. Wilbur waved over Monsieur Vaudin once more and asked how he might arrange for some time with the young woman in private.

The proprietor stiffened and informed Wilbur that he misunderstood. His girls were professional performers. This was not a *maison close*. They were not available to the customers for any other services—at any price, he added, as Wilbur pulled the roll of winnings from his pocket.

"Ridiculous!" Wilbur muttered as he rose. Pushing his hat onto his head, he walked unsteadily out the door. Backstage, Rupa would not tell the girls why she was crying. Gasping for breath between strangled sobs, she could not have spoken if she wanted to. They patted her shoulder and did not press her. Each of them had reasons to cry and none that they would want to explain.

# Chapter 50

What a joy it is when man's inventiveness produces something truly needed. Mrs. Williams returned from town with ten bottles of Mr. Nestlé's miraculous new infant formula, which was all the Chesterton Market had on hand. She proceeded to mix some with boiled water and filled a baby bottle with it. Agnes and Vera watched closely as she fitted the bottle with a rubber nipple, then Agnes gratefully handed her the screaming baby. Sitting down in a kitchen chair, the housekeeper offered the substitute breast to the squirming child in her arms. So great was his distress that he entirely ignored the nipple she touched to his open mouth. She rocked and clucked and coaxed, but little Henri only wailed with renewed vigor as Agnes, Vera, Stella, Fettles, and Dahlia stood together watching anxiously.

"He doesn't know what it is," said Mrs. Williams over the din. "Dahlia, get the molasses."

Dahlia pulled down the jar of sweet, thick syrup and swabbed the nipple generously. Mrs. Williams offered it again, touching it to the baby's tongue. Gradually his little mouth closed around it and his sobs trailed off as he began to suck. The onlookers clutched one another in relief, and Vera started to send up a cheer until Mrs. Williams stopped her with a finger to her lips. The famished child drained the bottle to within the last ounce before falling asleep against the good lady's comfortable bosom. One little arm lay across his chest, the other dangled free, and in this silent state he looked like an angel in their midst. Mrs. Williams threw a kitchen cloth over her shoulder, put the child against it, and patted him gently. A bubble of gas escaped his parted lips, and satisfied, she rose carefully and took him upstairs to bed.

Agnes, Vera, and Stella followed her on tiptoe and stood around the crib watching his sleeping form. Agnes whispered to her housekeeper, "How will we hear him when he wakes up?"

"Oh," replied Mrs. Williams, "we'll all be checking on him, won't we? I'll move into the adjoining room so that I'll hear him at night."

Agnes protested, but Mrs. Williams put up her hand and would not allow any discussion. "Only for this first week," she warned. "After that you ladies can manage everything yourselves."

Stella followed Mrs. Williams out of the nursery, but Vera held Agnes back. "Agnes," she said quietly, "the formula is expensive. Mrs. Williams says he will drink a lot of it, and at fifty cents a bottle the cost will mount quickly. I'll leave you some money for it, and don't scrimp. In a couple of months she says he'll be ready to try cow's milk. But by then you will probably have found another arrangement, God willing."

Agnes looked at the tiny boy, his fist curled beside his tranquil face, the black hair lying in careless disarray about his head. Another arrangement. What would that be? The orphanage? Or maybe Phillip would take him back. She put a hand on his warm head and felt her heart sink.

"Don't get attached to him," warned Vera gently. "He may disappear to another home before we know it."

Agnes sighed and assured her that she herself was simply caring for this child as any Christian would, nothing more. She had no plans to attach herself to one more thing that might soon be snatched from her.

The week passed quickly. Each day Mrs. Williams gave the three ladies pointers on handling a baby and feeding, diapering, and washing it. Stella observed each operation closely and took every opportunity to practice on little Henri. It made the advent of her own child more real, she said, and her excitement was obvious. She talked more and more about her husband William and began arranging her departure. After all, she had used up all her art paper, and traveling to Chicago would only get more difficult for her the longer she waited.

But the first to leave for home was Vera. On the morning of her departure, a few early-turning leaves had already fallen and lay thinly about in a dull yellow scatter. Ned loaded her trunk onto the carriage once goodbyes had been said three times all around, and still the ladies stood on the front steps with little Henri bundled up on Agnes's hip. Vera was promising to return before Thanksgiving. Thanksgiving—the very word sent a twinge through Agnes.

"Better yet," said Vera, "you must come to New York. Get away from all this for a while. I can introduce you to my friends, whose strange situations and dreadful problems can't help but improve your spirits."

Agnes said yes, maybe. In any case, she would certainly be there for Christmas and Vera's wedding. Everyone indulged in one more hug, the tearful aunt kissed the baby again, and Ned helped her into the compartment and closed the door. Agnes and Stella stood in the cool morning air and watched her disappear from sight, feeling her absence already.

Vera had been gone only an hour when Phillip arrived. Every few days he had been stopping by faithfully to inquire about the baby and ask if anything was needed, leaving a stipend even though he was always told that nothing was wanting. These visits were always short and somewhat strained. A cup of tea, remarks about the child's health and feeding habits, pleasantries about the weather and brief reports on Phillip's activities. Then he would be gone. Agnes saw more and more that something had gotten broken between them, like a bone that had been snapped and never set.

This visit was no different but for Phillip's announcement that he himself would be gone for a couple of weeks or so to take charge of a small farm to the north that he and his father had just acquired. He handed Agnes a packet containing funds sufficient for the care of the child until his return. Although the boy was not his, he repeated, he was at present responsible for his maintenance and was deeply in debt to Agnes and her family for their care of him. He was earnestly searching for a permanent home for the child and would relieve Agnes of him as soon as possible.

Agnes walked outside with him and watched as he swung up onto his horse. Standing just a few feet from him she felt a yawning chasm between them. It had become impossible to picture touching him again, sitting wrapped in his arms, kissing his mouth. From his saddle Phillip gave her a long look. For a moment she saw the old Phillip, his eyes full of a thousand thoughts yet to be spoken, a promise of brilliance, a deep well of sweet affection waiting to be plumbed. Then he vanished, and the sad and preoccupied man returned to wave farewell and ride away.

The next day the rain began in earnest and continued for two weeks. Agnes and Stella sat inside like new prisoners unused to confinement, now and then walking to the front door and looking out at the puddled drive, wondering how deep the clouds were and how far they stretched west and how distant was a clear blue sky. They tried to remember the feel of fair weather, dry garden paths dotted with shade, soft grass to sit on, the warm slate of the terrace in late afternoon.

Agnes's thoughts often strayed to the mother of the child in her arms. She wondered how a woman, even a frightened one without resources, could leave her own child behind. But Rupa must be still a child herself, trying blindly to survive by her own wits. Where did she go after leaving the convent? Was she even still alive? How much of her sad story would this child ever know?

Then the renewed patter of drops striking the windows brought her back. Henri's teeth had begun to push through his tender gums, turning the sweet baby into a fussy, whimpering thing who could not be pleased. Through the long hours of these soggy days, Agnes and Stella took turns picking him up and walking slowly through the dim rooms.

# Chapter 51

A man alone on the night streets of Marseilles was not necessarily in peril. Even if he were unsure of the way back to his hotel, he had little to fear if he kept his wits about him or if his obvious poverty told thieves he was not worth robbing. However, a well-dressed stranger who swayed as he wandered the tight streets, each of which appeared in the dark very much like the one before—a man who had just won an enviable sum at a poker table—this man ran a good chance of falling into mischief before reaching the bed he so keenly longed for.

Wilbur, on this late summer night, with a light salty breeze blowing in from the sea, was just such a man. Indeed, the night was so pleasant that he hardly minded that he seemed to be getting no closer to his destination no matter how many blocks he walked. The wine and rum—of which he had imbibed considerably more after leaving La Violette and stopping into a bar a few doors down—had worked together to dull his sensibilities and tranquilize his habitual suspicion so that he did not notice the three shadows dogging his steps at a precise distance.

If we were there to watch the progress of these silent Corsicans, who had followed their prey out of La Coquette, we might well imagine that they were only waiting until they reached a sufficiently dark and deserted part of the city to engage the gentleman in a short debate as to who should most properly be in possession of the roll of bills that filled his trouser pocket. The trio might also have wished to relieve him of the heavy silver pocket watch they had seen him consult more than once during the evening.

Fortunately for our little band, Wilbur eventually strayed into just such a quarter as befit these transactions. Mr. Brown paused on a dreary corner and pulled out the watch just mentioned, straining to see in the pale moonlight that the hands pointed to ten minutes past two. It was at this moment that his attention was arrested by the sharp end of an object pressing much too harshly against his lower back, while two pairs of strong hands gripped his arms, the better to steady him. The man directly behind him spoke a few words that he did not understand, while one large hand closed around his watch and another jerked the chain from its loop. At this Wilbur let out the first quarter note of a shout before another hand, no doubt belonging to the remarkably coarse face that flashed before him, cuffed him squarely under the jaw, indicating that these men preferred the universal language of silent negotiation. Wilbur felt a blow to his stomach that, in combination with the previous one to his chin, brought him fully awake, so he felt with perfect clarity the impact of the brick wall against his spine. Deftly, two of the men emptied his pockets in a blink as he lay against the wall, gasping for breath.

Remembering the knife deep in an inner pocket, Wilbur pushed his hand down inside to see if it was still there. Somehow the men had missed it. He drew it out and opened the blade awkwardly as the companions drifted down the street, seemingly confident that the well-dressed gentleman would be resting for some time in the heap he had fallen into. Wilbur was not ordinarily a brave man—quite the contrary. So it is hard to explain why he chose to gain his feet and follow his new acquaintances, or why, when they turned, he lunged at the ugly one and planted his knife in the man's upper chest. Maybe it was his fury at being robbed, for this was his first experience receiving rather than inflicting that injustice. Maybe he was at the point in his barren life when he no longer cared if it continued another day or not. Or perhaps the alcohol urged him forward in a way his sober mind would never have allowed.

In any case, his rash reprisal was quickly met with a counterattack. All three men, being sentimental creatures at heart, carried long, sharp knives with them at all times, souvenirs from their homeland. While the ugly man fell back to nurse his wound, his companions made quick work of Wilbur, stabbing him once each with an exactitude that testified to their experience in this profession. As Wilbur crumpled with a look of astonishment on his face, the men wiped their blades briefly on his coat, returned them to their sheaths, and hooking arms with their damaged comrade, hurried off into the dark.

It all happened with barely a sound. Wilbur lay across a doorstep looking up at a starry sky, aware only of a creeping coldness in his limbs and an inability to move. After a few moments or hours, he could not tell, he became aware of someone standing beside him. With great effort he turned his head. A man, darker even than the darkness around him, stood as though waiting. Wilbur wondered why this person was here but found he could not speak. Still, the man responded as though he had.

"It's almost time to go," the dark man said quietly. *Where?* Wilbur thought, staring at the face he could not make out.

"Somewhere you have never been but will always be."

*I hate riddles*, Wilbur thought. He could no longer feel his body.

The dark man pulled Wilbur to his feet. He held him up easily and looked deep into his puzzled eyes. "I'm very sorry." He spoke the simple words with such compassion that a thrill of terror ran through Wilbur, a terror that could have filled the universe. Immediately, a powerful whirl of warm but noiseless wind pulled him from that dirty street and the world it lay upon.

In the first gray light of day, a charwoman shuffling toward the counting house of Frères Lafèvre squinted at the dark shape before the door. Coming up to it she cursed and set down the tools of her trade. This would be a fine mess to clean up, she grumbled as she pushed and pulled the stiff, well-dressed gentleman out of the way, unlocked the heavy door, and began the day's chores with more than her customary ill humor. Nearly an hour would pass before a gendarme, walking his usual morning patrol, would find Wilbur and round up a cart to take him to the morgue.

# Chapter 52

Rupa barely got through the second show. Her legs dragged when they should leap, the pert angles of her shoulders drooped miserably, and her eyes met no one's gaze. But the men applauded as always and Monsieur Vaudin said nothing. Back in the dressing room she hurriedly wiped off her makeup and hung up her costume, then ran up the steep, narrow stairs to the safety of her little room. Fortunately the other girls were still downstairs visiting with clients or helping at the bar—they relished the tips that a swish of the hips or a knowing laugh could earn them. Their customers would happily drink and play cards until early morning, when Monsieur Vaudin started blowing out lamps and ushering lingerers out the door.

Rupa flew to her little dresser and pulled out the top drawer. All the way in the back, under a worn out silk scarf, was a tiny ivory box no bigger than a walnut. Her father had given it to her when she was a little girl. She rubbed her finger over the procession of carved elephants marching around the edge of the lid, then opened it and drew out a piece of paper that had been folded many times over. She read the address on it as she had a thousand times before: *Fellcrest, Route 7, Dutchess County, New York, United States*. She refolded the paper tenderly and held it to her chest. How he must be suffering—to have her child delivered to him as though it were his. Imagine what people must be thinking of him. As young as she was, Rupa knew enough to understand that the event may well have shattered his life.

A wave of rage filled her and she clamped her hands to her head. She spun this way and that and, with no outlet for her distress, threw herself against the wall with the little window to the sea. Weeping, she raised her eyes and looked out desperately over the red roofs of the mostly sleeping city. She never dreamed her father would go to such lengths, following their tracks himself, even to America. Foolish, foolish man! Now Phillip was paying for her silence, paying for the wickedness of her brothers. But how could she have told anyone? Her mother would have blamed her, and her father—there was no telling what he might have done in his rage. The whole family would have twisted every which way to avoid facing the truth: that her brothers had handed her over to a stinking British soldier for a little drink. She had seen that soldier before, hanging about the edge of their property with her brothers. They liked him for the gin he shared, and she had caught the big, dirty foreigner more than once eyeing her with a sickening smile. Then came that night . . . She would never forget the smell of him as he came toward her, nor her terror the moment she realized what was about to happen.

She saw again the four of them just inside the doorway to her room, her three brothers looking nervous behind the soldier. She saw his pale skin and matted beard as he stumbled toward her. He had gone too far. Arihant, the eldest, grabbed his arm as the soldier started to pull off her sari, but the large man took out his gun and pointed it at him. Arihant fell back with the others, and all she was aware of was this beast on top of her and the sound of Anil, her youngest brother, sobbing and arguing with Arihant. Viplav, the middle brother, kept his mouth shut as always and did whatever Arihant said.

When it was over and the soldier had shuffled out the door, Arihant threw her clothes at her. He leaned close to her face as she hid herself, crying, behind her hands.

"Look at me, Rupa," he insisted. "Look at me!"

It took all her strength to lower her hands and turn her eyes toward his.

"This did not happen, my little river rat," he whispered. "Do you understand? It was a bad dream, nothing more. I know you won't tell anyone, will you? It would not be good for you." His beautiful brown eyes were fierce and frightened, all at the same time. She knew he would do anything to protect this secret.

"Will you keep quiet or not?" She could smell the alcohol heavy on his breath and slowly nodded. The next day at dinner her father announced her betrothal to Manindra, the notorious local aristocrat. A fine match, he said, the son of a prince—reason to celebrate. Arihant shot her a warning look. No, she would not tell. But she could run away. She would not spend another week in this dreadful home or be traded off to a lunatic nobleman for the rest of her life. This American man Phillip was leaving their house soon, and he was so kind. Maybe he would help her. She had to take the chance.

Now that story must be told, she realized. Rupa calmed herself, breathing in the cool night air, taking control of her thoughts. She must send a letter. Phillip's Hindi was poor, and she knew no English, so she would write in French. Elise the barmaid had been teaching her for months now and said she was learning well. Everyone who was anyone knew French, Elise said, so that would include a high-born man of Phillip's class, surely.

But while Rupa could make herself understood in Marseilles, she could not spell, and she struggled to form the strange letters of this foreign alphabet. She would need Elise's help. And for that, she would have to tell her the story.

The next day Rupa rose earlier than usual and walked to a stationer's to buy a few sheets of paper and an envelope. When Elise arrived for work, Rupa drew her aside and asked the favor. The generous barmaid readily agreed, so the two decided to meet at the city's main post office the following morning, where Elise would write out a letter from Rupa's dictation.

Never having set foot in a post office, Rupa did not know what to expect. Imagining a chaotic scene that would require well-placed bribes to get her mail into the right bag and onto the proper ship, she was surprised to find the main post office in Marseilles a smart and busy place, with polished counters you could write at, complete with pens and bottles of ink, and all kinds of people coming and going with packages of every description. When Elise arrived, they found a corner away from the hustle and bustle, and spread out Rupa's letter paper on a counter.

Rupa looked earnestly at her friend. "What I tell you is not good, Elise. Maybe you will not like me anymore after I tell you. But it is necessary."

Elise looked down at the girl matter-of-factly. "My dear, you can't tell me much that I have not heard or even done myself."

"And you will not tell anyone? Not the other girls or Monsieur Vaudin?"

"Of course not. It's none of their business, is it?"

Rupa relaxed for just a moment to smile in innocent gratitude at her friend, then she began her tale. She interrupted it only once near the start to ask her scribe to please write it down in good French, not in her exact words with all the mistakes (to which Elise, raised by a literary mother until her early death, told her not to worry—that when the letter was finished, Dumas himself would find nothing to quarrel with.)[4]

Eventually they had covered three sheets of paper and said everything Rupa felt necessary. Elise blotted the pages carefully, folded them into the envelope, and inscribed the address from Rupa's little piece of paper. She handed the envelope to Rupa. She had written everything down without comment, and only now, as Elise gave the young girl a tender pat, did Rupa see how sad she looked.

"Take this to the window and send it off," Elise instructed, pointing across the room. "You are a very brave girl." Elise cleared her throat and touched the corner of her eye. "Now I'm off to *La Jambe Pendante* (the *Hanging Leg* had become the staff's name for their cabaret since M. Vaudin's installation of the new sign) "so I will see you soon." With a brisk smile, Elise left Rupa to conclude her business.

Rupa walked to a window where a small, yellowed man sat, smelling strongly of tobacco. He examined the address and stamped the envelope forcefully in the upper corner, then tossed it into a gray sack behind him. Rupa handed over the price demanded, then ventured to ask, "Please, Monsieur, do you know how long it will take?"

"Is it urgent?" snapped the man. Rupa pulled back involuntarily, squeezing her little purse. "If it was urgent, you should have said something," he chided her. The poor girl stared at him, not knowing what to say.

"Well, urgent or not, it's all about the same to America. Two days by train, seven days by ship, then what they do over there, God only knows. So maybe two weeks, maybe three." He sniffed and glared at her as though daring her to ask another question.

Conscious of people now waiting behind her and too afraid to satisfy her curiosity further, Rupa murmured her thanks to the violent little man and hurried away. Three weeks, she thought. So much can happen in three weeks. But it would have to do. She only hoped that the ship carrying her precious letter made it to New York harbor without sinking in the middle of the Atlantic. Two ships had gone down just a week earlier after colliding in a fog, and she wondered now how many important letters and fat packages tied up with loving care had sunk to the bottom with them. At this thought, a gloom settled over her in which she spent the rest of the day. She had to

---

[4] Alexandre Dumas, popular French novelist of the mid-1800s.

believe that her story would reach Phillip and that it would make a difference. Having included no return address—she must not be found— she would never know.

# Chapter 53

Eleanor pulled the damp cloth from her head and very slowly opened her eyes. She knew it was late afternoon by the light slicing between the barely open drapes and by the special quiet outside, when those used to living in a hot climate wait for the sun to slide low so they can finish their chores or simply stroll about the cooling streets. She recalled the sleepy region's motto, *"Deucement le matin, pas trop vite le soir."*[5] Gradually she pushed herself up and lowered her feet to the floor. Yes, the ferocious pain was gone. Only a dull soreness remained and a subtle ache that might simply have been from hunger. She dimly remembered someone knocking at the door the night before, telling her to open up for her dinner, but she had sent him away with something like a threat. So she had eaten nothing for at least twenty-four hours.

She looked at the other bed. Its coverlet was unwrinkled, the pillow still round. Just as I thought, she mused, Wilbur had not returned. She had enjoyed the quiet, but had to admit that it was unusual for her husband to be gone on a foray this long. He usually stumbled back around dawn and collapsed into bed. Once he was gone for two days, but that was because he had gone to gamble in a neighboring town and lost everything, including coach fare, and had to walk home, an experience which included spending the night under a tree and very nearly being attacked by an owl.

Eleanor washed her face and arranged her hair. She would have a meal downstairs and then find the baths. Nothing was more salutary after a bout with such pain than a gentle scrubbing and a soak in warm saltwater. Putting on hat and gloves, she descended the main staircase in search of the dining room. She found the room empty aside from a short man in a long apron spreading white tablecloths. Clearly she was too early for dinner, so she addressed herself to the front desk, inquiring in flawless French where she might find a quality bathhouse. The round, pale clerk with crooked spectacles referred her two blocks away, assuring her that it was the very best in town. He pulled a coupon from below the counter, imprinted with the

---

[5] Gently in the morning, and not too fast come evening.

hotel's name, added his initials in the corner, and urged her to present it for extra special treatment. And he hoped she would return for dinner, served at seven, tonight featuring a seafood bouillabaisse—the house specialty—with sweet melon.

Eleanor took a deep breath, delighted at the prospect of a good bath followed by a hearty meal, and walked to the door. A small sign posted just beside it made her stop. The word *Attention* appeared in bold letters across the top, so she paused with one hand on the door and read the short notice. All travelers were advised to be cautious after dark in consequence of the murder of a gentleman, possibly American, in the Faubourg Gastonnier, most probably at the hands of foreigners, who remained at large. Any information regarding the crime or the identity of the gentleman would be most appreciated. Kindly report any and all knowledge to the Prefecture of Police, rue Saint Etienne.

A gentleman, possibly American. She looked back toward the counter. The bespectacled man was bent over a ledger, making notations. Eleanor retraced her steps.

"Excuse me, Monsieur." The round man straightened, marking his place with a finger.

"Do you happen to know any more about the incident reported on the notice there?"

"I can only tell you what the gendarme who posted it this afternoon told me. The deceased was a man about two meters tall, lean, with graying hair. He wondered if we were missing anyone of that description. I told him," the man recounted with a look of satisfaction, "that physical descriptions of our guests are not the sort of thing we record in our books. And since I was on leave the last two days, I could not answer for the attributes of our clients who had checked in during that time."

Eleanor made sure her face reflected the fact that she found nothing exceptionally clever in what the clerk had told the officer. "How did they know he was American?"

"I asked the same thing," declared the man. "They said his clothes all had American labels, New York City, I believe. But the boots were English."

Eleanor stared at the man. Like an avalanche, one mighty thought fell upon her mind: While she lay in bed waiting out her headache,

Wilbur may have moved from being the nettlesome man who strutted and smirked and burned through their fortune to the softened and harmless status of the past tense. *His clothes all had American labels, New York City, I believe. But the boots were English.* Those silly boots he insisted on buying the last time they were in London even though he had three fine pairs in his trunk. And his clothes, all from Percy Haberdashers on Sixth Avenue—for years the only tailors he would buy from.

"Does Madame possibly know the gentleman?" The clerk's voice came from far away.

She hesitated only a second. "No, I don't believe so. Thank you."

Eleanor found the baths as good as the clerk had promised and more. As she lounged in the briny tub, inhaling the sharply scented steam, the accumulated anxiety of the past year melted into the water. It did not matter that soon her money would be gone. She would have to find another man quickly or work—a fate that, until this moment, had horrified her more than any other. Either way, she would wake every morning without having to set eyes on Wilbur Brown. Of course, this was only if his really was the corpse lying on ice in the Marseilles morgue. He might walk into the hotel tonight and fall into bed, only temporarily the worse for wear. But something told Eleanor that he was dead, and she was alone in this gritty town, indeed, in the entire world.

She turned over in her mind matter-of-factly how she might determine if this were true. Should she go to the morgue and ask to see the body? They would want identification. She would have to fill out paperwork and answer questions. No, that was impossible. Maybe she should conduct her own private investigation. But where would she begin? He could have struck off in any direction that night. She decided to wait a few more days and trust that his absence would confirm his fate.

She arrived at the hotel dining room at seven o'clock precisely, freshly dressed and wonderfully famished. The maitre d'hotel bowed and asked if her husband would be joining her.

"No," she smiled, "I am dining alone tonight." At a small table by the window, she took her time over each course, savoring the Mediterranean flavors, enjoying a glass of sweet wine that Wilbur would never have allowed (sweet grapes were a waste of vineyard space, he maintained), and altogether taking twice as long as she ever had at dinner with her husband. His nerves always propelled them forward to the next thing, whatever that was, before coffee could be served. When the dessert cart rolled up, she examined each magnificent confection before pointing to the largest one, a tart covered in berries and rich cream, and ordered a *café au lait*. She pushed her fork slowly into the tart, splitting a strawberry in two. In her mind Wilbur grew more certainly dead with each delicious mouthful.

# Part V. The Bells of St. Monica's

# Chapter 54

We sometimes find that those things we fought most fiercely become the very delight of our days—if our pride does not keep us from changing course. So it was for Fettles and the unwelcome kennel guests. For the first several days of their residence, Empress and Napoleon drew only burning glances from the butler, who saw them as a daily reminder of their felonious owners. He did his best to ignore the animals as Isaiah took them for daily runs or let them lap thirstily from the fountain. Still, this alert man could not help but notice when, by degrees, the dogs stopped running and only padded about listlessly until Isaiah led them, heads down, back to the kennel. Fettles, with his heart as soft as a feather pillow, began to worry despite himself as the dogs grew gloomy and the days turned cooler.

One morning, just after dressing, he crept to the kennel as the sky was lightening. He found the pair half buried in the straw and tight against each other. Picking up a new scent, they raised their heads and looked at him, but did not venture forth from their nest. Summoning his courage—Fettles had no natural affinity for animals—he stepped slowly toward them and crouched down on his heels. To his surprise, Napoleon stretched his head forward and laid his narrow chin on the butler's bony knee. From this simple expression of gentlemanly good will, Fettles drew the conclusion that the animals were far smarter than he had thought all along. After stroking their heads and speaking words of encouragement, he left the kennel determined to improve their situation before another night fell.

The sun was up by now and the sparkling dew lay heavy upon the lawn. As he trudged to the house, he was surprised to see Stella, wrapped in a shawl, walking slowly across the terrace, lost in contemplation of the scene before her.

"You're up very early," chirped Fettles as he stepped up to join her. "Fine morning."

"It is incredible, isn't it? It was getting hard to believe we would ever see the sun again."

"That's very true. So much rain is bad for the joints and bad for the spirits."

"Fettles, I'm leaving next week. I've already written to William—he wants to come out and accompany me home. But I hate to tell Agnes. Everyone has left, and now me."

Fettles' heart sank within him. "Our house does seem to grow quieter every week. If it weren't for the baby, of course. And Lord Phillip, I trust, will soon find him a home and take him away as well."

Stella turned her pale blue eyes earnestly upon the butler. "I think she should keep him, don't you? We have all grown so attached to him—I wish I could take him myself. It will be horrid to give him away."

"Miss Stella, you have a great heart, much like your aunt. But it wouldn't do to keep the little fellow. It would be quite impossible, you know."

Stella frowned and turned back to the brightening landscape, where here and there a rabbit nibbled its breakfast lit by the long rays of early light. "I shall miss this place so much." Her voice was almost a whisper. "I can't believe that I may never see it again. How is it possible that some other family will live in these rooms and play games on the lawn? They'll carry in their furniture and plant things in all the wrong places. It's too sad, Fettles," she said, looking at him as her eyes brimmed with tears, as though asking him to say that it need not be so. But he was fighting down a lump in his own throat, and all he could do was take her hand.

They stood gazing at the luxurious piece of Earth that would surely go on without any of them. But exactly how they would all go on without it confounded them into silence, and it was not until Isaiah noisily threw open the kennel door to let the dogs out that they started from their reverie and went wordlessly in to breakfast.

Thoughts of how to approach his mistress regarding the dogs kept Fettles' mind busy the entire morning. He played through a dozen different scenes, discarding one after another. He consulted Mr. Somerset's collection of books on dog breeds and their characteristics, mentally noting the winning attributes of the greyhound as well as the warnings about their need for warmth, stability, and their master's company. He sought out Ned and asked how near he was to finding the dogs a home. Fettles was surprised at his own gladdening when Ned replied that so far no one had expressed an interest.

If it weren't for Agnes being allergic to animals, the butler's task would have been easier. But since she was a child, his mistress was reduced to misery in the company of cats and horses and their band of hounds. She had long ago forbid any animal in the house, allowing only small caged birds. Still, Fettles had built his arguments, and something had to be done.

After lunch he found Agnes in the music room, playing the piano softly to little Henri, who sat in his chair in the sunshine of a tall window, chewing on a little rag doll Marie had fashioned for him. As she finished the sonata, Fettles stepped forward and cleared his throat.

He excused himself for raising the topic, and certainly she might be surprised after his earlier misapprehension, he admitted, but he had noticed a change for the worse in the dogs, and a little research explained why it was so, and an improvement in their situation might be effected with little stress on the household, and after all, he was sure Agnes would agree that bringing them into the house was the humane thing to do.

Agnes looked at him blankly. "Fettles, you're serious."

Fettles tried to straighten himself, but being already in a posture of the greatest possible rectitude, he settled for raising his chin. "I am, Madam."

"What about my allergies?"

"Madam, the breed is short-haired and sheds little. I have read that many people who cannot tolerate other breeds are perfectly comfortable with the greyhound."

"Has no one responded to Ned's posting?"

"No one, ma'm." Fettles locked his fingers and looked at her with deep concern. "They don't look well at all. Ned says they barely eat. They need human contact, Miss Agnes. Apparently it's in their nature. I know you have been terribly occupied with the affairs of the estate and with the baby. It's no wonder and no shame that you have not noticed their condition, especially with their coming to us uninvited as they did—indeed, ever so much more than uninvited. But

I feel a short trial in the house would show us whether a change in surroundings would improve their health."

Agnes ran her fingers thoughtfully over the intricate gold lettering above the smooth ivory keys. "What about the baby?" she asked, looking at Henri as he leaned out of his chair to study the doll he had dropped. "I don't trust them around him. We don't know how they'll react. They might see him as a large possum."

"They are intelligent creatures," Fettles assured her. "But your caution is wise. We could keep them in the kitchen."

"That hardly sounds sanitary."

Fettles thought. "The library?"

"They might chew the books."

"My room, perhaps."

"So much for company—you're never in your room. You barely sleep."

Fettles had run out of ideas. Agnes took pity on him and offered him the kitchen if he could work it out with Dahlia, and under no circumstances were they to be fed anything intended for the family or staff.

So began an unlikely friendship between man and beast. Within forty-eight hours of being admitted to the cheery warmth of the great kitchen, with its comforting activity from early morning until well after dark, with its nourishing smells and constant chatter, Empress and Napoleon showed undeniable signs of improvement. They both began eating again (even, despite Agnes's strict prohibition, tidbits of meat that somehow fell from the table while carving) and once again displayed their original energy on their morning runs. Napoleon, by some means that could not be discerned, understood that Fettles was his savior and rose to greet him whenever he entered the kitchen— which was very often these days. Empress took the new situation as her due, and while she watched everyone and everything attentively, displayed no particular gratitude for her happier lot in life.

One afternoon Agnes and Stella were coming downstairs with their arms full of old gowns and coats for the poorhouse, when they spied Fettles walking briskly through the foyer with Napoleon at his side.

"Fettles!" cried Agnes with an inquiring look that was not without reproach.

"Ah," replied the butler, "I was just taking him back to the kitchen. He somehow slipped out."

Agnes looked at him coolly. Fettles was a poor liar.

"He seems to have adopted me, madam," Fettles confessed, patting the dog's neck. "He stays by the kitchen door for the longest time after I leave and sometimes sets to whining. It strains Dahlia's nerves."

Agnes turned to Stella. "Can you take the pair home with you? Wouldn't William like some dogs?"

"Oh, no," cried Fettles involuntarily. "That is, I'm sure they could not find a better home than yours, Miss Stella. It's just that, with a baby on the way, this might not be the best time to introduce a pair of animals into your household."

Agnes approached man and dog and stood looking down at the hound, who gazed up at her brightly. "Have they made any messes inside?"

"No, not one," enthused Fettles. "They are very tidy animals."

Agnes considered. "Keep him away from the baby."

"I guarantee it," Fettles replied, clasping his hands together. "Thank you, ma'm."

From that day forward Fettles was seldom seen without the black-and-white canine hugging his side or trailing just behind, as though eager to assist him in any duties that a creature with four legs and no hands might be capable of.

# Chapter 55

While the last three months had seen people leaving Brookside in a steady stream of fastened trunks and wistful encouragements, one person had just arrived. William had come from Chicago to take his wife home. To Stella's surprise, he had made the offer himself to come and accompany her; indeed, he had insisted upon it despite her telling him that she was quite well and did not want to be the cause of any interruption in his business.

Great was his surprise when he saw his little Stella grown to such a diameter in his absence. To his wife's delight, William laughed and threw his arms around her and congratulated her on doing "such a first-rate job" of bringing their little one along. (The two made a darling pair, he a slim, strapping German just over six feet tall, and she barely grazing the five-foot mark.) This conjugal celebration was a joyful relief from the gloom that had settled upon the house, and everyone caught the spirit. It lasted a blessed three days while William remained with them, telling harrowing stories about the meatpacking trade, recounting the wonders of Chicago, and passing along such jokes as were suitable for ladies' ears.

Stella, like all the women of the household, had in her heart adopted little Henri and took pains to show off his most lovable features and precocious accomplishments to her husband. Her own growing child within her had lately provoked new pains in her lower back that kept Stella from holding Henri for more than a few minutes these days. But in fact, he wriggled so, struggling to be let down to explore on his own, that it had become difficult for anyone to hold him for long. The ladies usually put him into his little wheeled chair that he pushed around the room with his smooth, bare feet, crying for rescue whenever he worked himself into a corner. Empress, who had tired of the kitchen routine and somehow gained the run of the house along with Napoleon, often was the first to reach him in such times of distress and would lick the tears from his face until someone arrived to set him in motion again. Napoleon took small notice of the strange little human, and, like his master, preferred to keep his distance from the noisy, sticky bundle.

Wednesday came, and Stella was packed and dressed for the trip home an hour before they needed to head for the train station. She sat with Agnes once more on the terrace, wrapped up against the chilly morning air and taking in the view for the last time.

"I can't think about not seeing this again," she said without turning her head. "I find myself pretending that Mr. Rockwell will still find a way to save the estate. He might, you know."

Her aunt smiled at her and said nothing.

"Do you remember when I first arrived and I told you that I would not want to leave? I've been here nearly four months now and I was right; I still don't want to go."

"And I, more than I could have known then, am not ready to let you." The two women gripped hands. "Oh, Stella, I will miss you so."

"But, Agnes, tell me, why can't you keep Henri? I have to go, but why must he? You have Mrs. Williams and Marie to help and I know how fond you are of him."

Agnes looked away.

Stella continued, "I really can't picture you losing him, and I think you would be a wonderful mother!"

"Oh," Agnes replied slowly, "you cannot imagine how many times I have run through all this in my mind. Over and over and over. But the answer comes up the same every time. The child needs a mother and a father—that is so important, Stella. And here I am entering a state of near penury, which it would be wrong to inflict on that child. No, he must go to a good, solid family where he can get a fresh start and have all his needs seen to as the years go by."

Stella sighed. "You might be right, I don't know. This is just so hard, and I hate to leave you like this. I'll write as soon as I'm home, and you must come once the baby is born and help me."

"You won't need help," Agnes smiled. "You have had Henri to practice on and you are marvelous with him. Plus you'll have the governess William engaged. But I will come just the same—you won't be able to keep me away!"

The time came for leave-taking. Ned and Isaiah loaded all of Stella's things onto the coach. So prolonged were the hugs between Agnes and Stella, Stella and little Henri, and Stella and the remaining staff, that her husband at last tapped his watch and warned that they would miss all the day's trains if they did not get started. Everyone stood on the front steps and watched the carriage lumber off, with Stella waving a white handkerchief out the window all the way to the bend where they passed out of sight.

Agnes spent the rest of the day playing blocks intently with the baby and personally taking care of all the tasks she had shared with Stella. She pushed away the keen awareness that one day soon Henri, too, would ride away.

\* \* \*

In the lazy light of late morning, Claudia lay stretched across her favorite burgundy divan reading the *Dutchess Chronicle*. As usual, she had turned immediately to the notices. They were invaluable for learning whose fortunes were rising and whose falling, what new households were forming and which others going to pieces—a successful betrothal here, a business closing there, a fire sale, a new butler needed, horses for sale. She knew that behind each terse notice lay a story. So the small paragraph at the bottom of page six announcing that an estate was being offered up, whose brief description matched Brookside's exactly, caught her attention like a fishhook. She pulled herself up straight on the couch.

Impossible, she thought. My luck cannot have reached such mountainous proportions. Or could it? The exquisite scandal Claudia had engineered to extinguish her neighbor's romance had proved eminently satisfying, but a crisis of the heart does not bring about the sale of a family home. The woman must be ruined, thought Claudia, but how? The timing might be coincidental. By degrees, she realized that total victory over Agnes might be within her grasp. She had already disgraced her man Phillip, making him an untouchable of the lowest sort, one who consorts intimately with savages. Any chance for a union between him and the House of Somerset lay in a thousand pieces. And now the family seat of that same noble name could, just possibly, be hers.

Her own Beaujour was fine but it was not Brookside. Claudia's home possessed less acreage, little water, no view, a minimal garden, and a house—no matter how she dressed it up—far less imposing than Agnes's. That visit she had paid Agnes early in the summer to suggest that Brookside might be for sale (using the trusted "I heard from friends that possibly . . . ") had been a lark, just something to provoke the girl, or at best put a seed in her mind. Could that seed have sprouted?

Money for the purchase should not be a problem. Claudia's recent sale of her share in the railroad had netted even more than she had hoped, and the fact that it was not entirely hers to sell would never be proven.

She would need to move quickly. Brookside had a reputation as one of the premier properties in the county. She would pay a visit immediately to her men at Sutterfield Brothers and have them make inquiries for her. And, of course, she would drop by Agnes's on the way back in an act of perfect solicitude to convey her sympathy at seeing the estate put on the block. Claudia knew that Agnes would not see her today, just as she had refused all of her visits since the night of the ball. But again, she could leave her card.

That afternoon, as the sun slid behind an unbroken layer of clouds, Claudia called for her carriage and paused to smile at herself in the hall mirror, tucking her beautiful hair under one of her showier hats and buttoning on a pair of rust-colored gloves. "Time to take it all," she whispered, and stepped gaily into her coach with instructions to head for Chesterton at a quick trot.

Had Claudia gotten away only a few minutes earlier, her carriage would have crossed Phillip's, his turning into Brookside as her own passed the great estate on her way to town. Mercifully for him he was already up the long drive and knocking at Agnes's door.

# Chapter 56

Phillip raised the heavy knocker and tapped it twice, gently. In the quiet of the gray afternoon, it sounded sharp and resolute against the brass plate. Almost instantly Fettles opened and admitted him into the gloomy foyer. Napolean stood at attention, eyeing the guest eagerly.

Phillip looked at the animal with a mixture of surprise and distrust. He was struck for the first time at how dog and butler shared the same spare frame, both bodies appearing nearly weightless. "I see you are getting along well with the dogs?"

"Very well, sir." Fettles replied, restraining himself from telling the story of how their relations had warmed. Instead he offered their visitor tea, which was declined, and before he could step away to summon his mistress, she appeared on the stairs. She was pulling baby Henri's rag from her shoulder, having just put him down for a nap.

"I have good news," Phillip announced without smiling.

"Yes?" asked Agnes. She knew why he had come and could feel her stomach contract.

"First," said Phillip, remembering himself, "How are you? How is the baby?"

"We are both very well."

"It seems we have found a home for him," he declared, "at least for now."

Agnes stared at him for a moment, then walked slowly to a chair in the parlor and sat down.

"How soon?" she asked, looking at the swirling leaf pattern of the deep green carpeting.

"Friday." He took a step toward her. "They are good Christians. They attend the Methodist church in town and are very well spoken of. They have only one girl and are anxious for more children."

"Who are they?" asked Agnes.

"Reverend and Mrs. Thoroughgood. And they understand that the child is not—well, that he has one foreign parent. They are very broad-minded." Phillip turned his hat another revolution in his hands. "We're terribly fortunate, really."

Agnes raised her eyes to his. "Are we?" Absently she rose and walked to the Swiss music box beside the sofa. She traced the mother-of-pearl inlay with a finger, then raised the lid and slowly cranked the golden handle back and forth. A bright, tinkling melody filled the room. *Fortunate*, he had said. No, we are certainly the two unluckiest people in the entire world. Torn apart in the full bloom of romance, we are like victims who survive a hurricane only to find that everything they had built lies in splinters—indeed, that even the ground itself has been carried out to sea.

Philip came close beside her. "You must let the little fellow, go, Agnes. . . . And me," he added.

"Ah, so you finally say it!"

"You must find someone else, Agnes." Phillip looked impatiently at the cheery music box and abruptly shut it. "I'm no good to anyone now. I cannot possibly ruin your future with my own taint of scandal. You deserve so much better than that."

"My future?" Agnes said pointedly. "What would that be, precisely? The home I have poured myself into will soon fall into other hands. I have no money. I am nearly past marrying age, and now even little Henri—" she broke off.

"So how would you have it, then?" Phillip asked with unmistakable iciness. "We should get married, live with my father, and raise the little bastard child? Would that work well?"

Agnes looked at him, startled. "Why are you speaking like this?"

Phillip had taken on a hardened look. "Because one of us has to say it. You know as well as I do that it cannot happen, not in the world we live in."

"We could go somewhere else," she heard herself saying.

"No! I have been dashing all over looking for a safe place my whole life, Agnes, and I am tired. I'm sick of it!" He circled her chair. "You know I've started managing the farm father bought up north. I pray God that I finally succeed at something. The place has a terrible little house on it, more sunken than standing, but it will do for me. But you—you deserve so much better, in every way. I cannot put you there. I cannot sentence you to a life with me."

"Why can't I decide?" she cried.

He had passed behind her and now bent slightly to put his cheek against hers. "Let go, Agnes. You must let go—you know that."

Agnes stiffened and drew in a long, slow breath. "I am disappointed in you, my love. I thought you would have more courage than this." Agnes felt Phillip pull back but she continued without turning. "Do you understand how many things I am giving up right now? That's all I seem to do anymore."

Phillip walked around to face her. His features were stern. "I am sorry if I disappoint you, Agnes," he said hollowly. "I do this more for you than for myself. I hope one day you will see that."

As she looked at him standing pompously upon that ludicrous statement, a new idea seeped into her mind. As it advanced, it cleared away all the useless detail of the past several weeks. One truth stood alone on the raw landscape, naked before her. Of course—this was never going to work, not from the very first day. You silly girl, why didn't you see it sooner? Oh, what a fine disguise it has worn all along. She had prided herself in recognizing this feature even under the many costumes men cloaked it with, but not this time. Somehow this man had completely fooled her.

"What is it?" Phillip asked, uncomfortable beneath her silent and wondering stare.

Agnes clutched her skirt and wandered halfway across the room. She stood with her back to him, wondering how much to say. What if she was wrong? She turned to look at him in this new and dismal light. No, this explained too much.

"I have been very foolish," she said at last. She saw Phillip's face begin to relax almost imperceptibly. "But not for the reason you think." She moved behind the sofa and fingered the Italian lace runner that lay across its back, another gift from her father to her mother. What a wonderful life they had, she mused, reminded again of the precious thing that was fleeing once again beyond her outstretched hand.

"This was never going to actually happen, was it?"

"What do you mean?" Phillip asked cautiously.

"This lovely romance of ours. A wedding. A life as man and wife and children and all those things that a girl dreams of in her idle time."

Phillip waited.

Agnes toyed with an ivory rosette between her fingers. "You have reasons for not having married by now, Phillip. Something always happens to ruin it, I imagine. And something always will." She looked up.

"What are you saying?" he asked, searching her face.

"A summer of amusement was fine—some rendezvous in the garden, a new person to make the time pass pleasantly . . . But you are simply not the matrimonial type, are you, my dear?" She looked at him. "Vera was right, and I should have listened."

"You're saying that I never meant to marry you, then?" Phillip stammered. "That I was merely leading you on for my own pleasure?"

"Maybe you didn't mean to. But you also were never going to let it end in marriage."

Phillip took a step forward. "Do you really dare to speculate this way about my feelings, my motives? Why, you are accusing me of toying with you, like the lowest sort of scoundrel! You can't mean it, Agnes." Phillip turned away, then back again. "All this time I thought I had finally found someone who could really know me. A woman who could love me with all my flaws and my quirks, and the good parts, too. I have some good qualities, Agnes. My God, I thought you knew me." By now he stood over her, nearly shouting.

"I thought so too," Agnes replied without moving. "But note this well: You are ending this, not me. Ask yourself why."

Drawn by the loud voices, Fettles arrived at a trot and stopped in the doorway. Agnes warned him off with a look.

Phillip stepped back, studying her. At length he shook his head and picked up the hat he had laid on a table. "I will send someone Friday morning for the child."

The statement reverberated inside Agnes's head. She searched but found no words. She brushed past Phillip and retreated noiselessly up the carpeted stairs.

Donning his hat, Phillip found his own way out.

# Chapter 57

On the morning that the Duke's staff was to come reclaim the little boy, Henri sat in his wheeled chair, playing with the tassels that hung from the sofa cushions. He glowed from a fresh scrubbing and floundered inside a new suit of clothes that was a bit large for him. Agnes could not help looking out the window every few minutes to see if the Duke's carriage was in the drive. They had packed up all of Henri's clothing and effects the night before, and the black trunk sat somberly beside the front door.

Empress had parked herself a few feet from the baby. Maybe she sensed that today something threatened their hold on this child, and her posture seemed to tell everyone that she was prepared to defend the boy against all challenges.

Outside a stiff breeze troubled the gray day and sent fallen leaves scuttling across the ground. Agnes pushed the drapes as far back as possible to admit a little more light. It had been sunny earlier when she took Henri in his buggy for one last walk through the garden. She had stopped to pluck a lingering petunia and tickle his nose with it, a game that always made him laugh uncontrollably, squinting his eyes and pulling his little arms together. This morning she tried to store up the sound of that laughter for later, but it floated off on the wind, going the way of all tender things that make up the most precious parts of our lives.

Agnes pulled back from the window.

Mrs. Williams stopped dusting the curios. "Are they here?"

Agnes nodded gravely.

The two women waited for the sound of the knocker. It came, heavy and demanding. Empress raised her head and tensed. Fettles arrived, for once walking slowly, taking his time. He knew this child's removal would take from Agnes her last reason to smile. He allowed a full second round of hammering, then slowly pulled open the door to behold Mrs. Morgan.

In her long black coat, the woman closely resembled an iron rod. An admirer of the queen of England, Mrs. Morgan had chosen to imitate that great lady's continual mourning for the Prince of Wales. This marked the twentieth year of Mrs. Morgan's wrapping herself in black since the sudden death of her own husband who had fallen off the seat of his cab going at full tilt, probably in consequence of a too-liberal round of refreshment at his favorite tavern. (Mrs. Morgan championed her husband as blameless in the accident, although the driverless cab nearly killed two pedestrians, and she managed to make him the victim of this small tragedy rather than the cause in every telling.)

"Is the child ready?" she asked by way of greeting. Her small, dark eyes glistened beneath her gray brows.

Fettles said nothing but showed her into the parlor. She swept the scene with a critical look.

"I'm here for the child," she pronounced.

"You!" declared Agnes. "I did not expect Lord Phillip to send you on this mission." She remembered clearly the scene in front of Phillip's home when he had relieved the uncharitable woman of any responsibility toward the baby.

"Well, it wasn't my choice!" protested the woman. "The girl that was supposed to, she took sick last night and I was the only one to spare, though Lord knows I've enough to do."

Agnes and Mrs. Williams exchanged glances. Neither woman moved, transfixed by the awful prospect of handing their soft little darling into the courier's steely grip.

"Give him here, now. They're expecting him." Mrs. Morgan stepped forward and stuck out her black-gloved hands.

Mrs. Williams reached down and carefully lifted Henri from his chair. Agnes darted to her and took the baby. She held him tight against her and covered his dark, silky head with her hand. She looked around at the three people before her as they watched the color drain from her face and hands.

Mrs. Morgan shot a look at the others and pursed her pale lips. She turned to Fettles. "Put his things in the carriage, will you?"

Fettles looked at his mistress inquiringly.

Agnes shook her head slowly, her eyes pleading.

"For the love of Mary, what's the meaning of this?" Mrs. Morgan demanded. "I've not got all day. I'm taking the little burden off your hands, you know. We're lucky someone is willing to take him." She came closer and made a motion to take the baby from Agnes.

Pulling back and holding Henri more tightly still, Agnes suddenly turned, fled from the room, and raced upstairs. The startled party heard a door slam, and Fettles thought he could just make out the key turning in the lock.

Mrs. Morgan, gasping in outrage, made a move to follow her, but Empress had taken the hem of her dress in her jaws and held her fast. Napoleon, by nature every man's friend, stood at a yard from the woman and silently displayed his teeth. Fettles took charge and asked Mrs. Williams if she would please attend to Miss Somerset, then suggested to Mrs. Morgan that they deliver the child to her later in the day, apologizing for the great trouble she had gone to and assuring her that all would be made right shortly.

The widow's consternation was so deep that she could only stare at Fettles, then at the dogs, and back at the butler. Fettles, feeling that she had been sufficiently convinced of the enmity of the entire household, reproached Empress, who dropped the damp hem. He then stood between Napoleon and the visitor so she might exit in safety.

Locking the heavy door behind her, Fettles ran upstairs. Mrs. Williams and Marie were both listening at the bedroom door to Agnes's muffled voice.

". . . so who am I? I am invisible! Everything happens *around* me and *to* me and all I can do is sit by and stop up the bleeding. Now I am supposed to sit here, again, and hand you over to that monstrous woman? She'll take you away and give you to God only knows whom." Her voice went back and forth as one pacing about the room.

Fettles signaled the two ladies to make room and moved close to the door. "Miss Agnes, may I come in? Mrs. Morgan is gone."

There was silence for a moment. "She's gone?"

"Yes, ma'm. I sent her away. May I come in?"

The lock turned slowly, but the door remained closed. Fettles knocked a warning and went in, closing the door behind him. Agnes stood in the middle of the room, clutching herself. Little Henri was pulling himself to his feet with the help of her quilt, which he held in his fists like a man climbing a rock face. Fettles put an arm around her and squeezed her shoulders.

"I don't think I can stand this," she said, not looking up. "I'm exhausted and I'm angry and I don't know how to get my breath anymore. I pray for strength, but every day feels harder than the one before." She looked at her butler. "I feel like a piece of floating wreckage, Fettles—I can't steer myself in any direction, I'm simply tossed at the whim of the waves."

Fettles drew her over to the tall bed where little Henri was carefully working his way sideways in short, jabbing steps. The two friends sat on the edge side by side.

Agnes wiped her cheeks with her sleeve. "This all looks very irrational, doesn't it?"

"Not at all. I know how much you love this little boy. But it is true," his voice softened "that we cannot keep the baby. I think you know that."

"Yes, I know that. I hate it, though. I never dreamed I would get so attached to him. What did you tell Mrs. Morgan?"

"That we would bring the baby to her this afternoon."

"I can't do it, Fettles, I cannot physically place this child into her hands."

"We'll send Mrs. Williams or Maria."

Agnes sat silent and fingered the fabric of her soft skirt. "I want that family who's getting him to know that, if for any reason, they change their mind about him, we will take him back. Can we tell them that?"

"Yes, I will make sure they know." Fettles replied warmly. Agnes put her arms around his thin neck and hugged him as when she was a child.

"Fettles," she murmured, "do you remember when I fell from my horse when I was eleven? You were the one who read to me by the hour and bribed the kitchen staff to make me puddings and tarts. I know I was very gloomy and you tried so hard to cheer me up." After a pause she added, "You have been a wonderful friend to me all these years."

Fettles smiled and, pulling a handkerchief from his waistcoat pocket, offered it to Agnes. "I remember. And we played many games of hearts as well. You hated losing," he reminded her.

Agnes looked at him thoughtfully. "Yes, I hate losing. I've never been philosophical about it."

After several minutes the two friends straightened themselves, picked up Henri, and walked slowly downstairs to feed him one last meal in the warmth of the old kitchen.

# Chapter 58

With Henri gone, Agnes sank into a dark mood that clung to her beneath her clothes, like an extra skin she could not peel off. The terrible quiet made the house a tomb. Everything was so different now, as though years had passed since summer. Light and color drained away from the landscape outside her window, and she felt that winter was the natural state of things—that spring, summer, and fall were passing tenants with no real claim to the land.

In the fountain, leaves gathered around the edges, just a few at first, then dozens, then scores. From the window of her small study, Agnes watched Ned pull out dripping scoopfuls in his slow, deliberate way. She hated to see the fountain emptied. To her it signified surrender to winter, and for her sake Ned always delayed the task until the approach of freezing weather threatened the marble basin. He had already told her that today was the day, and this year he knew she would feel it more than ever.

There was a knock at the open door behind her. Ned entered, looking uncomfortable in his town clothes and holding a small assortment of envelopes that he set down beside her. On top lay a familiar calling card.

"The mail, ma'm," he managed through his whiskers. "And another card from you know who."

Agnes picked up the card by her fingertips and stared at it. "You would think that after being turned away for three months straight she'd know enough to stay away." Agnes looked sternly at Ned. "Did she say anything?"

"Marie took the card. She told me that she just said to convey her best wishes, like always."

"Viper," Agnes muttered, and threw the card into the trash basket beside the desk. "Well, let's see," she said, picking up the pearl-handled opener, "what else we have."

She slit open a long, gray envelope, unfolded the matching stationery, and began to read. Her face darkened. "Well, well," she said when finished. "Do you know of any firm in town called Sutterfield Brothers?"

"Yes, ma'm, I think they're new. I saw their sign on Main just today."

"Find out what you can about them, will you? They have sent me a letter of inquiry. It seems someone is interested in Brookside."

Ned's eyes widened slightly. "Do we know who?"

"Not for certain, but I could make a very good guess. The first vulture circles."

When Ned returned from a ride to Chesterton two days later, he walked into the kitchen with cheeks red from the cold. He found his mistress warming her hands beside the cook fire, with both dogs drawn up as close as Dahlia would allow. Ned set the mail down on a shelf and pulled off his gloves.

"Any news?" asked Agnes.

Ned, always slow to speak, took a little longer than usual to answer. A cold stiffness gripped him from his jaw to his toes, a result of the bracing ride home in an open buggy. Dahlia poured him a hot cup of tea, which he wrapped his thick hands around. He breathed in the rising steam and finally looked up at Agnes with misgiving.

"Not sure you'll want to know it," he warned.

Agnes looked at him impatiently.

"Sutterfield Brothers are out of London. Solicitors, real estate, all that kind of thing. They've got an office in the City too. Seems a gentleman who used to be in the tea business heads this location in Chesterton. Came back from India just this summer."

"India?" Agnes remarked.

"Um-hm." Ned slurped his hot drink. "There's something else," he said, staring darkly into his cup.

"Well?" snapped Dahlia reflexively.

"You'll never guess who I saw coming out of their office looking smug as a raccoon in a root cellar." He looked at Agnes. "Mrs. Claudia Thorne."

Agnes and Dahlia looked at each other.

"Well," said Agnes, "she was indeed my first suspect. Still," she continued, "there's no way of knowing what she was doing there. You said they offer several services. Maybe her lawyer quit just like her butler after finding out what kind of woman she is and now she's looking for a new one."

"Maybe," mumbled Ned.

Dahlia slashed open a squash on the cutting table. "She's a wicked woman! I wish she would disappear."

Whatever Claudia's connection with Sutterfield Brothers, Agnes could waste no time in responding to the firm's inquiry. Winter was coming on and money was running low. She would send word tomorrow that they could meet and take a look at Brookside. They absolutely needed to be out before Christmas.

So it was that within two days a pair of well-oiled and finely pressed gentlemen stood in the foyer, looking about. Fettles walked them through the house briskly, pointing out features that might escape the casual observer. It was only through a stern act of will that the butler brought himself to perform this task. If he let himself think about the consequence of these men purchasing Brookside for their client, if he pondered the scene of Miss Somerset and the remaining staff being turned out into the cold, he would have run groaning to his little room and covered his head with a pillow.

At the end of their tour, Fettles showed the Sutterfield representatives into the library, where Agnes had been unsuccessfully trying to read a book while waiting for them. The conversation lasted only a minute. They would convey the details of the home to their client, along with a list of the items in need of repair or replacement. If their client was still interested, they would communicate an offer.

This was the first of several visits to the estate by prospective buyers or their agents. Some were local; several were from Manhattan and Philadelphia. Of course, like all those who put their cherished home up for sale and must suffer its scrutiny by strangers, Agnes was dismayed at the lackluster reaction. It seemed that Brookside was either too large or too small; the décor was outdated and would take far too much work to redo; Greco-Roman was over; the estate included too much acreage; the buyer wanted more acreage; Chesterton was too close; Chesterton was too far. In the end, two buyers were interested. One offered a price slightly below what Agnes had expected to sell for. The other, offered via Sutterfield Brothers, was for a good deal more, with the understanding that all the furnishings, save a handful of heirloom pieces, would remain with the house.

Mr. Rockwell was consulted and, since it was now early November, he advised Agnes to accept the higher offer under the condition that no repairs were to be included for that price, and the purchaser must accept the estate as is. Besides, this offer would save them the sad task of conducting an auction. Agnes conveyed this acceptance to Sutterfield Brothers. Within forty-eight hours Mr. Rockwell himself arrived to negotiate the exact terms, and by the end of the week the house was considered sold. Agnes had until the fifteenth of December to vacate.

After signing the papers, Agnes and Mr. Rockwell rode back to Brookside from the Sutterfield offices in a cold drizzle. They were halfway home when Agnes broke the silence.

"I don't seem able to grasp what I just did," she observed, staring blankly at the empty fields and crowds of naked trees outside the carriage's rain-specked window. "I do wonder, though, why they won't say who the buyer is. That disturbs me very much. I'd like to know to whom I am handing over my home."

"You're quite right," agreed the accountant, bundled thickly to his chin. "One hopes the purchaser is a decent person who will take good care of the property and preserve its best features. I know of an estate in Ulster County that sold last year. Tremendous house. The buyer cut it up into a hotel. Tore up the gardens and put in tennis courts. Dreadful shame."

He noticed Agnes looking at him in dismay. "No reason to think anything of the sort will happen at Brookside," he added. "No reason at all."

They passed the rest of the trip lost in their own thoughts. The next morning, Mr. Rockwell enjoyed a final meal in the wonderful old house, sitting with Agnes over a steaming breakfast of eggs, coffee, hot apples, and biscuits. He had seated himself in the chair closest to the blazing fire, apologizing for his selfishness.

"The cold is my enemy, dear girl," he told Agnes, spreading Dahlia's famous blueberry jam over a moist biscuit. "There was a time when I flew out the door on the bitterest day, undaunted, with hardly a scarf around my neck. Now I can't seem to put enough clothes on to keep off the chill. I'm almost afraid to leave the house after October." He turned his head stiffly, chewing slowly, and looked out at the pale day.

Agnes smiled wryly. "So you don't agree with Mr. Lowell about winter: "There is a crabbed generosity about the old cynic that you would not exchange for all the creamy concessions of Autumn."[6]

"Ho, ho! Crabbed, yes; generous, I don't see it."

"Well, maybe generous in that he gives us time to rest. We are supposed to stay indoors and let the fields sleep while we read old books by the fire."

"I don't doubt that was the plan," acknowledged Mr. Rockwell, helping himself to another spoon of eggs. "But look at us now. Our labor knows no season. We hurry through summer and push ourselves through the paralyzing cold of winter. We have become unnatural beasts driven by a heartless technology. There seems to be no end to it and we cannot keep up, not in the long run. You see," he added, "I speak like an old man."

"Not at all," Agnes assured him. "I wonder all the time where all our progress is taking us."

Mr. Rockwell wiped his mouth. "Real progress, my girl, real progress, is that which takes man closer to God's plan for him. There you have it—the most profound thing I am ever likely to say. Write it down for me, would you, and put it in a jar." He leaned back in his chair. "Have you decided where you will live?"

"Yes, with Vera, at least at first. She's getting married, you know, at Christmas."

"To the lucky Mr. Schmidt."

"Yes, and I am so glad. Well, that means they will only need one of their two townhouses, so I may take one of them for a time."

"A very good plan. That will give everyone time to think. And now," he said, pushing back his chair and rising, "I must pack myself up like an Eskimo and be on my way. Will you come for Thanksgiving? Mrs. Rockwell told me not to return home unless it was with an acceptance of that invitation."

Agnes hugged the small man. "I am too distracted and would only spoil your holiday. Besides, there is too much to do here in the next month to spare the time."

Mr. Rockwell looked at her with a mournful face. "I am so very sorry, Agnes. I can't say it enough."

---

[6] James Russell Lowell, *A Good Word for Winter*, 1871.

Thirty minutes later, wrapped nearly to the point of immobility, Mr. Rockwell pulled himself up into the coach, waved a last good-bye, and left Agnes to the methodical task of bidding farewell to a hundred years of family history.

# Chapter 59

We often find that joviality is measured out to a person in inverse proportion to his competence. So it was with the thorny clerk in the Marseilles post office. As forbidding a man as he was, no one could accuse him of any lack of acuity or thoroughness in the execution of his duties. He assigned the correct postage to Rupa's letter and tossed it into the proper bin, *À L'Étranger*.[7] In the great sorting room behind him, however, a large North African with a ready grin found himself so frequently distracted while telling stories about his youth and asking details of his co-workers' love lives, that packets he handled regularly found their way into the wrong bag, headed to some remote and unintended destination.

Two hours after Rupa left the post office, this same Ahmed began sorting the foreign bin into bags by country. He would take these down to the docks later in the day, where workers would load them onto the restless ships. As he tossed the pieces slowly into canvass bags, a moment of hilarity eclipsed his attention long enough to let go of Rupa's tender letter above the sack bound for Egypt. And so, in fulfillment of her fears, the letter found itself jostled among hundreds of pieces it had no business associating with, thrown into the hold of a small ship headed east, and tossed ashore at the distant port of Alexandria some two weeks later.

We might well wonder at the ultimate fate of a letter that has been sent in the very opposite direction of its true destination. Carrying only enough postage for the intended trip, how could it double back on its tracks and move on to where it should go? And since Rupa had put no return address on the envelope, it could not ever come back to her. A letter so far afield was destined for the rubbish heap, or just as bad, the back of the sorting house in a barrel for dead letters.

It was to just such a barrel that Mahmood was directed when he asked his supervisor what to do with the small letter bearing an American address. Mahmood had been working in the great Alexandria post office for only a week, having gotten the job by a stroke of luck: a low-level superintendent owed his uncle a favor. The

---

[7] Abroad.

same uncle had himself hired the young man with the sweet eyes and soft heart a month earlier to help in his produce market, but quickly found his nephew dismally unsuited to the task. He was unable to haggle and, as a result, sold everything from carrots to couscous for half what he should. No amount of threatening could transform the young fellow into a shrewd salesman, and the desperate uncle got rid of him at the first opportunity.

Dressed proudly in his new postal uniform, a troubled Mahmood walked with the  envelope to the barrel, nearly full of dusty parcels and envelopes of every description. He stood turning it over in his hand, studying the handwriting. It was a woman's hand, and he imagined a dozen desperate situations that might depend on the arrival of this letter. Mahmood walked back to his supervisor, who would not like being asked the same question twice, especially since he was trying to drink his afternoon tea and win an argument with his brother-in-law over the age of the Prophet's youngest wife.

Nevertheless, Mahmood excused himself and asked what happens to things in the dead letter barrel. *Nothing* was the terse reply. What do you want to happen to them? Would you like us to send you around the world to deliver each one yourself? The supervisor returned to his discourse.

Mahmood slid the letter into his pocket and thought about it all day. When he got home that night, he pulled it out and showed it to his wife. Maybe it's something important, he explained. It did not seem right to throw it aside and forget about it. His wife, a young woman with an equally soft heart, examined the letter and suggested they open it.

"That's against the rules," Mahmood said sternly.

"Well," she said, thinking, "it's probably against the rules to bring other people's mail home with you, isn't it?"

Her husband ignored the question. "Besides," he pointed out, "you see it's from France. It's probably in French or some other language we can't read. What good will opening it do?"

The two left the mysterious letter on the table while they ate their simple dinner. After clearing the dishes, his wife put it on a shelf next to the door so Mahmood would remember to take it back to the post office in the morning.

"How much would it cost to send it to America from here?" she asked.

"Too much," he answered. For three weeks the envelope lay on the shelf where the two glanced at it each time they left the house, Mahmood hoping that inspiration would strike on what to do with it. One evening after cleaning up from dinner, his wife went to a small clay pot and took out some coins.

"Would this be enough for the letter?" she asked.

Her husband looked at the coins in her hand and the concern on her gentle face. "You saved these?" he asked.

"You are not angry, I hope,"

He smiled and shook his head. The next morning Mahmood went to work early. The first thing he did was buy enough postage to send the letter to America, which took three of the four coins his wife had given him. Trusting no one, he personally walked the letter to the back of the sorting house, to the outbound section, and shoved it deep into a bag marked *America*.

# Chapter 60

Thanksgiving came to Brookside on a gray day with cold sprinkles dotting the deserted terrace and flecking the windows. Dahlia, under orders to make a simple meal with no excesses, produced three succulent chickens stuffed with cornbread and raisins, a pile of roasted potatoes, green and yellow squash, and both pumpkin and apple pies. Fettles set the table for the whole household using the family china and crystal. With all the lamps lit and the fire roaring, the dining room sparkled as it used to, and everyone gathered to thank God for what remained and to pray for the days ahead.

In an effort to banish all gloom in this oasis of warmth and good fellowship, Agnes encouraged everyone to tell stories of their days at Brookside, especially those of a humorous nature. So they sat for nearly three hours, the ten of them—Agnes, Fettles, Mrs. Williams, Dahlia and her nephew, Marie, Ned, Isaiah, and the two junior staff—feasting and reliving their favorite memories. For this short time, disappointment was barred from the room, old friends long gone lived again, and all that was most precious was brought back into the light.

Meanwhile, just up the road at Fellcrest, the Duke and Lord Phillip shared a quiet meal together, alone at the long dining room table surrounded by the tumultuous peacock wallpaper. Phillip had acquiesced to his father's invitation to join him for the holiday meal. His two sisters and their husbands were sorely missed, being unable to come home this year as one was recovering from a bad flu and the other had just delivered her third child. Left to themselves, father and son exhausted discussion about the new farm and how Phillip was getting on in the little house and all other possible topics well before dessert. After coffee and a game of cards, Phillip pleaded fatigue and excused himself. His room was just as he had left it several weeks earlier, and he welcomed the comfort of his old bed. He stretched out with a worn copy of *The Life and Strange Surprising Adventures of Robinson Crusoe* and escaped into its pages until sleep overcame him.

The next morning he rose early to the sound of icy rain at the window. By ten o'clock he had dressed, breakfasted, and said good-bye to his father. The rain stopped as he headed back up the road toward his little kingdom of self-imposed exile, but a damp chill remained. He reflected upon how the presence of people made him increasingly uncomfortable and wondered whether he was on his way to becoming a recluse. He seldom saw anyone besides Richmond, the wiry former slave from Virginia who helped him around the farm, and Natalya, a Russian immigrant who had lost her family in a tenement fire as they slept. She now cooked for the two men and kept the house swept.

Phillip had sunk to a place that he could no longer pray himself out of and found solace only in physical tasks such as fixing broken wagon wheels and digging in the raw earth. Every day reminded him that he was thirty-seven years old with nothing to show for it save a collection of stories to tell.

Sometimes at night as the fire burned low and he sat alone with his boots on the fender, Phillip let himself remember his days with Agnes. For a little while, his numbness would retreat, and he felt again her cool hands in his, her hair against his cheek; he heard her laugh again and saw the violet night sky spread wide above them as they sat pressed against each other, whispering about all their tomorrows. Slow tears traced a path down his face and his lips murmured bits of remembered conversations. In this way he strove to hang on to at least the memory of her, knowing how time rubs away the details from even the most vibrant pictures.

A week after Thanksgiving, as Phillip struggled to rouse himself one morning after just such a late vigil, he thought he heard his father's voice downstairs. Dressing quickly, he splashed water on his face, brushed his hair with three strokes, and went down. He found the Duke seated at the old round table that came with the house, its surface bearing witness to the hundreds of forks and knives that had dug into it over the years and all the hot kettles placed upon it. The Duke clasped a large cup of tea in both hands, which Natalya had just set down for him along with some biscuits and peach butter.

"Hullo!" the elder cried, grabbing up an envelope from the table and waving it at Phillip.

"What have we here, oh father of mine?" Phillip smiled wanly as he pulled on his jacket in the drafty room.

"A letter for you. It arrived yesterday, but old Morgan didn't tell me until this morning. You're up rather late for a farmer, aren't you?"

Phillip took the dirty letter and examined its worn corners and strange notations. It looked as though it had gone around the world at least twice. He studied the odd handwriting and postage.

"From France," put in the Duke. "By way of Egypt from the looks of it."

Phillip took up a knife from the table and cleanly slit open the envelope. He unfolded three pages of common stationary covered in a small hand. He read the date. "This was sent nearly three months ago." Then he looked at the last sheet. His features froze as though he gazed upon a ghost.

His father was on his feet, looking over his son's shoulder. "What is it? What's wrong?"

Phillip held the signature out.

His father squinted, then looked at him in consternation. "Rupa? The Indian girl? But how? How did she know where to send it?"

"I gave her my address."

"Why did you do that?"

"I don't know. In case she needed it at some point. I don't know really."

The Duke looked down at the letter. "How is your French?"

"No better than before. Can you read it?"

The Duke put a hand inside his coat and drew out his spectacles from a slim case. Fitting them on, he took the letter, and both men sat down. The father took a sip of tea, smoothed the pages on the table, and began to read, translating as he went:

*17 September 188_*

*Dear Phillip,*

*I know you will be surprised to get this letter, and I hope it reaches you. I feel that I must write to you now that I know what is happening there in America at your home. I hope that maybe this letter will help make everything right again, and it is truly the least that I can do for someone who risked so much for me.*

In simple words, Rupa recounted how she had met Wilbur at the dance hall (without naming the city) and what she learned from him about her father coming to America and delivering the child to Phillip. Then she told how Henri had really come to be, about the terrible night at the hands of her brothers and the soldier. The Duke stopped reading several times to look round-eyed at his son. At last he reached the end of the letter:

*Maybe you can show this letter to people who think badly of you and think that the child is yours. I hope you do not think I am terrible for leaving him with the nuns. I never dreamed that my father would do what he did, even coming to America with the baby.*

*If I can ask you one more kindness, dear Phillip, it is this. Please put the baby with someone who will love him. I do not want him to suffer in a cruel family like I did. I am very sorry for all the trouble I have made for you. You are a very kind man. Do not worry about me. I am happy here and every night I thank your God that He sent you to India to save me.*

*Rupa*

*P.S. I am sending this letter from a city where I do not live* [she lied], *so the postmark on the envelope does not signify anything.*

The Duke pulled off his spectacles and laid them on the table. Both men sat quietly for a moment. Then the father stretched his hand out to his son, who clasped it in his own. Phillip looked from the letter to his father's face and saw to his surprise that he was crying.

"Forgive me, Phillip," said the father, reaching for his handkerchief. "I was never sure the boy was not yours, even though you told me he wasn't. Why did I doubt you? I should have known better."

Phillip rose and closed his arms around his father.

"And that poor girl," the Duke stammered, "what brutes she had for brothers!"

"It is disgusting," breathed Phillip. "I never liked them, but I never suspected they were capable of such monstrosities."

"But now we know!" declared his father, tapping the letter where it lay. "We know the truth."

The Duke wiped his face and cleared his throat. Phillip asked Natalya for more tea, and the two men attacked the biscuits and butter with vigor, as well as the sausages she had just set down beside a bowl of piping hot applesauce. When the first wave of relief had passed, the Duke began thinking practically about the next steps.

"As good as this news is, it might not be a solution to your situation, Phillip. I'm afraid everyone within a radius of a hundred miles thinks this boy is yours. It will be hard to undo that with just this letter—a letter from a girl who left him at a convent and went on her way. What would we do, take out an announcement in the papers?"

Phillip folded the letter and slid it back into the envelope. "It doesn't matter," he said, smiling. He rose and took his coat from its hook. "There is only one person who needs to see this."

"Oh! Do you mean . . . ?"

Phillip nodded, pulling on his gloves.

"Shall I give you a ride there?" asked the Duke. "I'd be very happy to."

"No, I don't want you to have to bring me all the way back here. I'll ride alone. You take your time, father. I'll stop by your house on my way back."

"Do!" The Duke rubbed his hands together. He gave Phillip a hug, wished him Godspeed, and shut the door behind him. Of all the things he wished for his son, a good wife—and Agnes would surely be that— was at the very top of the list.

# Chapter 61

Phillip rode to Brookside with a stiff wind behind him. The ground was hard, and he let the restless Queen Anne run at full tilt as long as she wanted. He could not lose a moment in sharing Rupa's revelation with his great friend, the woman who might yet be his bride if she could put all the harsh words behind. He could not imagine what would happen next, but an assurance of the truth, proof that he had not lied to her, must help dispel the cloud that hung between them.

Below an iron sky the fields lay bereft of crops, with harsh stubble where green stalks had stood. Bands of bare trees broke the open land, and here and there small gangs of sheep and cows nibbled off the last of the summer growth. Scenes of that awful night at the ball ran through Phillip's mind, the night his world collapsed. He saw again Dhanesh's sneering face, inches from his own, saw the carriage drive away, the stunned crowd, Claudia's smile. *Maybe you can show this letter to people who think badly of you and think that the child is yours.* Phillip passed his father's house at a quick trot and rejoiced that Agnes's was not much farther. He tried to hold himself back, but he could almost feel her arms around him again. There, just over that rise, was the drive.

Phillip turned in past the familiar stone pillars and pulled Queen Anne back to a slow walk. He had to collect himself before seeing Agnes. He must not scare her, arriving like a man on fire. He felt his pocket—yes, the letter was still there. He smoothed his moustache and straightened himself, breathing in and out, but his heart continued to beat wildly. Just around the bend would be the great house, and inside would be Agnes. It would be good to see Fettles again, too, and have tea in the green parlor. A wave of nostalgia for days past and a yearning for the days ahead filled him nearly to bursting.

He rounded the bend and saw again the square mansion beyond the twin rows of shivering trees. Dry leaves flew across the front drive and spun around in circles, but otherwise all was still. Phillip approached slowly, looking for Ned or his helpers by the stables. He scanned the windows for faces or any other sign of life. Pulling Anne to a stop, he looked up at the stone façade, at its blank windows and smokeless chimneys. He slid from the saddle, approached the massive doors, and knocked. He heard the sound echo ominously within. Again he knocked, harder, but drew no response. Tying Anne to a post, he took the path that led around the side of the house, ending at the back terrace. Phillip looked from the silent house to the tumbled garden, to the fields beyond. The fountain sat still with a blanket of wet leaves in its basin. Only the native wildlife went on about its business, the gray squirrels darting across the lawn and skittering up and down the stiff trees.

Phillip walked mechanically to the garden, down paths overgrown with the debris of last summer's glory, past the thorny arms of old rose bushes and brown nets of withered honeysuckle. He walked as in a trance until he found himself standing once more between Venus and Vulcan. There they kept their vigil, half-clothed in the damp chill, still separated, still yearning. He lowered himself onto the familiar stone bench, but its stark coldness drove him back upon his feet. Below him stretched the dull landscape stripped of all magic—could this be the same place he sat with her in the deep blue night, wishing for more than one lifetime? He felt the wind whip his face and cut through his clothes.

Yes, it was here. And she was gone.

* * *

Agnes had been careful to exempt from the sale of Brookside any of the finest family heirlooms. Whoever these buyers were, they would not be enjoying the cream of the Somerset's collection. The buyers had fussed, but Agnes held firm. Some items had been packed and sent to Stella, some went to Vera, and a few tokens found a home at the Bairnaughts' and Rockwells'. Vera had agreed to store some pieces in her cellar for the time when Agnes had settled in somewhere and could take them back again. The last horses were sold off, the chimney flues closed, and the remaining furniture stood draped in white sheeting.

Agnes walked slowly through the cold house one more time. The intensity of silence struck her. Everyone except Ned had gone away in the last two days, all to new positions or to the homes of family members until they might find a new post. Only Fettles, Marie, and Ned would remain with her, and Fettles and Marie had left for Vera's house in New York City yesterday with the furniture and the dogs. Agnes wanted one last morning to say good-bye, to make sure she had left behind nothing she did not intend to. Dressed in her coat and scarf, her hands tucked into a fur muff, she checked each room, pausing to open dresser drawers and look behind doors for things left hanging on hooks. A glance in the music room reminded her painfully of the one piece she would most deeply miss. Shrouded in white, the Chickering stood alone by the windows, its conveyance a condition set down by the home's buyer. Where would Agnes put a grand piano anyway where she was going? Closing the double doors, she moved on.

She came to her last stop, the green parlor, now a mere collection of cloaked forms. Pulling back the sheet from an old chest of drawers in the corner, she opened each one. In the back of the second drawer, nearly escaping her notice, was a small box. Its corners were chipped, and over its satiny red cover ran irregular scratches. Agnes recognized it immediately as her mother's collection of miscellaneous teaspoons, gathered over many years. Gently lifting the lid, she smiled to see the still-shiny spoons lined up in their tissue wrapping just as Mother had left them. A memory rushed over her of tea parties for her dolls, when she would carefully choose the fanciest of these spoons to set in each saucer. What delightful days those were. Her heart swelled with gratitude to her mother, gratitude for all the lovely, sun-streaked days of her childhood in this home. Taking the box, she went to the front door and placed it beside her traveling bag.

She heard Ned come in the kitchen door, and a moment later he was in the foyer with a small crate under his arm.

"Your collection?" she asked.

"The last of it. Rest is in the carriage." Ned looked at Agnes uncertainly. "Maybe I should have sold it all to the museum. They offered a pretty fine sum for everything . . ."

"No, indeed!" Agnes remonstrated. "Your butterflies and birds' nests will take up very little space in Vera's basement. You are right to keep them."

They looked around.

"Are the doors locked?"

"Um-hm. Locked up the stable and kennel, too, so's nobody decides to move in before the new owners do."

Agnes frowned. "Well then," she said, picking up her box of spoons. She meant to say something of a concluding nature but found she could not.

Ned took her bag and followed her out, stowing it along with his boxes, then handed Agnes up into the compartment. She watched as Ned pulled the home's heavy front door shut and turned the key. Turning up his collar, he squinted toward the indifferent sky as the winter's first snowflakes drifted down. He pulled on his gloves, pocketed the big brass key, then climbed slowly onto his seat and clucked to the horses.

Agnes sat back and tried to look fixedly out the far window. But before they had gone twenty yards she could not help lowering the glass and leaning her head out to look upon her home one last time, pale against the towering pines, until they rode around the bend and the grand old house disappeared from view.

# Chapter 62

Claudia passed her hand over the contract, examining again the signatures and seals. She hardly heard Mr. Edwin Rood, branch manager for Sutterfield Brothers, repeat her name. Looking up at last, she saw him extending a large key toward her.

"They dropped it off just this morning on their way out," he smiled.

Claudia took it from him and felt its weight. Brookside. The key to the front door.

"There are many others," Mr. Rood continued, picking up a bag that jangled as he placed it on the table before her. "They are all labeled. Very thoughtful people, the Somersets."

Claudia folded the contract, grabbed the bag of keys, and rose. "So they are completely done there, are they?"

"Yes, ma'm."

"Good. A week from today you'll put Beaujour on the market. And I don't want any surprises—viewings will be by appointment only, you understand."

"We will need to work up a complete listing agreement and proposed terms of sale—"

"Of course. We can take care of all that when I come by next."

Mr. Rood glanced at his associate as much as to say "What can one do with the woman?" but only replied, "Very good."

Claudia paused. Recalling that she still needed these men's help to effect a profitable sale of her own mansion, she extended her hand to Mr. Rood and bestowed a smile. "I can't thank you enough, Mr. Rood. To do all this in the absence of my husband, well, it's been difficult, and you've been wonderful."

The lawyer blinked slowly and smiled. "It has been our pleasure, Mrs. Thorne."

With a final warm look for both men, she gathered herself up and exited. Mr. Rood looked down from the front window as she boarded her carriage, then tugged two windows open to dilute the thick smell of lilac perfume.

* * *

Phillip rode home from Brookside with the reins slack, letting Queen Anne set her own pace. She seemed to sense his despondency and walked gently, now and then turning her head to the side as though checking that he was still in the saddle. The trip north took over twice as long as the joyous ride south, and Phillip rode past his father's house without stopping.

The day was waning as he reached home and walked into the barn. To his surprise, he found that his father was still there, hardly recognizable in old dungarees and a rough jacket, helping Richmond toss fresh hay into the stalls with the gusto of one who has at last found his true calling. Phillip was only a few feet from his father when this hearty laborer caught sight of him, uttering a cry of greeting. The Duke planted his pitchfork in the ground, narrowly missing his own boot, and beamed at his son. Although he could not make out the young man's face clearly in the dim barn, the droop of his shoulders and drag in his step told him that things had not gone well.

"What's wrong? Did you read her the letter?"

Phillip sat down heavily on a milking stool. Richmond lit a lantern and hung it from a low beam, then led Queen Anne away for a good brushing. The lantern cast a golden light over the two men, the pile of soft hay, and the old wooden stalls. The Duke pulled a short bench over and sat facing his son, his hands on his knees. He listened as Phillip recounted what he had found at Brookside.

"Do you know where she's gone?" asked the Duke, frowning.

"No. Maybe to the City, maybe to Chicago."

"We can find out."

Phillip hung his head. "Maybe we should let it be. Maybe the letter will not make such a great difference after all. She only thought I was toying with her anyway--"

"Let it be?" exclaimed the Duke. "Are you ready to give up? Are you really? On a woman like that?"

"Do you forget our last conversation, Father, hers and mine? She called me a cad. She didn't even believe I loved her. I wonder why I even went back today."

The Duke sat silent, as one fighting to control himself. Then he grabbed his son by the shoulders and pulled him closer. Startled, Phillip stiffened and looked into his father's eyes.

"If you let this woman go, Phillip, so help me God I'll have no sympathy for you ever again. None!" He squeezed his son's shoulders until they hurt, glaring at him ferociously. The accumulated frustration of many long years flowed into his grip.

"People say things they don't mean. They say cruel things when they cannot bear the pain any more. Put it aside. Do you want to be alone your whole life? I am alone and I ache from it. But I had the joy of your mother for the years we shared. I have you children. But you, this indecisiveness, this, this—" he seemed to struggle to let the word out "—cowardice!"

The Duke released his son and stood up. He passed a hand over his mouth as he glared at Phillip. "You're a far bigger fool than I ever thought if you let her go this easily." With that the Duke grabbed his coat off a nail and marched into the twilight. But before Phillip could collect his thoughts, his father appeared again in the open doorway.

"I'll expect a visit from you within the week to let me know what you have found out." Then he turned abruptly and was gone.

# Chapter 63

On the outskirts of Chesterton, the fine houses looked much like their counterparts in the city but kept their distance from each other as well as from the road. Among these self-contained kingdoms sat the square, red-brick residence of Mr. and Mrs. Thomas Thoroughgood. Mr. Thoroughgood held a high position in the town's Methodist church and, by virtue of his confident manner and persuasive powers of speech, was asked to preach the Sunday sermons while the congregation waited for their new pastor to arrive from Liverpool. The remaining days of the week Mr. Thoroughgood spent running a well-ordered office for the largest lumber company in the state, not unlike the well-ordered home he presided over.

Mrs. Thoroughgood admired her husband almost to adulation, and certainly to the point of self-deprecation. She felt deeply guilty for not having furnished the family with more than one child, a daughter, whom she lavished all of her loving attention upon. Indeed, Mrs. Thoroughgood could have had ten children and made each feel like the most precious, being a woman with a nearly bottomless reserve of affection.

Their daughter, Lavinia, despite her father's stern but infrequent efforts to form her into a selfless, no-nonsense young woman of faith, showed at the age of nine no characteristics tending in that direction. The servants had witnessed the scamp making faces at her father behind his back and telling bald lies to her mother to escape punishment for broken dishes and ruined clothing. The family cat, an otherwise friendly and affectionate creature, ran at the sight of her.

It was into this household that little Henri was carried one afternoon by Mrs. Morgan, who handed him unceremoniously into the arms of Mrs. Thoroughgood.

"You're to be praised for taking this one in," Mrs. Morgan pronounced soberly. She pointed to a corner of the foyer and the driver set down the child's meager luggage on the gleaming floor. Mrs. Thoroughgood took the baby and began cooing and rubbing his soft cheeks with her plump finger.

Mrs. Morgan resumed, "There's not many as would give a Christian home to such a child. He's a mistake, you know, and by rights ought not be here to burden the likes of you and me."

Mrs. Thoroughgood looked at the dark courier in mild reproach. "Oh, no," she declared. "My husband says God does not make mistakes, and he made this little angel." She bounced Henri gently in her arm as he studied her gentle face. "Would you like tea?" she asked Mrs. Morgan brightly. "We were just serving."

"No, madam, I'm a working woman with no time for tea. I must be getting back straight. These are all his things," she said, nodding toward the trunk. "If you don't have what's needed, it's none of my doing. He was sheltered by single ladies before coming here, and heaven knows how they made do.

"I'm sure we'll get along fine," Mrs. Thoroughgood assured her. "Thank you so much."

Mrs. Morgan stared at her for a moment and turned to go.

"One more thing," she muttered, turning back around and pulling a card from her coat pocket. "If it don't work out, I'm told to tell you to send word to his lordship and someone will come fetch him."

Mrs. Thoroughgood took the card bearing Phillip's name and address, examined it briefly, and dropped it in a small urn beside the door. She assured Mrs. Morgan that she would keep the kind precaution in mind. With that the housekeeper left, letting in a sharp gust of cold before the door shut behind her.

A stout manservant carried the trunk upstairs to the nursery that had been newly decorated in blue for the little boy. Mrs. Thoroughgood and her maid stowed his little outfits into a mahogany chest of drawers, laying one out on the changing table for after his bath, which the lady of the house said must be their first order of business. In the kitchen they set a shallow tub on the table before the fire and filled it with warm water. Mrs. Thoroughgood had already put in an extensive supply of bathing products and lotions, which she arrayed beside the tub, and had the maid lay out a thick towel to receive the sparkling child. Mrs. Thoroughgood carefully laid Henri down and unfastened his clothes, talking to him all the while, as the cook and the maid admired the little boy, ready to assist in any way. Testing the water with her wrist, Mrs. Thoroughgood lowered the boy into the tub, then shampooed and soaped and rinsed him until no bit of uncleanliness, however minute, could possibly remain.

It was during this procedure that young Lavinia quietly entered the kitchen, unnoticed by anyone, so firmly concentrated were they on the operation at hand. Leaning against the sink, she twirled the end of a braid and listened to the excited warbling of the three women, watching their backs against the glow of the great fireplace. As her mother lifted the baby triumphantly out of the water, she drew closer to observe the new curiosity.

"Oh, Lavinia, dear, look at your new brother," said her mother, wrapping him in the soft, white towel while the maid rubbed his wet head industriously with another. "Isn't he a little doll? We are going to have so much fun with him!" Mrs. Thoroughgood put out an arm and drew her daughter closer. Lavinia stood beside her and eyed the newcomer.

"I wish it was a girl. Then I could dress her up."

The ladies chuckled. "He has darling little suits you can dress him in, dear, just wait until you see them," assured Mrs. Thoroughgood. "And we can go into town tomorrow and get him a few more, as he doesn't have much. You can come and help pick them out."

Little Henri turned his brown eyes upon the girl and lifted his brows. Lavinia took this to mean, "Who are you? No one important. At least not any more." She had not wanted him to come into their home, and now she knew she was right—he was a wretched little thing and already taking her place in everyone's heart. She looked up at the faces of the three happy women as they beamed at her, their cheeks red from the warmth of the kitchen. The cook handed her a pair of tiny knit booties to put on the baby's curling feet. Lavinia felt the soft yarn and ran the blue ribbons between her fingers. She tossed them one by one into the soapy water, threw a daring look at her mother, and stalked upstairs to her room to rearrange her piles of toys.

# Chapter 64

Fettles was sulking for the third straight day, and Agnes did not think she could bear one more hour of it. She had expressly asked him to be at tea that afternoon, but he stayed away once more. Agnes was able to drink only half a cup before making a quick apology to Vera and going in search of him. She found him in his room, sitting in a straight-backed chair reading Augustine, which he only did in his blackest moods. Napoleon and Empress both lay at his feet with their noses on their paws, the scene feebly lit by the room's only window. Fettles looked at her testily above his reading glasses.

"Why are you closeting yourself like this?" she demanded, clutching the sides of her gray silk skirt with both hands. "We've hardly seen you for the better part of three days."

"I don't see why that would pose a problem," he returned. "The household is fully staffed—I'm not needed as far as I can tell."

Agnes dropped onto the edge of the perfectly made bed. Within three feet was a second bed, whose covers were casually tossed over it, partially covering a dented pillow. Vera's house was modest, and Fettles was sharing a room with Ned.

"You know this is temporary," said his mistress. "It's hard for all of us."

"Is it?" he replied archly. "You are reunited with your delightful aunt, with whom you spend happy hours each day, and I am indeed glad for that, Agnes." Things were truly out of kilter—he was calling her by her Christian name. "Marie continues to attend you as your personal maid, as she should. Ned busies himself fixing hinges and repairing cellar walls. But no home needs two butlers."

Fettles adjusted the pillow behind his back and set his glasses on a small table at his elbow.

"You know, I tried to be helpful," he continued. "I understand my reduced position as a guest. Several times I offered to organize the wines or dust chandeliers, or whatever that drudge of a butler might want my assistance with, but every time I open my mouth he seems to suffer some affront as though I am criticizing his abilities. So I've concluded that this is the safest place for me, where I cannot offend anyone or get in the way."

Agnes slid closer. Fettles was right—of all of them he was the most out of place at Vera's house, largely due to the ungraciousness of Vera's butler, a young man Vera had employed out of sympathy for his unemployment. Sullen and insecure, the young butler had indeed rejected all of Fettles' overtures to help, and a man of Fettles' constitution found the keenest torment in sitting idle. In addition, the topsy-turvy character of Vera's home, where coats were as often thrown over chairs as hung on hooks, and dirty plates cluttered the table long after meals concluded, made Fettles' little room the only refuge for the man's delicate nerves. And even in that space, he had to contend with his roommate's casual habits. Agnes decided to repeat what they already knew.

"The wedding is in early January. That's only two weeks away. Then they shall be in Mr. Schmidt's house and we shall have this one to ourselves. Besides, in three days it's Christmas. You don't want to spoil my Christmas with a sour spirit, do you?" A smile played around her lips.

In any other year, Fettles would have been in his glory at this season. Christmas lit him up with a perennial excitement the whole household looked forward to seeing. Every year he applied himself to choosing the perfect tree and improving on the previous year's decorations, with the result that Brookside had become famous for its sumptuous displays of evergreen garlands and complicated nativity scenes. People used to find excuses to visit the Somersets just to gawk at the glorious testimony to Christmas that Fettles put on exhibit each December.

"I've talked to Vera about the need for a tree in the front parlor," Agnes continued. "She puts up little more than a wreath each year, as you've seen. It's all right by her if we go get one, so why don't you and I go out tomorrow and select the best fir we can find and hang it with some of our decorations?"

Fettles looked fixedly at Agnes. Conflicting feelings seemed to contend within him, and after a moment he asked pointedly, "Why doesn't she decorate?"

"Oh, you see that she decorates the house handsomely in general. But she says she cannot be bothered with seasonal decoration, mostly because it saddens her when it must be taken down. Still, she said she won't mind provided we do it."

"Well that's something, at least," said Fettles, sitting up and closing his book. "I know where the trimmings are, at least, so we'll have no trouble there. This house is badly in need of some yuletide cheer!"

Agnes clapped her hands and rose. "I'll want to go early. With Christmas almost here we must get the best of what's left. I saw some trees for sale two blocks from here—"

"Yes, on Grand, next to the cab stand!"

"That's the place. They don't have many, but you can work magic with whatever we bring home."

Fettles stood, passed a hand over his rebellious hair, and straightened his jacket. "I'll bring up the decorations. We could use with a few more candleholders; some are old and don't clamp anymore."

"Do we still have tinsel?"

"Plenty left from last year."

As evening fell, the two friends sat before the parlor fire sorting through the decorations and deciding which they would use on the one tree. (In its heyday, Brookside had up to three glittering trees gracing the foyer, main parlor, and dining room.) Agnes pulled out the garlands of glass beads and the tatted snowflakes. Fettles found the tinsel and a sampling of his favorite ornaments from across the years. He also brought out the carved nativity scene Mr. Somerset had brought home from Portugal when Agnes was a tiny girl. After all this time, the only signs of wear were one broken shepherd's hook and a three-legged donkey.

After dinner the sorting continued, as Vera and Frederick sat with them drinking warm punch and commenting on Christmases past. As Fettles inventoried the working candle clips, Vera asked if they intended to light the tree, to which Agnes said it would not really be a Christmas tree without lights. This brought from Frederick a full account of Mr. Johnson's all-electric tree that appeared in the papers last Christmas to the wonderment of all. Vera said she supposed that candles would be all right if they kept the usual bucket of sand close by and spread an old rug under the tree to catch any wax. As the clock's hands hovered near midnight, Mr. Schmidt took his leave. The remaining three decided to rearrange the parlor furniture to make way for the tree, then went to their separate rooms in delightful anticipation of the next day's activities so peculiar to that cheerful season.

The following morning, in a slicing wind, Agnes and Fettles repaired after breakfast to the tree seller and picked out a respectable spruce nearly nine feet tall whose only fault was an undeniable bald spot on one side. The two determined that the flaw could be turned to the corner and hidden, so they happily ordered it tied to the roof of the cab and brought it home. Ned sawed off a piece from the bottom of the sticky trunk, trimmed up the lower boughs, and set it in the space cleared the previous night. To everyone's surprise, it took up an entire corner of the parlor, proving again that Christmas trees become twice as large when brought inside the house. It proudly stood where passersby would see it from the street (something Agnes insisted upon, as she loved riding down the street herself and looking for glittering trees in people's front rooms).

Marie arrived with two boxes of candles and new candleholders, and the three—Ned excused himself as one not gifted in the art of embellishment—set to work transforming the plain but rich-smelling tree into a wonder of white lace, red glass, gold, and silver.

When they had finished, everyone stood back and admired the effect. Outside the wind had slacked, and snow had begun falling in large flakes past the front window. Fettles finished setting up the Nativity figures on a small round table draped in white and turned to Agnes. "I think I shall go to Mass on Christmas Eve," he announced.

"Really!"

He cleared his throat and looked back to the tree. "I have hardly gone since leaving home as a boy. There was no Catholic church in Chesterton, you know."

"I never realized it mattered to you."

"It didn't." He looked at her bravely. "I am wondering now if it should have."

Agnes felt the depth of his words and a sense of slow but certain turning, like that of a great vessel whose captain has realized that they have sailed fully half their route several degrees off course.

"I noticed one just down the block," she observed.

"Yes, St. Monica's. I thought I might go."

"Well, you should," Agnes agreed. "You're overdue."

Fettles nodded and applied himself to removing the empty boxes and tissue paper to the cellar. Napoleon trotted after him, leaving Empress to guard the wondrous tree before falling asleep, curled in a semicircle on the old red rug beneath it.

# Chapter 65

The holidays came and went at Vera's house as pleasantly as could be hoped under the circumstances. Then, in the first frosty days of January, Vera and Frederick Schmidt took each other as man and wife at a simple ceremony in the old First Presbyterian Church. Vera took up her place as Mrs. Schmidt at Frederick's handsome townhouse, losing no time in transforming the bachelor's dark interiors into a vibrant landscape that he hardly recognized as his home. His library, however, remained his, all deep red leather and green, and served as a comfortable refuge from the unexpected intensity of conjugal living. Having taken in the better part of Agnes's cherished books from the shelves of Brookside, he spent many a glad hour pouring over the old volumes, taking particular delight in studying Mr. Audubon's spectacular feathered subjects while Vera flew about the city on her many missions.

Agnes and her small staff made Vera's old house their own, arranging the few pieces of furniture and decorative bits of art they had kept from Brookside so that, little by little, the house began to feel like theirs. The sale of Brookside provided Agnes sufficient funds to run the household for some time, and Mr. Rockwell had invested part of the proceeds to afford her a small but steady income.

Agnes was wise enough to be grateful for the simplified life required by her narrowed circumstances. With no gardens of her own, she learned the practical pleasure of strolling through public parks obligingly maintained by the City of New York. Without stable or carriage house, she employed public cabs and found they did the job admirably. She knew she was fortunate to have her duties reduced since she had still not recovered the strength, either of body or spirit, that she enjoyed before her illness. When she pictured managing the estate once more, with all that it entailed, her heart failed her, and she could not imagine governing again such broad affairs.

However, the loss of Brookside created a hole in Agnes that could not be denied. Life on the estate was all she had known from her birth, and that life constituted the measure of everything she would later meet with. The home of our youth becomes the archetypal home—its feel, its furnishings and customs—and every other home is an odd thing that sits, as at a strange angle, and must be analyzed and studied to be understood. And as much as Agnes studied this city life and applied herself to taking advantage of its good features, still she longed for the green view out her bedroom windows and wet grass in the morning, for breakfast on the terrace where early sparrows jumped forward for fallen crumbs, and for a thousand other pleasures and unexamined details that were exactly what *should* be but were no more.

This break with all she had known would have been enough to constrict Agnes's heart, but her loss had taken on a more bitter taste still. Scarcely a month after moving out, Agnes heard from Chesterton friends that laborers and craftsmen were at work on the rooms of the old mansion, painting and wallpapering. Masons had been commissioned to build a showy portico onto the front, and carpenters were adding lavish details to transform the stately home into a model of the latest architectural fashion.

These changes hurt and confused her; after all, Brookside was perfect just the way it was. But when Ned and Fettles (who together had the unhappy task of breaking the news) told Agnes that the new owner, the woman who pulled into the buzzing estate almost daily to check on the progress of its transformation, was none other than Mrs. Claudia Thorne, they confirmed what Agnes had long suspected but did not want to know.

When finally able to speak, she asked, "Do you think that she was behind everything somehow, just to get Brookside?"

"Very possible," declared Fettles. "That woman is capable of anything. Satan himself takes lessons from her."

Ned stroked his thick moustache and thought. "No. What happened to Phillip—and also to you, ma'm, if I may say—bore her mark. But losing the family money was beyond her reach. That was surely all Wilbur's doing."

Wilbur. Agnes liked to imagine that he and Eleanor were living meagerly in one of the dirtier European cities, getting by somehow on a mixture of lies and bravado and forever looking over their shoulders.

Agnes believed that Ned must be right. Even the Thorne had her limits. She probably just took advantage of a situation she could only have dreamed of: The Somersets reduced to penury; all assets to be liquidated at sacrificial prices. Suddenly she remembered the piano, the grand family heirloom, now forced to provide music for Claudia's garish parties. A sick feeling spread through her and remained the rest of the day. She spoke not another word until bedtime, and retired without her dinner. The staff avoided speaking of Brookside again.

As for her other great loss, a day did not pass without Phillip walking through Agnes's mind. Now he was laughing at one of her stories over tea, now patting down Queen Anne after a galloping ride, now unfastening his damp necktie in the afternoon heat. They had not spoken since that ugly scene in the parlor, which felt like years ago, although barely five months had passed. She wondered how little Henri was getting on, whether Phillip was making a go of the farm, or whether he had already moved on to some other idea. Maybe farming did not suit him any better than all the other work he had tried. She wondered if she had been too hard on him in their last conversation. But his long silence told her no. He had not visited nor sent any letter since that last day (she felt that she was easy enough to find for anyone who wanted to), reinforcing her conviction that he was relieved to be shed of her.

Winter dragged on well into April. But near the end of the month, Spring arrived like a mail train running late. It exploded onto the city as though atoning for its tardiness with a vigor that touched every corner of the metropolis. Green tips shot up from even the smallest patch of dirt, and leaves popped out on branches overnight. The sudden currents of warm air sent people diving into trunks for their summer clothes, and the city's population of children, now running in shirtsleeves through the streets, seemed to have doubled in a season.

Walking out one Saturday morning with the sun on her face, Agnes pulled in a deep helping of the mild air. She stood on the front stoop feeling for a moment a fraction of that old feeling that always came to her in spring, the wild sensation of unlimited possibilities. These days, she knew better. Still, watching a troop of wispy clouds flowing by against the blue sky, hearing the frantic chatter all around of birds building nests, and stunned by the sudden color of daffodils and flowering crabapples, she was reminded that life must surely resume.

She could not help imagining this same spring, of which she saw such a narrow wedge here in the city, washing lavishly over

Brookside. The gardens were no doubt erupting in a jubilant show of blooms. The lawns would be turning green again and the fountain splashing in the dazzling way it did when first turned on. But these wonders now lay in Claudia's hands. Agnes shook herself and turned her attention back to the pavement beneath her feet as she headed for the Schmidt's house. Today, with the weather so fine, she was walking rather than riding the six long blocks to her aunt's home. Vera was taking her shopping for a spring dress—something bright, Vera said, just the thing to welcome a new season.

Agnes knew her aunt referred to more than the weather. Vera, with her indomitable personality, seemed to be growing impatient with her niece's subdued spirits. Agnes tried. She had accepted many of Vera's invitations to concerts, operas, and charitable events around town, but nothing took root. She considered volunteering for a host of good causes that Vera proposed, but failed to pursue any. Even her attendance at church had grown spotty, something for which Fettles, with his renewed dedication to Rome, gently chastised her.

Even the children dashing past Agnes on their way to the day's adventures failed to lift her heart. They only reminded her of little Henri, who should be walking well by now and beginning to talk. She prayed that the Thoroughgoods were loving him as least as much as she did. She was sure that if she saw him now she would hardly recognize him, nor he her, so quickly does Time work upon the body and mind of little children.

And so spring gave way to summer, summer to fall, and fall to winter. All the while Agnes could only imagine the two greatest loves of her life moving in their own worlds, their memories of her dimming even into darkness, as their lives played out in places she would probably never set foot. Several times, when the memories became too much, she had almost written to Phillip. But then what? Wait every day in torment, looking for the postman to bring a reply? Better to leave it all alone and trust that another year might close the wounds.

# Chapter 66

Lavinia knew that she would have to answer for her little pranks, but she did not care. It would follow the usual pattern: Father would come home and, hearing of her crime, would bring her into the parlor and give her a stern dressing-down, his lanky frame towering over her and his mouth set in a deep frown. He would sentence her to several hours of Bible reading, usually from Proverbs, and extended time in her room without visitors. By the next day her mother would have managed to commute the sentence and everything would return to normal.

No, the punishment did not concern her. She had a bigger problem, which was the expulsion of the child with whom she had been forced to share her parents. "Heathen brat" was her new nickname for him when no one was listening. (Lavinia was not sure what *heathen* meant, but one day she heard women talking in the mercantile about how her parents had agreed to take one in, and the way those women said the word, she concluded it must be something bad.)

After the bath incident, Lavinia bided her time. She even pretended to warm up to the urchin, dangling things playfully in front of him and pushing him through the house in his little wheeled seat. Mrs. Thoroughgood had begun to relax a bit as she watched them, and the cook mused optimistically that it only needed time for Lavinia to become attached to her new brother.

Months passed, and Lavinia watched her mother grow ever fonder of the little boy. She felt herself barely noticed anymore. Now and then her mother made a feeble effort to compliment her or pull her into some silly game with the baby, but she remained convinced that it was just for show. The half-breed was completely eclipsing her in her parents' affections.

Spring came, then summer, and in the first chill, damp days of autumn Henri succumbed to a serious bout of cough and fever. His illness turned the house upside down with worry and frantic fussing around his bed. As days went by and the child continued to lie flushed and listless, Lavinia dared to hope that the illness would carry him away. But slowly his little body rallied, and he was once more toddling about talking his usual gibberish.

Christmas was only days away. The greatest present Lavinia could imagine would be the absence of Henri. Still, she had not found a good way to bring it about, and her frustration, which she had learned to keep carefully concealed (a frightening ability in one so young), continued to mount. One blustery afternoon, on the day set for Henri's weekly bath, Lavinia hung about the kitchen after school, watching and thinking. Her mother was at a meeting of the ladies' charitable society. The cook had just set the boy in the tub of warm water by the fire and proceeded to carry out a brisk washing with arms lean and muscled from years of lifting kettles and beating stiff dough. Henri kept busy banging a spoon against the edge of the tub, making such a racket that Lavinia was about to march away when the cook, glancing over her shoulder, called to her.

"Child, go fetch a gown for this one, will you? I thought I had everything, but . . ."

"I don't know where they are," Lavinia lied over the din.

"Of course you do. They are in the little chest just beside his bed."

"I hurt my ankle and Mother told me not to go up and down the stairs any more than I really must."

The cook cast a suspicious look on her. "Well, you stand right here and make sure he doesn't climb out while I go get it. Don't turn your back on him for a moment, do you hear?"

Lavinia almost made a face but thought better of it and took the cook's place beside the tub. Henri was now mercifully sucking on the spoon and splashing the water with his plump little hand. An idea came to her as the cook's steps retreated down the hallway. He might slip. His face might go under. She reached into the tub and shifted the wet child backwards, supporting him on her arm. *Bang* went the spoon against metal. She cradled him lower still and the child's arms went out, dropping the spoon into the murky water.

"Down you go," she cooed.

Frightened, the child stared up at her and began to cry. Lavinia pulled him upright and pressed the spoon back into his hand, urging him in whispers to be quiet, but she managed only to increase his distress. He let go the spoon and wailed louder, looking all around through his tears as though for a savior. Grabbing the wet washcloth, she covered his mouth to muffle the crying, while breathing dire threats into his little ear.

"Lavinia!" It was her mother's voice, but twisted into a shriek as the girl had never heard. Lavinia froze and looked up to see her mother's face contorted in horror. Mrs. Thoroughgood stood over her, still in her hat and coat. She pushed her daughter aside and grabbed the boy out of the water. Clutching him against her shoulder, she threw a towel over his back as he sobbed and spluttered. She could only stare at her daughter, her lips trembling.

The cook hurried into the kitchen with the gown in one hand and stopped. "What's happened?" she cried. She looked from mother to daughter and asked again, louder this time.

"He slipped." Lavinia pushed the words out as through a small crack, grudgingly, like one who knew she would not be believed. She let the wet rag fall to the floor and ran from the room with tears of anger burning her eyes.

The cook came close to Mrs. Thoroughgood and looked at her directly. "We can't keep him, ma'm. Not with Miss Lavinia in the house. It's not safe. One or t'other of them has to go."

Her mistress raised her eyes to hers, huge and unbelieving.

"He's not safe even another night here unless you put his bed in my room," warned the cook.

Mrs. Thoroughgood nodded weakly. "Yes," she murmured. "And I thought she was doing so well with him . . . ." Then she took a step closer to her cook and half whispered. "You won't say anything, will you, May? You won't tell what happened?"

"How could I tell? I didn't rightly see it. But no, I won't say anything. Still," she said, "you're going to have to do something one day with that girl, and you know it's so."

Mrs. Thoroughgood made no reply but wandered into the foyer, where, as in a daze, she reached her hand into the small urn by the door and retrieved the card she had dropped in when the child arrived just over a year ago. Within an hour, Henri was dressed and bundled in two blankets and a hat. The cook and maid loaded his belongings into a cab at the front door. Mrs. Thoroughgood placed a long kiss on Henri's cheek and handed him to the cook, who settled back in the coach with her arms around the child.

"What should I tell them, ma'm?" she asked her mistress.

Mrs. Thoroughgood, wearing only a velvet dress against the chill evening air, clutched herself. "Just tell them that we are not in a position to keep him. Make sure they know—" her voice caught—" that he is a wonderful boy and it is not his fault that we must give him up."

The good woman put her handkerchief to her face, shut the cab door, and hurried inside. The cook and little Henri rode together to Fellcrest, back from where he had come, as the first stars pricked the cold, pink dusk.

# Chapter 67

Of all nights in the year, none can surpass Christmas Eve for its warmth of feeling and general merriment. And so it was at the Schmidt's home that twenty-fourth of December, with all members of the household as well as Agnes and her small staff crowded around two tables for a dinner of roast duck, oysters, baked squash, cakes, puddings, and more delights for the tongue than can be named. After hearing how Agnes had celebrated her last Thanksgiving at Brookside with her own staff around the table—rather than invited guests—Vera adopted the practice enthusiastically as embracing the true spirit of the holiday. She set up extra seating in the adjoining parlor to accommodate everyone and reserved for her use only those servants who were indispensable to preparing and serving the meal.

Mr. Frederick Schmidt presided at the dining room table with the rosy glow of both benefactor and blissful newlywed, as Vera described her various ideas for celebrating their first anniversary (which included, to her husband's obvious discomfort, plans for ice skating followed by high tea in their home for several dozen close friends).

The couple's German cook worked miracles with every course that evening, sampling each one liberally along the way to ensure its perfection. The Schmidt's impeccable but aloof Italian butler—hired by Vera upon moving into Frederick's house to replace her own incompetent young man—in the spirit of the season, acquiesced to Fettles' offer to help serve, and the latter shone with this return to duty at a "real" dinner, as he described it. The two butlers poured wine and set out new courses, all to exclamations of wonder and declarations that they, the diners, could not possibly eat another forkful, which was disproved time and again through the testimony of another empty platter.

When everyone had done all possible justice to the dinner, they adjourned to the parlor to sing carols and light the tree. (Agnes and Fettles had convinced Vera the previous Christmas of the happy benefits of putting up a tree.) Vera, Agnes, and Fettles lit the tall spruce's forty candles with care, straightening each one to drip as little wax as possible. Outside the window, the occasional cab drove by conducting what remained of the business and bustle of the day. The bells of St. Monica's had long ago rung nine o'clock, and everyone in Vera's parlor who was not touching matches to candle wicks sank into chairs or leaned heavily on the piano with the sweet satisfaction of being warm and well fed. A robust fire blazed on the hearth and, along with several lamps, bathed the room in honey-colored light. As the candle lighters finished their work, a cheer went up, and the congregation admired the great tree with its wonderful ornaments and gleaming silver tinsel.

"What shall we start with?" asked Vera, taking her place at the piano.

"'Hark the Harold'!" declared Fettles, handing around sheets of Christmas lyrics. "Or," he said, slightly embarrassed, "whatever you wish."

All those present endorsed the choice, Vera found the page in her book of music, and the room rang with the carol's bright chords. Such was the gusto of the singers that no one noticed that another voice had joined theirs during the second verse. It was not until they concluded the final refrain of *Glory to the newborn King* that Fettles, looking around in satisfaction, uttered a simple "Oh!" Everyone followed his wide-eyed gaze to a figure standing just inside the parlor doorway, still wearing his coat and holding his hat. The man's sandy hair gleamed dully in the light of the lamp just beside him, as he turned his hat in his hands and smiled uncertainly.

Agnes gasped. Frederick came forward to give Phillip a genial handshake, and Vera got out from behind the piano to hold Agnes's cold hand. "It's alright," she murmured to her niece, "be a good girl and don't faint for us." Mr. Schmidt introduced Phillip to the household while Fettles took his coat and hat. The cook served him a glass of warm punch and fetched a plate of food from the kitchen, and Vera returned to the piano. The festivities resumed with renditions of several more Christmas favorites while Phillip took a seat beside Agnes and shared her sheet music. She did not look at him—a direct gaze might reveal that he was not really there at all. She sang in a whisper, listening to his voice and reeling inside from a hundred imaginings as to why he had come.

As midnight approached, Fettles and the young Italian butler donned their hats and coats, shook hands all around, and headed up the street to Mass, having discovered that they both belonged to the same ancient and venerable Christian institution. Mr. Schmidt politely decided it was time for him to retire, bowed to his wife with a wink, and headed for his room. The rest of the party blew out the Christmas candles, taking care not to spatter wax onto the precious glass ornaments. The partiers then broke up to put away the last of the refreshments or retire to their rooms, leaving Agnes, Phillip, and Vera alone. Vera trimmed the lamps, sinking the room into a collection of large shadows cast by the still-vigorous fire. Phillip crouched to turn a log, and Agnes fiddled with the tree trimmings.

After adjusting the last lamp, Vera turned and smiled at her niece. "Lord Phillip wrote to me that he had some news to share with you. He offered to come after Christmas, but I said why wait? *I* certainly didn't want to spend the holiday wondering what it might be! But I'll leave you two to discuss it." Vera glided from the room and slid the pocket doors closed behind her.

Agnes looked at Phillip, who stood half-lit by the orange light of the fire.

"Will you sit down?" he asked, indicating the deep red sofa beside the fireplace. Agnes came over and sat, absently gathering her skirt into her hands. Having once dared to look at him directly, she now could not take her eyes off him. Phillip sat beside her and drew Rupa's letter from his breast pocket. "You read French, don't you?"

"Yes."

"I'd very much like you to read this."

Agnes tilted the pages toward the firelight to examine the handwriting. "Aloud?"

"No, please, I have been over it many times."

Agnes drew the letter closer and read silently. Halfway through she took his hand and squeezed it and kept it until she had finished.

At last she lowered the letter and looked at him earnestly. "He's not yours, just as you said."

"No."

"That poor girl."

They stared at each other. "My father said that if I didn't come after you he'd never speak to me again—or words to that effect."

"So you're here because he told you to come—yet judging by the date on the letter, it has taken you more than a year."

287

"Well, there's a reason for that. Two reasons, really. I'm sure you remember the accusations you sent me off with the last time we talked."

Agnes worked to hold his gaze. "I remember."

"That I was merely amusing myself with your company, toying with your affections. Never seriously intending anything like the marriage we talked about."

His words cut into her. Agnes dropped her gaze toward the shimmering green folds of her skirt.

"You were a pleasant game to pass the time with," Phillip continued. He broke off and looked to the blazing hearth. Rising, he slid his hands into his pockets and took a turn around the room.

"A man does not push such words easily aside. I tried to—when this letter arrived I rode the same day to show it to you. Like a madman I rushed to Brookside only to find the house empty. I can't describe how that felt—to find you gone and not even know where. Father said I should pursue you. Said some rather harsh things about me that day, in fact.

"Well, I can't quite say why I didn't do what he said. Somehow I just could not work up the will to risk it, I guess. Which probably makes Father right about my being cowardly."

"Your father called you cowardly?"

"I can't blame him. I imagine *you* felt the same. Father and I are so different. And look what I have put the poor man through. Anyway, that doesn't matter. We come to the second reason why I am here only now." Phillip came around to face Agnes. "My bargaining position has unexpectedly improved."

Agnes looked up at him, puzzled.

"I'll explain," replied Phillip. "But I must know if you would still consider going in with me on that idea we talked about last summer."

"Which one? The one we agreed to keep secret so you could quietly back out?"

Phillip's face darkened.

Agnes grabbed his hand impulsively. "I take that back, I'm sorry. I have told myself for a long time that you never were serious. I had to."

"Why?"

"Because it was too much otherwise." Agnes's face contracted as she searched his eyes. "To think that what we felt was real and might have worked, that we might have married, was too awful. Better to believe that it was only an illusion all along."

At this Phillip's defenses fell, and Agnes saw the man she remembered. He sank onto his knees before her where she sat and pulled from his coat pocket a tiny velvet box. "What a fool I have been, Agnes! I should have shouted our news in the streets. I should have given you something like this." He set the box in her lap and clasped both her hands. "I have the farm, Agnes. It's not what you are used to, but I'm improving the house and by summer it will be very sufficient. I have ducks, cows, and a couple of good horses—I think I might actually be able to make a go of this."

He searched her face. Agnes sat motionless, her eyes wide. "Is that the improvement in your position?"

"No, no. You see, I understand if I am not sufficiently appealing on my own. But if you should say yes, dear Agnes, if you are still agreeable . . ."

Phillip let go of her hands and stepped lightly to the doors, sliding them open just enough to pass through. Agnes heard him walk upstairs and wondered if he had left her alone to work out the riddle he'd just given her. She rubbed her fingers over the soft surface of the box, then timidly opened it. Inside gleamed a dainty ring of rosy gold with a circle of tiny diamonds surrounding one dark ruby. She gently pulled out the ring to examine it, turning it toward the firelight, and judged it the most beautiful ring ever made. Unable to resist, she slipped it carefully onto her finger. The fit was exact. Hurriedly, she pulled it off and set it back in the box. She was so overcome with feelings that her mind felt suspended, unable to make sense of what she had just learned or the army of possibilities overrunning her. One thought stood out, however, from the wild throng: He loves me still.

Tears filled her eyes, and she pulled a handkerchief from her sleeve. Hearing the sound of Phillip's returning footsteps, she quickly wiped her cheeks and set the little box on her lap. She looked up to see him slip back into the room and then step to one side. Behind him came Vera leading a small boy whose huge brown eyes shone in the firelight as he approached on his sturdy little legs. Agnes rose with her handkerchief to her mouth, then slowly knelt down to look at the lad. The boy's wondering gaze moved from the fire to Agnes, and their eyes met. She made no sound as she took his little hand in both of hers. Then she began to laugh in short, broken pieces as tears ran freely down her face. Vera let go of Henri's hand and Agnes gathered him into her arms. She held him there, stroking his soft, dark hair, and shaking in quiet sobs, as Vera withdrew from the room.

From outside in the darkness, they heard the clangorous bells of St. Monica's announcing Christmas Day to the sleepy city.

It was into this scene that the two butlers returned, their noses reddened with cold and their faces lit with a convivial cheer that only the yuletide season can bestow upon two such dissimilar people. Vera quietly explained what was happening, and the two men let their mouths drop slightly open in the mystified way that bachelors do when the high emotion of matrimony is in the air. They crept on tiptoe to the kitchen where they knew hot cocoa and gingerbread awaited them. Along the way they held their breath like people afraid of catching some life-changing contagion.

# Chapter 68

Phillip described how the Thoroughgoods had returned Henri to Fellcrest without explanation just two weeks earlier. He also explained why he hoped to keep the little fellow this time rather than turn him over to an orphanage or seek another home. He did not trust anyone now with the child, he said, after the callous nurse he had first hired and then the mysterious events at the Thoroughgood home. But he needed a mother for the boy—he should have a family.

"So," Agnes summed up, leading Henri to the Christmas tree and handing him a strand of tinsel, "it's the both of you or nothing, is that what you're offering?"

"I thought about letting you, if you insisted, take just Henri and leave me to my fate, but then I came to my senses."

"And how did you find me?"

"I had help. When they brought Henri back to my father, he not only brought him to me directly but, unknown to me, he penned a letter to your Aunt Vera. He had been furious with me for a year, you know, for hiding on the farm. But when Henri reappeared, my father took it into his hands to make one last try for us. Your aunt sent back a short note that, well . . . ." Phillip looked for a word. "Encouraged me."

"Vera did that?"

"Thank God for those older and wiser than we, eh?"

Phillip reached a hand into his pocket, forgetting for a moment that he had already given the box he brought to Agnes. "The little box —"

In her jubilation at seeing Henri, Agnes had let the box roll from her lap. Phillip scanned the dark carpet lit only by the fire, now burning low. Finally he spied the black velvet box just inches from the grate and snatched it up. With an uncertain smile, he opened it toward Agnes.

Phillip felt a tug on his trouser leg and looked down to see Henri raising both arms imploringly. Phillip handed the box to Agnes and picked up the child, who leaned against his shoulder and rubbed his little fists into sleepy eyes.

"I know, old fellow, it's past time for bed." And turning his eyes to the woman before him, standing so close that they nearly touched, he asked, "So here we are, two men wretchedly in need of you. What do you say, Agnes Eileen Somerset?"

"I wonder," Agnes nearly whispered, looking from the ring to Phillip, "if I should feel manipulated."

"Oh, I would."

The tiny flames that clung, wavering, to the spent logs cast a dull glow upon their faces. Henri began humming lazily into Phillip's shoulder, signaling that sleep was near.

Agnes took Phillip's free hand and pressed the velvet box back into it. She watched his features freeze.

Then she stretched out her left hand and lifted her finger.

That Christmas, for the rest of their lives, stood as the greatest of all—at once the darkest and most radiant, the thriftiest and most lavish, a time both impossible and perfectly inevitable. And the miracle of that night in Vera's parlor seemed to the participants hardly less astounding than the one so many centuries before that brought the whole world to its feet. One could say that Phillip and Agnes themselves never stopped celebrating, and all who were fortunate enough to know them in the many years to come were undeniably the richer for it.

# *Epilogue*

Agnes and Phillip married quietly less than two months into the new year. They installed themselves, along with little Henri, at Phillip's farmhouse. In the spring they expanded the old homestead to accommodate a guest or two as well as Fettles, Ned, and Marie, who had in the meantime been making themselves useful at the Duke's home. Phillip enthusiastically tended the small farm with the help of Ned and Richmond, and everyone became so absorbed in their new duties that they found themselves thinking back less and less upon the lives they left behind.

For Empress and Napoleon the move to the country was perhaps one too many, and whether out of confusion or pique, they showed little enthusiasm for the great outdoors and spent most of their time patrolling the house or dozing on the front porch.

Vera and Frederick made regular visits to the farm. Two years into Agnes and Phillip's married life, these two arrived one sparkling autumn afternoon—as usual, a day earlier than expected. As they approached the house arm in arm, they rejoiced in the pure country air and broad sunshine. At a wooden table beneath one of the maples, they sat down with the family to tea (hastily prepared by Fettles with the enthusiastic help of Henri, who assumed his habitual duty of urging more butter onto the bread). Vera caught herself almost forgetting to give Agnes a letter sent to them by Mrs. Bairnaught, who lacked Agnes's address, and had asked the Schmidts to forward it. Rummaging in her purse, Vera at last produced the letter, which Agnes opened and read aloud.

*October 5, 188_*

*Dearest Agnes,*

*I felt I should write to tell you that Mr. Bairnaught left us last month, on the 3rd day of September. I have not found the strength to write to you until now. I am sure that I do not need to describe my feelings at this time, plunged into the void that his absence has created. The silence is almost unbearable, but I read my scriptures, and somehow time passes.*

*You may have heard by now the news of your old home. In case it has not yet traveled to you, I will share it. Shortly before my dear husband's passing, Mrs. Thorne had fallen under suspicion of foul play. It was widely rumored that she had conspired with several others in high places to maneuver her current lover into the office of senator in Washington. Two weeks ago she was placed under house arrest at her cousin's, where she was staying, on charges of tampering with the election (in which our dear friend Mr. McMeed was defeated—or was he?). This new trouble, coupled with the dwindling of her fortunes since acquiring Brookside, has apparently forced her to offer the estate for sale.*

*It would be a great delight to me if you chose to return and resume your place at your family home. With this wish in my heart, and with the considerable means left me by my husband, and lacking any children to bestow them upon, I would like nothing more than to purchase the estate and will it to you. My assets will also become yours, by immediate transfer, if you are inclined to accept my offer. The only condition is that you allow me, a very old and confused woman, to live among your precious family in that great house until the end of my days, which I sense may not be far off.*

*I await only a word from you and Phillip to put my solicitor to work.*

*God bless you all. I remain, in anxious anticipation of your response,*

*Beatrice Bairnaught*

No one knew about Claudia. Vera and Frederick had only returned from London a week earlier and had not yet caught up on news. And they had not spoken with Mrs. Bairnaught in months, having been abroad at the time of her husband's funeral.

Discussion of Claudia's fate and Mrs. Bairnaught's proposal dominated the next two days. Vera and Agnes chattered over the possibilities as they took Henri for long walks, during which he stopped to examine every late butterfly and wandering worm. Frederick got a taste of farm work while turning over with Phillip the advantages of re-inhabiting Agnes's former home or staying their present course. It was hard to comprehend that Brookside could be returned to the family—the gardens, the secret bench, the grand terrace and library, all theirs once more to enjoy.

But Brookside had been changed, who knew how much, by Mrs. Thorne and her legion of carpenters and decorators. And to install themselves again on the estate, Agnes and Phillip would have to turn their backs on what they had built together on the farm. Phillip would have to lease the land and manage it from a distance. Gone would be the early morning rooster call, the smell of fresh hay, and the joy of watching the crop he planted break through the spring soil. Fettles would no longer ride ten minutes each Sunday to the little chapel of Saints Peter and Paul, and Agnes would leave all her friends at Covenant Presbyterian, where she had just been elected head of the Ladies Relief Board.

So it was that the evening after Vera and Frederick's departure, Agnes and Phillip decided over dinner that Brookside in all its beauty could not pull them from their rustic home at the end of the birch-lined lane. Agnes felt that the long chapter of her life lived in the great mansion was closed. Their decision made, Agnes wrote to Mrs. Bairnaught with an alternative to that lady's generous offer, which was promptly accepted by return post.

Their benefactor came to occupy the guest room and begin her new life with them in the first days of a particularly icy winter, happy in the bosom of the busy, noisy household. Agnes was especially grateful for her when spring came, when she herself lay confined to bed for days on end by doctor's orders as they awaited the birth of baby Emmet. When Mrs. Bairnaught was not sitting by Agnes's bed or sharing a sunny corner of the front porch with the two dogs, she could be found in the nursery reading to Henri or warmly admiring his skill at building wooden block towers.

With the help of the widow's copious funds, the couple built a guest cottage just behind the farmhouse the following summer, where both children spent many hours enjoying the attentions that only a grandparent—actual or adopted—wise and patient with years, can shower upon the young. As for the bulk of the Bairnaught money, it was jointly agreed to set it aside in ironclad accounts for the children's future.

The Duke found his way to the farm two days out of seven, and on Sunday afternoons the young family came to Fellcrest. These were always pleasant visits, largely because Mrs. Morgan had been replaced as housekeeper by Agnes's own Mrs. Williams, who despite her efforts to remain unaffected, worshipped the children in her own stern way and slipped them sweets when their parents were not looking. (As for the discharged housekeeper, the much-relieved staff had observed the Duke, as Mrs. Morgan's black cab rolled away, raise his arms and contort his face as though ensuring by some dark art that they should never set eyes on her again.)

So the years turned, with children growing and everyone getting older through the passing seasons. On winter days as Agnes helped Marie hang laundry by the stove, she would sometimes look out the kitchen window and see her husband heading for the house, his hair blown back and his cheeks red from the raw November air. Above him gray clouds would be scudding southward, and for a moment, in the narrow spaces between them, the sun might shine through and light up his face. Then the old green kitchen door would squeak open, admitting him in a whirl of air rich with the smells of cold and animals and damp leaves.

Stella remained in Chicago, separated by many hundreds of miles from her beloved Aunt Agnes, a distance reinforced by the arrival of several children in quick succession, which delighted Stella and William, but kept the Molls close to home. Still, the aunt and her niece wrote faithfully to each other every week no matter what domestic calamities tried to keep them from their pens and paper. They became closer than ever now as they exchanged common sympathies over a child's illness or a husband's forgetfulness or the price of little boys' shoes.

As for Abram Rockwell, the whole affair of the lost fortune shook him so profoundly that he retired from practice and spent most afternoons at the club, renewing his friendship with the classics. He was, however, a little soothed in seeing how happy Agnes's life had become. He was further comforted by a somewhat puzzling letter that arrived one day from the south of France. It read simply *"Wilbur is probably deceased, apparently at violent hands. I thought this might provide some solace to you and the Somersets, although it does*

*nothing to restore what was lost. I myself am moving on somewhere*
*as yet undecided. Farewell. [Signed] Eleanor"*

The indomitable Mrs. Rockwell, as the years went by, increased
her stream of letters to congressmen, senators, the First Lady, and
even the President, exhorting them to support the cause of women's
suffrage. Accompanied by her daughter, she paid several personal
visits to these same luminaries in Washington and may well have
been a force in moving to the forefront of possibility the radical idea
of women casting their own vote.

Just outside Chesterton, the home of Mr. and Mrs. Thoroughgood
burned one evening, all its occupants barely escaping in their
nightclothes. An investigation quickly showed that Lavinia had
started the inferno while trying to incinerate an uncomfortable dress
her mother had insisted she wear the day before. Afraid for their own
lives, the couple sadly turned the young woman over to the county
home for wayward girls, where she continued her reign of terror. Her
parents left Chesterton for a pastor's post in Alabama, where they
adopted three orphans and lived as happily as parents can who have
lost a child to wickedness.

Far across the Atlantic, a young woman known as La Violette
turned twenty. She had, after four years at La Coquette, lost the draw
she once enjoyed, although she had never been more beautiful and
still cast a spell on those who saw her for the first time. A month
before her birthday, twins from Tunisia had taken her place as the
main attraction, performing their provocative Arabian dance to roars
of approval. Watching them she had suddenly felt old and prudish.
She seemed to see her audience run past her, arms extended, wild-
eyed and insatiable.

Fortunately, an agent from a club in Paris had visited and
expressed interest in her, and two days later she packed up her few
things, kissed Monsieur Vaudin and all the girls, and left Marseilles
for a finer room and a larger window to lean against. As she stood
there musing on sleepless nights, she felt the company of the Virgin
Mary, whose likeness stood nearby atop a tarnished dome. Mary,
white in the moonlight, constant and imperturbable, held out her arms
above the rooftops in that ancient town of saints and scoundrels, of
orphans and thieves; and together in this silent communion, the two
women watched over the slumbering city.

THE END

Made in the USA
San Bernardino, CA
28 March 2017